Comes Around

BY
Michelle S Morris

ISBN: 979-8284807187

Table of Contents

For Loree Ann Richardson Noel, matriarch, artist, mother, patron, grandmother extraordinaire, who takes kindness to an art form. You've always believed in me. If there were more mothers like you, the world would be less dysfunctional and a MUCH better place.

Chapter 1

EYES WIDE OPEN, THIS COULD HARDLY BE THE PLACE she left – NO, LET'S BE honest – the place she fled. The compact small town was no longer contained within the city limits, neatly kept houses arranged in neatly imagined blocks. The cute Victorian-style buildings on the main street, unique in color and unique in what hid behind the charming facades, some faded with age, some pristinely maintained, holding the dreams of new occupants, found competition beyond the original boundaries. Some called it progress, and maybe it was, for a while, but she saw the start of decay. Decay of the town. The traditions. The values. The soul – as much as a town telegraphed its soul. She wanted to cry out, "Beware false prophets who are here only for profit!" But she would not. Melodrama wasn't her thing.

Not sure of her place any longer, she *was* sure this had certainly not been it for years. Yet, cautionary tales she carried as warnings in abundance in her mind. The big box stores would come, and go, maybe others would come again. The all-in-one giants would stick around long enough to drive out the local grocer, the corner butcher, the family pharmacy. The expressway connecting the country's North to South corridor brought opportunity. Those well-known places that were the same, regardless of where one stopped along the route, crowded beyond the city limits, overtaking farmland and wooded copse.

But eyes shut, the familiar was there. The sounds of birds in the trees overhead first screeched danger before settling into routine chirping and singing, when they realized she meant no harm. The children walked by the gates laughing and shouting on their way home from school. Squirrels scurried in the tree branches and possibly raccoons, or opossums woken from their daytime routine. Bees buzzed as they searched for nectar to satisfy their queen. The smells were there, olfactory senses brought to the surface that which was long ago buried. Deeply. Mown grass, car exhaust, diesel fumes, fresh cut roses on a plot nearby, fertilizer to maintain the surreal green, cow dung floating on the breeze from a nearby farm, freshly cut wood burned her nose with its rawness, those were the smells that belonged here, the smells of her childhood – the good, the bad, all familiar and as deeply engrained as tying her shoes.

Halley McCarthy, Hal to her father and his family, opened her eyes to the trees swaying in the wind, leaves rustling, as the fore drop to an impossibly high blue sky. It made her a little dizzy, the motion. She, herself, lay inert on her back, canvas cargo pants protected legs spread apart as if making a snow angel, heels firmly grounded in the grass-covered soil, arms straight out to the sides, covering as much of the earthy plot as possible. Her wavy light-brown hair with "sun-touched" highlights, as described by her stylist, splayed around her head like a Renaissance halo.

"Uhh," she groaned, though no one was nearby. She was so tired, bone tired. It would not surprise her if she would lie in bed any day soon and simply not get up, just drift away. Dead. Not by her hand, never by her hand, but drifting away sounded right. Peace from her mind would be a relief. No more self-recrimination. No more regret. Wasn't it bad enough that she had to endure the humiliation of her own failure, without anyone else knowing?

She pummeled the ground with flat palms. "Are you listening to me? Do I have to go back there? Can't I stay here with you?"

No answering voices resounded. She sat up and spun around, tucking her legs into one another in crisscross applesauce fashion.

She stared at the headstones in front of her. Two larger slabs in the center for her grandparents – her mother's parents – five smaller ones, three to one side, two on the other, representing three of her uncles dead before their time, one for an aunt who died in a freak accident during childbirth, and another blank stone where she thought her mother should rest. Her father had other ideas. He bought the plot for her mother a couple of rows over, with an empty one for him – his name already on the stone, with no expiration date – for when it was his time. Halley wondered how that would work since he had a second wife now. In the row behind her grandparents, she saw the tasteful headstones of her great-grandparents, some of their children buried around them. There was comfort in the past.

Halley ran her hand over her grandmother's name carved plainly and clearly in the stone. "If you're not going to talk to me, I guess I'll have to leave. Wish you'd tell me what to do."

On her last word, the wind kicked up, blowing her hair in her face, disturbing dried leaves from the previous autumn, swirling in a mini tornado next to her, and then losing its grip, sending the leaves flying across pristine gravesites.

"Okay, okay, you're listening. I'm going now. I'm not putting it off," Halley smiled a close-lipped smile, the edges tilted upward at the sign sent by her dead relatives. They never believed in putting anything off. Neither did they believe in "shoulda" or "coulda." No second guessing – pick a side, pick a direction, and move. That was one thing her father had in common with her mother's family.

Halley strode back to her car parked haphazardly on the side of the cemetery's drive, a silver performance vehicle that cornered as if she never made a turn and sped up smoothly and quickly – just as she liked it.

That was something she had in common with her father – the thrill of speed. She especially liked it when she rode her motorcycle in the country, up and down deserted hills, around deep bends. The freedom was undeniable. Not that her father knew she followed his passion for the two-wheeled beasts. Though he should not be too surprised since he bought her the first dirt bike – and the second – after she crashed into an elm tree when Bobby Lyle dared her to take a jump on an unfamiliar trail. How was she supposed to know a tree was center bottom on the other side, down a short but steep hill? Her father was not happy after he realized she was not dead, or brain damaged. He said, "What were you thinking? If your mom and I wanted a numbnuts for a kid, we woulda had a boy." That one still made her smile. He and her mother had one girl; he saved all the boys for his second marriage, and two more girls. For now, her Harley was safe in storage. Until she figured out her life. Or left it to someone in her will.

The top of a shoebox spun up in another micro-burst of wind and hit her across the back of the head. "Ow," she shouted and rubbed the sore spot. She glared back at the graves, no trash in sight, peaceful when she came, peaceful as she was leaving, but she knew better. "No fair getting inside my head! I'm not going to do anything to cause my demise." However, you could never tell. One day someone seemed perfectly fine and at peace and the next the body was found dead. Or sometimes people got hit by the proverbial bus – it happens. "I'm only allowing for all possibilities," she grumbled.

Halley drove down the main drag, staring at the shops that were not here when she lived in the town and some of the boarded-up storefronts. The Five & Dime was gone. No surprise there. She was pleased to see a couple of new restaurants in the very heart of town. If the bodies she could see inside the windows were any indication, they had some business. Her crawl through downtown, under the speed limit, was her last attempt to stall. She told herself she was re-familiarizing herself with the area, but that was a thinly veiled ruse.

There were choices. Show up at the house. Show up at the shop. Show up at the bar. The house was quickly crossed off her mental checklist. Halley realized too late she should have devised her plan of attack long before she entered the city limits. Maybe she could leave and come back tomorrow. A night in a hotel was not going to kill her; in fact, she would probably end up at one anyway.

She had to figure this out: Where was she going? What did she want to do next? All she could feel was the metal-tasting tinge of failure in her mouth, threatening to empty the contents of her stomach. She, Halley McCarthy, had never failed in her life. She felt like a failure, showing up, unexpectedly, in her hometown. No plan in place. No time limit on her "visit." She *had* to stop thinking about it or she would lose her mind.

Before Halley could make her way out to the highway, she heard the familiar sound of pipes, motorcycle exhaust pipes, to be specific. She often heard the same sound as motorcycles had driven by her place in the city; it always reminded her of home. It also made her feel a little paranoid, wondering if her father had spied on her.

A man pulled alongside her car on the left. He was dressed in jeans, heavy black boots, and a black thermal shirt with a black leather vest over it. His longish chestnut hair was covered in a black bandana, and dark aviator sunglasses hid his eyes. He looked over at her and a quick smile lightened his facial features. Either his facial hair was a couple of days' growth, or he kept the fashionable stubble. He waved her over and now the choice was not hers. *What was she thinking?*

Toward the less developed end of town, she pulled into the bar and restaurant's dirt and gravel parking lot and rolled down her window. The biker slowly – at least it seemed slow to her – turned the engine off, kicked down his kickstand, and threw his long leg over the seat in a fluid dismount. She kept her sunglasses on. He pulled his off as he looked carefully inside the vehicle, at the dash, the leather seats, the manual transmission – that was not very practical living in a city, as she did – evaluating every amenity it offered before he met her eyes, well, her sunglasses.

"Hal. You're home," he said, an unspectacular observation of the obvious.

"I'm here. Hasn't been home in a long time," Halley replied, then inwardly winced at how snide that sounded.

"Ouch," the man grimaced. Then he nodded, as if he should have expected that answer. "Old man know you're here?"

"Just arrived. You're the first person I've seen," she shrugged, knowing she had not answered his question.

He nodded again. "Are you at least gonna get out of that death trap and give me a hug?"

She stared at him for a few beats, then hit the electronic button to close the window and carefully folded her designer sunglasses into their case, before opening the door and stepping outside her car. She reached up – he was tall, seemed taller than the last time she was home, especially to her five-foot-five height – to put her arms around his shoulders. He leaned down so she could reach and picked her up with his arms around her waist and swung her around. He whispered in her ear, "About time you showed up, big sister."

Halley kicked up one booted foot behind her, trying to regain some control, or at least balance. Other than a half dozen motorcycles and a few pickup trucks, the parking lot was empty, no people milling about. She supposed that was to be expected before five in the afternoon during the week. After he set her down, one arm still around her waist, the young man grabbed her key fob from the car's cup holder, shoved it in his front pocket, engaged the lock, and pushed her door shut.

"Hey, give me those," Hal demanded.

He swung his hip away from her grabby hand and smirked, pulling more than walking her to the side door, arm still firmly around her waist.

She noted the red brick and concrete building was faded with age, though it was neat and clean outside, including a side patio that had been added since she last visited. The bricks that built this building were handmade in a local factory decades before, the factory long since shuttered. She acknowledged to herself she was impressed the sign announcing *Raiders Roost Tavern* had been upgraded.

The bar-restaurant had been in her dad's family for at least four generations – five if she counted her half-brothers, who more than likely worked here now. That's something she should have known but did not and found that embarrassed her.

Inside the heavy door, she noted the reinforced metal covering it. It took more than a few moments for her eyes to adjust to the dim lighting. The bar curved, forming the U-shape, proudly carved by her great-great-grandfather. He also designed the hardwood shelves and carved intricate scrolls on the small endplate columns that held the shelves. Mirrors still reflected behind the liquor bottles, as they had since the bar opened. The scarred tables and chairs that sat on the worn hardwood floor and took up most of the middle of the room looked the same, as did the wooden booths along three walls. There was still a small black and white tiled dance floor off to the right, the white more yellow now, with room for a live band behind it. Her great-great-grandmother loved to dance and insisted there be a dance floor. It remained throughout the following generations. She took all this in as she casually glanced around.

The bar was lined with bikers in their leather cuts – vests, to her friends in the city. They all turned as one when brother and sister entered. One of the younger guys whistled, "Yo, Conman, who's the new chick? You finally gettin' some?" He punctuated the question with lewd hip movements. A couple of others laughed. Eyes widened on some as they belatedly realized who she was and moved slightly away from their rude brother.

"Watch your mouth, Munch. This is my sister," Conor replied heatedly.

"Munch? I can see that," Halley said and made sure to appraise him, eyes raking over him from toe to head. "It's for Munchkin, right? That's why they call you that?"

The red-headed young man was a few inches shorter than the others and a little on the pudgy side, but still taller than her. He sucked in his gut and took a step forward, eyebrows knit in anger, "You callin' me a *donut*?" Munch sounded highly offended.

Halley did her version of confusion then acted like a light went on over her head, "Oh! That's the name of those little donut holes. No, not at all." She waited a beat and then continued, "I was talking about the Munchkins in the *Wizard of Oz*, you know, the little people?"

"Okay, Hal. Enough," her younger brother whispered out of the corner of his mouth.

"You callin' me *short*, lady?

Halley shrugged and before she could answer, a hand reached over the bar and grabbed a fistful of Munch's T-shirt collar. The man behind the hand whispered in a menacing voice, "Enough, Munch. You respect our sister, or you get out." He ran his other hand through his long chestnut-brown hair that had come out of its ponytail.

Munch blanched, “She’s your sister? I ain’t seen her ‘round here before.” He turned his head to Halley, deflated, “Sorry for the misunderstandin’. And they call me Munch because I get the munchies when I party.”

“No worries, Munchkin,” Halley soothed and laid him out in the same sentence. She smiled broadly, hoping no one would realize it was forced. She should never have come in here. *What was she thinking?*

The tall bartender came out from behind the bar and picked her up in a brotherly bear hug. He would not let go until she beat lightly on his back, “I can’t breathe, Scottie.”

He put her down and held her at arm’s length, taking a good look at his older sister. Scottie was the oldest of her father’s second family, four years younger than she. Halley figured out when she was in her pre-teens that her dad had to have impregnated her stepmother before they were married and not long after her mother had died. Priscilla, her stepmother, used to hang around her dad’s motorcycle club when she came home from college – taking a walk on the wild side. It was not long before they were married in a hurried ceremony, most likely at Priscilla’s insistence, because Halley could never see her father caring about propriety.

One day Halley was skipping down the street between her father’s parents’ house and their own, saw the flashing lights of the police cars, smoke billowing from the living room window, and the next thing she knew she was whisked away to her mother’s parents’ home on the other side of town, made to sit through a funeral – her first – and then later brought to a new home and introduced to her father’s new wife. A few months later she had a baby brother. At least that’s how she remembered it.

“What ‘cha want to drink?” Scottie asked, pulling her toward the bar, near the end that lifted upward to open, and away from the bikers.

“Umm. Tanqueray and tonic?” she decided on simple rather than the martini she really wanted.

“Lime, right?” he asked. She nodded. Just as he set the drink in front of her and she drank half of it down, the mixture of crisp sour and burn welcome against her tight throat, the side door opened, and the bar became eerily quiet. She glanced in the mirror and tried to see who entered, without turning around. She caught a small glimpse of the tall man, still hard-bodied and cut, though he was closer to fifty than forty these days. She turned on her bar stool and watched him stride across the floor toward her. His hair was the same thick, chestnut brown as her brothers, though shorter, and a little gray beginning to show at the temples. The goatee around his mouth was neatly trimmed. His eyes were the mirror image of her own, dark blue with yellow flecks, the iris ringed in an even darker blue. He had a few more lines around the corners of his eyes than the last time she saw him.

"You should have called," he said, stopping a few steps from her.

"Hi, Dad," she replied, making no apology, and then slid off the stool, moved the few feet forward, and wrapped her arms around him, head buried in his chest. Just as she had when she was younger.

James "Irish" McCarthy stiffened for a moment and then his muscled arms enfolded his daughter, holding her tighter than she held him. The man no one crossed, the man always in charge, melted with his daughter's hug. It was more than a hug; he could tell that. It was as if she needed a lifeline. But he knew she would never ask; the apple did not fall far from the tree with this one. It was just his sense, but he learned long ago to never dismiss his instincts.

The bar relaxed again as James led his daughter back to her stool and took the one next to her. Scottie put a beer bottle in front of him without a word spoken between them. Conor took the stool to her other side, sitting quietly, hoping no one told him to go.

"You stop and see your grandparents?" James asked his daughter. He knew her routine. The cemetery was always the first stop when she reached the city limits, no matter if it was the middle of the day or the middle of the night. Sometimes she stopped to talk to her mother, but she always stopped with her grandparents.

"I did," Halley replied. She took another drink and grinned. "They told me to go find you."

"You didn't listen too well," James smirked. He was sure his sons were confused by this point.

"I didn't have a chance. This one forced me off the road here," she gestured toward her brother Conor.

Conor immediately looked alarmed and held up his hands, "Hey, that's not right. I waved you over to the parking lot before you could escape." The flash in Halley's eyes proved he guessed right; she *was* trying to escape.

"I wasn't escaping. I was thinking," she protested. Her father's raised eyebrows told her he did not buy her explanation. He knew his second son spoke the truth, a truth by which his oldest daughter was embarrassed.

The three quietly drank, the silence not uncomfortable, which Halley found odd but reassuring – maybe you *can* go home again, no matter what Thomas Wolfe claimed. Maybe she would be luckier than the twentieth-century author.

Luck – huh, so much of life came down to luck, she thought bitterly. A person can study hard, work harder, do everything right, and still be no further ahead than they started. All she had to do was look around at those who stayed in her hometown to deduce that truth. Even in the cities where she lived her entire adult life, the underbelly of the metropolis devoured the young that gave it its vibrance, its lifeblood, spitting them out as so many stripped and useless chicken bones. Only a lucky few came out unscathed and even fewer came out on top.

She thought she was one of the lucky ones. She survived. She thrived. But maybe it had been an illusion, an illusion created by her willful desire to succeed, to leave everything behind except what she created on her own. Silently she shook the thoughts from her head. Philosophical exploration of her recent days, moreover her entire adult life, was not going to change a damn thing.

She took the last swig of her gin and noticed Scottie had silently backed it up with another. She met her brother's blue eyes and smiled her thanks; she saw the questions in his, but she was not yet ready to answer anything for anyone. A waitress came out of the kitchen with a plate of fries and silently put them in front of Halley, along with the salt and pepper shakers and squirt container of ketchup, before retreating to take refill orders from a couple of booths where patrons sat drinking and eating the bar food. This time

Scottie smiled at her and pointedly stared at the plate, telling her with his eyes to eat.

In the life she left behind, Halley's former fiancé used to steer her clear of all things fried, all things potatoes, all things that might add to her curves. She often wondered why he was with her to begin with, given his eyes more often than not raked over the model-thin, long-legged, long-haired beauties who crossed their path at restaurants, clubs, and even walking down the street in the middle of the day. That should have been a red flag; she had dismissed it by attributing it to all men having wandering eyes – as long as that was all that wandered.

At least there would be no awkward explanation of his absence to her father or his family. No one knew he existed. He had not asked her father before he proposed. He had never been to her hometown. He never asked about her family or her history. It was as if everything started when they got together. She had thought it was romantic and perfect, since she chose to live in the present and future, leaving the painful past long behind where she would not have to explain anything to anyone. She had been a fool.

Scottie pushed the plate closer to her, bringing her out of her reverie and putting a stop to the mental self-flagellation she had practiced for the last weeks. Halley reached out, squirted ketchup on the plate, and dipped a single fry, bringing it to her mouth, eyes on her brother the entire time. *See, I'm eating – satisfied?* she asked with her eyes. He winked, amused.

Enough with the silence. James could be very patient when it meant getting what he wanted or waiting out less patient men in business and interactions with other clubs. Not so much with his children or his club members – in other words, family.

"I'll let Priss know you're here and to make sure your bedroom is ready."

Halley felt a slight panic hit her chest. The closer the proximity to her father and family, the harder it would be to keep her secrets and get her head straight. Before she could protest, James raised an eyebrow, a move she practiced for years and could not master – one would never move alone.

"Don't even think about it. You're staying at the house."

Halley tried anyway, "Really, Dad, I'm not staying with you. She didn't know I was coming, and I don't want to cause a problem. I'm set. Really." She tried sitting straighter and smiling confidently, letting her father know the matter was settled. Unfortunately, while that move worked on corporate executives and sometimes her ex-fiancé, her father was not having it.

"No." That single word from the large man's mouth was known to silence an entire room of rowdy bikers. But she was not a biker. She was not a biker's "ol' lady." She was an independent woman.

Gaze narrowed, lips pursed, Halley stared down the man. It was all she could do to not jump off the stool and put her hands on her hips, dishing out the attitude, and brooking no orders from any, even her father. *Yeah, that would go well for me*, she argued in her mind. Scottie and Conor watched in fascination, eyes moving like a tennis ball from daughter to father and back – Scottie enjoying the show and Conor worried she was going to put their old man in a bad mood.

James broke the standoff first and pulled out his phone, texting someone quickly, staring at the three dots while the person on the other end typed, got his response, and then stowed his phone in the back pocket of his worn jeans. "Done. You're all set." He turned back to the bar, picked up his beer, and tipped one side of his lips in what might have been a small smile at Scottie.

Scottie reached out and shoved a ketchup-covered French fry in his sister's open mouth before she could argue. She glared at him but chewed when her mouth watered at the salty, crisp goodness. The *Roost* always did make the best fries. It was so much better than the kale salads her fiancé – ex-fiancé – ordered for her. When, she wondered, did kale become a thing? When she was a kid, it was a garnish and not an appetizing one.

"I'd feel more comfortable at a hotel for a couple days," Halley mumbled.

"What? You're only staying a couple days?" Conor asked, clearly surprised. She had not been home in years and to stay only a couple of days would be an insult.

"I didn't say that," Halley protested, willing her brother to shut up. "I've been driving pretty much non-stop for the last thirty-six hours and thought I could get a couple days to unwind before I'm sociable."

"You didn't stop at all?" Conor said incredulously. "No sleep?"

"Not like you haven't pulled all-nighters before," she groused. "Probably partied that long of a stretch."

"That's different," Conor protested.

"You didn't stop to sleep at all?" Scottie questioned her, eyes narrowed, reminding her of their father.

"I did. I pulled over for a couple hours when I got tired," she admitted.

"Pulled over? Not a hotel?" Scottie pressed.

She sighed, "No hotel. I pulled into a well-lit parking lot with lots of people at a 24-hour fast food joint. Doors locked. Satisfied?"

Her brothers looked horrified, and her father's eyes narrowed as he bit his tongue.

"Shit no!" Conor exclaimed. "Anyone can easily break into a car, pick you up, and shove you in a white van to be sold to the highest bidder. Would have been a piece of cake since no one knew you were coming so no one would have known you were missing until it was too late." The twenty-five-year-old painted an oddly explicit picture of the dismal circumstances in which she could have found herself.

"I'm fine, obviously. Don't get your panties in a bunch," Halley huffed. "I've been on my own since I was sixteen."

"Not true," James growled. Sure, his super-smart daughter had graduated high school at sixteen and gone to college, where she proved again to be determined and intelligent, graduating with her bachelor's degree in two-and-a-half years, rather than the usual four. From there, she moved immediately into the corporate world and got her MBA while working full-time. But at no time was he not looking out for her. At no time was she on her own as a teenager, no matter what she thought.

The look on her father's face made her stop before continuing to push the point. Instead, she opened her mouth and shoved in more fries. She held her empty gin and tonic glass up to her brother. Scottie looked to their father before moving. James shook his head to the negative.

Okay then, no more gin and tonic, she thought. Though she was sure she would get through this entire day and night much better if she had another drink.

Chapter 2

HALLEY NOTED THE SECURITY CAMERAS DISCRETELY placed in the trees as they drove through the high, electronic, iron gate. No one would see them if they didn't know they were there. More seemed to be placed along the public road before they came to the drive, too, and up the long drive to the house that had been her second childhood home.

The first, damaged by the fire set to cover her mother's brutal murder, was not beyond repair, but her father and grandfather had bulldozed it anyway. Not that she could blame them, looking at it from an adult perspective. Who would have wanted to buy a "murder house?"

But from her reasoning as a child, it had been home, and she had wanted to go back there. Back to where the master bedroom smelled like her mother's faint citrus perfume, where the scent of crisp linen permeated the first floor from the laundry room, where her dad's tools hung neatly on the garage walls and the cement had faint oil stains, where she sat on the countertop and her mother pretended to let her stir the cookie dough, and where her mother and father had gathered her between them in their arms and loved her, loved one another.

It made no difference to her stubborn mind that this was the property her parents bought and the house they had been building when it all went wrong, that her mother had wanted this as much as her father. Because, instead of her mother, it was another woman in her place.

The door to the large house swung open and a teenager with long chestnut hair, the color of their father's and brothers', raced outside, not stopping when she spotted Halley and threw her arms around her, running into her with such force Halley fell back against Scottie, who had driven her car here, with her as the passenger. No one drove her car except her, but apparently her over-protective father and brothers had not gotten that memo. Even the ex-fiancé was not allowed to drive the car. Not that he could even if she had wanted him to; he could not drive a manual transmission to save his life, and she was not going to let anyone strip the gears of her baby.

"Oomph," Halley lost the air in her lungs and staggered backward as the teenager plastered herself to Halley's body.

At the same time, Scottie put his hands on Halley's shoulders to steady her. "Whoa, slow down. Don't knock her over."

"You're here! You're really here!" the girl squealed in excitement, hugging her eldest sister even harder.

Halley's eyes were wide with surprise. Even though her youngest sister texted often, and she followed the teenager on social media like a stalker, she was still surprised at how tall and shapely she had become, more woman than little girl. Rationally, she realized that happened to fourteen-year-olds, but her mind was having trouble crossing that time divide. She really had been gone a long time.

"Yes, she's here. Now let us get her in the house," Scottie said, peeling the girl's arms from Halley's body.

"Wow, Scarlett, you're taller than me now," Halley said, looking the teenager up and down.

"I know. I made varsity basketball this year!" the girl blurted proudly. She was a freshman, so that was quite an accomplishment. Scarlett always was more relatable to Halley than their sixteen-year-old sister Tiffany. Where Scarlett was smart and a sports star, bowing to no one, Tiffany was more interested in her hair, fashion, and boys, smart too, but tried not to show it too much if her latest crush was in the room. It was all Halley could do to not scream at Tiffany's social media pages to never hide who she was. But guiltily, she realized she did the same thing, albeit in a different way and for different reasons.

Tiffany was only a year old when Halley left for college and Scarlett was born while she was gone. Somehow though, Scarlett still managed to get under her barrier walls and built a long-distance relationship with the eldest sister she idolized. The girl planned to go to college and live and work in whatever exciting city Halley was located.

Tiffany? Not so much. Halley kept her opinions to herself, but she secretly expected Tiffany to purposely get pregnant in high school, or college, at the longest, to whomever the favorite jock of the season was, and tie her family-sized wagon to the poor sap until death did they part. *Yeah, best to keep those thoughts locked up in a vault.*

"I know. I'm proud of you," Halley said, meaning it.

Scarlett pouted slightly, "But you didn't make it to any of my games."

Scottie hooted, "Guilt much? She lives across the country, Scar!"

"I know. But I still hoped. She gets vacation time," Scarlett huffed. "We made it to States."

Halley nodded, "I know. You texted me, remember? And I did find it on YouTube and watched the entire series. You were awesome." Her fiancé – ex-fiancé – wanted to know why she was watching a kids' basketball game, especially one from another state, and of girls, no less. She kept the secret and watched anyway, while he shook his head and poured himself an expensive whiskey on the rocks, before disappearing into her home office. She remembered thinking every time he did that, that her grandfather would have been appalled by the audacity of someone to water down an expensive single malt. Maybe that's why she never told anyone from her hometown about him; they would not have approved. She knew unequivocally that he would not have approved of them.

"Thanks!" Scarlett flushed at the compliment. She pulled her sister's arm, dragging her toward the house.

"Wait, let me get my bag," Halley stalled.

"I've got it," Scottie waved her off as their father and Conor dismounted their bikes.

"No! I can do it," Halley pulled away from her sister. But Scottie beeped the trunk open before she could grab the keys. He took a step back, turned to stare at her, and then back at the trunk, "Uh, Hal, what's going on?"

James and Conor stood beside Scottie and stared inside. Halley shut her eyes and counted for a few seconds, seeking to calm herself, before facing the onslaught.

"What? Just shut that. My bag's in the back seat," she huffed and raced to the driver's side back door and opened it, hoping to grab her bag under the duvet she had situated on top of the things in her overflowing backseat, which had remained hidden from Scottie when he drove her to the house. But before she could reach inside, Conor pulled her favorite duvet with her favorite red cover out of the vehicle, exposing the mishmash of personal and household items, along with artwork, artfully loaded into every available space, an efficient storage container, of sorts, for what she considered her most important things.

Halley reached in and grabbed a soft-sided leather case with a shoulder strap and a leather backpack with her laptop and important papers. Scottie immediately took the bag and backpack from her and started toward the house, without another word. She stood there staring at the ground, not sure what to say.

James reached behind her and grabbed a pillow, another favorite, and tossed it to Conor, who struggled to catch it and not drop the duvet in the dirt. "Take those to her room." Then he carefully moved Halley away from the rear door, shut it quietly, steered her around the vehicle, pushed the trunk closed, and shut the passenger door on their way toward the house. He did not say a word, but his hand was gentle against her back. Scarlett stared with an open mouth and would have expressed what she was thinking had Scottie not bumped her as he walked by and quietly ordered her to follow him.

All Halley could think, as her brain threatened to explode and her eyes promised to leak, was that this was not at all how she intended this to go. She was not prepared for their questions. She was not ready for their sympathy or their anger – worse, pity. She needed to leave. Once they were all asleep, maybe she could make her way to a hotel for a few days.

"Who's here?" Tiffany asked as she peered outside the door. She looked confused and then realization dawned, "Well look who the cat dragged in. Hal, is that you? What on earth brought you to our podunk town?" Tiffany's words were sharp, while her voice remained sweet. It was not lost on her provincial brain that their older sister seemed to think she was too good for them and never returned home. Tiffany reigned as princess – at least in her own mind – of the school, the club, and their home, and did not relish any competition. Little did she realize that Halley had no desire to compete for anything Tiffany considered important.

"You calling Dad a feral cat?" Conor smirked as he pushed by the girl.

"Of course not. It's an expression, Conor. Haven't you ever heard the expression?" Tiffany rolled her eyes as only teenagers and club girls could, not realizing her brother was teasing her.

Another motorcycle pulled into the drive, followed by a late-model pickup truck. Inwardly, Halley groaned. It looked like a full family reunion. The only ones missing were her father's parents and her uncles and aunts. Her youngest brother Danny stepped out of the truck and Drake, the third brother in line, dismounted his Harley.

"What, no sled for Danny?" Halley asked, using the bikers' colloquial term for motorcycle. Danny had to be seventeen now, almost eighteen, if she did her calculations correctly.

"Crashed his being stupid. Not getting a new one until Dad thinks he's mature enough," Conor informed her over his shoulder, before he headed across the house to the first-floor bedroom that had been Halley's most of her youth. Her dad and Priscilla were on the other side of the main floor, in an extra-large master's suite, while her brothers and sisters had upstairs bedrooms. She was surprised no one had claimed her bedroom as their own.

"Well, guess you got your numbnuts after all." Without thinking, Halley joked with her father, belatedly surprised the familiarity so easily passed her lips.

James threw back his head and laughed hard. "That I did, Hal, that I did. I learned from you not to get the second one right away." He raised his eyebrow at his daughter, a knowing expression on his face.

"Hey, I did not crash the second one. I was too afraid you'd take it away," she said. Then she admitted shyly. "Well, I crashed it, but it was fixable."

"You crashed it the *day after* you crashed the first one," James reminded her. He remembered the look on her face as she stood next to the dirt bike, helmet off, trying to pull it out of the tree it was wedged into so she could push it with a mangled tire back to the house. She had ignored all their shouts looking for her, too embarrassed by crashing twice in two days, too mad to let anyone help her with her mess. She had been stubborn then and that trait only seemed to grow with age. It took three grown men to free the dirt bike and get it back to the garage. She was right; it had not taken much to fix, but he had made her wait a full two weeks for the new tire and the guys to fix it for her.

She shrugged and smiled sheepishly at her father. In that moment, he saw the girl she had been, before she quickly erected her protective walls and forced herself to follow Conor to the bedroom. It was not much, but he would take what he could get, for now.

The inside of the bedroom had changed. Her high school art and the motivational and favorite band posters were no longer on the walls. The paint color was different. But her same old quilt was folded at the end of the bed and the comforter was the same red and black plaid she left behind.

"Sorry. I was gone on club business and Priss got it in her head to redecorate the room," James said apologetically. "I couldn't find the posters, but the oil paintings are in the closet for you to rehang. And your old trophies are in a box in the closet; wasn't sure if you'd want them out anymore." He had been livid when he returned to the chaos and saw what he felt was an effort to eradicate his oldest daughter's presence from the house.

"I wanted this room, but he said I couldn't have it," Tiffany pouted.

"You've got your own room, Tiff," James reminded her.

"Yeah, and I'm older. I should have it before you," Danny added. He was two years old when she left for college. Another sibling with whom she had no real connection.

"Right. I'm going to let a teenage boy have a first-floor room. In your dreams," James replied.

Halley had not realized they all followed her through the house. "It's okay. You could have given it to one of the others. I don't live here anymore. Haven't in a long time."

"See! I call dibs!" Tiffany shouted triumphantly.

"Enough! Go see if your mother needs help in the kitchen," James ordered. All three teenagers left without argument, though the two discontented ones mumbled under their breaths; what they said, he did not know and would not ask.

"You always have a home to come back to, Hal. Told you that," James said. That's right, she thought, when James McCarthy made a promise, it was binding. But this one certainly did not endear her to her younger siblings, or his wife. Conor set the now folded duvet and her favorite pillow on the bed before silently following his younger siblings. The only one who had not followed her to the room was Drake.

"I think dinner's almost ready. I can hear Gramps and Gram pulling up now," Scottie said, listening to the distinctive sound of their grandfather's Harley, as he placed his sister's bags on the trunk at the end of the bed. The old trunk had belonged to her mother's mother, so she was grateful her father had rescued it from her stepmother's purge. She always meant to come back for it, but there never seemed to be time. When she infrequently did return to the smalltown, she flew, and the trunk needed to go by land. She hoped its contents had not been touched. It would not surprise her if Tiffany rifled through everything. But nothing in the trunk would interest her sister, or anyone, really, except her. Memories. It held memories and pieces of the past upon which she no longer dwelled.

"Let me freshen up and I'll be out soon," Halley said.

"Don't be long. Everyone wants to set eyes on you," her father admonished before turning on his heel and leaving.

Scottie squeezed her elbow. "Hey, I don't know what's going on, but we've got you. Always." He bent and kissed the top of her head, just because he could, and followed James down the hall toward the living area and kitchen.

Absently, as she brushed her teeth and splashed water on her face, Halley wondered if they already planned a family dinner before she arrived, or if this was put together once her father told everyone she was in town. It had to have been planned before her arrival, which meant they would add an extra place setting to the oversized dining table. It had to be big, given the size of the family and the grands. She knew they used to gather once a week at her grandparents' house but was not sure if that still happened or if her dad's house was the new gathering spot. She had a hard time seeing her grandmother voluntarily relinquishing her place in the kitchen, especially since Priscilla's culinary skills could not hold a candle to the older woman's. She spoke with her grandmother at least once a month but never thought to ask if the old traditions still held.

"There she is," her grandmother cried and everyone else turned to stare her way. The house was large, mostly open space with each area serving a different function, so everyone saw her coming. Halley almost stumbled, not wanting all eyes on her. Her grandfather, as tall and broad as her father, even in his seventies, took three giant steps forward and picked her up in a bear hug.

"Gramps," she sighed, shutting her eyes as she took a deep breath through her nose, breathing in the fresh air that clung to his thermal shirt, along with the leather of his old cut, and the faint smell of burning wood, and held tight to his familiar frame. She was shocked he could lift her, or that he would want to.

"Put her down. Quit hogging the child," she heard her grandmother protest.

When he reluctantly lowered her to the floor, she looked up to him and saw the adoration in his eyes, before they hardened again as he stared down at her. "Been too long, baby girl."

"Gramps."

Before she could say something that would put her in the proverbial doghouse, her grandmother wedged herself between the two and hugged her granddaughter close. She whispered in her ear, "I'm so glad you're home."

"Are we going to eat soon?" Tiffany grumped in the background, dragging out her chair and plopping down. "I have things to do."

James slowly turned to the teenager, "And what would that be, on a school night?"

Tiffany flushed a light shade of pink under all the makeup she sported and looked at her plate before replying, "Meeting some of the girls downtown in a while. I don't have any homework. I finished it in study hall."

Halley doubted that. She remembered her junior year. With Tiffany's penchant for socializing, homework would not be what she did in study hall.

Priscilla moved next to James and put a hand on his lower back as she spoke in a quiet voice, "Let it go, James. I already said it was all right." Then she called to Halley, still held by her grandmother and crowded by her grandfather, "Welcome back, Hal." Halley noticed Priscilla didn't say "home."

"Thanks, for having me on short notice," Halley said lightly as she pushed back from her grandmother's embrace. Her father scowled; she knew he didn't believe she needed an invitation.

"Let's eat before it's cold," Priscilla called to everyone, gesturing to the food already on the table.

Halley saw her grandmother grimace. The older woman guided her to the seat next to her own and pulled her into the chair. Her dad sat at one end of the table, and she watched as her grandfather took the other end. Priscilla dropped next to James, but the look on her face said that Halley's grandfather had taken her spot. Scarlett edged Scottie out of the way and sat next to Halley, grinning broadly in Halley's direction.

All through the dinner of dry baked chicken, limp asparagus, and lumpy mashed potatoes, Halley made sure her mouth was full, chewing very slowly, so she could listen and not talk. There were enough young people around the table that there was never silence.

She learned Scottie and Conor had their own place now; well, Scottie owned the house and Conor rented from him. She wondered if she could stay with them. Drake, now twenty-one, had moved into the clubhouse, though it sounded as if he regularly came around for meals and sometimes stayed in his old bedroom upstairs. Tiffany denied having a boyfriend, after she told everyone Danny skipped baseball practice to drive a girl home, and he outed her in retaliation. By the end of dinner, Halley was ready for bed. Thirty-six hours in her car was finally wearing her down. She tried to hide her yawn behind her hand, but her grandmother caught it.

"I think our girl needs some shuteye. Get some sleep, Hal. I'll expect you at the house for breakfast," the older woman said.

"Breakfast? How about dinner, Gram?"

"Breakfast."

"You got it," Halley relented. She looked directly at Priscilla and said, "Thanks for dinner. I'm sorry, but Gram's right, I need to sleep." She pushed away from the table.

Even though she had been in Halley's life since the girl was three years old, Halley had never called her Mommy or Mom, which she knew bothered her stepmother. She quit calling her anything when Scottie and Conor began calling their mother Priss rather than Mommy because they followed their big sister's lead and Priss had complained loudly to their father. It was easier to call her nothing.

She gave her grandmother and grandfather side hugs and then Scarlett jumped up and hugged her before she could make her getaway to her bedroom. The youngest McCarthy whispered, "It means so much to me you're here." Halley felt the guilt roll in her gut before she pushed it away, telling herself it was a useless emotion. A few minutes later, dressed for bed in yoga pants and a sweatshirt, Halley promised herself she would sleep for a few hours and then get up and find a hotel after everyone else was asleep.

Once they heard her bedroom door close, the table erupted, everyone talking at once.

"How long is she here?" Tiffany whined.

"Why didn't she call?" Priss asked.

"Why is all that stuff in her car?" Conor wondered.

"Does this mean I can't have her room?" Danny looked to his mother.

"Has she said anything, James?" Gram asked.

"I want her to stay for a long time," Scarlett declared and glared down the table at Tiffany, where she sat next to their mother.

The others added their comments and questions; everyone except James, middle child, Drake, and James' father, Mitchell. James sat back and watched the chaos unfold, waiting to let them get it all out. He folded his arms across his chest and stared at his father, who mirrored his image at the other end of the table. Scottie took his cue from the two men, disengaged from the speculation, leaned back, and folded his arms across his chest; the others were giving him a headache anyway. Drake ate another roll. One by one, the rest of the family noticed the silence and tension radiating from the three men and sentences died off in the middle.

"Are you all done now?" James asked quietly. Scottie always worried when his father spoke so quietly and precisely; at the club, that meant the hammer was coming down. No one replied, all waiting to see what he had to say.

"We don't know what's happened with your sister. We don't know how long she's staying. She can stay forever, if that's what she decides. We're going to wait until she tells us. Everybody clear now?" James slowly looked around the table and met each of his family eye to eye.

His father nodded in agreement, adding his weight to his son's decree. Everyone needed to leave his granddaughter alone, except him and his wife.

"Can I go now?" Tiffany broke the silence as she stood from her chair, clearly bored with the family dinner turned family meeting.

Her mother nodded for her to leave. James added, "Be home by ten." Tiffany rolled her eyes once she was out of her father's line of sight, and Danny smirked at her.

James saw his father gesture with his head toward the front porch and got up to follow him. Once outside, the door shut behind them, and Tiffany sped too fast down the driveway in the new car her mother had bought her against James' wishes. His father turned his hard look on him.

Before he acknowledged his father, he watched Tiffany a little longer. Oh, Priscilla claimed she thought James was not thrilled with buying a new car when the teenager turned sixteen but did not realize he meant *absolutely not.* James thought Tiffany was too immature and reckless. When he came home after more than a week away on club business, Tiffany had already had the vehicle for a week. He suspected Priss waited no more than an hour after he was out the door, not that she would ever admit to it.

The woman always acted like she listened to his every word, but he knew she often twisted those words to her liking. Still, they had been together a long time now and shared six of his seven children; never was his first-born counted in the number Priss related when she talked to anyone about their children. He supposed he couldn't blame her; Halley's mother was the love of his life. Priss was the sweet thing he got pregnant one drunken night in the midst of his grief. Priss had been home from college on her summer break. He honestly did not even remember having sex with her and insisted on an in-utero paternity test before he agreed to her demands for marriage.

He had been in such a bad place at the time, after his first wife's murder, that he supposed he should be grateful to the woman who helped pull him out of the dark place he had gone. Always bound by duty, he placed a high regard on integrity, more so than most. He loved Priscilla, a love born from years of familiarity and compatibility, but he had never been in love with her.

James would never allow himself to fall so far again that if something were to happen, he could not crawl out. Now that he was president of the club, too many lives and livelihoods depended upon him, just as his father and grandfather before him; the same duty he expected someday to pass to Scottie.

"Done stewing on little miss uppity and her car?" his father asked, tired of waiting, his own eyes on his son and away from his demon of a granddaughter. The old man called them as he saw them. Tiffany had way too much of her mother's family in her DNA, if her actions and attitude were anything to go by. The girl played the motorcycle club princess role to the hilt, though the men kept her away from the club as much as they could; she was far too tempting for the younger guys.

"Yeah," James sighed and met his father's hard gaze. "If you're going to ask me about Hal, I don't know what to tell you."

"Tell me you got people checking," Mitch's gaze stayed hard. James knew his father was an intimidating man, even at his age, but he learned long ago to meet him step for step and not back down. That others saw James the same way they saw his old man was always a surprise.

"I made some calls, yeah. Nothing concrete yet. Seems that company she works for may be in trouble."

"Is our girl in trouble?"

"I don't know yet, Pop. But I will," frustration evident in James' voice.

That was all Mitch needed to hear. He turned back to the drive Tiffany disappeared down and changed the subject. "Priss got Tiff on the pill yet?"

Just when James thought his father could not rattle him, the subject change left him reeling. "For fuck's sake!"

"That's what I'm talking about. Unless you want to raise the next generation of McCarthys, get her on the pill."

"She's sixteen." Even to his ears, James knew his protest was lame. The girl was a walking siren. He suspected the only thing that kept most of the town boys from dipping their wick was fear of him and her brothers. But even that was not a guarantee on a night filled with teenage hormones and pilfered beer. "Fine. I'll get Priss on it." He inwardly winced. Priss would not take that conversation well; she babied Tiffany. He had no idea why his wife was so protective of that daughter, but Priss handled her as if she were fragile.

The front door opened, and the four boys walked onto the porch, Scarlett not far behind. From the look of his sons, they were ready to leave.

"See you tomorrow. I'm heading back to the *Roost*. Jana says everything's quiet, but you never know if it'll stay that way," Scottie informed him, mentioning their best waitress and a great bartender in her own right. He turned to his grandfather and grinned, "Bye, Gramps. Don't give the old man too hard a time, 'kay?" His grandfather lifted his chin in his typical goodbye. Well, that chin lift could be a hello, goodbye, a challenge – pretty much anything the old man wanted was communicated that way.

"I'll give you a lift," Conor offered. That's when Scottie remembered he drove Halley's car to the house. He quickly thought about taking her keys – she was up to something; of that he was certain – but decided against it and walked back inside to dangle her keys on one of the hooks left for that purpose inside the door. Back outside, he strode toward his brother's Harley, and the two of them left down the long drive, the trees and winding path eventually hiding them from sight, but the others could still hear the pipes as they hit the road and sped faster.

Drake had been quiet most of the night and his departure was much the same; he silently waved behind his head as he mounted his Harley, an older model than his brothers', and rode down the driveway without a backward glance. Danny was next, taking the three porch steps in one, and jogged toward his truck.

"Whoa. Where do you think you're going?" James demanded.

Danny froze mid-step. "Uh, thought I'd meet Drake at the clubhouse?" His response was more a question than a statement. He did not yet possess the confidence of his older brothers, and his swagger was limited to the high school halls, football field, hockey rink, and baseball diamond. His father and grandfather intimidated him, though neither had done anything but bark and set boundaries. It worked for them.

"Not tonight. Back in the house. School night," James hitched his thumb toward the door while Scarlett snickered.

"Tiff's out," Danny protested.

"Yep, but you won't be."

The boy sighed deeply and stomped back into the house. Scarlett leaned against the porch railing, standing close to her father. Both men were silent, as usual.

"Don't stop talking on my account," she said lightly.

Her grandfather's lips twitched. Her father tried to keep a straight face and glare at her, but she knew it was faked. No one was going to ruin her night. Her oldest sister was home, and it was the best surprise ever.

Chapter 3

PURE DARKNESS FILLED THE ROOM. IT WAS DISCONCERTING. SILENCE. This was not her life; her life had no silence or darkness. This was not her bed. Before panic set in, Halley remembered she was in her father's house. She was in a different state. There was no traffic noise and no light pollution because she was no longer in San Francisco … or New York, the place she wished she never left.

That was not true either. She loved New York, loved the way it vibrated and pulsed as if the city had its own heartbeat, loved the restaurants and shows, the museums, the people. But then she was bored. Friends coupled up or looked to couple up. No potential partner she met lasted; no one could handle her ambition or her success or, maybe, just her.

The San Francisco opportunity arose, and she grabbed it with both hands, upended her life, and moved across the country. The chance to rise with a startup appealed to her sense of adventure, something desperately missing in her life in the last several years.

Halley was used to being the youngest one in the room, the brightest one in the room, and having the best mentors. She was used to having the most original and farfetched ideas. She was used to leering men and jealous women. She was used to success following her wherever she went. She was used to being sought after for the best positions. She was used to leaping and had the faith and confidence to know she would land well.

When she was young, very young, but after her mother died, her mother's mother told her that with great tragedy came great joy because life was about balance. She, Halley McCarthy, would be granted great heights and would also have to endure the deep valleys. That was simply the way of her life. Other people seemed to live in relatively straight lines, not too much tragedy, not too much joy, not too much adventure. Understanding those people was hard; it did not compute for her.

Her grandmother was right, so far. All she craved now, in this moment, was for that upswing, for the joy to come back. Preferably soon. For the first time, she also felt a tinge of fear. What if her time as the golden girl was up? What if she peaked early? She *was* in her thirties now.

Unable to sleep, Halley rose and took a shower in the ensuite bathroom, her father's gift to her younger self. Her room was far enough away from the others that she knew no one would be disturbed by the sounds of the water. Hair towel-dried and hanging to her shoulders – there was no taming the waves and curls, not that she wanted to – she brushed her teeth one more time, then dressed in jeans and a sweatshirt and her black motorcycle boots, threw the two bags over her shoulder, and as quietly as possible closed her bedroom door and crept through the living area to the front door. Relief filled her when she spied her keys hanging on the hook; *thank you, Scottie*. The security system keypad was next to the hooks. Luckily, Scarlett gave her the code, which she knew her security-conscious father changed regularly.

As she reached for the keypad, the weight of the bags on her shoulder disappeared and a deep voice caused her to jump, back flush to the door, a small eek escaping from her throat, hands at her sides flat against the door's surface. "Where you going, Hal?"

Halley mentally scolded herself for not being aware someone was in the room. Since when did anyone get the drop on her? Situational awareness. She had been raised on it, drilled into her head her entire life. But tonight, she was too much in her own head. She had dwelled there the last few weeks and it was hard to get out of the mess she tried to untangle in her brain.

James stood in his dark boxer briefs, waiting. Her father's tattooed chest, abdomen, arms, and shoulders stood out in the low light cast by the security panel. He might be closer to fifty now, but the ridges of his abdomen still sported the six-pack that had made her friends' mothers and her teachers – women and men – drool her entire life, and she could see the definition in his arms even as they hung at his sides. Her father in his underwear was nothing new. No one was body-shy in this house, and everyone ran around in their underwear for as long as she could remember. She also knew she saw more at the clubhouse than her father probably ever realized. Several of her friends first understood the mechanics of sex from the animals on local farms, but she witnessed actual human intercourse on couches and picnic tables at the clubhouse parties between young members and club groupies.

"Uh, couldn't sleep."

"So, you're taking your bags?" the man walked away from the door, with her things. He turned toward the kitchen and expected her to follow. Once there, he put her things on the other side of the black, granite-topped island, opened a cupboard, and pulled out two low glasses and a bottle of scotch from another cupboard high above. He waved her to a seat on a stool and poured two fingers into each glass, neat. She smiled inwardly – no ice watering down that nectar. He pushed one glass toward her and raised the other in front of his lips.

"This your solution for insomnia?" she asked and took a small sip. Yep, the good stuff.

James tilted his head to the side and narrowed his eyes in response. No words were necessary. She took a bigger sip.

"Am I under house arrest?" She tried the defiant route. Then quieter, "I really think I need to be alone."

"Been alone too long," he responded.

"Seriously, Dad. I'm a grown woman."

"Then act like it."

Well, there was that. Independent, grown women did not usually sneak out of their fathers' houses under the cover of darkness. She sighed and slumped with her elbow on the counter, head in her hand.

"I don't know what you want me to say," Halley groaned.

"There's a lot to say, Hal." He waited. She sat silently.

James continued, "How about start with why your car is packed with all your stuff."

"That's not *all* my stuff," Halley replied heatedly. "I lived in a house, you know."

"No, I wouldn't know; I've never been there. But *lived* is past tense. Where do you *live* now?" he pushed harder. Rationally, he knew he was throwing the plan of waiting until she talked to them out the window. Anger raged in his skull when he realized she was trying to sneak out – hurt and disappointment clenched in his chest.

Halley looked up, belatedly realizing her mistake. The fight went out of her. Right now, in the middle of the night, after more than thirty-six hours on the road, a tense family dinner, and only a very few hours' sleep, she really just wanted her dad. That realization hit her hard and shocked her. It was easy to keep him and his overwhelming personality at bay when she was across the country in another state or in another country; in front of her, she remembered how safe he made her feel, how loved.

In a small voice, Halley said, "The stuff in my car is important to me. And some other stuff I threw in because I had room."

"Where do you live, Hal?"

"I'm not sure yet," she met her father's blue eyes with her own. "I kind of gave up my place. Everything else is in storage."

"Why?"

"Some stuff happened," she skirted the heart of the issue.

"And?"

"And I need time to think and figure out what I want to do next."

Suddenly she recognized the look on her father's face, the pain. It was hard for a man who made decisions on the regular and ruled with an iron fist to hold back his opinion – hold back his desire to order her to tell him *exactly* what was going on, preferably in painstaking detail.

"You're killing me here, Hal."

Halley fairly exploded, "What do you want from me?! What do all of you want from me?! To tell you I'm a failure? That yeah, Halley McCarthy is a failure?" Determined not to shed the tears that welled in her eyes, she swallowed harshly and blinked rapidly, shoving the feeling of desperation and panic back where it would not hurt her just yet.

The stunned look on her father's face was not what she expected. "What the hell are you talking about? Failure is not a word anyone would associate with you – ever. Gotta give me more, Hal."

"Well, I'm here, aren't I? Car stuffed to the brim. No one ever expected me back. Not even me. I left a great job in New York for San Francisco and now my new company's in trouble. *I* may be in trouble. While we're on my failings, you might as well know my personal life is a complete failure, but that's nothing new, and probably not a surprise, but at least I always had my career," Halley suddenly slumped on her stool, the fight going out of her. Following her rant, her voice now sounded small and hallow, "I just didn't know where else to go when I started driving. The car kinda headed here. Maybe that's my biggest failure of all. I didn't handle it myself."

James was visibly shocked, which was never the case. Just as quickly as she had exploded, he processed what she said, and a furrow set between his brows. He moved quickly around the granite island and hugged her, holding her head to his chest with a hand stroking the back of her hair. He placed a fatherly kiss on top of her head and whispered, not wanting to upset her more than she already was, "You got that wrong, baby girl. This is exactly where you come when your world turns upside down." After a few moments of soothing his daughter, with a finger under her chin, he lifted her face to his, "No matter what you think, no one will ever see you as a failure. You're already a success and you aren't even halfway through your life, Hal. That means something. To me. To this family. To anyone who knows you. It should mean something to you."

Halley searched her father's eyes, looking for the lie. Looking for the "Dad Goggles," she saw no confiming signs, not that she expected him to placate her; he never had when she was growing up, she supposed he would not start now.

She asked slowly, "In the morning, can I tell you about the startup I was working for? I know you and the club own small businesses, but maybe you can help me figure this out?" Even as the words came out of her mouth, she realized she was feeling raw and her father's acceptance at this moment meant the world to her. This was not something she would typically share or on which she would expect help, though this was brand new territory, nothing she had experienced before in her corporate career. She suddenly comprehended the loneliness she had been feeling, the utter isolation, and no one to whom she could turn – most of the friends she made in her adult life were left behind on the East Coast, when she moved to the West Coast. Her work colleagues were all turning on one another. Her ex-fiancé left her with suspicion hanging over her head and several thousands of dollars lighter. Her father, on this dark night, was her lifeline. She may regret it in the morning, but for now, it was everything. He was everything.

"Nothing I want to do more," James assured her. In his mind, he thought more vicious thoughts, such as vowing to make whoever hurt his daughter and attacked her flagging confidence pay and suffer a great deal in the process. But those thoughts he kept to himself.

He carried her bags across the dark living area and back to her bedroom. He waited while she kicked off her boots and laid on top of the made bed. He pulled the old quilt over her still-dressed body. She was completely drained by the little she already admitted. He tucked the quilt over her shoulders and under her chin, then kissed her forehead, just as he had so many times when she was a child.

"Don't forget you have to meet your grandmother for breakfast. Come to the clubhouse after and we'll talk more. For now, sleep," James ordered gently.

"Love you, Dad," Halley mumbled and was asleep before he closed the door. He was not sure she even realized she said it, but his heart expanded anyway; he could not remember the last time he heard those words from her. The guys would be shocked three little words from a daughter he had not seen in a few years could tie him in knots. Good thing they would never know.

As he made his way across the dark living area and toward the master suite on the other side of the house, he changed course and headed to the front door. He picked her keys off the hook and stared at them a moment before palming them and backtracking to the great room, where he placed the keys under the pillow on the end of the couch and laid down, pulling a blanket from the back over his tall body. Halley was fine for now and clearly spent, but once she woke and realized the extent of her nighttime admission, he expected she might backtrack and try to bolt. *That* was not going to happen again. The keys and his presence in the living area were his insurance policy, because the reality was that he needed some shuteye too.

Halley woke to her father's voice, "Better get up, Hal. Don't want to keep Gram waiting." She groaned and sat up, realizing she slept in her clothes, further remembering her late-night confession to her dad, and groaned louder. Oh well, she would brush her teeth and head over. No need for another shower.

"I'll be in my office at the clubhouse when you're done," he tossed her keys through the air; she caught them with ease.

"Will do," Halley agreed without hesitating. That made James' smile reach his eyes. He closed the door.

Once in her car, Halley pulled around on the paved road through the woods that led to her grandparent's house. James ensured the security of both homes kept behind the perimeter fence and monitored with cameras. Halley had explored every inch of the thousands of acres owned by her family and the club: on dirt bike, horseback, and on foot. She could have walked this morning, but her grandparents were just far enough away she would have been late. As it was, her grandmother was finishing the eggs benedict, Halley's favorite, as she walked in the kitchen door and breathed in the scent of home cooking. Her ex-fiancé never understood her love of cooking and preferred to eat out and be seen or order in and not have to wash pots and pans. She missed this.

A head now full of white hair and more wrinkles around her eyes, her grandmother's stature seemed smaller, though she moved with the spryness of a much younger woman. Still, the fact her grandmother was aging, not stuck in time like the images in her mind, was jarring. One more reason she should not have stayed away so long.

"Your tea's steeping on the counter; should be ready," Gram pointed with her head as she carefully poured the hollandaise sauce.

Halley grabbed the mug from the light granite counter and topped off Gram's coffee, before setting both on the butcher block farm table and sitting down, stomach growling in anticipation. When the plate slid in front of her, it was all she could do to wait until the older woman took her place at the head of the kitchen table.

The kitchen was Halley's favorite room in this house. The distressed antique white cabinets looked functional and fashionable. It was a comfortable space, with warm accents; filled jars and ceramic containers stood at the back of the counters, cooking utensils within reach of the high-end, stainless-steel stove – a kitchen used often, not a showpiece for minimalist modern form.

After her mother's death, James convinced his parents to build on the property near the house they were building. Why live on the same street and every day drive by the spot where their daughter-in-law had been murdered? Security became their number one concern. She spent many happy days of her childhood learning to cook next to the woman beside her now. It was strange how those memories had been in the recesses of her mind for so long that she forgot, but now thcy camc rushing back.

"Feels like you never left," Gram said, delighted with the young woman in her kitchen. "You finally decided to leave San Francisco, didn't you?" Her grandmother was not known for beating around the bush.

Keeping her mouth full was not going to work this morning. The eggs benedict sat in her stomach, more rock-like as she decided what to say, how to explain.

"Just out with it. Quit trying to spin it," Gram prodded.

"Not sure I have a spin yet," Halley replied. She was good at the spin; it came naturally. Even with all the tragedy in her life that began with her mother's death, Halley learned to look for the best and the positive. That made her good at her job, but those words, that strategy, eluded her now. Halley breathed deeply and expelled slowly, gathering her courage along the way. "I'm not sure I'll ever go back. I may have to. My company is under investigation for fraud and some of the executives for embezzlement. I didn't do anything wrong, but I may be painted with the same brush since I'm on the executive team. All our jobs are gone – or temporarily on hold; I'm not sure. Who knows what will happen? I didn't hang around to find out. I was so upset, I packed up my house and left the keys on the counter with a note for the landlord. I took what I could in my car and put the rest in storage. Then I started driving. At first, I thought I'd head south and maybe visit New Orleans, maybe go back to New York, and see if I could get my life back, but somehow Henry headed here. Now, here I am. I'm as surprised as all of you."

"Is that your fella?" Gram picked up on the most innocuous part of the explanation.

"What? No!" Halley replied, startled. She quickly went over what she said in her head, but no, she did not refer to the ex-fiancé.

"Who's Henry?" Gram persisted.

Halley giggled, "My car, Gram. Henry is my car's name."

"You named your car Henry?" Gram snorted and slapped the table with her hand.

"Yep. Good old-fashioned horsepower called for an old-fashioned name," Halley reasoned. Her ex-fiancé got unreasonably vexed when she called her car by name and treated it like her best friend. He always said cars were supposed to be named after women, if at all. That should have been another red flag for her. Looking back, maybe she was so desperate for a friend she overlooked all the red flags and let someone in she should not. That was probably also why she subconsciously decided not to tell her family about him. They would have insisted on doing background checks, investigating, and then sizing him up in person. That would never have done; they would have picked up right away on the red flags she dismissed. Then she would have been alone. *Like now.*

"Ha! Gotta tell your gramps that one!" Gram was still chuckling. Then she picked up where she left off, "But what about a man? You would never leave just because of a job. You put too much of yourself into your work. There had to be a guy. Or a girl?"

"Gram! People may go to prison! This *is* a big deal," Halley insisted. Now that she opened the door to this conversation, she wanted her grandmother to understand.

"I'm hearing you, Hal. I'm also feeling what you're not saying."

"No girl, Gram. I like guys."

"Nothing wrong if you did," Gram said stubbornly.

"I promise; if I discover late in life I'm a closeted lesbian, you'll be the first to know," Halley rolled her eyes for dramatic effect. The eggs benedict was going down easier now and the boulder in her stomach disappeared.

"And? Your guy?"

"He's history, Gram. Good riddance." It wasn't a lie. She may have omitted some truths, such as that they were engaged and he had all but moved in with her, and he may have disappeared, but those details hurt too much.

"Hhmmm. I think there's a story there. But you get a one-time pass today since you're probably still tired from that drive."

"Thank you," the relieved tone evident in Halley's response.

On the drive to the clubhouse, Halley used the main road rather than the "secret" trail inside the property line. Not having been here in years, not everyone would know her and the possibility of angering a bunch of testosterone-heavy bikers was more than she could handle today. At the front gate, the tall man in his mid- to late-twenties with cropped blonde hair and aviator shades looked in the car and recognized her from the day before at *Raiders Roost Tavern*. The name patch on his cut read *Handsy* and she realized he was one of the guys who used to play football with Scottie. While his road name could be for something more sexual, or even violent, she grinned, remembering he had magic hands receiving the football her quarterback brother threw him. That high school nickname apparently followed him to the club.

"Nice to see you, Doug," she grinned up at him. "When did you patch in?"

"Been with the club since I got back after college," Handsy grinned back. He had gone on a football scholarship and, if she remembered correctly, was a good student, too. "Didn't think you remembered me, Hal. And no one calls me Doug anymore."

"Didn't want to take that education somewhere else?" she pried, genuinely curious.

"Nah. Club has plenty of businesses that use my skills. And I get to help coach football too. Can't beat the life." He rapped the roof of her car with his knuckles and stood back, "Better get going, Irish is expecting you." It had been a long time since she heard her dad's road name. He was always "Irish" around their club family growing up and then that or "Prez" or "President" when he took the helm from his father.

The clubhouse was hidden from the road by a winding drive and a stand of pine trees that stood green in all seasons and blocked the view from curious or prying eyes. She parked next to a row of motorcycles, paint gleaming in the sunshine, most with custom jobs. When she got out of her car, she walked by each one, admiring the custom paintwork and wondering who the artist was. It was someone she wished she had on her creative team, that was for sure. There were flames, skulls, abstract visions of women, tribal-like swirls and lines, all obviously customized to the individual owner. She ran a hand over one gas tank in particular, the subtle lines of a woman's head and hair blended perfectly with the rest of the image, giving the impression of fluid movement and beauty. It was breathtaking. Reluctantly, she moved away when she heard a throat clear and saw her father standing at the door with his muscled arms crossed over his broad chest.

"Did you go into the custom painting business?" she asked before he could say anything.

"One of the young guys does it as a hobby," he replied.

"Dad, the work is beautiful. You could make a lot of money with that as an actual business." Halley's wheels turned in her head in a way they hadn't since she first got to San Francisco, excited about the new job and the prospects for the startup she had joined.

Her father sent her a questioning look, "You want to run that business, Hal?"

"Who? Me? No, I mean I'd love to work with artists of that caliber, but I don't even know what I'm doing with my life."

"Could be that; if you think it would be profitable." James noticed the flare of interest in his daughter's eyes. Before he added anything to their portfolio of businesses for the club, he would ensure the due diligence to determine the market viability and potential profitability. A bonus was if he could keep his eldest daughter in her hometown. Right now, she looked at him with her head slightly tilted and her lips in a straight line, the same look he gave club brothers when he knew they were trying to pull something over on him and he wanted them to know he thought they were dumbasses. He headed inside to his office, knowing she would follow.

In her mind, Halley thought of several questions for which she wanted answers, such as, if the custom painter could work in other mediums, as well. Was he formally trained? Did he paint on canvas? How long did it take for him to finish a piece? Did he do the designs himself? She was so inside her head, that they reached the office without her noticing anything of the hallway and almost bumped into her father's back when he stopped to open the door. Once inside, James sat in the leather office chair – one of the expensive ones, she noted – behind the big, scarred wooden desk that had been her grandfather's. Before she could close the door, two people slipped inside. She narrowed her gaze.

"This wasn't the deal," Halley said, heat rising.

James held up a hand and shook his head, "Hal, nothing goes beyond these doors. You know that."

One of the men lifted her off her feet in a bear hug, "About time you came home, princess." For the first time, she looked at the faces of the two newcomers and broke out in a grin at the man who held her. He was her dad's age, longer dark auburn hair and more of a beard than her father's neatly kept goatee, gray liberally spread in his beard and at his temples.

"Uncle Red," she squeaked as he squeezed her.

"I wanted to send a search-and-rescue party two-and-a-half years ago when you headed to the Left Coast, princess." Red set her down but kept hold of her shoulders. "Your dad nixed it. Said you expected independence or some shit." The look on his face said he didn't agree. He pulled another chair to the side of the desk.

"I'm an independent woman. Haven't been a princess in a long time," she said firmly. Give these guys an inch and they took a mile; she knew the score. She was back to staring at her father. She asked to talk with him, and she supposed Red was okay – he was her father's lifelong best friend and the club vice president – but she had no idea who the younger guy was. He quietly took a seat on the couch against the wall and watched the interplay between her and Red.

"Hal, this is Wire, don't think you've met before," James indicated toward the young man with short blonde hair, a clean-shaven face, and intense dark eyes. "Wire, this is my daughter Hal."

Wire nodded at her in greeting.

Halley stared at her father, asking with her eyes who the new guy was and why he was there to hear her business. James sighed, "Wire handles all tech for the club and businesses." He left Halley to read between the lines; it sounded like "hacker" to her. His posture spoke former military.

"Why do I need a hacker?" Hal asked, hand on hip, still standing in front of the desk.

"I don't know, Hal; you haven't told me anything yet except that company you worked for might be in trouble. Easier to have Wire here than me explain later," James cut off her protests and gestured for her to take a seat.

"This isn't club business. It's personal," Hal attempted lamely as she dropped into the chair in front of the desk.

"Club *is* family, Hal, you know that. Personal includes family, in case you've forgotten," James made his point.

Halley was already sorting through what she would and would not divulge. Nothing about the fiancé. It was bad enough that she had to contend with it; the embarrassment would be too much.

"From the beginning, start when you accepted the San Francisco job," James prodded.

With eyes shut, she launched into her story, watching it unfold again behind her eyes. The offer had seemed to come right at the perfect time. She was getting bored with her job in New York; nothing was new or exciting any longer. She had taken the company's marketing and communications efforts as far as the company's C-suite would allow, proving to be more on the conservative side than when they hired her. One of the founders of a tech startup in the San Francisco Bay Area approached her at a glitzy charity auction in Manhattan. He was in town raising money with potential investors. In conversation, she animatedly talked about ideas off the top of her head for campaigns and brand building, willingly giving him the benefit of her experience. It was always fun to talk with someone who appreciated what she brought to the table and seemed as excited about the prospects as she was. The following week he called, a surprise, since she didn't expect to see or hear from him again. She still remembered the phone call.

"I was impressed when we met last week. My company's ready to hire a Chief Marketing Officer and I think you could be just who we're looking for. Interested?"

"I hadn't expected this call," Halley said, scrambling. "Why me?"

"You need to ask that? I loved your ideas, Halley. You're such a fresh voice. I work with a bunch of techies and money people all day; you made me remember why we started this company and its possibilities. Then I asked around and checked you out. You were one of the '30 under 30' to watch in business. You'll easily stay there and are going to be on the '40 under 40 list' with us. Say you'll listen to our offer."

Craig Martin had been persuasive. Meeting his two partners a week later cemented the deal. She would make considerably more than what she was in her current position; she would have an equity stake in the company and be part of their executive team. C-suite at not yet twenty-nine-years-old was hard to turn down. They were interested in her ideas, even the far-out ones; ideas and realizing the possibilities they promised were always most important to her. She could explore a whole new part of the country and meet new people, at the same time.

After doing what due diligence she could, including verifying the company was well-funded and investors still interested, she gave her notice and less than a month later moved across the country – to the protests of her friends and co-workers. They told her a startup was too big a risk. They told her she was going somewhere she had no support system. Her friends who were newly part of a couple told her they had someone for her to meet; she couldn't go. But she went. For two-and-a-half years, she put her heart and soul into ensuring the company built its brand, raised its profile, sponsored the right events, and spotlighted the founders and their genius.

Along with the rest of the team, she was happily losing sleep and moving them closer to an initial public offering (IPO). Taking the company public was a huge step and would make the founders instant billionaires, her own stake significant. The financial coffers were flush, investors plentiful, and revenue from sales teeming. Her team won award after award for their marketing and advertising campaigns – not that she ever cared about awards, but the outside validation was gratifying.

Then the calls came from vendors. They hadn't been paid. Checks bounced and bounced again. The chief financial officer (CFO) said he would check into it; there had to be a mistake, a banking glitch. Two of the three founders disappeared and weren't answering their phones or answering their doors, including the CFO, not long after subpoenas began arriving. Then the regulators got involved. One of their biggest new contracts was with the federal government, which, along with angry investors, had elected officials up in arms. For her part, she was asked over and over if she knew what she was promoting was built on financial dynamite, if she knowingly lied to customers and the general public.

"I didn't. I didn't know. I didn't lie," Halley shook her head and looked at her father, begging him with her eyes to believe her. "Our products are sound. It's the finances that were shaky, and I had nothing to do with that side of the business." She hadn't, but her ex-fiancé had. He was the CFO who had disappeared, and with him, files, money, and her dignity.

"But I don't know how they could be shaky. There were investors. We were selling – a lot," Halley said and still could not wrap her head around how everything crashed around them.

For the first time, Wire leaned forward, elbows on his thighs, and directed his comments to his president rather than the princess; that's how he thought of her – MC royalty and out of bounds.

"Tracks with the financials. About ten months ago funds went missing, but not enough for anyone to notice. That continued once or twice a month until big chunks disappeared over the two months before it blew up. Investors expecting their contractual cuts started making a fuss about six months ago, when the money wasn't in their accounts."

"Wait, hold up. How do you know this?" Halley waved her hand in the air. "Were you spying on me all this time?" she looked accusatorily at her father.

"No, but we should have been. This might not have gotten so far, if we had," James ground out.

"How do you know when the money went missing? I didn't even know that!" Halley said, still staring a hole in her father.

"Because I'm good at my job," Wire answered evenly, looking her in the eye for the first time, when she turned to him. "I spent all night and this morning pouring through records."

"You hacked our system?" Halley accused the man.

Wire's face didn't flinch or even move a muscle. He merely stared at her like she was a child too innocent for her own good and then turned his attention back to his president. "I haven't traced where the money landed – yet. I suspect the government and the investors' attorneys are trying to do that too, based on the digital trails I can see."

"You can see their digital footprint, so they'll see yours," Halley protested. "I don't want to put the club at risk, Dad. I didn't ask you to do this."

Wire looked at her one more time. "They won't. Not that you need to know, but it will look like someone inside the company, if – and that's a big *if* – anyone notices at all."

Before she could argue more, Red cut in, "Wire's that good, Hal. Don't doubt it."

Halley did doubt it. Why else would he be here, in small-town America? If he was that good, he would be making a killing in Silicon Valley. Faced with her own prejudice, she stopped before speaking and remembered what her grandmother once told her. *Everyone has to find their own path to peace and happiness, Halley. Yours may not be here, but your dad's is. Mine is.* At the time she thought peace and happiness sounded overrated. She wanted excitement and adventure. Maybe Wire couldn't find what he was looking for somewhere else and found it here. He wasn't local; she knew that. He was too close to her age, which meant if he was from the town, she would have known him growing up.

"Anything else you can tell us?" James asked, breaking her trip inside her head, yet again. She really had to stop all that internalizing.

"Not that I can think of," Halley responded, hoping her father didn't see through her omission – not a lie. There was no reason for them to know she had been seeing and was engaged to the CFO.

Chapter 4

SITTING IN THE COFFEE SHOP ACROSS FROM THE office building proudly bearing the logo of the startup the two founding partners conceived five years prior, hidden behind dark sunglasses, and a wide-brimmed fedora covering his wavy black hair, clad in a flannel shirt, jeans, and hiking boots, the man blended with his surroundings. His choice of clothing was so different from his usual tailored trousers and blazers, bespoke button-down dress shirts, hand-made Italian leather loafers, that no one would recognize him or even give him a second glance. He drummed his manicured fingernails on the side of his over-sized ceramic coffee mug, trying not to squirm. The manner of dress alone was giving him hives. Having to hide almost sent him into another rage. Staring at the building, he waited to see who entered and who exited.

"Is this wise? You shouldn't be here," a large man with dark sunglasses said, taking a seat next to him. His dress was casual but seemed more in sync with his own style, not uncomfortable.

"Intel. I'm gathering intel that's important," he replied, not taking his eyes off the building.

"You're trying to see the girl. That's not gathering intel. Is she that good a lay?"

"Watch it, Enzo. She's still my fiancée." He proved that when he refused to take back the ring she thrust at him when she childishly told him they were not a good match and tried to break their engagement.

"She dumped you, cousin."

"We disagreed. She'll see we're right together," he shrugged. No one ended anything with him, not business and certainly not personal relationships, until he was ready for things to end on his terms.

Enzo sighed heavily. He shook his head to himself. His cousin always was headstrong and arrogant. As their grandfather and Enzo's own father, now head of the family, said time and again, arrogance would be his downfall, and he needed to curb his darker impulses.

To Enzo's mind, his cousin always seemed to want to change his fiancée and would say how he would have her in shape to meet the family soon. Why change someone when it was easier to find the type of person you wanted in the first place? This woman worked too much for his cousin, even though they worked for the same company; she was too curvy for his cousin's liking, though Enzo thought she looked perfect and was beautiful, a real woman, though he'd never been allowed to meet her, he had observed from afar. She was also highly intelligent. He knew this from her resume, her elevated position at a young age, the other two partners falling over themselves to get her to work with them, and the bit he was able to eavesdrop from adjacent restaurant tables and bar stools. Halley McCarthy seemed, to him, to be the whole package. She wasn't Italian, but that seemed to be her only real flaw.

They had been keeping a low profile, working out of Enzo's condo on the water in the Presidio district of San Francisco, since the feds and subpoena processors were closely watching Anthony's upscale apartment and the office building. He spent most of his time at Halley's rented house, before the blow-up – Enzo never understood that either, given his cousin's penthouse was bigger and more prestigious, something important to the man.

"She's not there, Anthony," Enzo sighed again and stood up. "Let's go before you're spotted."

Anthony snorted. No one would recognize him dressed like this. He reluctantly relented and followed his cousin around the corner where the sleek, black Alpha Romeo was parked. He couldn't even take out his own vehicle any longer, for fear of being caught. Soon they would all see it was the other partner, Andres Murano, the Chief Operating Officer, to blame; the one who had disappeared mere days before Anthony.

The idea for the technology came from tech genius Craig Martin, the founder, who brought his friend Andres Murano in as a partner to run operations, the COO – Chief Operating Officer. Anthony was added as Chief Financial Officer, CFO, when his friend Andres bragged to him about the company – he knew they were looking for investors – and Anthony approached them with high investment dollars and further investors, with the caveat he would be made a third partner and CFO. He was good at persuading people to do his bidding.

That he used the startup to launder money from his family's less legal businesses, was no one's business – at least it shouldn't have been. Unfortunately, Andres, who uncovered several months ago what Anthony was doing, had a sudden bout of conscience and wanted out of their deal, a very lucrative one for Andres, and all he had to do was keep his mouth shut. The fragile house of cards Anthony was building came crashing down when he couldn't pay out the expected funds to vendors and investors and didn't have more investment dollars to cover the shortfall. His uncle and his close associates were withholding more funding, worried it would attract too much attention. That, and paying Andres, had been the start of his unraveling.

If Halley had not been so brazen as to try to break up with him, he would have ultimately shifted all the blame to Andres. As it was, he only wanted to destroy her reputation so she would have nowhere to turn in the end but him; he would waltz in and save the day. Then he could destroy her; apt punishment, in his mind, for having the gall to try to dump him…and, for being her.

"I think maybe it's time for you to leave the city for a while," Enzo broached the subject his father had pushed with his early morning call. “We could avoid the feds and take a private plane to Mexico until things quiet down.”

“I’m not ready to leave yet.” Anthony stared out the passenger window, scanning the sidewalks as they drove.

If his father and grandfather could not control his strong-willed cousin, how did they expect him to achieve it? When Anthony first suggested another avenue to launder large sums of cash, they were intrigued by the plan. Then Anthony had to get greedy and careless – Enzo’s private estimation of the chain of events that led to a federal investigation and angry investors, not that he had shared that with his father or grandfather.

He wasn’t sure what his cousin’s endgame was; Anthony had not shared that yet. What he did know was the man was keeping key details from the family. Anthony would not be arrogant enough to think he could supplant the current head of the family or strike out on his own, would he?

This thought crossed Enzo’s mind more often these days. He tried to push it to the back of his mind and ignore the niggling feeling growing in his chest. His father would not be happy, if that was the case, but he would act swiftly at even the hint of betrayal. So, Enzo kept the thoughts to himself. Enzo grew up with Anthony and wanted to give his cousin the benefit of the doubt. But those doubts continued to grow.

It was giving Enzo a headache. Sure, the California weather was agreeable. He found the women were willing, though the majority were either flighty – must be a leftover hippie vibe – or socially awkward, thank you tech industry for the change in demographic. Yet he was ready to move home where the winters were bitingly frigid; either that or get a new assignment that did not include his cousin. He had already spotted an opportunity for the family that would continue to expand the legitimate business operations and cover for some of the less lawful activities, if the family powers insisted.

“Drive by Craig’s house,” Anthony directed.

“He’s not there. We saw him enter the building.”

“I want to look at the entire perimeter. Double-check where the cameras are. There must be a blind spot.” Anthony insisted. As usual, it was easier to go along than argue with his cousin. They already did this with some of the muscle Anthony brought in, but, as Enzo's father always reminded him, be *absolutely* sure.

"Fine. But I want to check out some real estate in Sausalito after."

Anthony turned and studied his cousin's profile. "Looking for new business, Enzo?"

"Always, cousin."

"Patience, Enzo. We won't need to be here much longer."

"Maybe if you told me your whole plan, I would be more patient," Enzo groused.

Before Anthony could reply, his phone buzzed. His jaw tensed as he replied into the phone, "Stay there." He ordered his cousin to follow his directions to a new address.

"What's going on?" Enzo inquired.

"It seems my fiancée has moved out of her house, with no forwarding address."

Waves of rage emanated from Anthony, enough to keep Enzo silent rather than reminding him she was no longer his fiancée. How the goons Anthony hired to watch her place had missed the move, was beyond Enzo. His father's muscle was eminently more competent. But then, Anthony did not want anyone in the family to know about Halley, yet. Enzo was now revisiting why he agreed to keep the secret, only telling the people back home that Anthony was seeing someone.

They pulled up next to a dark SUV in an alley of an abandoned warehouse that was situated across from a large self-storage business. Enzo's head pounded; he was ready to go home.

Chapter 5

THE GROUND WAS DAMP, TOO EARLY FOR THE morning sun to warm and dry the earth at the end of its rays. The smell was distinctly that of sod and earthworms, the same odor conjured in Halley's memories from when her uncles took her fishing, and they made her dig for worms first. She could imagine the worms slowly eating through her clothes and then her skin. All she had to do was lie here long enough. Problems would disappear, the world would fade; she would fade and would last as, maybe, a footnote for a generation, then disappear altogether. What had she ever really accomplished? All those late nights, early mornings, media interviews, campaigns – what did any of it matter? Did she ever make her part of the world a better place, much less the greater world around her? She thought she would. She had been naïve, *so* naïve. She bought her own public relations; she bought into the corporate arrogance. For that, she was ashamed.

Lying atop the cemetery plot, she felt the only peace she had ever felt. Maybe this was the feeling her grandmother tried to tell her people chase. Here her mind quieted, somewhat. Here she could be still and shut out the world. *You don't belong here.* She heard the voice of her mother's mother in her head and tried to push it away.

Just a little more time being still. Not enough for the earthworms to do their job, but enough to rest.

The last few days had been a careful dance of disappearing to where no one would see her and going to the house after everyone was in bed. Her father had to leave on club business with Scottie, Conor, Red, and probably others, and she had nothing in common with her stepmother. If anything, Priss was probably grateful she kept to herself. Tiffany's open hostility was too much right now; she had no energy to explore the root cause. Drake hadn't spoken one word to her since her return. Danny was too busy with baseball and his new girlfriend to notice her. Scarlett was the one bright spot in the house, leaving notes on her pillow she would find upon return, but her youngest sister's adoration felt undeserved.

Gram and Gramps insisted on feeding her at least once a day. They tried to get her to look up her old friends, but why? They all had their own lives and friends; many of them had started their own families. How would she fit with that? How could she explain why she was in town? In the pit of her stomach, she knew she wasn't ready to face her present or her past. Maybe that hole in her chest would heal sometime, but right now it was gaping.

A raven landed in a great flap of wings on the branch of the tree above the plot on which her body rested. He stared down at her, eyes far more intelligent than should be in a bird. His beak opened and a long croak pushed forth.

"Sheesh! You want me to leave too?" she narrowed her eyes at the bird. Its solid black form shone in the sunlight. Such a pretty bird to be a harbinger of death. "Are you waiting for my impending death? Do you know something I don't?" The grand bird continued its staring match; she was the first to blink.

The winter wind had blown the day her grandmother was laid to rest – what a strange concept – "laid to rest." At the time, it made no sense. Now, seventeen years later, understanding bloomed. Maybe it was what preachers and funeral directors said so mourners focused on something nice rather than the earthworms and beetles burrowing through the soil. Ashes to ashes, dust to dust; no one wanted to imagine how the ashes and dust were formed.

Her maternal grandmother had been taken too soon for her granddaughter. Though not as violent as her mother's death, the woman's departure felt brutal to Halley. Her maternal grandfather, that quiet, gentle man, so different than the men in her father's family, followed less than two years after his wife. They both left Halley. But she never forgot the warmth and security of their love, their calm voices, or her grandmother's lessons – many not making sense until she encountered a situation where she needed them. Then the light bulb would shine bright, and she would have a moment of clarity – *ahh, that's what she was talking about*. She marveled at the woman's simple wisdom and her uncanny prescience to know what Halley would need later in life.

Over the years, sometimes Halley envied her friends, whose first memories were school age, and even those were vague. For her, the past was ever-present. She remembered everything, every moment, every detail, every word, every feeling. Some she pushed to the back of her mind and locked in a vault she conjured. It was easier that way, even though the good had been shut away with the bad. That was the price she paid. Now she was back, where all those memories were made and the impenetrable lock on the vault failed.

"Bye for now, Grandma," Halley whispered, as she pushed to her feet and brushed her hands over the back of her jeans and shook the back of her shirt the best she could, knocking small clumps of the damp, dark soil and blades of grass to the ground. She tried to startle the bird to flight, but he had moved and sat atop the gravestone, unflinching. She gave up with a shrug toward the raven and walked back to her car.

Resolute, the car, Henry, turned toward the main street and parked in front of the diner; at least she told herself Henry was taking her there. Once inside she was waved to a booth by a harried waitress. Halley would have been happy at the counter, but all the stools were taken. This was the first day hunger hit her. Over the last few weeks, food was not high in her priorities. Everything turned her stomach. Her jeans were loose and the cotton shirt she wore hung on her frame. She thought it was ironic that the one thing it took for her to start losing the extra pounds her ex-fiancé complained about was for him to disappear. Oh, and her life to fall apart; there was that.

"Halley McCarthy? Is that you?" a woman stood beside her booth. When she looked up, the woman's face lit up. "It is!"

"Sarah?" Halley stared at the girl, now a woman, who had been in the circle of her closest friends growing up. Sarah seemed genuinely delighted to see her.

"Meeting someone or can I sit?"

"Please," Halley said, gesturing to the navy-blue booth bench across from her.

"I heard a rumor someone saw you in town, but I didn't believe it," Sarah said.

Halley felt the slow crawl of heat up her neck as she flushed. Why she was embarrassed, she didn't know, but she was. "I'm here," she replied lamely. "I know it's been a long time, but it's really good to see you. What's been going on in your life?" She desperately hoped to keep Sarah talking about herself.

Sarah laughed, "You mean in the last fifteen years since you graduated early and left me? Well, let's see. You know I went to college and grad school. Then I came back and have been working at my parents' financial planning business. We also do some stock trading and tax prep for businesses and individuals – kind of need to branch out in a small community."

Halley nodded and smiled, "Yeah, I remember that was your plan. You did it."

"And you got out. Every time I see your brothers or dad, they growl at me when I ask about you," Sarah laughed again. Halley remembered this, her friend's easy nature and cheery personality. It was as if they were teens again.

"That sounds like them," Halley rolled her eyes.

"So, are you still in New York?"

"Nah, I moved to San Francisco a couple of years ago."

"Oh wow! Conquering both coasts! How multi-cultural of you," Sarah joked.

"Yeah, not so much. Mostly I see techies and venture capitalists these days. I kind of miss the diversity of personalities and professions in New York. I also never thought I'd miss the change of seasons, but California makes me miss it. I do like wine country though. If it wasn't so far from my office, I would have lived in Sonoma or Napa," Halley said, warming up to the conversation.

"Ugh! Are you trying to make me jealous?" Sarah rolled her eyes and gestured to a waitress. "Are you meeting someone, or can I eat with you?"

Sarah was always confident, even in high school, when very few were confident and comfortable in their skin. Her hair was almost black, cut in a pixie style, which made her expressive brown eyes even larger.

"Please stay. I won't look so lame," Halley enthused.

"It's not high school. No one cares if you're alone or not. Just makes you look more confident," Sarah argued. Then she leaned forward and whispered, "But I agree, always more fun with a friend."

Growing up, Sarah Ferguson and their other friends Anna Chopin and Renee Winter, used to hang around the clubhouse with Halley on family days and the early evenings of parties, before the patch bunnies strutted their wares and came on to the brothers later in the night – at that point her father and Uncle Red made them go home. She and her friends knew what was going on, even if her dad tried to protect them and keep them young and naïve. Adults never did seem to realize how much kids picked up just by osmosis.

"Have you seen anyone else?" Sarah asked after they ordered.

Halley shook her head. What she didn't reveal was that she had purposely avoided everyone.

"Well, Anna got out of the Army after two enlistments and got her degree during the second. She met a doctor while she was stationed in Germany and now, they're married and in Chicago, both out and working at one of the university hospitals there. I think she does something in administration. Renee's still here. She got her degree and came home to teach at the elementary school and married Ross Winter," Sarah caught her up on their two other best friends from her childhood and youth. Renee's path was no surprise. She and Ross dated through middle and high school.

A waitress, not the one who took their order, came back and slammed their plates on the table. Halley's club sandwich slipped across the plate and half of it deconstructed onto the tabletop.

"Smooth move, Kath," Sarah scowled.

Halley's jaw dropped, "Kathy?" The woman before them stood in jeans, a pink t-shirt with the name of the diner, an apron with a wide front pocket at her waist, and white orthopedic sneakers. She had several fine lines around the outside of her eyes and her lips. Her blonde hair, obviously from a bottle, was pulled up in a bun at the back of her head. She looked much older than the two years she had on the women sitting in the booth. In high school, Halley beat her for valedictorian, even though Halley was two years younger and graduated at sixteen. Kathy, the head cheerleader their senior year, had dated the quarterback their final year, and was livid she lost the top academic spot. It seemed she never got over it.

"Hal McCarthy, what are you doing back here? Thought you were too good for all of us these days," Kathy snarled.

Halley was taken aback by the vitriol the woman spewed. Before she could summon any words – you'd never know she used words for a living – Sarah jumped in, "Back off, Kath. Halley isn't one of the women Brett slept with or the reason he left you. Get over yourself." Kathy gasped in outrage, spun on her heel, and disappeared through the swinging door into the kitchen.

Halley wasn't sure which shocked her more, her old friend's attack on the waitress or the waitress' fifteen year old grudge. When she could speak, she asked the most obvious, benign question she could muster, "Kathy married Brett Creighton, and they stayed here?" Kathy always said she was leaving the podunk town and was sure Brett was her ticket to see the world, once he got a place in the NFL. That must not have worked out for her.

"She did, but first they started college when you did, though they stayed in state. He played football until he was injured and lost his scholarship their sophomore year. She quit and followed him home. Stupid woman. He never could keep his zipper up. Not sure how she thought a marriage certificate and her lady parts were magical enough to keep him faithful. He never was before. He kicked her to the curb a few months ago for some young thing just out of cosmetology school. She's been bitter ever since. Not that she was ever nice, but now she's particularly mean. Only good thing I can see is they didn't have any spawn," Sarah spewed.

"Wow," was all Halley could muster. She quietly ate the half of the sandwich not laying in pieces.

"Yeah, wow. I figure eventually everything comes around. You know, like karma. Though maybe they were part of each other's karmic cycle, since they are both terrible people," Sarah mused. Halley didn't think karma worked that way, but kept quiet.

Sarah changed the subject, tired of talking about the negative people who didn't deserve their energy, "Your dad still has the horses, right? You been riding since you got home?"

"Not yet," Halley said guiltily. She wished she would have thought about that herself. It would be a good way to while away the time and not have to see anyone else.

Sarah grinned, "Remember when we used to go the back way to sneak into the club without your dad seeing us?"

"Oh yeah." The first couple of times she tried taking her dirt bike, while Sarah rode behind her, but quickly realized her dad, Red, or one of the older club brothers heard the dirt bike approaching the clubhouse from the back and headed them off. Horses were quieter.

"We should try that again," Sarah suggested hopefully.

"Seriously?" Halley laughed. "We can walk in the front door, you know. We are grown women now."

"Where's the fun in that?" Sarah challenged and joined Halley's laughter.

Chapter 6

ACROSS THE COUNTRY, JAMES, SCOTTIE, AND RED stood back and watched as Conor applied the bolt cutters to the simple padlock, after the key he took from Halley's glove compartment didn't work. It snapped in one try. He tossed the remains and lifted the garage-type overhead sliding door. What was inside caused all the men to pause.

Boxes were torn open, contents haphazardly strewn around the interior of the storage unit. The cushions and backs of couches, chairs, and ottomans were sliced open, the stuffing pulled out and thrown. James was pretty sure whoever ransacked his daughter's belongings did not find what they were looking for because plates and glasses were smashed on the concrete – there was no need for that other than anger. He supposed vandals could have destroyed the property purely for the high of destruction, but he doubted it. This looked more like a search turned frenzied and then vindictive. Someone she knew, was his guess.

Once they showed Halley's agreement contract to the guy on shift at the front desk and he showed his driver's license with the same last name as his daughter's, the young guy opened the security gate and waved them back to the outside units. It might have been their look, of which he wanted no part, or he really thought it was all right to allow them access to Halley's unit. He suspected the former reason, not that he blamed the guy. They were all over six feet tall, broad, muscled, tattooed, clad in leather jackets – they never wore their club cuts inside vehicles – and unsmiling, with four others waiting in the SUVs they had driven to California. They could have used the instructions on how to use the security code and open the gates Halley carelessly left with the padlock keys and rental agreement, but he wanted to make sure they cancelled her contract.

"What the fuck is this?" Red finally spoke for them all.

"Not the government, they wouldn't have destroyed so much. Doubt it was vandals," James responded.

Conor had moved inside the unit and picked his way to the back. He knew Red and his father were unlikely to call the police, but he didn't touch anything in case. "Uh, Dad? You might want to take a look." Pinned to the back wall with duct tape, someone had taken a picture of a laughing Halley, blown it up, and drawn a red X through her face. There were several knife slashes through the picture, as well.

"Son of a bitch," Red muttered as he stared at the picture. "Irish, rather take care of this in-house, but you think we need to call the cops in case it has something to do with Hal's company?" James was wondering the same thing. He pondered a few moments and gave a quick shake of his head.

"Get pictures of this entire place and everything we can see, exactly like it is now. Take that picture of Hal down carefully and put it in an envelope – use latex gloves or hold it with your shirt sleeve or something. I don't want any of our fingerprints on it. Maybe someone left a calling card Wire can identify. Then, get the prospects in here to clean it up. They can buy fresh boxes and tape from that dumbshit at the desk. Make sure they label all the boxes. Toss the broken frames but keep her pictures. Just clean up the broken plates and glass and throw it away. Everything else have them box up for her and we'll load it in the trailer to take home. Call Wire and get him on the security footage – I see cameras here," James barked out his orders clearly, barely able to keep his anger contained. One of the SUVs pulled a long horse trailer. James figured Halley's possessions should fit in that, but if not, he would rent another moving trailer.

"I'm going to check out the other unit she rented," Scottie said, backing out of the trashed concrete and steel cubicle and grabbing the bolt cutters from the ground. Conor began taking pictures with his phone while Red had his phone to his ear.

"I'm coming with you," James replied. He wasn't sure what was going on, but he didn't want anyone alone right now. If whoever did this was not able to find what they were looking for, it was possible they might have someone sitting on the unit waiting for Halley to return. He didn't sense anyone watching though, no prickle up the back of his neck, and his instincts were usually infallible, proven by years of working for the club and watching his and his brothers' backs.

The other unit was set off to the back of the property where a high fence with razor wire topped it. It was one of a line of twenty or so small units. The entire facility had been built on what appeared to be the desert floor. It was amazing how the west side of the Oakland Hills could be cool and damp while heading east on the other side was hot, former desert turned into town after town, with houses built on the sides of canyons and amidst the dry, red-gold grass that grew on rolling hillsides.

They did not have to cut this padlock, one of the two keys worked. Whoever ransacked the large unit must not have known she rented another. When they rolled up this door, Scottie turned to his father with a large grin that reached his eyes. His father peered around his eldest son and a slow smile took over his face. There, sitting in the center of the unit, was a deep red Harley Sportster. Pristine, other than the fine layer of dust on the black seat. The sun hit the inside of the unit, making the paint sparkle on her ride. Her helmet, the same deep red, with a black face mask, sat on the seat.

"Did you know?" Scottie asked.

"No." His daughter was keeping a lot of secrets. He knew she was holding something back about her situation. The destroyed storage unit proved that. He had been giving her space to tell him in her own time, while Wire continued his search for more information. Now he knew one more secret. This was no dirt bike. He wasn't sure if he was proud of her for keeping up the family tradition or if he was peeved she hadn't told him and asked his advice on her purchase.

Scottie reached inside one of the unlocked saddlebags and pried loose a false bottom, coming up with a key. He grinned, "Maybe I should ride it back." Halley followed the trick for a spare key they had both learned when they were younger.

"It's too far and we're not stopping much. Let's get it loaded in the trailer and tied down. Wouldn't want anything to happen to it. She calls that car Henry; bet she has this named too," James' laugh rumbled throughout the mostly empty unit. "Besides, you ride that twenty-five hundred miles without asking, your sister will kill you."

There was that. And the fact she didn't know what their mission was or that they were here at all. They were all already bracing for her wrath when they returned with all her worldly belongings. She didn't ask them to do it; she wouldn't. She would have done it herself or called a moving company, of that, they were sure.

James wanted a little time to see the entire situation up close and personal. With four people in each vehicle, on the way out they drove straight through and only had to stop to switch drivers, get gas, and use the facilities. They spent time looking over Halley's old home, the neighborhood, and surveilling the building where she worked, watching the people who came and went.

James had members of another charter club from the Bay Area watching the building and its occupants since Wire first gathered information on the wrongdoing. He wanted to know who was still around and what their habits were. He wasn't sure what he would do with that information, but every little bit laid more pieces in the jigsaw puzzle he saw in his head. At some point, it would all click into place. It always did.

They looked to make sure there was nothing left in the unit, rolled the bike out, and pulled the door down.

"I'm going to ride it to the trailer," Scottie grinned and started the machine. "Want to come with me?"

James lifted his chin, threw a leg over the seat behind his son, and held the helmet and bolt cutters in his hand. Even though not a comfortable ride with two grown men, he could tell in the first couple of turns and by the sound that his daughter chose well. The others were standing tense and guarded as father and son turned the last corner. They heard the rumble and weren't sure who was descending on them – friend or foe. All relaxed when they saw the two approach.

"That Hal's?" Conor asked, appreciation clear in his tone.

"Appears so," James answered after he dismounted. Scottie rode it up the ramp to the front of the horse trailer and began tying it down.

"Can I take it for a ride?" his second son asked. He was itching to ride after being caged in a vehicle for the long trip, and then the long hours on surveillance.

"Nope," James flatly refused.

Conor frowned but gestured toward the larger unit. "Anything fabric – couches, mattresses, chairs, stools – are pretty much trashed. A leather loveseat looks intact, but I think the way it's constructed they could see nothing was hidden inside. The wood pieces seem okay. She'll need all new plates, glasses, barware, canisters, and bowls, if she moves into her own place again."

"She's not going to be able to claim insurance without a police report," Scottie suddenly realized.

"I know. I still think it's better this way. Gives us free rein, and no one knows we're even looking," James argued. He had given Scottie and Conor the overview of the situation, mostly so they would quit asking Halley. He had not divulged any of the details Wire found.

"We headin' home?" Red asked. "Or are we going to take a look around the boss guy's house?" They had seen the partner who hadn't disappeared, Craig Martin, many times coming and going from the office building and followed him to his home but hadn't searched his office or the house.

"Don't want to risk it. If we do that, we'll send someone in from the other charter club," James replied.

The four prospects, young guys who still had to prove themselves and act as general unpaid labor at the beck, call, and whim of patched members, before they earned the club patch and the right to call the members brothers, dragged the destroyed pieces to the dumpsters and finished boxing and loading, then swept the place clean. It all fit in the long horse trailer.

The horse trailer and its predecessors had been used for many purposes over the years, as well as transporting the various horses they owned to horse shows and races, and to buy and sell. James' great-grandfather was a moonshiner during Prohibition in the United States in the nineteen-twenties and early nineteen-thirties. The man hid stills deep in the forest in northern Michigan to make moonshine and gin and then transported the illegal liquor. He found the false bottoms he built under the horse's feet in the trailers provided a great compartment to transport the boxed-up bottles of booze. He also ran boats, bringing in alcohol from Canada and rum from the Caribbean, and transferred it to the horse trailers once it hit U.S. soil.

It was his son, James' grandfather, who started the motorcycle club after World War II with his best friends who made it home from the European theatre after victory was finally declared. They wanted a lifestyle that continued to respect the brotherhood they formed in the Army. Given James' great-grandfather's penchant for criminal activity, it made sense that tradition fell to the MC. It wasn't until toward the end of James' father's time as president, and after Evie's – James' first wife – murder, that the club began to place more emphasis on their legitimate businesses and de-emphasized the criminal activity.

Once James became president, he moved them completely out of the criminal zone and started even more new businesses. Everyone in the club worked in at least one of the club-owned businesses. They all did well, and they all stuck together as brothers. Even though they gave up their one-percenter patches (the patch representing an outlaw club), they still adhered to their lifestyle, and the club still preferred to handle its own issues and security threats. They were a tight-knit group that lived by a code and unbreakable rules. Family supported family. No one else would ever take care of them as well as they took care of one another.

Halley was family, and it was time she remembered that.

"Let's head home, brothers," James announced.

They loaded into the SUVs, Red driving the one pulling the trailer. James stopped at the front desk on the way out and told the young guy who backed away from the desk when James walked through the door, that the units were empty. He assured the contract was cancelled and no more charges would be made to his daughter's credit card.

That done, they hit the road.

James' phone rang. By the ringtone, he knew it was Wire. "What you got?" he asked, with no polite salutation. He listened and then said abruptly, "Putting you on speaker."

"Looks like whoever it was killed the power before they made it to the units, but the cameras are battery-backed. Still, the video is dark. I enhanced it, but they're dressed in dark clothes and hats. Looked like one is in a suit and the other two in cargos and turtlenecks – who wears turtlenecks in that heat?" Wire asked in a derisive aside.

"People who try not to be identified," Scottie gritted out. "Maybe they have neck tattoos."

"They turned on flashlights when they were searching, before they started destroying. The camera across the way points directly at her unit, so I could see what they were doing. I don't think they knew it's there because they were less careful once they were inside. The suit is the one who had the picture in his hand before going into her unit," Wire said. "I watched him stab the picture with a long knife. Multiple times. Seemed personal. Knife didn't look military issue. I've got one of my contacts working on facial recognition – one of them had his face turned up and we got a side shot and a couple other possible captures." Wire stopped before he added, "Might want to show this to your daughter, she might be able to identify them."

"Don't show her. I want to see it first. We'll decide when we get back," James commanded, his voice low and menacing.

"I'll let you know when I get anything else."

James ended the call.

"Why would a suit be there when his guys are doing the dirty work?" Scottie asked.

James concluded, "Because it's personal for him, and he may have needed to identify whatever they were looking for. Probably didn't want to get his hands dirty or he could have done all that destruction himself."

Conor grimaced and then said to his father, "We're going to leave it to you to tell Halley we got her shit." Conor grimaced again, "I think I'll skip family dinner that night." He could already picture the smoke coming from his sister's ears when she found out they invaded her privacy. The invasion and destruction were on a whole other level.

This time they split the drive into two segments, ensuring they all got a good night's sleep for one night on the road and a hot breakfast the next morning. Scottie was sure it was because his father wanted to be fortified to talk with Halley. His sister could be more stubborn than their old man, which said something.

Chapter 7

AT THE BACK OF THE WALK-IN, CEDAR-LINED CLOSET, HALLEY found her old, worn, brown cowboy boots crammed in a corner. Priss must not have gotten to the closet before James stopped her changes to Halley's childhood room. Up high on a shelf, she saw her great-grandmother's hat box that should contain Halley's old cowboy hat. Now wasn't for reminiscing. Now was for practicality. She needed boots to go riding. Her motorcycle boots would do in a pinch, but the chunky front and rubber sole would not suit the stirrup as well as her cowboy boots.

For a short time in Halley's childhood, Priss thought they could bond over showing horses and equestrian competitions. Priss had ridden her whole life, even competed on the equestrian team at her college, and thought she finally found something to which she and her stepdaughter could relate. Unfortunately, Halley's equestrian days were limited. While particularly good at show jumping – Halley was nothing, if not competitive – she preferred the independence…and clothing…of western riding, as well as the saddle and style of riding – pretty much everything. If it had been an option, she would have been a rodeo competitor. She wanted to gallop free for hours in her jeans and her father's pilfered T-shirts and denim button-downs. It was the same to her as the feeling she got on her early dirt bikes.

It never made sense to Halley as a child and not now as an adult, how her father and Priscilla ended up together. It truly must have been a weekend for the woman to walk on the wild side and lasso a bad boy. Why they stayed together was a mystery. Maybe Priss only wanted the comfort of a good-looking man with money and to stay home and raise a family. Though that seemed at odds with the Priss she knew too; the woman was vain about her body. Having children wasn't easy and having six should have wrecked her smooth skin and toned abdomen. But every time, Priss fought her way back with more determination and a trainer on call.

Priss preferred her parents' country club to her husband's clubhouse or her in-laws' table, and shopping to parenting. Halley realized she didn't know the woman at all. A little bit of guilt seeped in as she took some of the responsibility for keeping the woman out of her life. Which probably meant she pushed her father away for bringing the woman into their lives when it should have been only them. *Selfish much?*

Over the years, she spent zero time examining her motivations or dwelling on a past she couldn't change. She kept way too busy to revisit the place she left behind, as she built her career. Now, being back where it all began, she could admit, if only reluctantly to herself, what she denied most of her life. Halley McCarthy was not an island. She was not forged from earth and fire.

Who she became was shaped, molded, and loved by the family who raised her and the community that watched her grow and encouraged her hard-charging approach to life. This was where her character was etched into the fiber of her being. She was not reborn at sixteen; she simply moved to the next phase. She was not an orphan by circumstance but by choice, in a far-flung city at age eighteen when she combined her first job and grad school, sleeping rarely, and socializing less.

Yet, now, in the battered state in which she returned, not a victor but a shadow of her former self, her family welcomed her and only saw the returning champ, not the prodigal she saw herself.

She held the boots upside down and shook them violently. Putting her hand inside to check for spiders was not an option she relished. Nothing came out except a small pebble that had probably been there since the last time she wore them before she left for college. She sat on the closet floor and pulled them on. She marveled they fit. Was she really still the same shoe size as when she left fifteen years prior? That seemed unlikely, yet here was the proof. She ran her hand over the faded denim shirt hanging in the back of the closet, behind clothes she hadn't worn in years and never would again. This was one of her dad's. She pulled it over her T-shirt. It was still oversized, hanging loosely over her thighs, though her curves had become more pronounced over the years and made it not quite as large as it had been. Still, it dwarfed her frame. It made her feel warm inside. Leave it to her father and his big presence to consign his imprint to an inanimate object, abandoned years ago.

Ready, she headed for the stable. A young man shoveled old straw and horse manure from an empty stall into a wheelbarrow. His cut said "Prospect." A horse, presumably one from the empty stall, was tied to the outside rail.

"Should I saddle one of the horses for you, miss?"

Wow, a polite prospect, that was an interesting twist to her day. Or maybe he knew who she was and was trying to ingratiate himself to Prez's daughter.

"Thanks, but I can do it," Halley told him.

He leaned on the shovel and watched her walk down the long building in front of the stalls, perusing the horses her father now kept. Pirate, her long-time friend and first horse of her own, had died years ago. Now she had a choice of which one to ride. She stopped and rubbed a few heads on her review of the stock, promising carrots the next time she visited.

"If you want spirit, Lightning hasn't been exercised today," the prospect smirked. "If you're looking for something more sedate, you could take Lola."

Halley turned slowly on her heel and stared at the young man with a vocabulary. He was probably baiting or making fun of her. "I'm more of a spirited woman." She wasn't going to let him rattle her or know she hadn't been on a horse in a couple of years. The last time was at a property that rented riding horses outside of San Francisco. There had been no time since and her ex-fiancé didn't understand her love of riding – horses or motorcycles.

"Oh, I don't doubt that," he quipped. "Just wasn't sure 'bout your riding skills."

"Don't worry your pretty little head, Prospect," she said in a sickeningly sweet tone.

"Not worried, just don't want my head handed to me if you land on your ass or break your skull."

This was fun. In her long-gone past, rarely did prospects have the courage to talk to her. "I'm Halley; what's your name? I can't call you 'Prospect' if we're going to run into one another in the stable."

"Tyler. Nice to meet you, Halley."

Halley turned her attention back to the horses and her eyes settled on the one with "Lightning" on a wooden plaque above the stall. "I think Lightning and I are going to be good friends."

The prospect watched the woman calm the feisty horse with gentle strokes and soft whispers. When she had him saddled and easily swung up into it, even as Lightning tried to spin around on himself, Tyler turned back to mucking the stall, more confident she knew what she was doing, and he would not have to take his president's daughter to the emergency room. That would suck.

Halley leaned down in her old saddle – it seemed her dad had someone oil it regularly, waiting for her return – to open the gate at the back of the stable and then close it behind her once she and Lightning moved through it. They started at a trot; then finding her seat, Halley gave the horse his head. He seemed to need the freedom as much as she did and galloped beyond the tree line to where a natural field opened to the top of a rolling hill. The grass was a vibrant shade of green. The spring wet brought out nature's flora. Wildflowers grew up in between blades, dotting the countryside with splashes of color.

From the top of the hill, the valley that sheltered her hometown sat below looking much like it had when she was younger, mostly straight streets, neat buildings low and colorful. Beyond the city limits, she could see the new sprawl where forest and farmland once sat. Both were still there, just further flung. She watched the cars in the distance as so many ants on a trail as they raced along the curving expressway, heading north and south, wishing they were at their destination.

She had been the same, she thought ruefully. The destination had been everything. The degrees. The first job. The fashionable city apartment. Mimosas for brunch with climbing friends. The promotion. The headhunters. The better job. The ever-higher salary. The even better job. The expensive clothes. The new city. The city rental house. The stylish boyfriend. The ring. The equity promise of a public offering. It had always been about the destination for her.

"Arghhh! What did I do?!" she bellowed at the top of her lungs with her head thrown back, staring at the blue sky with high white clouds. Beneath her, Lightning danced nervously at the unexpected bawl. Halley leaned down and patted the stallion's neck. "Sshhh, boy. I'm sorry."

Her maternal grandmother's voice rang in her head, another memory of something she should have remembered, spoken when she was twelve, but pushed to the back because she didn't want to hear it. She had told her grandmother, not for the first time, that she was going to escape this town as soon as she could. *It's not the destination, Halley; it's the journey. It's all about making the most of your journey. The destination is just a placeholder; it's overrated.* She was determined to make it on her own, which, she now knew, meant making her own mistakes – even the mistakes that would have been avoided had she believed anyone knew as much as she did – and having to live with those consequences.

Huh. Here was another area her father agreed with her mother's family. If only she had taken to heart the words she read on the wall her entire childhood and teenage years inside the entrance to the clubhouse. It was repeated above the bar in the same clubhouse. It was still there when she met her father in his office the other day, along with the wood-carved club logo for the *Phantom Raiders* and their motto *Live & Die, Family, Fidelity*. She harbored no naïve notions that fidelity referred to the brothers' relationships prior to taking an ol' lady; she knew it meant fidelity to family – the club – was everything. There were other words inside the entrance that spoke to the heart of the club and maybe, for the first time, they spoke to her: *It's not the destination; it's the ride…live free…always.*

"Guess that makes you the perfect match for Lightning," a deep voice said from behind her, amused. "You're the Thunder."

Halley lurched forward in her seat and twisted to see who was there, startling Lightning in the process – horses always sensed the emotions of their riders. The horse reared up and she barely held her seat. Before he could bolt and unseat her, she pulled in the reins, gripping with her knees and speaking softly. Once Lightning calmed, she spun toward the stranger.

"You shouldn't sneak up on people!" she huffed in the most annoyed fashion she could muster. She threw all the attitude of her Manhattan friends behind the words.

"You should have more situational awareness. Didn't sneak," the man replied evenly.

Halley quickly assessed the stranger. His mount was from her family's stable. He wore a *Phantom Raiders* cut over a black thermal Henley. His brunette hair that curled up lightly at his shoulders held flecks of red where the sun shone on it. His eyes were a deep blue and never left her face. The way he held his arm, relaxed, wrist resting on the saddle horn, she couldn't read his name patch. What was it with the men she met today? They both were articulate, and tan, even though it was only spring, and most people this far north were pasty white from the long winter they hoped was behind them. And she recognized neither of them.

"Are you following me?" Halley asked suspiciously.

"I'm out for a ride, Thunder. I was supposed to exercise Lightning, but someone beat me to him," he said, amusement still threatening to turn his lips to a full-blown smile.

Halley subconsciously ran her hand over her thigh – her father's shirt had pulled up to the top of her thigh during the ride – and narrowed her eyes at him. Haughtily, she said, "Are you calling me thunder thighs? I'll have you know, that's mean. I won't be body-shamed."

In high school, she overheard two of the boys, one on whom she had a crush, talk about her thunder thighs and how she might be hot if she did something about those. From then on, she never wore leggings in public, and even in jeans, usually had a long shirt or sweater hanging low on her frame, covering as much as she could.

Much later, her ex-fiancé once told her he was afraid of her crushing his head like a nut with her thunder thighs and that was why he was not so into cunnilingus. He wasn't that good at it anyway, but she still never forgot the embarrassment.

The hint of a smirk disappeared from the man's lips. His gaze moved from her face down her entire body and stopped on the way back up to examine her thigh. "Of course, I wasn't. Why would I do that? I was referring to how loud you were bellowing. Could give the thunder competition." This time his eyes narrowed as he met hers again, "Some idiot say something to make you feel bad, Thunder?"

Halley shook her head, more embarrassed now. She knew better than to let her own insecurities leave her mouth. It was a rookie mistake. Confidence – always; if not, then fake it until it's true. "Never mind, forget I said that. Who are you?"

"I won't forget, Thunder, but you get a pass for now. I'm Maverick and this girl is Lady," he said as he patted his mount's neck. In actuality, he was following Halley. It was fortuitous she chose to ride this morning because he had promised to help exercise the horses. When he received the call from Irish to fill him in on what they found at the storage unit and requested Maverick shadow his daughter and keep her safe until they returned, he thought he was going to find an entitled princess and was glad he could keep his distance and watch her from afar. When she had shouted so loudly, he thought there was danger on the other side of the rise. Luckily there was not, but now he'd shown himself. Part of him was intrigued. He was a fast study of people and body language. Hers said there was no entitlement – unlike her younger sister Tiffany – and possibly even unsure of herself, though she covered it well.

"Maverick? A non-conformist? Irish give you that road name?" Halley asked, not sure if the man knew she was the president's daughter, and if not, she wasn't going to tell him.

"Nah. I came with it. Got it in the sandbox," he replied, referring to Iraq. He started there but ended in Afghanistan…with a few stops in between with the rest of his Delta unit.

"You were in the military?" she asked, surprised.

"I was. Army."

"Your accent says you're not from here. How'd you end up a *Phantom Raider*," she asked, finding she wanted to know. It wasn't simply polite conversation.

"Accent? I thought I got rid of that. Kind of like you. You don't sound like you're from Michigan," he countered but then answered. "Texas born and raised."

"It's slight. Texas, huh? Way you're sitting that horse I'd guess you grew up around horses. Ranch kid?"

Maverick laughed, a free sound that came from deep in his chest, not muffled or restrained. "Got it in one, Thunder. For that, I'll give you the other answer. I met Scottie when we were deployed. He was getting out and told me about this place and the club. Said I had a place to land if I wanted it." That was the simple story; she didn't need the longer version.

Lady pawed the ground impatiently and Lightning began to dance. "Okay, girl, I gotcha." Then to Halley, he said, "I still need to give Lady some exercise, want to ride together?" He urged Lady forward, not waiting for her response.

Halley pushed Lightning to match the other horse and rider's pace. After an hour, mostly in companionable silence, they headed back toward the stable. When the building came into view over the final hill, Halley shouted, "Race you back!" She dug her heels into Lightning's side, not that it took much to get the stallion to run, and didn't wait for Maverick to agree. She heard Lady's hooves pounding close behind. She whooped loud enough Tyler came to the barn door to see what was causing the commotion. He opened the gate so they could fly through before pulling up short of the stable. She won by half a length.

"Woo hoo! She beat you, brother?" Tyler hooted. He held Lightning's bridle while Halley dismounted.

A line formed between Halley's eyebrows as she turned from one to the other of the men. She could see Maverick's name patch now, so knew he wasn't a prospect. "I thought prospects aren't allowed to call members 'brother' until they're patched in? Did the rules change?"

Maverick laughed and got the other man in a chokehold, rubbing his knuckles over the brunette hair that Halley now noticed was the same color as his own. "No rule changes. He's a prospect all right. But he's *actually* my blood brother. I got him to come up here and join me." When Tyler pushed his older brother away and stood straight again, she saw his eyes were the same shade of blue, too.

"Wow, two Texas boys. Wouldn't think you'd like the winters much."

"Better than the heat," Maverick countered. He'd had enough heat – and cold – in his time served to last a lifetime.

"The club has two of you working at the stable? Is this part of the business now, too?" Halley asked, curious what else had changed in her absence.

"I go where I'm told," Tyler said, the appropriate response for a prospect. "I'm glad when it's with the horses. Get to use my experience."

"No, Thunder, I don't work here. But I do help out sometimes, like everyone else. And exercising the horses is a bonus for me," Maverick smirked.

Though club business was never discussed with anyone outside their brotherhood, Halley heard enough when she was growing up to do the math and understood far more than anyone knew she did. She knew all about her great-great grandfather's Prohibition business and what that morphed into later, as well as how her father, grandfather, Red, and some of the older members worked so hard to make sure all the businesses were legitimate.

She had hidden in a corner next to a sofa in the clubhouse where she pretended to be asleep the night the brothers came out of the room where they held church – their official club meeting – and watched through lidded eyes as they each cut their one-percenter patches from their cuts. That night she also watched a few who didn't denounce the one-percenter patch walk away and never come back.

She suspected many of the ol' ladies knew club business, too – whether they were legal wives, like Gram, or not; though, it wouldn't be a surprise if Priss did not know the club's business. Halley assumed as long as Priss could shop, keep a nice home, drive a nice car, and have the best horses, she wouldn't care to learn where the money was earned.

"What do you do?" Halley questioned Maverick. He was smooth, but she recognized when he didn't directly answer her questions.

"He runs the security business," Tyler told her proudly. His brother backhanded him in the gut. "Oof. What was that for? I didn't tell club business. You have a website and everything!"

Halley made a mental note to get up to speed on all the club's businesses. They didn't own a security business when she lived here. "I take it this is a new business. What do you do – install security systems at houses and businesses?"

"That and a few other things," Maverick said lightly.

"They also do threat assessments and sometimes act as bodyguards and –" Tyler stopped with a sideways shove from his brother. "Stop! What? It's on –"

"—the website," both Maverick and Halley finished for him. All three laughed.

"I can brush down the horses and put them up for you," Tyler said, reaching for the reins.

"Thanks, but I can do that," Halley said and led Lightning into the stable. "All part of bonding with the horse."

"She can do that," Maverick repeated in a quiet voice to his brother and nodded, glad to see she still didn't act like the princess he expected.

Halley felt her face flush as she slid the saddle and blanket off Lightning's back. Both brothers were gorgeous, and she had no business staring at them like they were a couple of sides of beef. When anyone did that to a woman, she was highly offended, whether it was her or not. Now that she thought about it, maybe sometimes they were admiring beauty, but no, that was objectifying another human, it was never right. She stroked the horse with the brush and startled at Maverick's voice, sounding amused once again.

"You can stare all you want, Thunder," Maverick smirked as he began to groom Lady.

Her face turned full-blown red. "Did I say something out loud?" she asked as casually as possible.

"Yep," he replied and didn't expound. He didn't even look her way.

Halley kept brushing and then lifted each of Lightning's feet to check his hooves, before leading him into the stall, latching the gate, and giving him the usual feed and a portion of sweet grain. She then stretched her back and arms. Oh yeah, she was going to feel this tomorrow. Not using those muscles for years, she would be stiff and ache – her rear, thighs, back, and arms. Going to the gym with her ex-fiancé was not the same workout as truly doing work or riding. She would have to spend a lot more time in the saddle to get back in shape; that was one of the best ideas she'd had since she returned. She'd missed riding and didn't know how much until she was on the back of a horse galloping across their property once again. Now, if she could just get her motorcycle here before summer.

In the meantime, she was going to search and see if her old dirt bike was here and in working order. No time like the present. She marched off and began checking rooms off the main stable and in the traditional barn next to it.

"Here you are," she said as she pulled a tarp off her old Yamaha where it was stored in a small, dusty room in the old barn. She gave a cursory check of the spark plugs, tires, brake line, and gas tank. She'd know better if any work needed to be done after she saw if it started. She threw her leg over the seat and pushed the bike forward off the kickstand, crab-walking it to the less enclosed part of the barn where fumes wouldn't overpower her if she got it started. She put her right foot over the kick start and prepared to jump down.

"What do you think you're doing?" Maverick stepped beside her.

"What does it look like?"

He put his hand over the throttle on the handlebar. "It looks like you're going to try to start an old dirt bike."

"Yeah."

"Not yeah," he said, sounding annoyed. "You don't have on protective clothing or a helmet. You can't go racing out in the woods on a dirt bike like that."

Now she was annoyed, "I can do what I want. But for your information, I just want to see if it starts."

"Irish had it tuned up a month ago."

Halley knitted her eyebrows. She hadn't thought that maybe one of her siblings might be who rode this now. But that would make sense. Why have it sitting idle all these years? She always thought of it as hers. It had been a gift when she was younger and racing motocross in summers, members of the MC taking her to races, acting as her pit crew, and cheering her on. Another memory she had shoved away came barreling through her synapses.

"Is someone else riding it now?" she asked, trying not to let the disappointment show in her voice. "I mean, I understand if they are. And I guess I should ask if they mind if I take it out." She babbled until Maverick stopped her.

"No one else is riding it, Thunder. Irish makes sure it's maintained. Danny and Scarlett have their own bikes. This one is an older model." He tried not to smirk at the last part of his statement.

"Oh. Well then, get out of the way," she ordered. He didn't move. She sighed, "I won't take it offroad. I'll just go to my grandparents' house." If he didn't know who she was, he did now. She suspected he already knew. He moved from the front and stood off to the side.

"You haven't done this in a while. Want me to kick start it for you?" he asked.

She gave him a withering look and jumped on the kick start. On the third try it fired up. Maverick watched as the huge smile transformed her face. "See you around, Maverick." She headed out of the barn at a fast pace, back tire careening out to the side until it found purchase, leaving him in the dust to shake his head at her retreating back. At least he knew where she was going. There was little chance anyone would get to her inside the perimeter. Now, if he could just trust her to stay close to the houses. He didn't.

Chapter 8

THE TOWN WAS BUSTLING THIS MORNING. EVERYONE seemed ready for summer to start. After a cold winter, the residents were out and about, social creatures free from their seasonal hibernation. While the citizens of San Francisco would have had their puffy winter coats fully zipped at a balmy 60 degrees, the people here were in T-shirts and peasant tops, their bright smiles surely as much part of the outfit as the cotton and polyester on their backs. The sun cooperated today, though it was Michigan, so the skies could darken, and rain appear at any time.

Halley parked around back in the parking lot since on-street parking was taken. Henry, her car, was still full of her possessions, so she would rather have had it visible on the street. However, this was a place where a lot of people didn't even lock their cars, so how big a risk was it really? Her mind said her father would say not to tempt people. He was always security conscious. But he would be, wouldn't he? And her grandfather too. Her back windows were tinted, so that should help with the looky-loos. With one last glance at Henry, she walked to the side street and around the corner to the diner.

Sarah was already in the booth when Halley arrived. Across from her was another familiar face, one that lit up when she spied

Halley walk in the door. "It *is* you!" The other young woman jumped from her seat and threw her arms around Halley, squeezing her tight.

Halley should be used to this – hugging – but it had been a long time since anyone touched her. Friends in New York were more likely to kiss her on both cheeks, copying the French greeting, or squeeze her hand lightly, not the full-on bear hugs of her hometown. In San Francisco, she didn't have close friends. Her ex-fiancé was more likely to kiss her cheek in public or hold both her hands in greeting. Surprised, she realized she liked it. The exuberant human touch made her relax a little. Somewhere she read a study about that recently. Human touch was good for health and longevity – at least that's what she thought she remembered.

"It's good to see you!" Halley enthused, realizing she meant it. As they settled into the booth, she turned to Renee and said, "So, Ross Winter, huh?"

Renee blushed and looked down for a moment, "We didn't have a big wedding, only justice of the peace. We wanted to put the money into the house, not on one day. Otherwise, I would have invited you."

"Oh no, I'm not upset, Ren! I was just thinking about how you've been together since middle school. You knew what you wanted, and you got it. I'm so happy for you," Halley assured her old friend. "Is he still the perfect gentleman and hot?" she added mischievously.

Renee's laughter peeled like church bells. Even that was sweet with the woman – there was not a bad bone in her body. "Yes, he is. Both." Then she giggled. "But I'm not the only one. We all got what we wanted. Look at us, successful women. Just like we planned," Renee lifted her Coke glass in salute. Sarah grabbed her diet Coke and, more slowly, Halley raised her water glass.

"You're one step ahead of us, Ren," Sarah acknowledged. "You've got the guy too. We have lonely beds to go home to."

"But remember, that was always part of my plan," Renee argued. "It was never defined in your plans."

Sarah rolled her eyes and exaggeratedly looked to Halley, "She's still doing those vision boards; yes, she is. Just sayin'."

Renee smacked Sarah's arm and said haughtily, "You two make fun all you want, but I've gotten everything I've manifested."

"We got what we set out to get too, right Hal?" Sarah nudged her friend.

Renee jumped in again, "That's what I'm saying. We all got what we set out to do as kids. You're going to take over your family's business. Halley's been climbing the corporate ladder and seeing the world."

Halley supposed it was true. Only now, she wondered whether she was a fraud, if she was a spectacular failure if she could never go back to that world. At one time, she thought people measured success by how much money you make, the size of your house, how much land you owned, if you were married and had children – a family – and how "big" you were between small ponds and big ponds. What she came to realize was there were ever-increasingly "bigger ponds" no matter how far you go. Now she didn't think any of that mattered so much anymore. So, what was success, really? Was there even a measure? She was pulled from her confused musing by Sarah's suddenly quiet tone.

"Now I'd kind of like someone to share my bed with," Sarah admitted in a hushed voice, not wanting any eavesdroppers to hear her confession.

"For a night or a lifetime?" Renee asked, forehead drawn inward, serious now.

"Jeez, Ren! I can have a night, though pickings are pretty slim here and I have to go out of town for that. I mean a lifetime. Maybe? Oh, I don't know!" Sarah groaned.

"How about we envision you with the right man for you and then a lifetime doesn't seem like a prison sentence," Renee suggested in all seriousness.

"That sounds right," Sarah agreed. Then her lips turned up in an impish grin, "Hal, how about you sneak us into the clubhouse? Some of those new guys are pretty."

"I told you we don't have to sneak anymore. But seriously? You want a biker?" Halley asked skeptically. "I don't know. I'm not sure they're for you. They're kind of overbearing. And please don't call them 'pretty.'"

"I think I can handle it, Hal. Besides, I'm not going anywhere and they're here, too. I wouldn't have to worry about some guy expecting me to move. This is home," Sarah tried to convince her friend.

"You know you can't take them all for a test drive, right? You can't be like a patch bunny. Some of those girls are delusional – if the guys have all had their roll in the hay, they'll never be an ol' lady. If there's *one,* who does it for you, that's another thing; that would be okay," Halley tried again to dissuade her friend.

Sarah grimaced, "I'm not sure I could be called an 'ol' lady.'" Then she added, "Sheesh, Hal, I'm not going to sleep my way through the club. I think your dad would put a stop to that."

Both Halley and Renee nodded at the truth in that statement. James McCarthy was a lot protective of his daughters and their friends. Halley said, "If you were an ol' lady, you'd wear it proudly, like my Gram and every other one of them. I don't know what happens when they fall for a member of the club, but they all decide it's okay."

Halley knew her own mother proudly owned the term that meant commitment from a biker and his MC family, as much as she was proud to be his wife. Halley remembered listening to a conversation between her mom and one of her friends as they sat in the kitchen on a cold winter morning talking about being with a member of the MC. Her mother was calm and glowed with love, at least that's what young Halley remembered feeling from the woman. Her mother was so much younger then than Halley was now and that suddenly struck her. Her mother exuded more peace and happiness then than Halley had ever felt in her entire adult life. She should have known by that measure her ex-fiancé had been wrong for her all along; her parents set the bar high. As did both sets of grandparents.

"Well?" Renee prodded, looking directly at Halley. The other woman looked like the sweet elementary school teacher she was. Her soft blonde hair was straight and hung down her back, a colorful scarf tied from the top of her forehead to the base of her neck, pulling it away from her face.

"Sorry, did you ask me something?" Halley asked, focusing on her friends and not her mind.

"What about you? Are you interested in someone warming your bed for more than a night?" Renee giggled.

"Well, considering I'm staying in my dad's house, *no one* is warming my bed. Not if they want to live to see morning," Halley deflected.

Both lowered their chins, tilted their heads, and stared pointedly at her.

"What? You know it's true."

"No one you left behind in San Francisco?" Renee pressed.

"I'd like to know that too, Thunder," an unmistakably male voice asked. The large man took a step closer to the table and leaned his tall body down, so his head was closer to the woman's. The smirk stood out on his usually serious face.

"What are you doing here? Following me again?" Halley asked suspiciously.

"In your dreams, Thunder. I'm picking up a carryout order. Some of the rest of us eat lunch too,"

"Who's this? Why does he call you Thunder?" Sarah leaned closer.

Maverick held out his hand to Sarah and introduced himself, "I'm Maverick." He repeated the action with Renee.

"I'm Sarah and this is Renee."

Halley couldn't help but hear the different tone in her friend's voice. Maverick didn't seem to notice and after making introductions, turned his attention back to Halley. "What is it, Thunder? Someone waiting for you on the West Coast?" He doubted it. He couldn't imagine any man with a lick of sense wanting this woman to walk out of his life.

"No," Halley replied primly. He could tell there was a lot she left out with that one-word answer. So could her friends. They'd press her later. "I spend too much time working to have a personal life." That wasn't a lie.

He turned toward the counter when the waitress called his name and held out a large paper sack. "Make sure you give them the real reason. Don't need any more females after my hide." He referred to the first question Sarah asked about her new nickname. Then he was gone, with a quick over-the-shoulder goodbye, "Nice meeting you both."

"Well, that was interesting," Sarah said, watching him walk down the street, or more specifically, his jean-covered ass. Halley told them why he called her Thunder.

"I could go for that one," Sarah said wistfully.

"No, you couldn't," Renee interjected. "That man would be a one-nighter for you. You said you want more."

"How do you know?" Sarah asked grumpily.

"Because he only had eyes for Hal," Renee said matter-of-factly.

Now it was Halley's turn to balk, "That's not true."

"Truth." Renee's reply was saucy, and she followed it with a grin.

The waitress – not Kathy – put their food in front of them, saving Halley from replying. Sarah made sure the surly former cheerleader was not their waitress and was assured she would not be allowed near their food.

"It's Saturday. Let's go to the clubhouse tonight," Sarah suggested.

James and the others hadn't returned from their club business yet. It might be a good night to be there. She knew there would be a party. Maybe even a band, given the nice day.

"Okay," Halley shrugged.

"Really?! Well, all right then!" Sarah grinned and dug into her sandwich. "You and Ross going to come?" The couple went to school with several of the members and would know most of them.

"I'll check, but probably," Renee agreed and took a big bite of her chicken sandwich.

Neither of her friends nor Anna who was now in Chicago, were prudes, so there was no worry about what they may witness at the clubhouse if the party got rowdy. Their open minds and those of their families were her saving grace as a schoolgirl. None of them minded their little girls were friends with the MC president's daughter; if anything, they seemed grateful her father looked out for her friends, too.

Across and down the street a ways, Maverick sat in a dark SUV eating his lunch, eyes on the front of the diner. He could see them sitting in the booth at the window. He knew the women couldn't see him and seemed to lose interest once his jean-clad derriere had moved down the street out of sight. That made him laugh. He caught the spark of interest from Halley's friend Sarah. He'd already known who both women were. Irish had been very specific about his daughter, her habits, and her friends, and left it to Maverick and Wire to discover anything new. They had quite a thick dossier that if the woman knew existed, he had no doubt the thunder would truly roll.

What he couldn't figure out was why one of the missing partners at the startup had mentioned her several times in deleted cryptic external emails Wire recovered. The tone was too familiar for his liking. All of Halley's work emails to the partner were professional in subject and tone. The recipient of the partner's emails was unknown, as of yet, the person buried beneath several offshore shell corporations. It was only a matter of time before Wire – or the government investigators – figured out to whom they belonged.

His money was on Wire. The former military intelligence operator was a tech prodigy, having hacked into several secure government databases by age twelve, usually on a dare from his geeky friends. By the time Wire was seventeen, it was either join the military, the CIA, or go to jail. It wasn't that he was easy to trace, but that they had been watching him since he was twelve years old. That hardly seemed fair to Wire – to him that was cheating – so he chose the military and built out his physique to match his over-sized intellect. There was no doubt he could have made a fortune in the Silicon Valley. Instead, he chose the brotherhood of the MC and was as loyal as they came. The man would do anything for his president and brothers, just as he had his team in the military. Both Wire and Maverick, and Tyler by extension, were fortunate to have met Scottie during their time in service.

Maverick saw Halley and her friends leave the diner. He noticed the sour-faced waitress with hair too blonde to be anything but from a bottle, the dark roots in stark contrast, standing by the window staring at them, then throwing the dirty dishes into a plastic tub to carry to the kitchen. He watched her pocket the cash tip until another waitress, this one older, came behind her and muttered words he couldn't make out with honed lip-reading skills, but based on her outstretched hand, palm up, he guessed she demanded her earned tip. That was one to file away for another time. The younger waitress who had something against Halley or her friends couldn't be trusted.

Maverick pulled the truck out of its parallel parking space on the main street and turned down the side street Halley walked to get to her car in the parking lot behind the buildings. He idled just before the alley she would have to exit, keeping her in sight as she got to her car.

She slipped inside and then stepped back outside and reached for something under the windshield. Maverick hadn't seen anyone handing out fliers. Halley looked around, doing a three-hundred-sixty-degree view of the area, before getting back in the car. She raced too fast out of the parking lot, flying in front of him and turning left onto the side street, not noticing where he sat across the street, not that he would expect her to see him through the dark tinted windows. If she was going to her father's place, she would have turned right.

He followed at a slower pace, several blocks back, until she turned into the cemetery on the hill at the edge of town. He was surprised she hadn't been stopped by a city policeman or county deputy, her speed noticeably above the speed limit. With his truck parked beyond the entrance, hidden by a stone mason's workshop, he made his way around the trees so he wouldn't be seen, but close enough he could see if she was meeting anyone – or if anyone laid in wait for the unsuspecting woman.

"Hi, Mom," Halley said as she stared at her mother's headstone, the dates for birth and death prominent. It was an illusion, a trick of her brain, but Halley was sure the death date was even more pronounced. The day of Eve McCarthy's death was the day Halley's life was changed forever. "Sorry, I haven't been by in a while. I'm sure Grandma and Grandpa said they've seen me."

Halley wondered to herself if spirits get together and talk; something inside her said they surely did.

Halley plopped down on the grave site; legs bent to the side beneath her weight. "Sometimes I feel guilty. If I'd been there that day, maybe whoever hurt you wouldn't have come in. If he did, maybe I could have hit him over the head with a frying pan. I know that sounds ridiculous, but I remember that day and everything I thought and felt. Grandma said she knew you were glad I was safe and not there."

After a slight hesitation, Halley's voice shook as she spoke again, "Mom, I'm not sure I'm safe now. I know it's not the same as being murdered, but what if they want to put me in prison? I think Anthony did something to make me look guilty. I don't know what. It's just a feeling. I don't even know where he is. He disappeared shortly after whatever was happening was discovered. You and Dad wouldn't have liked him. I guess I knew that and that's why I didn't tell anyone we were engaged.

"I came home with my tail between my legs. How lame is that? I was so sure I had to get away. Now I'm not sure I ever want to leave again. I can't tell anyone that, of course. I've cut myself off from everyone who ever cared about me. And for what? A bank account that was emptied by my conman of an ex-fiancé? A job where I'm *persona non grata*? Good thing I listened to Dad about at least one thing – I don't keep all my money in one place or where anyone can find it.

"I feel like such a failure, Mom. No one else may see it, but I do. I feel it to my bones. I made such terrible mistakes. No one will ever trust my judgment again. Then today someone left a message on my car. I don't know what it means or if it was meant for me. It said: *Waiting for me?* What does that even mean? No one signed it. I'm *so* tired, Mom." The tears began to flow down her cheeks. She moved to her side in the grass, letting the tears fall, sobs wracking her body.

Talk to Daddy. She was sure she heard the words whispered in the wind. Or maybe it was her own conscience speaking to her. But it sure sounded like her mother's voice. She didn't want her father to know the extent of her failure or stupidity. He had always been so proud of her. Now, she would let him down, too. That made her cry harder.

Ssshhhh. The wind picked up.

Behind the giant maple at the end of the row of graves, only a few yards from where Halley sobbed on the ground, Maverick slid down the massive trunk to sit against it. He wanted to comfort her, but that wasn't his place. He felt bad for eavesdropping on her personal conversation with her dead mother. It did answer a lot of questions he had – they all had. He wanted to get his hands on whatever she plucked from her windshield and have it dusted for prints or see if there were clues in the writing or the paper.

He was also sure Anthony was one of the two missing partners. It was doubtful two people named Anthony would be so intimately involved in this debacle. Now he knew Halley had been engaged. That realization made his gut clench. He wondered if she called it off or if he did.

The discussion with Prez was going to be interesting. He'd have to make sure Halley was far from the clubhouse when that happened. He'd get Wire on it and see what they could find, before taking it to the boss.

For now, he had a dilemma. It appeared Halley cried herself to sleep. He couldn't leave her lying on the grave, but she already accused him of following her; this would cinch it if he revealed himself. So, he waited. To save time and feel somewhat productive, he texted Wire instructions to look into any bank and financial accounts in Halley's name and to do a deep dive on the partner named Anthony.

He waited some more. He'd had to practice patience as an Army Ranger. It wasn't in his nature, but he learned it had its merits when used right.

Sometime later, Halley jerked awake and sat up, eyes red and swollen, grass indents on her cheek. The sun was still out, so she couldn't have slept for too long. She still had to get to her room and get ready for the club party that night before Sarah arrived at the house.

"I've got to go now, Mom. I promise I won't stay away so long next time. I guess it's just easier to stop with Grandma and

Grandpa. It hurts less. Now that I'm home, maybe once I figure out my mess I can work on your cold case and find out who really killed you. I don't believe it was a home invasion. Some drug-addled thief wouldn't have set the house on fire. There was no reason; they didn't find him anyway. I love you, Mom."

Halley stood and made her way down the row the opposite way from where Maverick watched. He was ready to make his way back to the SUV when Halley turned around with a puzzled look on her face and searched the area with her eyes. Not seeing anyone, she continued toward her car. Once he was sure she was moving forward, he quietly hurried out of the cemetery and followed behind her, staying many cars back, and then when the traffic thinned to almost nothing, letting her vehicle remain far enough ahead of him he sometimes lost her for a few moments on the curves, until he could see her turn into the private drive to the McCarthy house.

Halley rushed into the house. Maverick moved the truck forward from behind the tree line and got out next to her vehicle. With a glance toward the house, he tried her passenger door and luckily, she hadn't locked it in her haste to get inside. The note, written in block letters on a note card, was in her glove compartment. Rather than take it with him, he used a bandana to lay it on the seat and then took pictures of both sides. He'd let Wire work his magic. If that turned up nothing, he would take the actual card. The card back in the glove box and car door closed, he thought about it. To him, the words were taunting. But they could just as easily be a mistake or in jest. Maybe she had an old boyfriend in town who wanted to rekindle things. He doubted it, but it had to be on the list of possibilities.

Maverick moved his truck to the large pole barn garage. From there, he took his Harley to the clubhouse to talk with Wire and await the arrival of Halley and her friends. Tyler was working with the horses, so he would alert his brother when the women departed.

In the house, Halley looked through her clothes, discarding each piece with a frustrated shake of her head. Who was she trying to impress? It's not as if she was looking for a hookup.

Being at the clubhouse was going to be uncomfortable. She hadn't seen many people since she returned home, by choice. Now, attending a raucous party turned her stomach.

Breathing deeply and standing taller, head thrown back, she reminded herself no one cared who she was or that she came back to town. A friend's therapist once told her friend that everyone else had their own problems and insecurities, so they were not going to focus on hers. Halley didn't have a therapist, but she gleaned what advice she could when her friends recounted their sessions like it was their badge of honor. That one piece of guidance had served her well as she climbed the corporate ladder, and it would again tonight. Besides, tonight, she was a wingwoman for her friend. That's all this was.

With that decided, she pulled on a pair of jeans with rips in more places than not, showing skin but nothing indecent. Then a white tank top that showed more cleavage than she was used to exposing, but no one would notice, not with all the patch bunnies there blatantly displaying everything they had. She finished with a black leather necklace with a silver charm hanging down toward her cleavage, her black motorcycle boots, and a black leather jacket – spring was still cold, especially at night. She contemplated makeup, but again, why? She rarely wore makeup, so swiping on some lipstick and maybe some eyeshadow was all she was going to do for the night.

Sarah came tumbling into her room without knocking. Someone else must have been home to let her in the house. Her friend wore skintight jeans, and a cropped, lightweight, purple leather jacket over a black cropped top. Her boots were thigh-high and heeled. "I couldn't decide between the jeans and this skirt. What do you think?" Sarah thrust a short black skirt in front of her.

"Well…whatever you'll be more comfortable in. You're hot either way," Halley admitted.

"What will look better?" Sarah pressed and pouted, reminding Halley of the girl she once was. She wore red lipstick and with the contrast of her black pixie cut and dark eyes, she was stunning. Plus, she was always up for fun and was a successful businesswoman. Sarah was the whole package. Halley didn't know why she wasn't coupled up already; except, yeah, there were not many choices when you fish in a pond rather than the ocean.

"I only need one fish, Hal, the pond should have that, right?" Sarah said with hope in her voice. Halley realized she once again said aloud what she was thinking. She had to stop that habit.

"Sorry! But you do look fantastic. How about stick with the jeans this time?" Halley suggested.

Sarah threw the skirt on Halley's bed and grabbed her hand, "Let's go!"

Chapter 9

THE BACK WAY TO THE CLUBHOUSE WAS BARELY A trail and free of traffic and people, the ideal route, in Halley's opinion. She drove slowly enough there would be no damage to Henry, her car. She didn't even care if some newbie questioned her right to be on the property. As they got close, they could hear the bassline from the music. The party was in full swing. People spilled from the inside to the picnic tables and bonfire outside. That meant there was a good-size crowd. Halley wanted to turn around and go to the privacy of her bedroom, but the look on Sarah's face told her that was not going to be an option.

They wandered inside, Halley walking more slowly than her friend. Sarah threw an arm through Halley's elbow and pulled her inside, just as when they were kids. Near the bar getting drinks, they saw Renee and Ross and made a beeline for the two. There were a few wolf calls and whistles as they made their way across the room. Halley cringed; Sarah smiled more broadly. The patch bunnies, clad in barely anything and makeup thick, over the top, in Halley's opinion, sent derisive looks their way, wondering who the newcomers were and silently warning them they were on someone else's turf. Little did they know.

"Beer or do you drink something more sophisticated these days?" Ross asked Halley after he hugged her hello. She wanted to say a martini, but by the looks of the prospects behind the bar, that would be an unwelcome request.

"Beer's fine," Halley answered. She wasn't planning to drink much of it anyway. Ross handed both of them bottles, which was better than whatever was on tap.

One of the club brothers clapped Ross on the shoulder, "You interested in prospecting with us, buddy?" It was someone with whom they'd gone to high school who promptly pulled Ross toward the pool table, where several other boys, now men, they grew up with were gathered, proudly wearing their leather cuts.

"Now our chaperone is gone, let's have some fun, girls," Sarah wiggled her eyebrows.

Halley glanced around the room and was embarrassed to see her younger brother Drake leaning against a wall with a patch bunny clinging to his front, kissing his neck, making her way down his body until she was on her knees. When Drake's eyes met hers, he hesitated in what looked like defiance, before he pulled the young woman up by her arm and led her outside toward the bonfire. For that, Halley was grateful. She had no desire to see her brother's wares. The club brothers may not have any modesty, but she was a much more private person.

"Looks like you scared young Drake off," Handsy laughed beside her.

"Not my intention. But yea?" Halley replied weakly.

Handsy laughed harder and turned to look at Sarah, "You girls okay with drinks? There's food set up too, if you're hungry." His eyes looked Sarah up and down, clearly appreciating what he saw. Halley felt like an unwanted accessory.

"We're good, for now," Renee replied, holding up her bottle and giggling. Sarah was peering out at the crowd, seeing who was there. She wasn't paying attention and hadn't noticed Handsy's interest. Several of the guys looked their way. Halley guessed neither had been to a party here since high school when her dad kicked them out after family-appropriate hours. But she could be wrong, Renee and Ross seemed comfortable.

Halley elbowed Sarah lightly in the ribs and gestured with her head toward Handsy. "Doug, you remember Sarah from school, right?"

"Of course. And from around town," Handsy nodded and reached a hand politely to Sarah. "The club does a lot of business with your family."

Sarah shook his hand and nodded, "It does, but it could be more. Doug Lennox, all grown up and now a *Phantom Raider*. I expected you to stay away like Halley here."

"Been a grown-up for quite a while now," Handsy allowed.

Before he could comment further, another man stepped forward, grabbed Sarah around the waist, and twirled her around. "Come dance with me, Sarah Ferguson. It's been too long," the club brother, someone else with whom they had gone to school, spun her away. The band was outside, on a raised platform in the pavilion that hadn't been here when Halley was growing up. Back then, the band would set up inside the clubhouse in a dark corner of the common room, sometimes until daybreak.

"Well, that was interesting," Renee laughed. "Does she have a sign flashing on her head that says, 'Take me now' only men can see?"

"I'm not sure this is the place for you and Sarah," Handsy said to Halley, concern lacing his voice. "Maybe you should wait until Irish and Scottie are back."

"Thanks for the concern, but we can take care of ourselves, Handsy. Been doing it a long time," Halley said, making sure to emphasize his road name. She wondered how long she was going to have to keep reminding men of that fact. "You go have fun with the patch bunnies." She wrinkled her nose. Renee stared at her with green eyes wide. Handsy looked as if he would say something; instead, he shook his head and left them where they stood, making his way to the outside door.

"That was a little harsh. He was being nice, Hal," Renee protested.

"Maybe," Halley lifted one shoulder in a half-shrug. She took a swig of her beer and decided that maybe finishing it wouldn't be the worst thing she did tonight.

Ross gestured for Renee to join him with the guys. A couple now had their ol' ladies leaning into them, hands around their waists in what Halley always saw as a distastefully possessive gesture.

"I'm being summoned. Come with me," Renee smiled again.

"You go ahead. I'm going to wander a bit," Halley declined. The last thing she wanted right now was to be around happy couples who made her examine her bad choice all over again. That, combined with the fact she was pretty sure the women had gone to school with them, and she would have to answer more questions about the last fifteen years, cinched her decision to remain alone tonight. She could do this. She could wander around and pretend to socialize.

Her wandering took her outside. She saw the patch bunny who had her sights set on Drake sitting on top of a picnic tabletop with a pout on her made-up face, seated with other patch bunnies, but no Drake in sight. For that, she was thankful. The bonfire was high and cast an orange glow on the people around it. Others were at the picnic tables. Even more were dancing. Some man she didn't know, wearing a cut, grabbed her hand and pulled her toward the pavilion dance floor. Rather than protest, she figured she didn't know him, he didn't know her, so what could a dance hurt? At least there would be no awkward conversation. She let the music carry her away.

They stayed on the floor for a few dances, her beer now long gone, and bottle moved to a picnic table by a prospect who brought her another. She allowed herself to feel free and moved her body, hips keeping time to the music. The next song she knew was a typical grind piece and she didn't even care when the guy moved behind her and grabbed her hips in his hands. At least someone seemed to think her body was okay. He was molded to her back and backside, and they moved together like the other people on the dance floor, some grinding four and five deep.

As warm as it had been in the cool night air, suddenly, her back was cold. When she turned around, her dance partner was standing to the side having a stare-down with Maverick.

"Hey, we're just having some fun, get your own girl," the man protested, and she could tell he was angry.

Maverick dropped the guy's arm and said something in a low voice Halley couldn't hear. The man, still clearly not happy, stalked away. Maverick stared at her for a beat, eyebrows raised in what looked like a challenge to her.

"What? Can't I have fun?" Halley glowered at him, hands on her hips.

"He wasn't just having fun. Thought you were a sure thing," Maverick stated.

"That's not true! And even if it was, what if that's what I wanted?" Halley yelled.

Maverick's eyes flashed, "Is that what you wanted? To be used?" He pointedly looked around at the other couples, many of the guys with patch bunnies.

"It's not being used if both people want it," Halley argued. She didn't want anything other than to dance with the guy, but Maverick didn't need to know that. As she glanced around, she saw Handsy pull the guy Sarah was dancing with away the same way Maverick had, with angry faces and low growling words exchanged. Sarah looked as vexed as she was.

Sarah stormed back inside; Halley followed. She saw her friend beeline for the bar and grab the shot glass from the bartender, downing it then signaling for another, pointing at the prospect to also give a shot to Halley. After three she grabbed a new beer bottle and turned to look around the room. Halley stood in front of her, expectantly.

"You okay?" Halley asked.

"Why wouldn't I be," Sarah huffed. "I was having fun. I wasn't going to sleep with Hairy John."

Halley's eyes opened wide, "That was Hairy John?" The nickname stuck from middle school all through high school when John developed faster than the other boys. He was proud of it. She remembered like it was yesterday when he stood in the hallway, shirt unbuttoned to his navel and pointed out the three dark hairs growing out of his chest and the five on his chin. She was relieved when he didn't unbutton his jeans, that show and tell was saved for the boys' locker room.

Sarah rolled her eyes, "Yes."

Renee moved to stand next to Halley. "You could dance with Handsy."

"He didn't ask. He just interrupted the dance I was doing for no reason," Sarah growled.

"Oh, there's a reason. You were getting pretty sexed up with Hairy John," Renee giggled.

"It was *just* dancing," Sarah insisted.

"I think Handsy may have a thing for you. He's *hot*," Renee said.

"He does not. He's four years younger."

"So? Scottie is four years younger and he's hot too."

"Scottie's into Jana, even though he won't admit it," Sarah argued, mentioning the female bartender and waitress from *Raiders Roost Tavern*.

"Wait. He is?" Halley turned to Renee.

"Not the point right now, Hal," Renee rolled her eyes. "Sarah, four years at our age is nothing. It's not like when we were in our early twenties or teenagers. Handsy is not only hot, he's super smart. And, Hal, Maverick hasn't taken his eyes off you all night."

"That's not true! He's just being protective, so my dad and brothers don't get pissed off when they hear about tonight."

Renee shook her head and looked toward the doorway. Both Maverick and Handsy stood there, arms crossed over their broad chests, staring at them. Rather than the angry look he had moments before, Maverick had a slight smirk. Handsy looked angry. Sarah narrowed her eyes at them, then turned abruptly toward the bar and ordered shots for her and her friends. Then another. Halley discreetly handed hers to one of the prospects sitting on a barstool. Both men moved closer until they crowded the bar, the women in front of them.

"Think you've had enough of those," Handsy said in a low voice.

"Not nearly enough," Sarah retorted and reached for another. Too slow. Handsy got it first and downed it.

"You're not driving, Thunder. How about you give me your keys and I'll take you both home when you're ready," Maverick said, holding out his hand.

Halley shook her head, the first shots going to her head. She realized she hadn't eaten since lunch. "I don't have a home."

Maverick sighed, "Your dad's place. Where you sleep."

Halley shook her head again. "Can't leave Sarah. I'm her wingwoman."

"I'll get Sarah back to the house, Hal," Handsy promised.

"What if I want to sleep here?" Sarah pushed her way between the guys and headed back outside, Handsy on her heels. Halley started to follow.

"Uh uh. You dance anymore you're going to fall out of that shirt, Thunder," Maverick said as he moved in front of her, looking at her chest and the tank top that had pulled down lower, revealing the top of her lacy white bra. She wondered when that happened.

Maverick gritted his teeth. No way did he want the brothers looking at that much of her body. It was bad enough that the jeans were sexy as sin, creamy skin peeking through the numerous, strategically placed holes, and he was serious about the tank top being too low. Without thinking, he reached out and zipped her leather jacket.

Renee sucked her lower lip between her teeth as she watched the interplay and tried not to gloat. She winked at her husband, who walked toward her and put his arm over her shoulders.

"Thanks, I was cold," Halley said, immediately feeling stupid that was what came out of her mouth first. Not a protest, not indignation, but gratitude. She was not good at this; whatever *this* was. Maverick smirked and kept his hands on the collar of her jacket.

"Ready to go when you are, Thunder."

Side-stepping the man, she started for the door, "Not yet." She had more dancing to do and her wingwoman duties to fulfill, though Sarah hadn't needed her help in that area. Her friend had been on a mission.

Many dances later, all the last ones with Maverick, the man led her to her car and opened the passenger door for her before moving to the driver's seat. Handsy steered a more subdued Sarah to another vehicle and got her inside, following Maverick to the house over the back trail so he could give his club brother a lift back to the clubhouse, though neither was in the mood to continue the party.

Handsy stared at Sarah, who fell asleep, or maybe passed out, halfway to the house. He would love to spend more time with the woman. He had a crush on her all those years ago when he was at the house with Scottie and Sarah was spending the night with Halley. Now they were both adults, he still felt the same. He had been trying to find the courage to ask her out. She didn't know it, but he was the one pushing Irish and the others to do more business with her family's firm. Seeing the work she did, he knew it was the right move.

Now, if she could see him as a man and not her best friend's little brother's best friend, he would be ecstatic. He almost went nuts when he saw Hairy John with his hands all over her on the dance floor. Hairy John was a club brother, but the guy dipped his wick in every available pot. Sarah was off limits to him, Handsy would make that crystal clear.

"Come on, Sarah, we're here," Handsy shook her arm a little. Sarah moaned but didn't open her eyes. Rather than watch her trip up the steps and down the hall – if she would even wake up – Handsy reached in and picked her up in his arms, following a wide-eyed Halley into the house. He and Halley were both surprised to find Maverick behind them. He laid Sarah on the bed after Halley pulled down the covers. Handsy carefully pulled off her thigh-high boots and leather jacket, then tucked the duvet up to her chin.

"Thanks for bringing us back. I could have driven though," Halley said. She walked both to the door.

"Don't forget to set the alarm when we leave," Maverick admonished. He surprised himself when he leaned down and kissed her forehead before striding out the door to the vehicle Handsy drove. He had surprised Halley and Handsy too, though neither said anything.

Once on the dark trail back to the clubhouse, Handsy glanced at Maverick. "You like her. She's Prez's daughter. You going to tell him? That could be tricky."

"Didn't say I'm interested. She hasn't said she's staying." That was it for conversation.

Chapter 10

"OHHH. HELL'S BELLS. TURN OFF THE LIGHT," SARAH groaned. She looked like a lump under rumpled bed clothes. Natural light came in the window, but there was no other light source turned on in the bedroom.

Halley poked her head out of the bathroom, toothbrush in her hand. "It's afternoon. Ibuprofen and water on the nightstand."

Hand outstretched, Sarah tapped the nightstand until she found the water bottle and the tablets. Eyes still shut, she swallowed the pain killers and drank most of the bottle of water. Maybe if she didn't move until the tablets did their job, she would feel somewhat normal.

Halley threw an oversized sweatshirt at her friend's head. "My jeans will be too big for you. Want a pair of leggings? I never wear them, so they're pretty much new." Without waiting for an answer, she tossed the black leggings in the general direction of her head. "Lots of hot water left. Why don't you shower; you'll feel better. Maybe."

"How did I get in bed? I don't remember coming back here," Sarah pushed up on her elbows and squinted. Her short black hair stood up in all different directions. Halley wanted to know how her friend could look cute, even in her hungover state.

"Handsy carried you in. He took care of you."

Sarah looked horrified. "He carried me? Did he undress me too?"

"He did. Well, your boots and jacket."

"I'll never be able to look at him again," Sarah groaned even louder.

"I don't think he minded," Halley grinned.

"Hal, I mind! How would you feel if some hot guy had to take care of your drunken ass?"

"So, you *do* think he's hot. Why did you give him such a hard time?" Halley would have to give Renee credit the next time she saw her.

"I don't like to be told what to do. You and I have that in common. I was hoping he'd notice when I danced with Hairy John and cut in. But he went all caveman instead," Sarah said. "You do know I would never do more than dance with Hairy John, right?"

"Glad to hear it."

"Yeah, I went to prom with Hairy John junior year – the year after you left for college. He's been trying to get in my pants ever since. No way. No how. I know where that boy's been and it's nasty."

"Maybe give Handsy a chance. Renee's right; he's super smart. He didn't just play football in college. He came back because he wants to be here."

Sarah tilted her head and asked quietly, "And why did you come back, Hal?"

Halley plonked down on the side of the bed, mattress dipping underneath her, and whispered, "I didn't know where else to go."

Sarah wrapped her arms carefully around her friend, "You know we're all here to catch you when you decide to talk. Got your back. Always. Doesn't matter how long you've been gone."

Sarah couldn't know how much those words meant to Halley, even though she wasn't ready yet.

"I figured when I got here everyone would have their own lives, their new adult friends, their routines, and there wouldn't be room for me," Halley admitted. That was certainly the case with her friends in New York. They all coupled up, settled down, and got into new routines that didn't necessarily include her.

"Hal, that may be the case for some people, but I would have had to have a life in the first place. All I have is my work and dinner a couple times a month at my parents' place," Sarah scoffed. "We both need a reset."

Sarah grabbed the clothes and headed for the large walk-in shower Halley's father had included in his first-born's bathroom. She marveled that several people could comfortably fit inside, or maybe this was what passed as normal in a family full of men over six feet tall, broad, and muscled. Halley never seemed to notice they were the exception and not the rule.

Half an hour later the two sat in the kitchen drinking coffee – really strong coffee – when they heard vehicles approach. Through the kitchen window, two black SUVs barreled down the driveway. James, Scottie, Conor, and Red exited and headed toward the house in long, confident strides. A prospect slid into the driver's seat of the SUV pulling the long horse trailer and disappeared behind the stable near the pole barn to park it and remove it from the hitch.

"Smells strong. Got anymore brew?" Red asked, heading directly to the newly filled coffee pot, not waiting for an answer. "Ahh. Perfect. Priss must be out; you made this, right?"

Halley snickered. Priscilla was known for making weak, barely colored coffee. Halley and Sarah both decided years ago that she did it so no one would expect it of her or ask her to make it. As far as Halley knew, her father never complained. He either did it himself or waited until he got to his mother's kitchen or the clubhouse for his caffeine fix. The other three filled their mugs, Conor doctoring his with mostly half-and-half and sugar – some habits never changed, Halley observed.

"No sleep?" Sarah asked innocently.

"No," Conor grunted. Even though they spent the night in a hotel, the drive was long.

Scottie slid onto a stool next to Sarah after kissing the top of his sister's head. "Lookin' a little peaked, Sarah. Have fun at the party last night?" He hid his smile with the coffee cup.

"How? … Ugh! Someone already called you. How embarrassing," Sarah groaned yet again, making it multiple times for the day.

Scottie had known his best friend's secret interest in Sarah for years. He hoped they would both own up to it soon and give one another a chance. They would be good together; he had no doubt.

"You two need to watch yourselves," Red cautioned. "Neither of you been around the club for years and a lot of the guys don't know you yet. You can't just flounce what you got."

"Flounce? Really, Uncle Red?" Halley shook her head. "We were fine. Not that your goons gave us a chance to prove it."

"Doing their job," James said.

"We're a 'job' to them? Good to know," Sarah prickled. Now she knew her girlfriends were all wrong about Handsy; he was just doing his job.

"Not a job, Sar," Scottie soothed, sending a glare his father's way. "Just concerned and taking care of family."

After more back and forth, remarkably comfortable, in Halley's view, James closely watched his daughter. He could see reconnecting with her old friends brought back a little of the girl who left. She didn't seem as determined to run, like a skittish colt with no destination, only the instinct to flee. He made a decision and opted to plow forward. It might help to have Sarah and the others here.

Leaning against the back counter, hands braced on the cool granite, James addressed his daughter, "Need to talk, Hal."

Before he could say anything else, both brothers jumped from their seats and made excuses to leave. "Gotta get back to the clubhouse," Conor said lamely.

"Sit your asses back down," Red ordered, smacking Conor in the back of the head and missing Scottie's when the young man ducked.

"I'm not going to like this," Halley sighed, and her shoulders slumped. The others might want to escape, but Sarah was eager to find out what was going on and made no move to leave. There always had been more excitement at the McCarthy house than the Ferguson house – apparently accountants, brokers, and financial planners didn't generate much drama.

"Is there anyone out to get you, Hal?" her father asked.

Halley's eyes bugged out of her head. Her mind scrambled, information zipping through her synapses like a motor speedway, overpowering her logic and desire to keep her own counsel. "Why would you ask that? I don't think so – unless you count suspicion by the investors' attorneys, the partners, or the feds." She slumped lower as she thought of that. Since arriving in her hometown, she hadn't received any communication, not that she expected any while the investigation commenced.

"No jilted boyfriends? No stalkers?" James persisted.

"No, of course not. No one is interested in me. I work all the time," Halley replied stubbornly. No one needed to know her ultimate humiliation. There was no way her ex-fiancé would look for her; he was the one who disappeared when the noose was tightening at the company. She was only glad she broke it off with him mere days before that happened; she was unhappy it wasn't soon enough to rescue her bank account. The bank was still "looking into" her dispute of fraud. Of course, he had told her it wasn't over until he said it was, but don't all egotistical jilted men say that?

"You don't have to worry about your storage facility anymore. It's all here, in the one the club owns," James changed tactics. The club had bought a foreclosed storage facility outside of town only a year ago, upgraded security, fixed the drainage problems, and turned it into an already profitable small business.

"How did you know where it was?" The answer dawned as soon as she asked the question. She then turned and glared at her brothers. They had been in her car. They must have searched and found the rental agreement. Stubbornly, she added, "I had two."

"We know. Both are empty and here now. Your boxes are in a storage unit. Your ride is in the pole barn – we'll talk about that another time," James replied evenly, as if they hadn't just invaded her privacy.

"Do you have another car?" Sarah asked, ever practical when it came to purchases, confused as to why her single friend needed two vehicles. Then she realized, "Nuh-uh, no way! You have a motorcycle? Sweet! When can I go for a ride?"

"Not the time, Sar," Halley gritted out and her friend sat back with a pout, curbing her enthusiasm. "You said 'boxes' – what about my furniture?"

All the men looked at each other. Halley felt left out of some silent conversation and didn't like it.

"Need you to think who might want to hurt you or might be looking for something you have," James persisted. His eyes never left his daughter's, as if he was looking for a tell.

"What makes you so sure someone is after me, other than in a legal way?" Halley questioned. "And what about my furniture? Surely my style didn't offend you enough to leave it behind."

Conor pulled his phone from his pocket. Scottie batted his hand down before he could pull up the photos. Conor was just as stubborn as the rest of the family. "She's gotta know. This will make her understand."

"For crying out loud! Let me see the pictures!" Halley demanded. James nodded and Conor pulled up the photos. Halley's face dropped, after the few moments it took to register she was looking at her belongings inside the storage locker. Conor pulled the phone away and she protested, "Wait, I want to see the rest."

Even Conor wasn't sure she should see the photo of herself. James moved around the counter and stood behind his daughter. He nodded his assent. Halley gasped while Conor held his phone. Sarah leaned over to look, and her gasp was far louder than her friend's. James watched his daughter slump further and reached around, hugging her back to his chest.

"It's going to be okay."

Not able to comprehend someone so vile as to defile the picture of her – a picture she had never seen before, taken without her knowledge – she turned to something on which she could focus. "I liked that red couch."

Red roared with laughter and the others followed, hesitantly at first and then louder. "I'll buy you a new couch, Hal. A better one," the hardened biker promised.

There were evil people in the world; she saw her mother's beautiful face in her mind's eye and knew it was true. Now one of them seemed to have his sights on her. *Lucky me*, she thought, full sarcasm in effect.

"Did you leave someone behind in New York, Hal," Sarah guessed, wanting to find the culprit and ensure her friend was safe.

"No, no one. Besides, it was almost three years ago. Wouldn't someone have tried something before now?" Halley shook her head. She was not going to lose it in front of her father, his best friend, and her brothers. She was not going to slip to the floor and cry – no matter how much she wanted to.

"Hal, who were you seeing in San Francisco? One of the partners? Is he the one who got you to upend your life?" her father turned her on the stool to look into her eyes.

Halley noted it was no longer "are you" but now "who is it." This was not going the way she wanted. "I don't want to talk about it. It's not him." She whispered the last part.

"So, he's one of the partners." James' voice took on a hard quality he rarely used with his daughters.

In that moment, she realized she was not going to be able to hang on to the shred of self-respect she still had. She sighed and looked directly into her father's blue eyes, mirrors of her own, though hers were shining with unshed tears. "There was someone. He was a partner and the Chief Financial Officer. But I ended it with him. We, uh, we were engaged. But he was all wrong for me. I know that now."

"Engaged? What the hell, Hal? You don't get engaged to someone and not tell your family. Not let us meet him!" Conor exploded, more hurt than angry. Scottie put a hand on his brother's shoulder to calm him.

Halley winced. She knew this wouldn't go well. Her father's face was frozen, unreadable; she knew he did that when he tried to control his emotions.

"I'm sorry. I was making it on my own. You know, living the life." She hesitated and then added with more honesty than she'd shown since she arrived back in town, "Yeah, what a life, huh? I guess I forgot who I was. Thought I could handle it."

Sarah threw her arms around her friend in a tight side hug. "I can't believe you didn't tell us, even if not me, since we haven't talked much in years, then your dad. But it's okay, we gotcha now."

Red nodded emphatically by his spot near the coffee pot, leaning against the countertop. "You're family, Hal. That means something here."

"Name, Hal. I need a name," James insisted.

Her eyes widened and she swallowed hard, "It's not him."

"Not going to ask again," James said evenly. She wasn't sure what that meant, but she didn't want to find out. He could easily look up the company and see who was listed as the CFO, so she didn't know why she didn't want to say it.

With a deep breath, she breathed out the name of the ex-fiancé, the one who had stolen from her and probably the company, "Anthony Martinelli."

"I think he may have been a con man," she looked at the floor and added it very quietly.

"Why would you think that?" Sarah asked.

"I don't think he ever really loved me. He wanted to change how I look, what I eat, who I saw," Halley confessed. "That's why I don't think this was him. He didn't really want me."

"Sounds like he was trying to control you," Scottie observed, his face and voice as even as their father's; he was learning well.

"That's not the worst of it," Halley continued. "I broke up with him shortly before the company came under investigation. When he disappeared, so did my bank account." She shut her eyes waiting for the onslaught. She opened them again, first one, then the other, when no one said anything. They were all watching her.

"You're broke?" Scottie asked, no reproach in his voice. She saw the hard line of his jaw and knew he was restraining himself.

"Not exactly. No. I did listen to you, Dad," she said, turning her eyes back to her father. "I didn't keep all my money in one account. I have a couple, plus stocks. And cash in a safety deposit box and a lock box in the house Anthony didn't know about. That's with me. My stock from NY has another six months to mature and I can cash it in then, if I need to. I have my portfolio stocks, but those were supposed to be long-term bets."

Sarah clapped her hands, delighted. “Yes! You’re speaking my language!”

“How much did he clean out?” Red asked.

“A lot,” Halley swallowed. “I hadn’t moved it in a while and it’s where three-quarters of my paycheck and bonuses were directly deposited. I got all caught up in the startup and my relationship. I was stupid. The bank is investigating the fraud I reported. He shouldn’t have been able to access my account. His name wasn’t on it; I promise, Dad.” She desperately didn’t want her father to think she was completely foolish. As an officer of the company, the CFO had access to employee records, where he could easily get her social security number, birth date, and bank account where her direct deposit went. That and he had free rein of her little rental house for months. She had moved all her direct deposits and automatic withdrawals to another account but knew it was too little too late. At least her bills were being paid.

Maverick moved into the kitchen. He’d been standing in the shadows near the hallway. On James’ bidding, Red had texted the head of their security business to come to the house. He had been listening quietly in the wings when Halley revealed her secrets; some he already knew from the cemetery. He was perversely glad when he heard Halley say she was the one who called it off with the former fiancé.

Halley groaned when she saw him and rested her head in her hands. Now he would have one more reason to think less of her. Would her humiliation never end?

“Dramatic much, Hal?” Conor teased, trying to lighten the situation.

James nodded his agreement, “You couldn’t know this asshole was going to take you to the cleaners.”

“Maybe he just got desperate when the company came under investigation and didn’t mean to hurt you,” Sarah argued.

Halley tilted her head toward her friend and frowned. “He set me up. I’m sure of it, Sarah.”

Maverick jumped in, looking at his president rather than Halley, “Wire looked further into all the partners. He found some emails from the CFO to outside people where he mentions Halley;

those make more sense now. Anthony Martinelli didn't exist before five years ago. Wire is doing some things with facial recognition now and hopes to get a hit."

"He didn't exist?! See, set up," Halley said ruefully. "I was *so* stupid."

No one said anything. Her brothers stood on a silent signal from their father and moved toward the door. "We'll see you at Gram's in a couple of hours for family dinner. Need to shower and change first," Scottie said. "Maverick, you're invited. You too, Sarah. Gram said. Don't argue with Gram."

Sarah beamed and Halley groaned.

"What? I love your Gram's cooking," Sarah said, her hangover dissipating.

Maverick seemed to find something humorous about the conversation and smirked from where he leaned against the refrigerator with his arms crossed over his chest.

Three hours later they all gathered at Mitch and Mary's house through the woods. The house smelled of roasting meat and vegetables, homemade French bread, and strong coffee. There was a faint scent of something sweet; Halley hoped it was her favorite pineapple upside-down cake. It had been so long since she tasted the gooey dessert. Dessert was never on the menu with Anthony. He could have his cannoli, but always tsk-tsked her if she ordered anything that would go straight to her hips…or stomach…or, heaven forbid, her thighs. Maybe she should forego dessert after all.

Priscilla arrived with her three youngest children in tow. They had been at her parents' house earlier in the day, much to Danny and Scarlett's irritation. What started as a trip to the store for new baseball and softball cleats was a bait and switch. Tiffany, of course, was delighted. Her grandparents doted on her, while they thought Danny and Scarlett were a little too much like their father's side of the family, too many rough edges.

Red and his wife pulled up on his Harley just ahead of Maverick and Handsy as they arrived on their bikes, pipes announcing their arrival long before they pulled into the driveway. Sarah blushed and looked away when Handsy walked through the kitchen door behind Maverick. Drake appeared without a word to anyone, just as they were sitting down to dinner. Handsy snagged a seat next to Sarah; he wasn't going to keep hiding in the shadows, and he wasn't going to let her do that either.

"Guess I owe you a thank you for last night," Sarah whispered under her breath to Handsy.

"Anytime," Handsy whispered back, and a small grin curved his lips. Gram watched the interchange and didn't try to hide her smile.

Tiffany frowned as she looked around the large farm table. "I thought this was *family* dinner?"

"We're all family here," Mitch answered his granddaughter, his scowl daring her to dispute it. She looked down at her food, but not before sending an unhappy eyeroll her mother's way. Priss gave her an almost imperceptible shake of her head; the last thing she wanted was an argument to erupt – she knew Tiffany would never win in that room.

"You got something to say, Tiff?" Mitch pushed her.

Tiffany looked to her mother again, avoiding her grandfather's gaze as she spoke up, "Just think I should be able to invite my friends, too."

"You'd have to have friends to do that," Danny teased her. "Something more than that posse of mean girls."

"Enough," James laid down the law and began passing food dishes. The food was eaten, and good-natured chatter got loud, everyone ignoring the pouting Tiffany. Halley was glad no one brought up her situation in front of the rest of the family.

Maverick watched as Halley took very little of the food, bypassing the warm French bread altogether. He was certain, once again, that her ex-fiancé had worked hard to lower her self-esteem. His eyes narrowed and he encouraged her, "Thunder, have some of your Gram's bread. It's still warm."

"I'm good, thanks," she mumbled politely.

"Hal doesn't need more food. Looks like she's been living it up while she's been gone. Might need to spend a few hours a day on the treadmill," Tiffany spoke up. The chatter stopped suddenly; forks halted halfway to their mouths. Halley's face turned beet red, and Maverick wished someone would put a sock in Tiffany's mouth.

He'd had to chase her away from the clubhouse more times than he could count, more for the sake of the young guys than hers. It wouldn't do for them to face the wrath of their president just because his second youngest daughter tried to seduce everything in a well-fitting pair of jeans.

"That was uncalled for, Tiffany Marie," Gram spoke up. She dragged out the middle name, which everyone knew meant she was displeased.

"What? She's thirty-one and not married – doesn't even have a boyfriend. Maybe if she cared more about her appearance. I don't want anyone to look at her and think I'm going to let myself go when I get to be that old," Tiffany argued her point.

Before anyone else could step in, Maverick spoke up, "Your sister is a beautiful woman. You could take a lesson from her. Very few guys are interested in – uh – holding a woman who is skin and bones. Give me natural beauty any day; your sister has that going on."

"Nice save," Conor snickered to Maverick, knowing "holding" was not the word he was going to use.

Halley wanted to crawl under the table. She didn't know what she'd ever done to Tiffany, but the girl was out to get her, of that she was certain. Could she get up and leave without causing a bigger scene? "You know what, I'm going to head back to the house. I could use a walk anyway and I'm not hungry," Halley pushed back from the table.

"Sit," Mitch ordered. Halley stayed standing, debating whether to go or stay. Her grandfather continued, "You're staying. I think Tiffany needs a walk to clear that bad mood she's in."

"I don't have my car here," Tiffany argued.

"I didn't say drive; I said walk. Get going and make sure you stay put in your room until everyone else is home. We don't need any more of your nasty mouth today," Mitch said firmly.

Priss started to rise from her chair, "I'll take her."

"No, you won't. She can walk," Mitch insisted. The man's blue eyes were hard as he stared at Tiffany. Halley was still standing, wishing she could sink through the floor. Tiffany got up in a huff and slammed out the front door.

Sarah pulled on Halley's hand to get her to sit back down. Nope, there was never drama with Sarah's family. She wanted to slap Tiffany for making her friend feel badly about herself; there was too much of that going around.

The chatter started up again as if it never stopped. No one felt awkward except Halley. She hated being the center of attention. Maverick had called her beautiful, but she suspected he pitied her because of her sister's attack and the debacle that was her life in general; he couldn't really mean it. He was a gorgeous specimen of a man. Every time she looked at him, he was engaged with her father, brothers, or grandparents. He fit in well here; far better than she did. Once again, she was the odd woman out – it was that way in New York, San Francisco, and even with her family.

Tomorrow, she would begin anew. It was time to take charge of her life again. Maybe somewhere along the way she would reclaim her dignity and find where she fit.

Her first call would be to the bank and see what headway they made on restoring the funds in her account. Her second call would be to Craig, the remaining partner, the man who hired her. Even though she was supposed to have no contact, she had to have answers.

Once she straightened out her professional life, maybe, just maybe she could be open to finding what her mother and father had shared; even if it was for a brief time, it had been real and passionate and unconditional. She wondered not for the first time: *was that too much to ask?*

Chapter 11

IT WAS STILL DARK WHEN HALLEY'S ALARM SANG HER awake. She hated buzzing and obnoxious alarms. The only problem was she sometimes incorporated the mellow song into her dreams and didn't always wake up – a fact her ex-fiancé pointed out many times. Still, it was a gentle way to rise in the morning and this morning she got up without hitting the snooze button.

She quickly showered and pulled on jeans and a light cotton sweater under her leather jacket. She was out the door before the teenagers were awake for school or her father or stepmother rose. Her first stop was the diner – the only place open this early in the morning. She made sure to park in the back lot rather than the main street, where her car would be conspicuous. The other patrons were truck drivers getting ready for their runs. Some eyed her hungrily, with interest, while others continued drinking their coffee and engaged in their light conversations.

There was a booth in the back corner, away from the windows and the door, a space where she could sit on the side facing the wall, hide, and write out her plan. Luck was with her when her least favorite waitress was nowhere to be seen. The woman probably had a later shift. Halley made a mental note to be gone before the woman arrived.

Hungry, after not eating much the day before – certainly not the pineapple upside-down cake, even though Gram put a piece in front of her – Halley ordered an omelet with cheese and vegetables and a side of bacon, along with coffee. Her jeans were a lot looser than they had been a few months before and she realized she had not been eating much for quite a while, even the once-daily meals for which her grandmother insisted she join them. Mostly she pushed her food around the plate to look like she made an effort. It was ironic that now she was done with Anthony, she was losing the weight that so disturbed him.

A pen and a hard-covered notebook sat on the table. Afraid to use technology that could be used against her or hacked, she went old-school and began with a to-do list. By the time her food arrived, along with more hot water and a new tea bag, she had her first tasks for the day carefully planned.

Convinced the protein would fortify her for the tasks ahead, she began to eat. After a few bites, she knew it was a waste of food. She had no appetite left and pushed it toward the end of the booth for the waitress to bus. She would drink more tea and wait a couple of hours, unless they needed her booth, but for now, there were others available. The West Coast was three hours behind and she wanted to catch Craig before he left for the office, if he still went in every day. His routine was get up, work out, and shower before the markets opened in New York. That routine never varied, even on the weekends when the markets were closed.

In the meantime, she logged into her bank account on her phone and saw it was still light by several thousand dollars. Depressing as that was, she hadn't expected it to be different.

On another page in her notebook, she made another list. This one was a possible next step for her career. As she looked at the words she wrote on the page, she felt no joy, only dread in the pit of her stomach. She was afraid the little she had eaten was going to come back up.

The list consisted of possible corporate positions in New York, Boston, Washington, DC, Charlotte, and Los Angeles. She tentatively added London as a possibility. One thing she did know is that she would not go back to San Francisco, with so many bad memories attached to the place. She listed the executive recruiters she knew and would eventually have to contact. The problem was, no one was going to touch her until the mess with the startup was straightened out and she was exonerated. Who knew how long that would take? She might even end up in jail.

A new list spelled out the wide spectrum of her possible outcomes: exonerated of any wrongdoing; offered a high-paying executive position with a great company; blackballed from any other corporate job; jail; dead, if someone was angry enough and blamed her; start her own business. The last one didn't make her stomach sick. It kind of intrigued her, which, after her experience with a startup, surprised her. But this could be something of her own. Something she would enjoy, working with people she liked. Something of which she could be proud. Something to do with art, like custom paint jobs on bikes, or an art gallery.

She was lost pondering in her head and doodling other ideas for a new business venture in her notebook, as a dark-clad body slid into the booth across from her. When she looked up, surprised, she met Maverick's deep blue eyes.

"Up early, Thunder," he stated the obvious.

"How'd you know I'm here," Halley asked suspiciously.

He knew because he pinged her phone, but she didn't need to know that. "I came in for breakfast and saw you. Mind if I join you?" Without waiting for her assent, he gave his order to the waitress who had approached the table.

"No, not at all," Halley muttered under her breath.

Maverick pushed her plate toward her. "You should eat."

"I already did," she said stubbornly and pushed the plate back to the edge of the booth.

Maverick was going to argue but decided against it. Instead, he spun her notebook and pulled it toward him, looking over her lists while she tried to grab it back.

"Nice. Glad to see you're considering all the possible outcomes, including jail and death," he deadpanned. "I do like this page though, where you start your own business. I think that's a great idea."

"You do?"

"I do. Be your own boss. Make or break on your own and no one setting you up. It's like what we do at the club. Our own businesses. Our own time." He looked more closely and added, "So you want to do something more creative. That sounds like a good fit, with your background. I'm pretty sure you'll be able to make anything successful, especially since you'll know how to position it and market it."

That sounded an awful lot like a compliment to her. She wasn't used to many of those from men lately. Cautiously she smiled and grabbed the book back. "Thanks. I think."

"Let me know what you decide. And if you need investors."

"You have money to invest?" she asked.

"For the right projects, yeah. Don't let the leather cuts and the bad behavior fool you, Thunder. Club businesses do well and so do the brothers," Maverick said lightly. What he didn't say is that they did *really* well. As for him, he didn't need much and had plenty left to save and invest.

Halley knew her father had a lot of money. She never considered if it came from way back with her great-great grandfather's Prohibition liquor-running business or if her dad made his own money. Now that she thought about it, it was probably both.

"You need to let us help you, Thunder. After you make that call to your bank, depending on what they tell you, Wire can probably do the investigating on his own and find where your money went."

"He can do that?"

"That and more," Maverick assured her. "We're going to be working on your case, so it's better if you're a willing partner. There's no way you're going to jail or end up dead. Got me?"

Halley, used to doing everything on her own, wasn't sure what to say. But the seriousness in his voice and the sincerity she saw in his eyes made her agree. "Okay."

"Okay?" Maverick blinked, then broke out in a wide smile, teeth straight and white. "Okay then. That's the first thing on *my* to-do list. Now we're going to start on yours." Irish was going to be pleased he'd convinced the man's daughter to work with them. He found he was more than pleased himself. This woman frustrated and intrigued him at the same time.

Hours later, Halley sat in Maverick's office, while he paced. She preferred to be still when she needed to think or when things weren't going her way. Maybe something inside her thought she could make herself as small as possible the stiller she sat, shrinking into invisibility. Maverick, on the other hand, needed to work off the excess tension. He was fluid motion, energy rolling off him in strong waves.

The office was neat and minimalist, mostly black and gray. It was located in a large building in town. For some reason, Halley thought the business would be run from the clubhouse and was surprised at the professional atmosphere.

Besides Maverick, Wire, Handsy, and Conor's offices, there was a small reception area; a large and a small conference room; a large room of computers and monitoring equipment; a gym, where the guys could work out and hone their takedown and defensive skills; a tactical room with weapons, vests, communications devices, and anything else a full-service security firm would need; an indoor firing range in the underground section; a storage room for all their home and business monitoring and security equipment; and a few closed doors, which she didn't know their purpose. There was an entire side with empty offices. None of that included the third floor; she had no idea what was up there. She was impressed.

When they had walked in, Maverick was either amused or offended by the surprised look on her face. "You can close your mouth now, Thunder. What did you think? We're not Silicon Valley or New York, but that doesn't mean we don't have it going on."

She had the decency to look contrite and followed him on the tour of the building. She learned a little more about their business as they went along.

Now, after sitting in the office making the first call on her to-do list, her phone on speaker so Maverick and Wire could hear the whole thing, she was already numb and exhausted. She had spoken with the bank manager and no, they had not traced the transaction to its origin and no, they had not restored her account; they were understaffed, and, unsaid, an executive under investigation herself was not a priority. "That was useless," she sighed.

Wire disagreed, "Not completely. We know what they haven't done. We do have more information and know the money was taken out in multiple transactions over a short window, some at ATMs, some with tellers, and the largest through online transfers. Now, I'm going to go in and search cameras to see if we can see who was in person and at the ATMs. I'm going to try to get the IP location for the online transfers and where it went." He left the office abruptly, mumbling to himself.

"He can do all that? And not get caught?" Halley asked, watching the door close behind the man they called Wire.

"He can. And more," Maverick assured her. "If there's anything to find, he's the man."

None of that should surprise her, given she had just left Silicon Valley, where they hired hackers all the time to try to infiltrate and break their systems, identifying fatal flaws. Her bias was showing again; she didn't expect to find that here, in her hometown. Nothing had seemed that interesting when she left fifteen years ago, and she hadn't paid much attention to anything other than her grandparents when she visited the few times since, quickly coming to town and just as quickly leaving. None of that did she say to Maverick, but by the look on his face, he knew exactly what she was thinking.

"Time for the next call, Thunder." He stopped pacing long enough to lean on his desk and look her in the eye.

With a heavy sigh, she leaned forward and grabbed her phone from the desk. She quickly pressed Craig's mobile number from her contacts before she lost her nerve. The phone rang through the speaker. She thought it was going to go to voicemail when Craig's voice answered the call with no preamble. "Halley?"

"Hi, Craig. What's the latest? I haven't heard anything from anyone," she tried to sound professional and nonchalant.

"You shouldn't have called, Halley. The feds are all over the office. I don't know where you are but stay there."

"Don't hang up on me," Halley almost shouted. "Have you heard from Anthony or Andres?" She almost choked saying her CFO ex-fiancé's name and the third partner, who was the Chief Operating Officer.

Silence seemed to scream at her through the phone line, but she knew he hadn't hung up. They could hear his breathing. Something was off. Maverick wanted to take over the call but was afraid the guy would disconnect. He was skittish. But why?

"Craig, please. My life blew up and I don't know why or how," Halley said evenly, trying to keep the pleading from her voice. She wanted to plead, but pride wouldn't allow it. She might have lost a lot, but she outwardly tried to maintain a grasp on her dignity.

Craig sighed and came to a decision. His voice was a whisper, "Andres is totally MIA. Anthony, I don't know. He's been in contact but then disappears. He hasn't found you?"

"No, is he looking?"

"He asked where you were. Said he went to your house, and you were gone." After a long pause, Craig continued with his whispered conversation, "I don't think he's who he said he was. I…I think he set up me and you to take the fall for this. He told me not to cooperate with the feds, if I knew what was good for me. What the hell, Halley?! You were engaged to the guy." The last part came out as a frustrated accusation.

"Don't remind me. But *you* should remember that I broke it off with him even before this all came crashing down around us. And don't forget, you introduced us," Halley argued and then sighed. Maverick handed her a hastily scribbled note.

"Yeah, I'm really sorry about that. He was friends with Andres and came with a lot of investment money and credentials. The FBI says it was all a lie, except the money, and that may be dirty. He was laundering money through *my* company. I started this with Andres. What we make is good, you saw that, right, Halley?" the man sounded desperate. He sounded a lot like she felt inside.

"I know, Craig. Great tech. Great products. Customers love them. So, he really set you and me up for this? Do the Feds believe the trail he left?" Halley continued the conversation, trying to discern if she was going to be arrested as soon as they found her. She guessed it was good Craig wasn't under arrest; maybe she had time for Wire and Maverick to figure this out. When she had begun to see them as part of "team Halley" she wasn't sure, but knew she needed them more than ever now.

"I've told them it couldn't be us, but unless they find the trail, they're going to need to blame someone," Craig's voice cracked.

Maverick poked her in the arm and pointed again to the note he had handed her.

"Uh, Craig. It sounds like we may need security. Like real security. Bodyguards, if Anthony is threatening you and dangerous, or if any investors are desperate."

"My accounts are frozen. I can't pay for some high-priced security firm," he whispered.

"Uh, the cl – my dad owns a security firm. They'll protect us. They can have people on the ground this afternoon," Halley recited and looked to Maverick with raised eyebrows, questioning if that were the case. Maverick gave her one quick nod. She didn't get into the club ownership, that was club business; saying it was her father's company made it simpler for all of them.

"I don't know. If his people think I've brought anyone in, it could be bad."

"They can blend in or stay in the shadows. They're good at that," Halley read the next note Maverick passed her. He didn't want to spook the young tech founder by jumping into the conversation.

"Yeah, maybe. Send them. I have to go, Halley. I think my house is bugged. But every time I have it cleared, it's back the next day. I don't know if it's the feds or Anthony's people. I'm sitting in my shower talking to you. Just stay safe and stay away. None of this is good. I'm sorry I brought you out here, Halley, I really am. You didn't deserve any of this," Craig said, his voice laced with regret. That was what the noise was in the background, water running.

"Well, it was a lot of fun until the last few months. But I'm glad to hear you say that and that you don't believe this was me," Halley said with feeling. It wasn't much, but at least one of the founders, the CEO, finally believed in her innocence.

"Stay safe, Halley." Craig ended the call.

Maverick was already on the phone, barking out orders. While he was talking, Wire, Handsy, and Conor came through the office door. Conor and Handsy sat on the couch and Wire leaned against the windowsill.

Maverick hung up and heard Conor ask, "What is it this startup makes, Hal?"

"Think of it as the connector that can make different technologies talk to one another. It works for smart homes or defense systems or even dating apps. Lots of uses and everyone is interested. The big thing about our company's products is that they are seamless and pretty painless to install. Unlike some of the other big tech who sell their painful, years-long installs as a badge of honor, the clients actually like working with us," Halley explained.

Wire shook his head and looked at Conor, simplifying further, "Think of it as having one app that does everything, and you don't have to switch back and forth among a lot of them."

"Got it," Conor nodded. "Don't know how you did it all these years, big sis; this corporate crap sucks."

Right about now, she tended to agree with him. That made her think back to her notebook and her ideas for her future. As she raised her eyes from her notebook on Maverick's desk, she saw he had looked the same place. That made her inwardly smile; they had something they shared no one else knew, yet.

The men began talking to one another as if she wasn't there.

"I got the San Francisco chapter to sit on the partner who hasn't disappeared, the CEO, until we can get guys out there. Conor, this is bodyguard duty, but in the shadows and blending for now; make it happen," Maverick said to Halley's brother, who managed the day-to-day of the bodyguard division of the security business. "Wire, we need to find out who Anthony Martinelli really is, like yesterday, and who his associates are. He seems to be at the center of all this and could be looking for Halley. I bet when you get the trace on her money it will lead to him or his associates."

Maverick gave them a quick synopsis of the call with Craig. Halley sat silently, slightly in awe of how he was able to sum up the situation and quickly get to the heart of it. Her emotions were still too raw, and she was too caught up in it all to see the forest for the trees. She had to break through the fog in her own head and put it in order. Otherwise, she was of no use to herself, or the men trying to help and protect her.

"I can take Halley," Conor said. She realized they were talking about bodyguard assignments.

Maverick shook his head, "I've got Halley. When I'm not available, I'll call you in." Conor looked like he wanted to argue but gave a quick nod to the head of the business. He trusted his club brother with his life; he would have to trust him with his sister's.

"The club must have grown a lot, if you have enough guys to have divisions of this one and still manage other businesses," Halley screwed up her forehead as she thought through it all.

"We don't only employ brothers, Thunder. We hire people in the community as employees. For the security business, we have full-time employees, some club, most not, and we have contractors all over the country, even some in Europe, mostly former military we can call in for bodyguard services or investigations," Maverick proudly informed her.

"Wow. I had no idea," Halley said, impressed with the direction her father and his club brothers had taken the club.

"You've missed a lot, Hal," Conor said. Whether he meant it or not, Halley could hear the hurt accusation in his voice.

"But she's here now and letting us work with her," Maverick jumped in, not wanting a sibling argument to break out in his office.

"I think I'll head out to San Francisco with the team to see things for myself. Got my go-bag here," Conor decided. "Handsy, if Mav needs help with Halley, you've got her back, right?"

"Absolutely," Handsy immediately agreed. He spent a lot of time working on the club books and investments, but also occasionally helped with security system installs and bodyguard duty. He was the best kind of brother, always willing to step up.

Halley was stuck on something else her brother said, which sounded incredulous to her. "You have a go-bag?"

Conor opened his mouth to respond, but Halley held up a hand and nodded, "I know, Conor; I haven't been around, and I don't know much. Got it. Please be careful. None of this makes sense, and from talking to Craig, I think it's dangerous."

"It's what we do, Hal," Conor smirked.

Before he could make the few steps to the door, Halley jumped up and impulsively threw her arms around him. “Please be safe, little brother. I love you,” Halley whispered.

Conor, stunned by her words and the hug, wrapped his arms tightly around her. Then he slipped out the door, a chin lift to his brothers.

Chapter 12

THE FOG WAS LIFTING OVER THE PACIFIC OCEAN IN A remote cove at the most western edge of Sonoma County, north of San Francisco. A couple hiked, off the beaten path, walking the narrow strip of sand, thinking they were two of the only people to ever see this place, this close. Maybe some made it to the towering cliff of the bluff overhead to watch a Pacific sunset after driving on the narrow, winding, mountain road, then hiking to the overgrown overlook, but there were no stores, no vineyards, no tourist attractions to lure anyone. There were plenty of other places to visit with tourist stops and still see the Pacific sunset. But to walk this pure sand, unmarred by human footprints, climb the rock formations far below the cliffs, was a whole other level. It had taken them days of camping and hiking to make this trek, to find this unexpected gem, as they made their way north along the ocean.

The woman wandered toward the base of the cliff, climbing over a large boulder, looking for a place to relieve herself. As she started to jump off the rock on the other side, her eyes grew large, and she placed her hand over her mouth and let out a startled yelp. She slipped down the bumpy surface, bruising her calf and slicing her elbow in a deep gash that extended up the underside of her upper arm, banging her head hard, before she hit the ground. One look to make sure she saw what she thought she had several feet ahead made her scramble on her knees and then lose the contents of her stomach.

"What's wrong?" the man called as he climbed to look over the top of the rock. He saw her on all fours vomiting, blood running down the back of her head and from her arm. Sliding down the rock himself, he hurried to her side.

"What happened?" he asked as he tried to staunch the head wound with a soiled bandana from around his neck. The elbow and arm would probably need stitches, too; he thought he could see bone and almost vomited himself. He pulled his T-shirt over his head and tied it tightly around her elbow, trying not to look at the wound.

Not able to speak, the woman pointed toward the area closer to the cliff and further down the base, without looking herself. There he saw what looked like a person's body, dead, definitely dead. He crab-walked backward, instinct taking over as he tried to get away from the brutality. After not speaking for several moments and not able to look away from the horror, he hurried to his girlfriend's side and cradled her in his arms, rocking back and forth in a soothing rhythm, whether for her or himself, he wasn't sure.

Finally, he let go and had her hold the cloth to her still bleeding head. "We've got to call the police. Or an ambulance or something."

"I think it's too late for the ambulance," she said, dry heaving. "Our mobile phones won't work out here. We're going to have to hike out." They were careful to use the solar charger for their smartphones. But a full battery wasn't going to help without a tower nearby.

The guy admitted with an embarrassed one-shoulder shrug, "I've got a satellite phone in my backpack. My dad made me bring it in case we got in trouble."

She stared at him, uncomprehending, and then laughed, the hysterical laughter giving way to tears streaming down her tanned face. "Of course, he did. I think I love your father right now."

He made his way back around the large boulder to where their packs sat on the sand, finding a longer but easier path that didn't require climbing, since the tide was out. After pulling on another shirt, the Pacific wind cold even in the sunshine, he called

911 and told the dispatcher they found a dead body; yes, they were pretty sure he was dead. He guessed it was a man, by the size and rumpled clothing. He had to stay on the phone while emergency services pinpointed their location. Then he remembered to ask for an ambulance because his girlfriend was bleeding from a head wound that didn't seem to stop and an elbow laceration that was deep and probably needed stitches.

When he got back to her with their packs, he found her curled in the fetal position shivering uncontrollably. Quickly, he unrolled a sleeping bag and wrapped her in it, holding her back to his chest, resuming the rocking motion.

This went on for how long, he didn't know but only stopped once he heard the roar of the chopper and "thunk" of its blades. The rescue helicopter hovered over the water, and he watched as they signaled they had to go to land topside. There wasn't room on the narrow strip of beach and rock. Soon he saw rappelling ropes drop over the cliff, paramedics with a basket and what looked like police officers beside them.

Once his girlfriend was secure in the chopper, they let him inside. Two of the police officers followed them to the hospital and would take their statements, beyond what he had already told them. There really wasn't any more to say.

Other police officers had arrived and then men and women in FBI jackets showed up in their own helicopter. He had overheard one of the officers while they were at the bottom of the cliff say they found the dead guy's wallet and he immediately called in reinforcements. He must have been someone important to stir up this much action.

At the hospital, he recounted what happened yet again, first to the state police and then to the FBI, when they appeared.

"We thought the guy must have fallen off the cliff," the young man surmised.

"Did you or your girlfriend touch the body, move it, remove anything?" one of the FBI agents asked.

His eyes widened in shock and then disgust, "No! We didn't get closer than where you found us. Sorry, if we messed up your crime scene, but Mae threw up as soon as she fell off the rock when she saw him. Then she was bleeding and went into shock. I was more worried about her and getting out of there. I didn't even think to check to see if he was still breathing or had ID or anything." He knew he was rambling now but couldn't help himself. "I mean, he had to be dead, right? It looked like maybe animals got to him."

"No, kid, you did the right thing by not touching anything and calling us right away," the agent assured him.

After the two agents talking with him and one with his girlfriend moved out of their range of hearing, the female agent said, "I sincerely doubt they had anything to do with Mr. Murano's demise. They both smelled so bad they had to be hiking and camping for the last several days like they said." Her nose twitched, still smelling their natural body odor, compounded by the adrenaline racing through the kids' veins at finding a dead body.

"I suspect you're right. That double tap he took had to be an execution. It was no accident, and he couldn't have shot himself twice. It also looked like bruising on his wrists, like he was restrained with duct tape or something similar. But we'll have to wait for the medical examiner's report on cause and time of death and any other details. In the meantime, let's get back to the city and keep an eye on the dead guy's partner," the senior agent sighed.

The team followed him out to the SUV for the ride back to San Francisco. Two of their colleagues were still at the remote cove, waiting for the body to be transported and to work with the state police, who searched the area looking for a weapon, not expecting to find one.

Several hours later, Conor McCarthy called Maverick's phone. The man put it on speaker because his president and vice president were in his office, champing at the bit for any new leads, along with Wire, Scottie, and Handsy.

"You're on speaker," Maverick told him.

"Sounds like a couple college kids found the body of one of the missing partners in a remote area on the Pacific north of here. We listened in when the feds showed up at Craig's house." They decided if they were going to remain in the shadows providing the man security, they would piggyback on the listening devices that were already in place in the house and his office, though it was still a mystery who planted them. “They don’t know for sure, but they think it was a hit. I could tell they didn’t have all the facts yet, like the medical examiner’s report, but they were feeling him out, checking his reaction to the news his partner is dead.”

“Did he seem surprised?” Red asked.

“I’m pretty sure he almost pissed himself. Yeah, he seemed shocked as hell. But scared. Really scared. Once the feds left, we could hear him puking,” Conor recounted. “Then Craig took a walk and called me from the burner I gave him.”

Conor and one of the contract guys were waiting in the dark in his house when he arrived home that first night after they agreed to provide protection; he almost had a heart attack but was glad they took precautions not to be seen, if Anthony or his associates were watching, until they could blend in like his usual driver or company security. They disabled the listening devices in his bedroom so they could talk and give the executive instructions.

“I don’t think Craig was involved in any of this and didn’t set up Hal. He seems genuinely concerned about her and feels guilty for bringing her out here,” Conor added, mostly for his father’s benefit, but thought, maybe, Maverick might need to hear it too.

“If we find out he did, we’ll take care of him when all this is over,” Irish gritted out.

All the men in the room nodded, jaws clenched.

“Any news on your end?” Conor asked.

Wire moved closer to the phone and gave an update. He had found the security and ATM camera footage he needed to show it wasn’t Halley taking money out of her account. It was Anthony. He could also show the IP address was not Halley’s at home, office, or an Internet café. It was registered to a shell corporation owned by a myriad of other shell corporations, but the one name that kept cropping up was Anthony, though not the last name Martinelli, that he had gone by as CFO of the startup. This was an Anthony Barone. Wire was able to find his picture in one of the shell corporation's paperwork and it was, indeed, the same man as Anthony Martinelli.

It wasn’t until Irish’s fist went through the plaster of the wall in Maverick’s office that anyone but Red noticed the president’s reaction to that name. Irish pulled his fist out and didn't even flinch. Scottie was sure his father must have broken his hand.

"What was that noise?" Conor asked, concerned, through the phone line.

"Your old man just tried to make a new window in my wall," Maverick said evenly. He'd have prospects in the next day to patch the wall and paint.

"What aren't you telling us?" Scottie asked, as his father moved angrily toward the door.

Red's voice stopped him, "We gotta tell 'em."

Their president slowly turned and took a seat on the couch, rested his arms on his knees, and looked at the floor. Maverick reached inside the freezer of his office refrigerator and grabbed a bag of peas, which he gently laid over Irish's swollen and bleeding knuckles. This wasn't the first time those were needed.

"Way back with my great grandfather, he and his buddies ran moonshine, gin, rum – anything they could make or bring in from Canada or the Caribbean during Prohibition. There was a split within a Chicago crime family, though he stayed in business with the original family. It ended up being a long and bloody rivalry. My family thought it went away when Prohibition was over, though they kept smuggling other goods that could make a profit, less and less with the same Chicago family. Then my grandfather and his buddies, the next generation, got back from World War II and started the *Phantom Raiders*. They wanted to continue the brotherhood they found in the Army, a chosen family they could trust, and they loved the freedom of the ride." So far, most of them knew this history.

"Turns out some families have long memories. Really long. Generations long," Irish continued.

Handsy nodded, "La Cosa Nostra families – Italian mafia."

Irish looked up and nodded at Handsy before looking back down at the floorboards as if he were mesmerized by them. Maverick had no doubt what he saw in front of his eyes wasn't the floorboards and that this story was about to get intense.

"My dad was president of the club. I was just twenty-one, married to my high school sweetheart, stupid in love, an intelligent, beautiful three-year-old at home. I wanted the world for them and pushed hard for my dad and the old guard to keep legitimizing the businesses and get us out of the illegal side. We would still honor our brotherhood and take care of things our way, but I really wanted the businesses to all be legitimate. I didn't want any of us to do a bid at the state pen or federal lockup, like so many of the previous generations had. I didn't see that as a rite of passage or anything to be proud of. Red here agreed with me and we pushed my dad and the executive committee hard. Pretty sure my mom was all over my dad too. She wanted her granddaughter and any future grandchildren to live in a different world. Yes, to the club. Yes, to the brotherhood. Yes, to the lifestyle. But make our money legally.

"Turns out the Chicago family was part of the supply chain for one of the businesses we were exiting. One of their guys went rogue. He decided to make a statement. He waited until I was out of town on a run. He entered our house, and he raped and killed Evie, brutally, frenzied. Then he set the house on fire, hoping to cover his crime. But someone saw the smoke and the fire was put out before it got to her. Halley was running home down the sidewalk from where my parents lived a few houses down and saw the emergency vehicles, lights flashing, chaos everywhere. Ma ran after her and grabbed her, not knowing what was going on, and took her to Evie's parents across town to keep her away until things calmed down.

"The police said it was probably a home invasion gone wrong, and some druggie attacked and killed her in a drug-induced rage. We knew differently. We got the messages sent to my father. The police eventually put it in the cold case file. We took care of the guy ourselves. His name was Carmine Barone." Irish looked up at this point, a haunted look in his blue eyes. He saw his club brothers make the connection.

"It wasn't allowed to go after families back then, no innocents, not in their world and not in ours. If we hadn't tracked down Carmine first, they would have taken care of him themselves. He apparently was trying to make his bones with the family and thought the attack up all himself. I think he was really just a sick son of a bitch, and I make no apologies. It had the downstream effect of getting us off the hook with the mob and they haven't come to us again. There's been a healthy respect between our families. My guess is that Anthony is either the son or nephew of Carmine. Carmine's wife was the daughter of the don back then – the head of their family, their syndicate. Barone's actions showed a lack of respect and dishonored his family. I'm wondering how long Anthony has been planning this. If it is him, Hal is not safe," Irish concluded the story and looked exhausted. Red reached out and squeezed his shoulder in support.

Maverick's jaw was set in a firm line. "Halley doesn't know any of this?"

Irish shook his head no.

Maverick said quietly, "I heard her in the cemetery, at her mother's grave. Once she gets clear of what's happening now, she wants to investigate her mother's murder herself and get the police to re-open the cold case. She made a promise to her mom." Irish blanched at the revelation.

"Let's get through this first and then we'll deal with that," Conor suggested over the phone. Everyone had forgotten he was still on the line. All voiced their agreement to his suggestion.

"We need to find out if Anthony's acting alone or is there someone new in charge of the family and he was sanctioned," Maverick said.

"I'll get on that electronically. See if there's a trail, now I have some ideas on where to look," Wire promised.

"Yeah, we can't go to the sons of bitches and show our hand if they already knew and it's some new game plan," Red proclaimed.

Irish shook his head slowly, "I can't believe they'd sanction this. But who knows? If there's new leadership, a new don, it could be a new ballgame. There seems to be a lack of moral code with a lot of the new generation. Except you guys, of course." He quickly added the last.

Red howled, breaking the tension of the last several minutes, "Yeah because we're still young enough to kick all their asses, if they step out of line. You never mess with family."

"We wouldn't," Scottie agreed. Then a small smile traced his lips, "We were raised right."

"Damn straight," Conor's voice came through the phone speaker.

***

At the clubhouse, Halley and Sarah sat at the bar. Since not many people were around tonight, Halley decided to try her luck and tell the prospect bartending how to make a martini. In the middle of her explanation, a woman in her twenties with beautifully coiffed straight dark hair hanging to her shoulder blades, flawless caramel skin, and mischievous gray eyes, dressed in jeans and a long-sleeved black t-shirt, walked in and stepped behind the bar. "Give that to me," she said and took the vodka bottle from the prospect. "Let the expert show you how to do it."

She looked at Halley and asked, "Do you want a dirty gin martini or a Cosmo?"

Halley blinked her surprise and said, "If you have the ingredients for a Cosmo, I'll take one of those. If not, a dirty one is fine." Halley's go-to drink was gin, but most flavored martinis were vodka-based, so she learned to be flexible, since she really liked the flavored ones.

"*Sex in the City* girl, my type of woman," the woman behind the bar quipped.

Halley wasn't sure if she was talking about the television show or making a lewd reference to her time in the city. Without thinking, she mused, "Wish I was getting sex in the city – or anywhere, really." Then, once again, realized she said what she was thinking out loud. The woman behind the bar and Sarah burst into laughter. The prospect looked like he'd rather be anywhere than with the women.

"Halley, meet Jana; Jana, this is Halley," Sarah introduced. "Jana works with Scottie at the *Raiders Roost*. Halley is Scottie's older and wiser sister."

"I heard you were back in town," Jana nodded her recognition. "I didn't grow up here like everyone else, but Scottie talks about you."

A jolt of guilt hit Halley's system. Her brother talked about her? She didn't talk about him to any of her colleagues. No one she worked with knew her story or anything about her family. Now that she really thought about it, she found it strange. She knew about everyone's family and personal situation, except her ex-fiancé's, who seemed just as happy to keep his past in the past as she had.

After college, where she tried only twice to explain her story of her half-siblings, how her mother was dead, how she graduated early, she either saw pity or horrified looks on the faces of the people she told. Since she didn't want to be pitied and didn't want people to avoid her because they knew too much and felt awkward, she quit sharing and kept her private life private. She reinvented herself to live the career-driven, corporate ladder-climbing, fast-life of her dreams. Only it made her feel empty. The work was okay, she even enjoyed it, but that became her life. Now she didn't have that anymore, she had no life – felt as if she lost her identity. She hoped Jana hurried with the Cosmo.

"If you're not from here, how did you end up here?" Halley asked Jana as the young woman set the perfect-looking Cosmo in front of her.

A momentary darkness showed in Jana's gray eyes, but it was gone in a flash. If Halley had blinked, she wouldn't have seen it. Then Jana smiled her white smile with perfect teeth and said, "I got tired of moving around. I was a military brat. Then I was in DC for college and worked there when I graduated, thinking I'd climb the corporate ladder at the real estate firm I was at. I bartended some nights on the side to meet people – I'm a people person. Then one night I met Scottie when he was in town at some military powwow, and I told him how I wanted to settle down in one place someday and never move. The city was kind of taking it out of me and the moving every couple of years as a kid all over the world took its toll. Scottie gave me a card for the *Raiders Roost* and told me if I got tired of living in the city and was ready to settle down, he knew a nice little town where I'd fit in. I moved here a year ago and never want to leave."

This was becoming a familiar theme. Scottie seemed to be building his own contingent in the town, one person at a time. Her brother was going to make a good president when his turn came. Not that she knew that was the plan – heaven forbid anyone but the brothers were clued in on club business – but she assumed he would take over for their father.

"Well, welcome. I'm glad you've found a home here," Halley said, raising her martini glass in a toast. Sarah and Jana both lifted their beer bottles.

At that moment, the men appeared from down the hall where they must have come in the front door. Handsy popped onto a stool next to Sarah. Wire immediately disappeared down a different hallway, where his bedroom was; it was set up with enough equipment that it rivaled his office. He could work efficiently in either place. James and Red walked in next. They said hello, grabbed the beers held out by the prospect, went back to the president's office, and shut the door, with no more conversation. Halley didn't have time to ask her dad what happened to his hand.

Scottie walked in next, with Maverick by his side. He scowled as he looked behind the bar. "What are you doing back there? Prospect, you're supposed to be serving, not getting people to do your job."

The prospect's eyes went wide. He held up his hands to defend himself, but Jana beat him to it, "He didn't ask for help; I like to do it. I was showing him how to make a martini for your sister. No big deal." She then turned that brilliant smile on the man, showing she was no worse for wear and having a good time.

"Well, come out from behind there and sit with my sister and her friend," Scottie grumbled. He nodded at the prospect, "Learn how to make the fancy drinks and I'll get you working at the *Roost*." That made the prospect stand straighter. His energy level picked up perceptibly, as he grinned his agreement.

Maverick watched the interplay from a few feet away. He knew his friend was worried about his sister and disturbed by what they learned tonight, not angry with the prospect or Jana. The whole club could be in danger, but definitely anyone named McCarthy. That was enough to make them all on edge.

Red came into the common room and announced, "Church at seven in the morning. Don't be late." Lots of groans met the announcement because of the time. Maverick knew that was coming. They had to fill all the brothers in on the danger that could be lurking.

"Your dad makes the guys go to church?" Sarah asked, confused.

Halley laughed. Sarah had been around the club, but only the family days and parties, not anything to do with business. Handsy was the one who answered her, "Not that kind of church. Church is what we call our club business meetings." That seemed to be the easiest explanation.

"Have you ever been to their church? I don't remember you talking about it," Sarah looked at her friend.

"No, it's just for the patched-in brothers. No one else allowed," Halley explained and had to fight to keep from rolling her eyes. At one point, when she was a child, she told her dad she wanted to be president of the club when she grew up. He had gently, but definitively, told her that couldn't happen.

"That's kind of caveman-y, isn't it?" Sarah asked in a low voice she hoped only Jana and Halley would hear.

"You could say so. It's complicated," Halley shrugged. And it was complicated.

She knew a woman couldn't be a member of the club, which she thought was all kinds of sexist bullpucky, but she also knew her father and even her grandfather respected her and her abilities. If she decided to open her own business, she was pretty sure her father would support it and maybe even put it under the club umbrella. They were overly protective and believed in taking care of their family, which included keeping some things from their ol' ladies, wives, women, partners, and children, which was often for their protection. Everyone worked together to make it work. But women couldn't be members. She thought that was more appropriate in her great-grandfather's and even her grandfather's era than now, when the businesses were all legitimate. But it was a lifestyle, and everything wasn't always above board; she knew that. It was complicated.

If Sarah ended up with Handsy, she would learn all about it. Until then, it wasn't Halley's place to educate her. She may have been gone a long time, but she grew up in the club and knew the rules.

Maverick heard every word. He always did. He saw how she held herself back from educating her best friend and maintained club rules. Halley continued to score points with him. He could see how she was the president's daughter and had the intelligence and understanding to be real MC royalty.

Tonight wasn't the night they would tell Halley anything new they learned. They would wait until they had more information, such as the report from the coroner. Tonight, she could relax and enjoy her time with her friends. Her protective detail was about to become exponentially bigger, and Maverick wasn't sure she was going to accept that.

Chapter 13

THE GRASS GREW LONG IN THE BACKYARD AROUND the large deck and patio four steps down. It was a deep shade of green, nourished by a long winter and spring rain. The fertilizer didn't hurt either. As the wind blew from the west, the blades bent and danced at a varied tempo. Soon it would take two passes with the lawnmower to cut it down to the expected manicured length.

Priscilla did not understand why James insisted his children mow the lawn. The club owned a landscaping business that could have added them to their rotation. Or there were certainly prospects who could do it. But no, her husband wanted their children to show responsibility. They each had their jobs around the property. She grew up two towns over, with a housekeeper, groundskeeper, and cook; no one who lived in her father's house lifted a finger. Was it any wonder she could not cook when her own mother was even worse at it than she? When she was younger, the difference in their lifestyles was part of what attracted her to the rough and handsome biker.

The home she grew up in was so quiet, so still, so … boring. Shades of beige were the palette of her parents' life. James' world had color, a vibrance that drowned everyone near in their radiance. As a college student, it was exciting. Oh, how she had wanted him.

How she had envied Evie all through high school and even when she was gone at college. Then that fateful weekend she got her chance. She was home from college and the young biker was mourning his dead wife. More than a few drinks and it had not been hard to seduce him. That she became pregnant was the bonus. She could move out of her father's house and have her own home.

Priscilla didn't expect to be overwhelmingly in love. She wasn't raised that way. She expected to be taken care of, have nice things, a comfortable life. That some people looked down on her, who were once her peers, was hard for her to swallow – they gathered at the country club, played a round of golf, drank champagne cocktails, and laughed politely with one another.

James refused to join the country club – not that her father's friends would have accepted him anyway. Over time, she realized he gave her what he could, but he would never compromise who he was for her. For that, she hid a bitterness. She joined his world – that it had been her young desire, was beside the point – yet he would not compromise on her world. So, she lived in this limbo. In a house designed by and for another woman, a fortress in the middle of nowhere, where she was allowed to decorate, keep horses – not that she rode much anymore – and shuffle their children to and from their activities. At times, she wondered what would happen once they all moved out. Would anyone notice if she faded into the background, perhaps disappearing altogether?

In Tiffany, she saw herself and poured her dreams into her daughter's head. More than any of the others, Tiffany showed promise to marry well and live a life of wealth and privilege. Possibly Danny could be persuaded, too. The others embraced her husband's lifestyle. With James, she was financially comfortable and had a certain degree of privilege as the wife of the MC president – an involuntary shudder accompanied the moniker of "ol' lady" – but it was not the style in which she was raised.

Having her stepdaughter back in the town, in this house, brought back the indignation that she was never enough, that James had not chosen her first, that Evie's ghost remained between them. She had envied Halley's life from afar – living on both coasts, the travel, the money she made herself, the independence she demanded. Halley was a success and now she was throwing that all away by coming home. Secretly, she subconsciously thought if Halley was out of sight, she was out of mind and no longer had a place in their lives. But she was wrong. Halley returned and they all treated her like returning royalty.

The wind blew again, and she watched the grass. She would have to get someone to mow it before James stepped onto the deck and saw it had not been cut. If that happened, not only would Danny lose his motorcycle, but would be in danger of losing his truck, which meant she would have to drive him to school and practice and whatever else the teenager wanted to do. It did not occur to her that Tiffany could easily take her brother with her. Tiffany resided in her own walled-off space in Priscilla's mind.

"I think we should get a couple goats." Scarlett's voice startled her from behind. She hadn't heard the French doors open. Her youngest held a mug of tea in her hands, warming them, even though the morning was warm.

"Goats? Why on earth would we do that?"

"Well, they're cute, especially those fainting ones. And mostly because this wouldn't need to be mowed if we had goats," Scarlett smirked over the rim of her mug as she took a sip.

Priscilla rolled her eyes, "Yes, I'm sure they'd eat this, all the flowers, the garden, and anything left in the yard."

"Can you take me to school? Tiffany left without me, and Danny had early baseball practice. I'd ask Dad, but he's not home."

No, James stayed at the clubhouse last night and they had that ridiculous meeting they called "church" at some ungodly hour this morning; at least that's what he said. It was easy for Priscilla to think the worst, since her own base desires tended toward deceit.

"Fine. Let's go," Priscilla sighed.

"I'll mow this after school. I don't have softball practice," Scarlett shrugged as she turned to go back into the house. It was worth it to have Danny owe her one, and, if she were being truthful, to not listen to her father lecture her brother yet again.

There it was, that involuntary shudder. Her daughter volunteering for yard work should have been a proud moment; it would be for James and his family, but for Priscilla, it was one more example of how different her daughter was from her and her other daughter. A tomboy to her Barbie, a worker to her privilege, a down-to-earth soul to her pomp.

"There's lip gloss in my purse," Priscilla eyed her daughter critically as they pulled out of the drive.

"No thanks. It makes my lips feel all sticky," Scarlett declined.

Why couldn't the girl take any tips? She wore her chestnut hair in a ponytail. At least it looked like she brushed it first. It was bad enough she wore ripped jeans – not the stylish kind with the rips strategically placed by fashion designers – and a T-shirt Priscilla was sure belonged to Drake.

Halley had waited to leave her bedroom until she heard her stepmother and youngest sister leave the house. While spending an early morning with Scarlett would be pleasant, the other would not. There was nothing Priscilla overtly said or did that made her feel uncomfortable, it was more subtle. It was a instinct, on Halley's part.

Now she moved swiftly to the stable and found the coffee pot already full of a rich, dark brew. Maverick's prospect brother Tyler must like it strong. She knew she liked that prospect. Though tea was her usual preference, there were days coffee was required. One strong mug later, and she lifted her saddle to the rail next to Lightning's stall.

"Morning, Halley," Tyler stuck his head out of one of the stalls further down the row. "Aren't you going to wait for Maverick? He said he was going riding with you this morning."

"He didn't tell me that. They're in church. I'll be fine on my own," Halley smiled as she put the blanket over the stallion's back and then the saddle.

Tyler looked unsure and set the pitchfork against the stall. "How about I go with you? I still have more to exercise this morning."

"You've already been out?" Halley said, surprised. The clock had just gone beyond the seven a.m. mark.

Tyler looked at his boots and blushed slightly, "Well yeah. I grew up on a ranch. If you weren't up by five, my dad made sure you never missed wake up again."

"Huh. Makes you a good prospect too, I would think. You don't need to go with me, Tyler. I know my way around," Halley declined, not wanting to get the earnest young man in trouble by leaving the stalls to clean later.

"It's no problem. I'd like the company. I'm starting to talk to the horses more than people and some of the guys are making fun of me," he said sincerely.

How could she turn down those blue eyes? "Okay, saddle up," Halley gave in.

Tyler made sure to send a quick text to Maverick while he was in the tack room getting his saddle. His brother was not going to be happy Halley was up and about without her escort. As expected, his brother texted back immediately, even though he was in church, where electronics were usually prohibited.

Maverick: Stick with her

Tyler: Will do

The grass was wet with dew as they set a sedate pace toward the far rise. Tyler was not comfortable being so out in the open. If anything happened to Prez's daughter, he was sure he would be shipped back to Texas, and that was a fate he could not bear.

"How'd you let your brother talk you into prospecting all the way up here?" Halley asked, making conversation.

"He and my dad thought it was best for me," Tyler answered.

Halley gave him a questioning look, waiting for a more complete answer. Tyler caved to the pressure.

"I got mixed up with some people I shouldn't have, and my family wanted me out of town. Straighten me out, I guess." He seemed embarrassed by the confession. There was more, but he did not want to share too much. Maverick told him over and over to keep his own counsel; he could not tell everyone everything just because they asked.

"Your family wanted you out of town and my family wanted me to come back," Halley laughed easily. "I guess we're both outsiders."

"Yeah, I guess we are," Tyler smiled, liking Halley's company. She was not the princess some of the guys made her out to be.

"Do you come from a big family?" Halley continued the conversation.

"There are six of us kids. Two sisters and then us four boys. Maverick's the oldest. I have one sister younger than me. Our other two brothers work the ranch with our father and my other sister is in college in Texas. Lots of uncles, aunts, cousins, grandparents – yeah, big family," Tyler explained.

"Must be nice," Halley said without thinking.

"What do you mean? That I got away or that I have such a big family? You've got a big family too," Tyler asked, confused.

Halley realized her mistake and a slow pink crawled up her neck. She always thought of herself as an only child. But she was not. Not technically. Staying away helped perpetuate the myth in her mind. It was a stupid myth. When she really thought about it, she genuinely liked most of the people in her family. She didn't know the younger siblings that well, and if she did, she was sure she would not like Tiffany, but for the most part, she was lucky. *Well, wasn't that a revelation?*

"I just meant you sound like you're all close," Halley tried to cover her mistake.

Tyler frowned. "We were. Maverick was gone a long time and then didn't move back home when he left the Army. Then I screwed up. I think they're glad I'm gone."

"I doubt that," Halley argued. She had a hard time seeing Tyler as anything but sweet and lovable.

Tyler changed the subject, "Want to let them have their heads for a few minutes?" Halley's response was to grin and lean forward; gripping her knees tighter she touched Lightning's sides with her boot heels. It didn't take much to get the horse to leap into action and take off across the field toward the next hill. Tyler and his mount were less than a head behind.

By the time they reached the edge of the far meadow, both horses slowed to a trot, seemingly knowing they would have to turn around and head back. Halley leaned down and patted Lightning's neck, praising and reassuring at the same time. Tyler rode abreast, as comfortable in a saddle as his older brother. He seemed to be an extension of the horse. Both men were naturals. It made Halley wonder how much they must miss their ranch.

"We better head back," Halley said, somewhat dejectedly. "I can help you with the others."

"That's okay, I've got it. I only have two more to exercise and I can put one on a lead," Tyler said. If Maverick wasn't there when they returned to the stable, he would stay close to Halley and exercise the others later in the morning.

"Fine. But I'm going to help clean the stalls. It's the least I can do," Halley insisted.

"Deal," Tyler grinned. No need to follow her, if she was going to muck stalls with him.

The two worked in companionable silence. The smells of the barn were pungent with the horse excrement, old straw, hay, and natural animal odor. She giggled to herself, unable to imagine her city friends standing knee-deep in the muck without shrieking. It came back to her as if she never left. There was a peace here she had not felt in a long time. Not that she was ready to acknowledge or examine that emotion.

After a while, Halley called over the wall where she could hear Tyler scooping old hay into the wheelbarrow, "What exactly drove you out of Texas?" She was having trouble imagining sweet Tyler doing anything knowingly that would cause him to be banished.

Tyler felt his heart drop to his stomach. He thought the woman had dropped her questions. He knew she stopped shoveling, waiting for his answer. Before he could respond, he heard Maverick's voice answer for him.

"He was a dumbass. Hanging around in town on street corners with thugs, driving them around in his pickup. It was more lucrative than good old-fashioned ranch work. Thought the money was easy. But those thugs were attached to one of the cartels. When Tyler realized what was going on, they didn't want him out. It was stay and eventually go to jail or come up here with his big brother and a bunch of other brothers who would straighten his shit out. Right, bud?" Maverick looked over the top of the stall straight into his brother's eyes.

The younger man, still a teenager, only eighteen, looked down quickly, not hiding his embarrassment. "Yeah, that was it." That his father saw him patching into a motorcycle club rather than staying, said something about how dire his situation had been.

Halley came out of the stall she was cleaning, glared at Maverick, and walked into the one Tyler worked. Planting her feet in front of him, she reached up, touching her hand to his shoulder. "Hey, we all make mistakes. I made a colossal one. Trusted people I shouldn't have, just like you, and ended up here. Guess we're in the same boat. We'll look out for each other, yeah?"

Tyler lifted his eyes from where he stared at the straw-covered ground and saw the sincerity in Halley's eyes, a small smile overcoming his embarrassment, and nodded in agreement. "Yeah."

Hands tucked in his front pockets, Maverick watched the interchange between the two. The sooner his brother owned up to his mistake and got a thicker skin, the easier his time as a prospect and eventual club brother would be. The guys could be brutal with their teasing and barbs when they smelled weakness. It was all in good fun, and they would always have each other's backs, but being on the receiving end could hurt if you didn't learn to let it wash off. Tyler knew that, growing up in a house full of older brothers, even the sisters gave as good as they got. Their father loved them, but he was not one for coddling, and when he told Tyler with unshed tears in his eyes that he needed to go with Maverick, Tyler knew there was no other choice.

What did surprise Maverick was Halley's reaction to his blunt explanation of his brother's story. She seemed to relate on the same level as Tyler, showing her vulnerability. How could she not see her situation was totally different? She did nothing wrong, as far as Maverick and the brothers had been able to learn. She had been going about her business, living her best life, successful beyond the wildest dreams of most thirty-one-year-olds – hell, most fifty-year-olds. Yet here she was, tail between her legs, hiding in the stable mucking stalls with his baby brother. That she offered her support in solidarity with his brother was yet another side to the woman, one he found he respected.

"You could pick up a shovel or pitchfork and help us," Halley stared at Maverick pointedly.

"I could," Maverick hid the grin that threatened to break across his face.

"Here, take mine, I'll get another," Halley shoved the pitchfork into his hands and pushed by him to take one from the wall where it hung. "Get moving, ranch boy, show us your big strong muscles."

"You think I have big strong muscles?" Maverick asked, not hiding his grin this time, and flexing his biceps in a show for her benefit.

Halley rolled her eyes, "Of course, that's the part you'd hear. Take the next stall down. We're moving that direction. Come on. Daylight's wasting." The truth was that they were almost done, but she wanted to shove the man a bit, on his brother's behalf; she'd do anything to get Tyler to loosen up again. If ordering his big, scary brother around was the way to do it, so be it.

Tyler's eyes bugged out and he raised a hand in protest, "That's okay, Halley. I've got this. It's my job. You two don't have to help me."

"No, we don't, but we will," Maverick winked at him and sauntered to the next stall. The horses were outside in the near pasture until they finished with their stalls. Tyler wasn't sure what just happened, but he was pretty sure Halley was watching his brother's ass as he walked away. He thought it best to keep his mouth shut and muck.

"I'm buying breakfast after this," Maverick called to the two of them.

"Why don't you take the last two out and we'll finish the stalls and get the feed set up. Then we can all leave together," Halley suggested to Tyler as she pulled the pitchfork from his hands.

"I think he meant the two of you," Tyler said.

"I meant the three of us. Listen to the woman, Prospect," Maverick's voice yelled good-naturedly over the stall.

He didn't need to be told again.

After the work was done, the horses munching hungrily in their clean stalls, Halley hurried to the house to shower and change. "Fifteen minutes and I'll be back," she yelled over her shoulder.

"No woman can be ready in fifteen minutes," Tyler scoffed. Maverick was wondering the same but kept his opinion to himself. He was pretty sure Halley always said what she meant and delivered. Both men hurried to take turns in the shower in the bathroom James had built in the stable. Maverick had a change of clothes in his saddlebag and Tyler had learned to keep a bag ready in the stable.

Halley swiped a circle in the fogged-up mirror and looked at her reflection. She quickly rubbed some product on her palms and scrunched her light brown hair with her fingers. She considered makeup, but why? There was no one she needed to impress and the two men she was going to breakfast with had just seen her covered in stray straw and manure. She was who she was, and unlike her ex-fiancé, these two didn't seem to care if she wore jeans, stood in knee-deep muck, or went out in public makeup free. Fresh-faced, clean jeans, and a men's white button-up shirt hanging to her thighs, she pulled on her boots and raced out of the house. She didn't even notice Priscilla sitting at the kitchen table staring into space. The two women co-existed, rarely crossing paths. They both liked it that way.

"Impressive, Thunder," Maverick nodded at her, looking her up and down. His own brunette hair was wet and dripping onto his fresh T-shirt. "You have two minutes to spare."

"Huh, and I took my time," Halley replied saucily, swinging her hips a little wider as she walked toward them.

"Keys?" Maverick held out his hand to her.

"What? No! I drive Henry," Halley said, hiding the keys behind her back.

"I gotta crawl in the backseat?" Tyler whined. His long legs would be cramped.

"You can follow on your ride," Maverick lifted his chin toward his brother's motorcycle. Tyler had bought the Harley well-used and in need of tender loving care. Luckily, Maverick and the club brothers worked with him to get it in shape once he and Maverick arrived in the town in his battered pickup truck his father gifted him in high school. He couldn't prospect without his own motorcycle; it was a rule of the MC.

Tyler looked relieved, "Okay, good."

Halley jumped into the driver's seat and grinned triumphantly. Maverick, rather than argue, dropped into the passenger seat – not his preferred position, but he would go with it for now. He was hungry and an argument would be one more delay. Without asking, Halley set a course for the diner in town, hoping Kathy was not working. Or maybe she would be working and would see Halley with two handsome men at her side. Where did that thought come from, Halley wondered? It's not like either one of them was hers, and Tyler was only eighteen, between her brothers Drake and Danny – *way* too young, though she envied who he eventually fell in love with; Tyler would be a keeper.

Parked in the back and once seated in the diner, Tyler sniggered, "Your car's named Henry."

"Yeah, what of it?" Halley jutted her chin in the air. "It's a strong name."

Tyler shook his head but didn't respond. Kathy appeared at their booth and threw a menu on the table in front of Halley where it slid and hit the wall with a slap. Before she could set down the other two, an older woman took them from Kathy's hand and told her she could take the booth across the room.

"Sorry about that. I'll be waiting on you," the owner of the diner smiled and poured coffee into two mugs already on the table and set one with hot water and a tea bag in front of Halley.

"Thanks, Nora," Maverick smiled back. He and Tyler ordered full breakfasts.

Halley was quiet and stared at her menu, no longer hungry. Kathy reminded her, yet again, that she did not fit in here and never would.

"I'll just take the tea. Thanks, Nora," Halley said with a small smile for the woman who had been in her father and mother's class at the local school. Nora was always kind to her, offering her treats when she was younger.

"She'll have a veggie omelet with a side of bacon," Maverick overruled her order.

"I'm not hungry," Halley protested.

"You are and even if you're not, you can't work as hard as you did this morning and not eat," Maverick insisted and nodded at Nora. The diner owner pursed her lips, trying not to smile, as she walked away.

Waiting until Nora was through the kitchen door, Halley hissed, "Stop bossing me around. I know if I'm hungry or not. I've got enough padding to last a long time without a meal, thank you very much."

Both Tyler and Maverick stopped mid-sip of their coffees to stare at her. Maverick set his down without drinking.

"You're a beautiful woman, Thunder. Whoever told you not to eat was a fool."

Tyler nodded in vehement agreement, "What he said."

"I'm well aware of my flaws, guys. It's okay. I'm okay with them."

"Not flaws," Maverick argued. "Stop talking about yourself that way. Skinny is so last century, Thunder. No real man wants a matchstick under him."

Halley felt her face get warm as she automatically pictured being underneath Maverick. Oh no, that would not do, she couldn't think that way. She berated herself in her head, reminding herself that she just got out of one very big mistake and jumping into another, particularly with a man who was in the MC and would live here forever, and, by the way, showed no interest in her other than as her protection – probably at the behest of her father – was stupid.

"Unfortunately, a lot of men do," Halley replied to him in a small voice, staring into her tea mug. Anthony's face flashed in her mind; then came the multiple visions of when he watched the form of another, more desirable woman. Too bad she remembered each and every time it happened. All had been one more chink to break down her self-confidence. They added to every comment she heard in high school and college.

"I said *real* men," Maverick said with emphasis. "You've been hanging around the wrong people, Thunder. I don't want to hear any more tearing yourself down. Yeah?"

Halley moved her eyes from the table and stared at him. Was he for real? She saw no malice, no lies. "Fine," she sighed heavily.

"Even I know when a woman says 'fine' it's anything but," Tyler observed.

"Look at you two, you're … well, you're you," she said as she shimmied her hands up and down in front of their forms and then pointed at her own body. "I'm just me. I'm okay with that."

Maverick shook his head, "Gonna work on that, Thunder."

In the nick of time, Nora brought their plates and set them down in front of them, the two men looking like they each got two breakfasts – one with eggs, meat, and hashbrowns, and the other a plateful of pancakes. Halley's omelet made her mouth water, and bacon, well, who doesn't like bacon? Her stomach rumbled loud enough that her companions could hear. Maverick dipped his head toward her with that typical "I told you so" look with which she was more than familiar from growing up with her father and grandfather.

"Yeah, yeah, all right. I'll eat *some*," Halley conceded. After a few bites of the omelet, she watched as Maverick poured maple syrup over his stack of pancakes and cut into it.

"Umm, could I, maybe, have a bite of your pancakes?" Halley asked quietly, fully aware of the irony of her request after stubbornly refusing to eat minutes before. But the pancakes looked and smelled divine. Her fork hovered in between her plate and his, waiting for the go-ahead to dig in.

Without hesitation, Maverick cut another large forkful and held it out in front of Halley's mouth.

"Oh, okay –" Halley started. As soon as she opened her mouth to talk, Maverick shoved his fork in and grinned at her, looking delighted to share his food. Tyler watched silently, shoving food in his own mouth before he said something to get him in hot water with his brother.

They all ate in silence, Maverick every little while pushing his fork toward Halley's mouth with more sweet pancakes. Each time, a hint of a smile turned up the corners of his mouth that reached his eyes. He seemed as happy to feed her as she was to taste something so decadent that she hadn't allowed herself to enjoy for the last couple of years. Amazing, something as simple as pancakes could make her feel more like her old self again.

Over Maverick's shoulder, Halley saw Kathy staring at their booth with narrowed eyes. As Maverick stood to pay at the counter, Kathy sidled up to him with a smile. "Anything I can get for you, Maverick?"

He barely glanced at her before turning to Nora, "We're all set. Thanks, Nora." Kathy scowled over at Halley, where she and Tyler more slowly exited the booth.

The three made their way around the corner to the back of the diner, stomachs full, and joking as they walked. Maverick snatched the keys from Halley's hand when she wasn't paying attention and held them over his head where she couldn't reach them.

"My turn, Thunder. I've been waiting to take that machine for a ride."

"Machine? His name is *Henry*," Halley said with fake indignance. "I'll *let* you drive – this time – since you bought breakfast, and Henry is magnificent to drive. You can drive stick, right?" She tried not to smile as she said the last, knowing no self-respecting MC member would not be able to drive a manual transmission, at least they'd never admit it.

Maverick scoffed and shoved her shoulder lightly, "I'm not going to dignify that with an answer, Thunder."

Tyler was ahead of them, his head on a swivel, taking his job as one of Halley's protectors seriously. Maverick noticed and felt a small swell of pride. Tyler walked around Henry, first visually checking in the back seat, then stopping short at the front of the vehicle. He pulled something from under the windshield wiper on the driver's side, carefully holding it by one corner. Maverick tried to get Halley into the car, but she saw Tyler's movement and stopped short, the color leaving her face.

"What is it," she asked in a soft voice.

Tyler looked up at Maverick and back down at the note card. When his brother and Halley walked around the hood of the vehicle, he held the note carefully, tilting it for Maverick to read. In block letters, it read: ONLY THE GUILTY RUN.

"What's it mean? Is it on the wrong car?" Tyler asked, confusion filling his voice, but he had a creeping feeling up the back of his neck and he knew it wasn't the wrong car.

Halley moved around to the passenger side and got in without saying a word. Maverick looked around, noting no camera at the back of the diner or the adjacent store. He quickly checked under the car, under the driver's seat, and opened the hood to examine the engine.

Maybe he was paranoid, but too many improvised explosive devices were in his military history and there was no way he was losing his president's daughter, no matter how farfetched the threat. There was a lot of money involved with the startup and a lot of unhappy people, including, apparently, the mob. Once he was satisfied they were safe, at least for the moment, he nodded to his brother. The younger man remained calm and alert throughout the entire car check; Maverick was even prouder of him.

"Follow us to the clubhouse," Maverick ordered and took the note from his brother, holding it by the corner, touching as little as possible, and set it in the car.

Though he had conducted the visual inspection, he still held his breath for a few seconds after the engine turned over and purred. He pulled out of the parking lot and kept his eyes alert for anyone paying special attention to their departure. Later he would ask the diner staff and store employees if anyone saw anything when they took the garbage out or were on a smoke break. For now, he needed to get Halley to the clubhouse.

"What's going through that brilliant mind of yours, Thunder," Maverick glanced at her profile as she silently stared out the window.

She was silent for so long that he wondered if she heard him. Finally, she said in a small voice, "Someone thinks I'm guilty. Someone blames me. What do they expect from me?"

"Someone wants you scared," Maverick replied confidently. He might not know who it was. He may not know why she was targeted. What he did know was that the unsigned notes were meant to inspire fear. That was unacceptable.

"Scared?" Halley looked at him as he drove. "I'm not *scared.* I'm confused. I'm angry. I want to know what kind of coward stays in the shadows instead of getting in my face."

"Angry?" Maverick homed in on the one word. He was good at that, picking out the one thing on which he wanted to focus. He smiled toward her, "We can work with that, Thunder."

Chapter 14

THE CLUBHOUSE BUZZED WITH ACTIVITY. SOME brothers sat in the bar talking among themselves and playing pool. Others were in the family room purportedly watching television, but the tension was palpable. No one liked not knowing what or who they were up against. Two were now assigned to the gate, which remained closed unless a brother pulled up or it was someone who had permission to access the property. If an old rivalry had come back to life, they had to assume it was not solely focused on Halley and the brotherhood was targeted, until proven differently.

Halley sat quietly on the leather couch, trying to keep her mind from thinking about what intimate activity may have taken place where she sat. There was a reason the patch bunnies and prospects were expected to keep the entire building, including furniture, sanitized.

Scottie and Handsy burst through the door and went straight to Scottie's sister. She held up her hands, "I'm fine." They looked at one another, jaws set firmly, reminding her of her father and Red. So much was communicated with those set jaws.

"In here," Red called from the doorway to the president's office.

"Me too?" Halley asked innocently, knowing they would all hear it if she allowed the snark to come out in her voice.

"You too, princess," Red affirmed and retreated into the office.

Scottie pulled Halley from the couch and the three made their way down the hall. Inside the office, James was behind his desk, Maverick paced by the bookcase, and Wire was on the couch with his ever-present laptop, Red beside him. Scottie gestured for Halley to sit in a guest chair in front of the desk, and he sat next to her. Handsy held up the wall with his arms crossed over his chest.

"Two notes, Hal. Any others?" James got to the point.

"Two? How –" Halley turned to Scottie and narrowed her eyes. "You've been going through my glove box again?" Her brother didn't correct her that it was Maverick this time.

"Hal, you can't keep things from us, not if we're going to get ahead of this," James drew her attention back to him and his stern face.

"That first one could have been anything or meant for anyone. It might be a mistake," she replied, trying to make them see why she did not bring it to them.

"Same stock. Same block lettering. Same delivery. Same car. No mistake," Maverick answered for her father.

"Now we're on the same page, no more secrets, Hal. None," James ordered. Other fathers may implore, but the unbending president of the *Phantom Raiders* ordered – and expected to be obeyed. No question.

"Got it," she said and met her father's stare with her own unblinking stare, then turned the same look on Maverick.

"You go nowhere without protection," James continued.

For this, Halley started to protest, "That seems a little excessive. We don't even know if there's any real danger."

"There's danger, Hal. Just a matter if it's found you here yet or not," Red responded.

Looking around the room, Halley sat forward in her chair, mind ticking over at a processing rate few could match. "What is it you all know that I don't. Tell me. Now."

She knew she was pushing it, sounding like she was delivering an order, here in the clubhouse, but she did not like being in the dark, particularly when it had to do with her life.

"Tell her," Conor's terse voice came over the speakerphone. He was the youngest in this meeting and his patience had yet to develop.

Wire waited for the signal from Prez and when he got it he started his report, "The startup partner that was missing –"

Halley interjected, "Which one? Andres or Anthony?"

"Andres. No one has eyes on Anthony yet," Wire answered. He continued, "Andres Murano was found dead at the bottom of a remote cliff."

"Dead?" Halley blanched. "Did he fall? Why would he jump? Was he the one embezzling funds from the company?"

"Didn't fall. Didn't jump. Was shot and then dumped there. Pretty sure no one thought he'd be found so soon. It was a remote cove accessed by hiking in many miles or driving to the middle of nowhere and rappelling down the cliff. Whoever got rid of him was unlucky because a couple college kids were spending weeks hiking up the coast. Well, maybe it was the kids who were the unlucky ones. The girl got spooked, fell off a rock, and ended up with a concussion and stitches in her arm."

Halley composed her features. She would not look like the helpless woman in front of all these testosterone-filled males. She waited for Wire to continue. When she didn't respond, he went on, "The authorities, led by the FBI, are investigating. And you should know it was, without a doubt, Anthony who drained your bank account. We have him on camera and can trace transfers to shell companies where he's a director."

Halley's only response was to stare at the wall and ask in an even voice, "Has my bank figured it out yet?"

"I've gone through channels to send them the results of my investigation. You should hear from them any day and get at least part of it back since they'll turn around and file with their insurance," Wire affirmed.

Maverick jumped in, "There's a good chance the FBI may try to find you to question you about Andres' death."

"Me? Why? I had nothing against the man," Halley said.

Maverick hurried to continue, "All depends when the time of death is established. They're going to want to know when you left the area and where you've been every moment from the time you last walked out of the office building. Wire is monitoring the coroner's office so we have some idea when they may show up." Wire also had his FBI connections.

Halley took in the new information and then turned to look between Wire and Maverick. "Anything else?"

"Isn't that enough?" her father responded before they could. Conor ground his teeth on the other end of the phone, but he did not divulge anything his father was not ready to disclose.

"Not really," Halley retorted.

"Listen carefully, Hal. A man who was being framed along with you has been murdered. Maybe he was involved, maybe he knew too much, but we don't know that. What we do know is that you seem to be in someone's crosshairs, and I am *not* going to let your body be found at the bottom of some lake somewhere. Got it?" her father's voice raised in volume.

Halley ground her own teeth together before she responded. "Got it. I'm under house arrest."

"Not house arrest," Scottie shook his head. "Just a protective detail. You can still go out. It'll make it easier to identify anyone after you."

"Oh, so now I'm the bait?" Halley looked at her brother.

"If that's how you want to look at it," Maverick answered for Scottie. "I would rather look at it as you get to continue living your life, but with appropriate defense."

Halley refrained from asking what life that would be. It was clear to her now she would never return to San Francisco. She knew it at her core but had not completely acknowledged it. She also didn't see a return to New York, at least not in the near term, more than likely never, if she could trust her gut. Maybe Boston, or if she could find a job in London that would sponsor her work visa, she would try somewhere new. Her heart wasn't in it though. She felt it.

She may never be accepted again in the corporate world. Was that such a loss? Probably not, if she was honest with herself. She had been bored and frustrated in New York, and San Francisco went sideways. Neither was in her control, and she was realizing control meant a tremendous amount to her and her sense of well-being and, yes, success. Her entire career, thus far, was a series of other people with no vision ultimately making decisions she was better able to address. That was not the life for her. She needed more freedom, more artistic input, more willingness to take risks. She needed to run her own show. There. She thought it. She articulated the desire.

"Damn," she murmured. Immediately all the men's eyes turned to her, waiting for her to expand her thought. She realized they thought she was answering Maverick.

"Never mind. I just had a realization that I'm pretty sure Dad and Gram already made a long time ago," she said cryptically.

"What's that?" James asked, no demand this time.

"I'll tell you more when I figure it out. Let's just say, I guess I never really belonged where I was, doing what I was doing," Halley admitted.

"Or it prepared you for what you'll do next," Maverick was quick to add. He was a firm believer in experience as the best teacher. Even when things didn't work out, you learned something – sometimes exactly what you didn't want to do and who you didn't want to be.

Halley met his eyes and smiled, "Maybe that. Have you been talking to Gram and getting positivity lessons?"

Maverick grinned back at her, ignoring the other men in the room.

"Well, that's a good start," James allowed and banged his palm against the desk, sounding more like his old man all the time. "Maverick is in charge of your security. You will follow his orders and that of his designated second if he isn't there. Agreed?"

Halley sighed, "Agreed. But that doesn't mean he gets to drive Henry all the time."

Maverick barked out a laugh. The others didn't understand but he did. Halley established her own rules to be laid down next to her father's. Maverick was taking it as a win that she had not walked out.

Halley stood and Maverick moved in step with her, "Where we goin', Thunder?"

"I get to choose?" Halley asked, surprised.

"You do," Maverick replied.

"How about *Raiders Roost*? I could use a cheeseburger and fries right now," she admitted, too emotionally tired to keep up the pretense of not eating. Maverick nodded his agreement.

"Now you're talkin'," Scottie grinned and jumped up from his seat to follow them. "Maybe we should all get some burgers." The others moved toward the door with them.

"Is this my new security detail?" Halley questioned Maverick, staring at the line of men walking behind them.

"No. They're just hungry," Maverick laughed.

They left Halley's car at the clubhouse and rode in one of the club SUVs. That might make it a little harder to find her. Maverick sent a text to one of the guys to sweep her vehicle for a tracker. He also asked her to let Wire look at her phone to see if any software had been added without her knowledge. Somehow someone knew she was in her hometown. It could have been a good guess that she would return to the home she had not seen in a few years, but doubtful.

Jana was behind the bar when they arrived and mixed a sour apple-flavored martini without Halley asking. She wasn't going to drink in the middle of the day but then decided "Why not?" since she was not driving, and by anyone's estimation, today was rough – it certainly would not make her all-time favorites list. Though, breakfast with Maverick and Tyler – and those pancakes – were close, until the rest of the day went to hell.

"Thanks," Halley lifted the martini glass toward the beautiful bartender before taking a sip.

Scottie gave the food order for all of them to the waitress on shift – cheeseburgers and fries. The group was getting loud as more of the brothers drifted in and took up places in booths and at the bar. Halley preferred it this way; she thought too much in the silence. It would be easy to have more than one martini and try to forget the day and what she learned, but she wanted to be able to think and respond quickly, should the situation call for it. So, she moved to a booth and nursed the drink she had, giving Jana no reason to mix another.

Andres was dead. She wondered if Craig knew. He must, she surmised. He would be the first one the FBI would approach. Maybe he knew already and that's why he sounded so skittish the last time she talked with him. She could not see Craig as a murderer, especially not of his best friend and co-founder. The two were closer than most brothers.

Maverick talked with her father and brothers, easily fitting in with the crew, much more so than she did, she noticed. Sometimes she wondered how different her life would be had she been born with a penis. Certainly, the corporate corridors would have been more welcoming and open to what she had to say – that was not bitterness talking, that was reality, even in this day and age. There was no denying she made it far at a young age, only to end up stymied by the powers that be, hitting the glass ceiling much sooner than expected.

The move to San Francisco was supposed to break that ceiling, and she thought she had, until she looked back and realized it could all have been a setup – there were still three men at the very top and she was ultimately a pawn for at least one of them, maybe more.

If she had been born with a penis, she could also have aspired to her young dream of becoming president of the *Phantom Raiders*. She laughed at that one because then she never would have left, never seen the world, never discovered where she fit in. Not that she had made that ultimate discovery yet, but she felt she was getting closer, if by sheer willing it to be if nothing else.

While she thought Maverick was paying attention to the guys, he kept a close eye on her. He noticed every time her facial expression changed. He saw moments of sorrow, pain, and more moments of courage and determination. When the food came, he made sure to slide into the large booth next to her, so she didn't change her mind and push the food aside. He knew today was a lot to take in. Scottie, Red, and her father slid into the other side and Handsy pushed him over to sit on the same side as he and Halley.

"Eat," Scottie admonished her as she pushed a fry around the plate. This made Maverick smirk behind his burger. Halley caught him and wrinkled her nose in his direction. Scottie, missing nothing, grinned broadly at his club brother, "Good, you keep on her too."

"How come I feel like I got another brother – an older one this time?" Halley whined to the table.

They all laughed at her expense and Maverick bent and whispered in her ear, "I am definitely not your brother, Thunder."

That should not have made goose bumps rise on her skin the way it did. She was his assignment. Even so, she could not deny she liked spending time with the man.

The bikers doubted any stranger would be foolish enough to come into their bar, but they stayed alert regardless. Red and James each had a beer in front of them that they nursed. Handsy and Scottie both had Coke, as did Maverick, not even giving the pretense of a light afternoon of partying. Scottie intended to take over the bar for Jana as soon as they finished their late lunch.

The door swung open, and Drake walked in with a couple of the younger club members behind him. It looked like they all came directly from the club-owned garage, if the grease on their shirts was any indication. When he walked close to their booth, Halley noticed the paint stains on her brother's T-shirt under his leather cut. He had a streak of blue paint above his left eyebrow and yellow paint on his hands. When he noticed his father, brother, and sister sitting in the booth with his club brothers, he visibly winced and then nodded before heading to the bar and taking a stool next to his two buddies. Drake still had not spoken to her, but then, she had not spoken directly to him either.

"Are you guys doing re-paint jobs now too?" she asked no one in particular. The garage always handled repairs and rebuilds, but they used to send the paint jobs to a shop down the road.

"Yeah. Old man Davis closed his shop and moved to Florida a couple years ago. We hired his paint specialist who was young enough to want to keep working. He trained Drake," Scottie nodded.

"And Drake does some custom paint jobs on the side for fun," Handsy added.

Halley's eyes darted to her father. Why hadn't he said it was Drake who did the custom art she'd admired on the bikes at the clubhouse when she first returned? James didn't look at her, but a grin played on his lips. "Those bikes, Drake did those?" she demanded.

"Yep," her father replied.

"Do you know how much money he could be pulling in with that? I didn't know he was an artist!" Halley exclaimed, her burger forgotten, excited once again by the art and the possibilities. Halley loved possibilities, almost as much as she loved new ideas.

Handsy lowered his eyebrows in earnest as he looked at her. "Seriously? Is he that good? I mean, he's good and what he's done for the brothers looks great, but that could be a job?"

"Hell yes, it could be a job. He is definitely an artist. I'd love to see more of what he's done," Halley responded, matching Handsy's seriousness. "Do you know how much people pay for custom art on their bikes? Or their cars? Or the designs they put on their bikes or cars as framed art for their walls?"

Handsy shook his head no. James had watched her carefully during the exchange. Her excitement was palpable.

Maverick moved her plate in front of her, "Eat, Thunder. Put the rest of it in that notebook of yours."

She frowned at him, but to his and Scottie's surprise, she took a large bite of the burger. Little did they know, when she was excited about a new idea or happy, she ate.

James watched her for a little longer, then turned to stare at the bar where his sullen son sat with his friends. Now, at twenty-one, Drake was allowed at the bar. He had no idea what ran through the kid's mind and wondered why he seemed to brood all the time. He tried to talk with Priscilla about it, but she didn't notice and only seemed glad Drake was not causing problems – quiet and well-behaved were things with which she could deal, or ignore, more likely. If it did not have to do with Tiffany or maybe Danny, Priss was not really engaged.

Drake did what was asked of him. He did a good job at the garage, without complaint. He had the mechanical aptitude and had also picked up the painting side with ease. James could see that son running that business one day. Now he wondered if maybe it was not what Drake wanted. Maybe he should have paid more attention to his son's art. But then, it wasn't as if Drake came to him and talked about drawing or painting or creating or whatever he was into. No, Drake rarely talked at all. That couldn't be healthy.

Movement brought James out of his thoughts. Halley excused herself to go to the Ladies and that side of the booth moved to let her out. On the way to the back hallway, where the toilets were located, Halley took a detour. Maverick watched, ready to move when she did. She stopped behind Drake and put a hand on his shoulder. He turned to her, and they could all see her animated face and hand gestures across the room.

Halley was nervous to approach her unapproachable brother but determined. "Hey, Drake. We haven't talked since I've been back." Drake stared at her without saying a word. Halley decided to plow ahead, "I just found out you're the one who did all those custom paint jobs on the bikes."

Drake's eyes narrowed, but he still didn't say anything. He wondered where this one-way conversation was going. So, he waited.

Halley continued talking undeterred as if he were keeping up his end of the dialogue. "You're really gifted, a true artist."

Drake's eyebrows would have jumped to his hairline, if he had not caught himself.

"I'd like to talk with you sometime in the next few days, if you have time, about how to make that a business, or part of the business you already have. You could be making a ton of money. And really, your art should be seen by a lot more people. I work with loads of artists and designers and I'm telling you, you're even better than most of them." Halley knew she was rambling, but it was a little disconcerting to keep up a one-way conversation with someone she should know well but, in reality, hadn't known since he was six years old. When she thought back, she did remember even at that age he was always sketching on any paper or cardboard he could find or painting with the watercolors people bought for the kids.

"So, what do you say? Want to talk about it?" Halley pushed.

Drake finally uttered the fewest words he could muster, "I'll think about it."

"Oh, okay. Well, let me know. And I'd like to see more of your art. You must have sketches and things I could see," she added. "You're extremely talented."

Drake gave her a single nod and turned back to place his elbows on the bar top. She thought she saw a spark of interest in his eyes before he raised the mask again. Somehow, she would get through to him. She hadn't been this excited about an idea in a long time.

When she came out of the Ladies' Room, Maverick was leaning against the wall opposite the door, knee bent and booted foot against the dark paneling.

"Are you stalking me?" Halley asked, only partly in jest.

Maverick nodded toward the end of the hall that led to the back of the bar, "Exit there. Someone could come in and I wouldn't have seen, or you could have tried to escape." He shrugged at the last part.

Halley glanced at the door and felt ice crawl up her spine. Yeah, that could be bad. "Well, thanks, I guess. I'm glad you're on top of it. I'm obviously not that observant or devious."

"You're welcome, darlin'," his Texas drawl more pronounced. He gestured for her to walk back to the booth. "Did you make any headway with Drake?"

"I don't know. He's hard to read."

"He is that," Maverick agreed.

"I'm not giving up," Halley stated.

"I wouldn't expect you would."

Handsy moved so they could slide back into the booth. James raised his chin to his daughter, "You're serious about this idea, aren't you?"

"I am," Halley smiled brightly.

James nodded once, "Let me know when you're ready to talk it over."

"Gotta see if Drake's interested first," Halley said.

James could make that happen but suspected Halley would be displeased if he coerced his son into cooperating.

For a while, sitting in the low light of the tavern, Halley was able to think about something other than her predicament. She was excited to find out her brother was an artist. She sat back and enjoyed listening to the guys' banter. She allowed herself to feel and not think, enjoying the simple moment. That did not happen often. In fact, never. This time one of Gram's lessons zinged into her brain. Both grandmothers seemed to have a lot of wisdom to share. The older woman always said, "Just be; you need to learn to just be." She never understood what that meant, but now she felt it. It felt pretty good.

Chapter 15

THE FBI AGENTS APPROACHED THE LARGE HOUSE ON the quiet block in San Francisco for the second time in less than a week. All these tech geniuses had more money than sense, one of the agents thought to herself. All this house for one man. Who was he trying to impress? He likely used two rooms, and the rest were seen more by the cleaners than him. All these people did was drive up the housing prices and, by default, the rental prices, in a city that used to be eclectic, artsy, and hip. Sure, the staid bankers were the stalwarts of the old guard, but they merely made up one end of the varied spectrum. The tech boom, bust, and boom again changed the face of the beautiful old urban center at a pace no previous era had come close to, much less matched.

The agent felt eyes on them and looked with a critical eye at the parked cars along the street and the trees planted long ago to provide shade to succeeding generations, to see if there was someone watching. She saw nothing. But she felt it. Her boss always said, "Listen to that instinct; it could save your life."

While she continued to surveil the area, her partner spoke into the intercom at the black, wrought-iron gate. When it opened, they walked through and up to the front door. A man with his shirt untucked, hair standing on end as if he had run his hands through it over and over, stood in wrinkled trousers and loafers with no socks. The loafers looked like they were a last-minute addition to his ensemble, given the way he moved his foot around inside to put it on properly.

He peeked his head outside and then backed into the dark interior of the house, holding the door open, urging them to hurry inside. He led them to what appeared to be an office with a single desk lamp lit and the blackout shades lowered. Her partner reached for a switch on the wall and flipped it upward to turn on the overhead light, or what looked to be a modern chandelier. Craig Martin recoiled at the sudden brightness, and she immediately wondered if he had been drinking.

"Do you have news for me? Have you followed the embezzlement trail to the end? Do you know where our money went?" Craig asked, trying to take some semblance of control of the meeting he did not call. Not one question asked if they knew who killed his partner, his closest friend. That was interesting.

Her partner stared at the man without speaking. Finally, he let out a breath and held an arm toward the grouping of sofa and chairs, "Why don't we sit, Mr. Martin?"

Craig scowled suspiciously. He guessed he should be happy they weren't taking him out in handcuffs. He'd seen that happen lately to other CEOs. The problem for him was that if he was in jail, he was sure he would be killed. His friend-turned-enemy had made that point clearly enough when he admonished him not to give any testimony to the authorities.

"Please," her partner nodded encouragingly. She fought rolling her eyes and wanted to tell the man to sit his ass down and quit obstructing their investigation.

Once the startup founder sat on the edge of the cushioned black leather chair, her partner sat across from him on the leather sofa. She chose to move around the room, picking up objects, looking around, making Craig uncomfortable. She noticed a painting by a famous modern artist on the wall. At least the man did not have the art locked up in a safe away from potential theft, where it was not enjoyed, like so many of his contemporaries. What was that saying? They "knew the price of everything and the value of nothing." Her grandmother said that all the time.

"Mr. Martin, would you go over again when you realized something was wrong financially with your company?" her partner said in his even voice. No threat, no promises, simply getting the facts. Their boss said that was his superpower, understatement.

"I don't understand. We've been over this multiple times," Craig began to protest.

"Sometimes you remember something else the more often we go over it," the FBI agent explained with a slightly apologetic smile.

Craig knew he should have called his attorney, but he walked through the last several months yet again anyway. He suspected they were no closer to answers than in the beginning and were trying to trip him up.

"So, you first became aware vendors weren't getting paid when your Chief Marketing Officer Halley McCarthy approached you. You said she told you she had already approached the CFO and COO in previous months but came to you when the invoices still weren't settled," her partner said, purportedly reading from the notes he took as Craig spoke.

Craig realized his mistake then. He had not mentioned Halley before, at Anthony's direction. This was a new "fact" for the investigators.

"Did Ms. McCarthy seem unduly agitated at the time or angry with your partners?" the special agent posed his follow-up question.

"Halley? No. She was concerned they were too busy with the investors to worry about the vendors. Since Halley's team dealt with the vendors most closely, she wanted to make sure they were paid for their services. Halley likes – liked – working with a lot of independent creatives and she worried about them. There was nothing personal in what she brought to me," Craig tried to explain, waving off any concerns with the young CMO.

Now, not only did he have Anthony's people listening to his conversations, but Halley's father's security team also listened in. He thought he might lose his mind before all this was over. Maybe

Andres was the one who had it easiest. He was dead and no longer had to worry or be frightened out of his mind. More than fear of Anthony and his criminal syndicate, he feared prison. A man like him would not last in prison, even without Anthony's promise to have him killed.

"We understand Ms. McCarthy was in a relationship with Anthony Martinelli. Is this correct?"

Craig scowled, "I'm not sure what their personal lives have to do with any of this. Anthony took an interest in Halley from the moment she was hired. Eventually, they were engaged, but Halley called it off before my company imploded."

"Is it possible she used Mr. Martinelli's position as CFO to gain access to sensitive information or company bank accounts?"

"No, absolutely not," Craig stated firmly.

"You sound so sure, yet you let Ms. McCarthy go after your company's difficulties went public," the female special agent entered the questioning.

"Yes, well, I shouldn't have done that. I wasn't thinking straight. There was no work for her for the foreseeable future, so it didn't make sense for her to stick around until this nightmare is over," Craig practically whined.

He was devastated, embarrassed, and angry when the company imploded. With his two partners gone, he could have relied more on Halley, but that seemed pointless. At the time, he was angry about her relationship with Anthony and blamed her with no substantiation. Since Anthony's secret visits, he knew how wrong he was.

His only consolation was that he never filed the papers with HR or had removed Halley from the payroll. Technically she was still the CMO of a sinking company, was still on the payroll, and would eventually get her equity if they went public or had to sell, not that she knew that, and the agents didn't need to know either. It had no bearing on their case. But it did assuage his guilt over Halley, if only a little. He brought her here and uprooted her life. He made her feel less than when he exploded.

"Do you know where Ms. McCarthy is, Mr. Martin?" the male special agent continued.

"No," Craig answered quickly. That was not a lie. He specifically did not ask her where she was the one time he talked with her.

The two special agents exchanged a look and then asked Craig to continue his recitation of his knowledge of all events.

"Andres Murano had not been in contact with you after he disappeared from your offices and was not at his home?"

"No. I tried calling him multiple times. I went to his house. No contact," Craig said bitterly. Andres was his best friend, yet he had not confided in him when he got himself in trouble. Maybe Andres was protecting him. He doubted it.

"Continue please," the special agent gestured with his hand to get on with the explanation.

By the time he showed the agents to the door, he had no idea what they gained from their inquiries. It seemed like a waste of time to him. They never did answer when he asked if they found the money trail.

The female agent turned around on the steps outside his front door as if it was an afterthought and handed him her business card – a redundancy since they had given him their cards on each of the previous visits. "Mr. Martin, if you hear from Ms. McCarthy or Mr. Martinelli, please contact us. We are most interested in talking with them."

Craig pursed his lips and shut the door before they were even down the steps.

The special agent turned to her partner and asked, "Did you get anything new out of that?"

He kept walking and said quietly, "A little. He knows more than he's saying."

"When do they not?" she scoffed.

"How did you get so cynical for someone so young?" the special agent shook his head at her.

"How are you not?" she countered. "All these rich corporate types are the same. In it for themselves. They flat out steal and think they can get away with it."

"Some are like that," he conceded. "Not all. Just like any other institution. Including ours. Power and money corrupt people."

They got in their government-issued black SUV and pulled out onto the street. Neither noticed the pickup truck parked amongst the other vehicles along the curb a short way behind them, nor the two men inside, hidden by the tinted windows.

Conor McCarthy sat in the pickup with Wolf, one of their contract security men, an operator who had served in the Army Rangers and on the Delta Force team with Maverick.

"What do you think that was about?" Conor asked. Both had listened in to the entire interview.

"Fishing," Wolf surmised.

"Too many damn questions about my sister," Conor griped.

"Yep. Relay to Maverick," Wolf said in the typical short sentences Conor was coming to expect from anyone involved in Maverick's former team.

"I wonder when they're going to send in the agents to find her?" Conor mused.

Wolf gave him a side look. "Ask Wire."

"You're a lot of fun on a stakeout, you know that?" Conor frowned, texting his quick report to Maverick. They would talk later when his father and the others were in the room.

Wolf snorted and shook his head but did not reply. It was more a protection detail than a stakeout, but the resulting boredom was the same. Wolf was used to sitting, unmoving, sometimes days at a time. Whatever the situation called for, he and his teammates learned to adapt. He applied that now to his civilian life.

Given a choice, he preferred the quiet. The kid next to him wasn't so bad. Wolf liked giving him a hard time, staying silent just to keep the kid off-balance. Kid. Huh. When did twenty-five-years-old suddenly become a kid to him? He was beginning to feel like an old man, and he wasn't even thirty-five.

He'd seen a lot in his time on earth, more than most saw in a lifetime, and a good deal of it was the underbelly of humanity, if you could even consider some of the animals he dealt with human. While his reactions became numb to what he saw, his brain could never reconcile the vile things of which some were capable. That's part of why he liked this job. He could help protect, and he could wield his and the brothers' form of justice when called upon to right wrongs. That mattered to him.

Maverick tried to get him to move to the small northern town his brother-in-arms now called home. He could not quite understand how a Texas boy could deal with the Michigan winters. Having grown up in California, being back was as easy a transition as he was going to get. He resisted the move to join Maverick, though he admitted when alone in his rack most nights that he missed the camaraderie of their old team, the brotherhood. Maybe he should move to Michigan, join the MC, and work for the security business full-time.

He glanced at Conor's profile. The young man watched the house and surrounding area with a careful eye. The kid wasn't so bad. Either were the others he had met over the last year doing contract work. There was a chapter in San Francisco he could hook up with, but his gut told him to go with whom he knew. Something to think about, though he knew if he made the move, thinking would have nothing to do with it. It would be pure instinct. There was a reason his name was Wolf. His instincts were supreme and his need for a "pack" and to protect that pack was deep-seated. Being a lone wolf was starting to grate on him.

"He's moving," Conor said suddenly. "Well, sort of."

Wolf looked toward the ostentatious mansion and saw their "client" close the front door and then pace back and forth on the front steps as if he could not decide whether to stay or leave. They had already replaced his driver with one of their own guys – his driver was on a surprise, extended, warm-weather holiday with his family – and Craig had not called for a car. Sometimes he drove himself, but he was more likely to use a driver. His genius brain, flitting around with new ideas, and now the added pressure of the investigation and threats against his person, did not make for a safe driver.

"Idiot. He makes a nice target."

Wolf nodded, though Conor wasn't looking at him.

Out of the shadows, another of their team appeared and walked toward Craig. The team member was dressed like a landscaper and pointed toward the perimeter as if discussing what the landowner wanted to do with the vegetation. Through their tiny ear communication devices, Conor and Wolf knew that was not the tenor of the discussion, but to anyone else looking on, it would look normal. Finally, Craig nodded, shook the man's hand, and went back inside his mansion. Their guy returned to the shadows, trowel in hand, disappearing among the foliage. Whatever mental crisis Craig experienced, would wait a while longer.

A high-end SUV with tinted windows parked across the street. A single nod toward Conor and Wolf through the front window let them know their team members were ready to take over or provide backup, whichever the team leaders needed.

"Don't you think it's strange we haven't seen the other partner? He regularly terrorizes 'McWussie' there and suddenly disappears altogether," Conor said as he continued to stare at the house. He'd begun to give Craig nicknames disparaging his level of courage and calm: McWussie, Spineless, Mr. Scaredy, Wimpy Dick. He was more annoyed with their charge as time went on, thinking about his sister's dire position.

Wolf tended to agree. Conor's sister had not stood a chance. As far as he could tell, she was the only one with a backbone in the entire outfit. Not only had she continued to defend her vendors, but she took it all the way up the chain, she dumped the creepy Anthony, she moved out of her rental house, and she did it all without a single call to her family. She was a woman he'd like to meet.

"Probably spooked by the feds' visit," Wolf surmised.

"So, you think he offed the partner?"

Wolf stared at him as if he were missing a few brain cells.

"Yeah, okay. Yeah," Conor conceded, slight pink creeping up his neck. Craig had said Anthony implied bodily harm if he made a complete statement to the authorities and continued to taunt him with the threat to end his life. Wolf made him feel like a dumb kid half the time, without even trying. He knew the man and Maverick had more experience in their thumbs than he did in his whole body. Not for the first time, he considered enlisting and gaining the experience and credibility these guys commanded by merely breathing. Sometimes he thought Scottie should be in the security business and he should run the tavern, but Scottie didn't want it that way. He didn't know why.

"Feds don't have the evidence," Wolf allowed.

"If Wire can find anything, he will," Conor said, holding steadfastly to that simple belief. His club brother could perform miracles with his cyber-digging, following the money, finding email and text trails, and putting together disparate pieces that would make it all fall into place. The regimentation required by law enforcement wasn't anything that impeded Wire. He hoped for that conclusion before something happened to his sister.

***

The next morning, Enzo sat alone at the coffee bistro across from the startup headquarters and watched as the usual dark SUV dropped Craig Martin at the front door. Sometimes they parked under the building in the private parking garage, but more often, the driver was sent on errands before returning to the bowels of the building. Enzo observed the CEO as he furtively looked around before entering the lobby with a quickstep that belied his fear. His cousin had surely done a number on this man. It was sad, really; they could have had a much longer run if Anthony had not gotten greedy. He was sure now that was what happened.

There was no need for the company to implode, particularly since the products were stellar, if everything he read in his research was correct, and he believed it was. Their competitors were far behind and scrambling to catch up, and before the implosion, Craig Martin was calm and confident. His cousin was a fool. He would have to tell his father and their grandfather soon. He couldn't cover for the man he had grown up with as a brother much longer without bringing himself down too.

Enzo sighed, resigned to his unpleasant task as the messenger. Maybe he could give Anthony a little longer, just a little. He still did not understand what role his cousin's former fiancée played in all this. He would like to have more answers before talking with his father and grandfather.

Today he sat alone. He was not comfortable with his cousin's hired muscle – they were sloppy and mercenary, with no principles other than allegiance to the dollars his cousin waved in front of them

– and did not want to alert his own family's partners or allies to his doubts and lack of knowledge. Time to think was time he needed alone. Perhaps not across from the building where it all went wrong. Staring at the building was not giving him any new answers. If anything, he was more frustrated.

Later he headed to the financial district near California Street to wait for the men with whom he had slowly made acquaintance over the last several months. Listening to them as they talked together, acting as if no one could hear their confidential conversations, except him, and he was no longer an outsider, he learned about current and upcoming deals, taking advantage of the research and due diligence their firms regularly conducted. They took him at face value when he introduced himself and slowly, over cultivated months, they believed the story he spun that he was a trust funder with his hand in many pies around the world. Not totally a lie, but not the full truth.

They were potential partners, or they pointed to avenues of business in the future, ones that might keep him on the West Coast and not be called back to the cold corridors of the northern Midwest by the next winter. As much as he thought he wanted to go home, he wouldn't mind staying in San Francisco if he wasn't babysitting his cousin. If he could bring in business or useful partners, his father may allow him to stay. Damn Anthony for screwing up a good thing.

The light in the speakeasy was warm and welcoming, lamps and overhead lights glowing through gold, orange, green, blue, and red stained glass, much like the Tiffany lamps they tried to replicate. It reminded him of New York or Chicago, not the modern, trendy bars dotting San Francisco and Silicon Valley. He liked it. Here, people still spoke to one another, only occasionally glancing at their phones.

He could no longer count the number of times he sat in almost silent bars and pubs where everyone was glued to their smartphone, even texting the person sitting across from them. Most of the time he felt like he was being punked or in the setting of a pre-apocalyptic film.

Here, in this bar, as its genre implied, it could still have been Prohibition times. People were laughing, flirting, conducting business, over martini and champagne glasses. This was a place where he felt comfortable.

Anthony hated it here and complained every time Enzo said that was where he was heading. He remembered the one time he sat in the background watching as Anthony brought his fiancée to the speakeasy. She loved it. He watched her flit from group to group, striking up a conversation with people he was sure she did not know. Maybe that's why Anthony hated it so much; he couldn't control her here; he wasn't her only option for conversation. From what Enzo saw, Halley McCarthy fit in this environment, as did he. That made him like her more and his cousin a bit less.

"Ah, Lorenzo, join us!" he heard from across the room. "Settle this bet."

His "friends" made space for him around the high-top table where they stood close to the bar. He could tell they had already been here for one or two drinks, based on the width of their smiles and the number of martini glasses littering the table. They must have left work early. A smiling waitress sauntered confidently to deliver more drinks and take away the empties, her hips swinging in the beaded flapper dress that did wonders to emphasize the curve of her hips, the front low enough to show substantial cleavage, though the waist was lost under the straight fabric. Even her short hair had the pin curls that matched the era. She was lovely. He would have to keep an eye on her.

Soon he would have to answer his father's calls. Not tonight. Tonight, he would pretend his life was the one he made up for the financiers who called him friend.

Chapter 16

THE HARDCOVER NOTEBOOK SAT IN FRONT OF HER, open, on the mission-style desk her grandfather had proudly made for her as a child – there was nothing beyond the skill of her father's father. The adult-sized desk looked out a large window that overlooked the forest and part of the pasture leading up to the first rise. It was easy to get caught up in the scenery, attention claimed by each new movement of a woodland creature, silence louder in her ears than the roar of her Harley. Someday she might get used to the peace, the quiet, the surface stillness, disturbed by all manner of fauna in the grasses and trees if only you paid attention.

Fifteen years away had wreaked havoc with her ability to be still, to sit in silence. Sure, the longer she was with Anthony, the more she sat alone in her little rental house in San Francisco when she wasn't at the office, but she was cognizant of the life outside, the neighbors talking, little lap dogs barking incessantly at each passerby and squirrel, honking horns – though far fewer than New York; New Yorkers considered the car horn a God-given appendage and used it liberally – and the utility motors of landscapers constantly in motion to cut back the grass or errant tree branches encroaching on the power lines of civilization. Here, no light polluted the night sky, unless the motion-detector lights came on when a deer wandered into the yard. She had almost forgotten how many stars dotted the heavens. Listening carefully, she could even hear the soft whinny of the horses through her closed windows. She felt like a child again, each sound, sight, and smell, new to her senses, causing a fresh round of marvel and awe.

Distractedly, Halley wondered if this is what Maverick, Jana, and others found when they followed her brother's pied piper tune to this town, off the beaten path, secure in its obscurity, though closer to the edges of civilization than when she grew up here – if the box stores on the outskirts and changed shopfronts on the main street were to be believed.

Sighing, Halley lifted her pen once again, jotting notes on the lines of the notebook. This was her process. Pen and paper. Ideas. Notes. Then she would eventually pull out her laptop and type up the plan forming in her mind.

Drake hadn't been in contact about his art and his interest in pursuing it as a business. That was not going to deter her. She would be ready when he was because she could see it, feel it, and knew it was the right path. Her father and probably the executive committee of the club would require actual market research, not only her gut instinct, but she trusted her intuition.

Too bad that intuition was on holiday when she met Anthony. Well, to be fair, it was there, but she pushed it aside because she was flattered a partner was paying attention to her, wooing her – did anyone say "woo" anymore? – and he was *so* sophisticated and good-looking.

The knock on her door was faint, tentative. It was so light she almost missed it, but in the silence, any sound was noticeable.

"Come in," she called quietly.

The door swung open, and her youngest sister stepped inside, hesitant, so unlike the hard-charging teenager she was. "Busy?"

"Never for you," Halley smiled, visibly relaxing at her sister's presence. That was a long way from the uptight woman who arrived weeks ago. She took note of how her body felt, how her brain was clear and not fritzing out over dealing with family. She liked this new version of herself. Maybe it was the old version coming to the fore again.

Scarlett hopped on the end of the bed and crossed her legs under her, hands resting on her thighs. "What 'cha doing?"

"Working on ideas for a business plan," Halley replied, surprising herself with her candor. It was not like her to divulge plans before they were fully fleshed out and ready to be discussed, examined, torn apart.

"Business plan? You're not going back to San Francisco? Or are you creating your own startup?" Scarlett looked equal parts confused and excited, with a side of trepidation. How would her sister's decisions have an impact on her planned future life? Realistically, she knew she would make her own way just fine, her father reminded her of that all the time and Gram reinforced it. But the child in her liked the idea of relying on her big sister a bit – or a whole lot.

"I'm not sure yet. But I'm figuring it out," Halley admitted, leaning back in her cushioned desk chair. Her grandfather insisted on a chair that matched the mission style of the desk but added a cushioned seat – courtesy of Gram – rollers on the feet, and a back that had a spring that allowed her to lean back. At least she thought it was a spring, she wasn't sure of the actual mechanics. What she did know was that a lot of time and love had been put into her specially crafted desk and chair.

"What's the new business you're thinking about?" Scarlett prodded.

Halley hesitated before launching into a simplified explanation. "Custom art for bikes and cars. Marketing the specialty first regionally and then countrywide. Maybe to higher-end clients in Europe, Latin America, and Asia eventually. I'd like to expand with more artists to create a marketing arm that specializes in unique campaigns with original art. Further down the road, I want to open an art gallery to display the art and possibly sell originals on different mediums than the vehicles. And, if all that works like I think it will, I want a not-for-profit that offers art classes and workshops for students and the community." Halley held her breath, waiting for a reaction. Scarlett might be fourteen years old, but she was the first to hear her grand design and she realized it was important to her how her sister reacted. Scarlett was very much like their father, and this would be a precursor to how he might respond, albeit from a younger perspective.

Scarlett did not react immediately. She seemed to be rolling the idea around in her head. Soon she sat up straighter. In a serious voice, no smile, she said, “This sounds like something you could do from anywhere – even here.”

Halley nodded, waiting for more.

“You should talk to Drake. His art is awesome. He doesn’t let anyone see it, other than what he does to the guys’ bikes, but I found a lot in his room. Don’t tell him I know, though,” Scarlett added hurriedly.

“He’s the first person I thought of as the talent,” Halley responded.

Scarlett let a grin spread over her young face, “This is *so* cool. And if you aren’t going to be in New York – I really didn’t want to live in San Francisco – then I guess it would be okay if you were here.”

“You think so?” Halley breathed out in relief.

“Yeah. I do. Dad’s going to need to see numbers and stuff, but I get what you want to do. I think it’s original and awesome. But what do I know; I’m a kid in a hick town, right?” Scarlett shrugged, only half kidding.

Halley was taken aback at how like her teenage self her youngest sister sounded. Then she scowled, “Don’t do that.”

“What?” Scarlett’s eyes grew wide. She was used to heaped on praise when this sister was in contact, which was not often, but still, the displeased tone was a surprise.

“Don’t demean yourself, your thoughts, your ideas – your worth. Don’t wait until you’re my age to realize some truths,” Halley took in a deep breath. Was she really going to lay her thoughts bare? Was she really going to admit to her misjudgments and failings? If it helped Scarlett to not make the same mistakes, she would woman up.

“Small towns do not have to equal small minds,” Halley continued. “I met with equally small minds and giant criticisms in the city. Just look at Gram. She's the most open-minded and savvy person I know. Dad runs multiple businesses and a giant family of blood and chosen, and he does it seamlessly. I know CEOs who can't keep as many balls in the air as he does. We're from here and we should be proud of that, our heritage, our family." She paused and then admitted, "Took me thirty-one years to figure that out. I wasted all this time I could have been with all of you and people who care about me – at least come home more often." Because as much as she hated being played for a fool and as down on herself as she was now, she knew the time away helped shape her worldview, her confidence, and her professional acumen. That was something she could take with her and use anywhere.

"Are you staying?" Scarlett asked, her voice low. The girl wasn't sure if the idea thrilled her or disappointed her. This is not what she expected to hear from Halley.

"I'm not sure yet. But I don't have anywhere to go back to, so I guess my future is wide open," she pasted on a smile for the younger girl's benefit.

"I'm going to be as successful as you when I'm done with school," Scarlett asserted, flopping back on the comforter and staring at the ceiling fan over the bed.

"You think I'm successful?" Halley asked, incredulous. She moved from her desk and flopped back on the bed next to her sister and likewise stared up.

"Of course! You graduated early – high school and college. You got a master's degree while you worked in New York. You've lived and worked on both coasts. You got recruited to move to San Francisco by a wildly successful startup. You're barely thirty-one and you've already been a Chief Marketing Officer for years. I'm not totally sure what that is, but I know it's a big deal. You are so successful I hope I can be half as much by your age," Scarlett gushed.

The teenager continued, "I don't know what happened in San Francisco, but I do know it's not your fault. I may be a kid, but I listen really well around corners, and Gram and Gramps and Dad and Scottie all say you got caught in circumstances and none of whatever is going on is your fault."

Halley felt around the top of the comforter and found her sister's hand. She held it in her own and remained silent. She wasn't sure she could speak around the lump in her throat, even if she knew what to say. They defended her, even without her being in the room. Her throat closed on the emotion that elicited. This was enough for now, lying next to her sister, staring at the ceiling, not feeling like a total failure for the first time in a long time.

Across the house, Drake sat at the kitchen counter drumming his fingers on the black granite, contemplating why he was there and whether he should leave. He had a mug of coffee in front of him – not made by his mother – running his finger up and down the heated ceramic. He had been up late working on a special project, one he hid in the back of one of the outbuildings to the rear of the clubhouse.

He had secretly cleaned the space and set up a makeshift studio hidden by abandoned bike parts and long-forgotten projects it looked like maybe his grandfather had worked on in his spare time years ago. He had washed the years of dust and grime off the windows that faced away from the other buildings to let in the natural light.

Sleep alluded him. Halley's praise for his work and her tease about a potential business opportunity that used his art popped into his head at the most inconvenient times, well, all the time – while working on the pretty nurse's engine so she could make it to her shift at the ER without mishap, to even working on his art in his studio.

In high school, his art teacher had encouraged him to go to art school. She sent some of his work to prestigious programs, all of which had come back encouraging him to apply. He applied, just to see if he would get in; he did. He never told his parents or anyone in his family. Then he decided to work at the garage and prospect for the club; it was more of falling into it than an actual decision. Art school was not in the cards for him.

Part of him was bitter, but he had no one to blame but himself. His father, brothers, and grandfather were all ensconced in the club. Even Scottie had done his time in the military but came home to the club, others stringing into town behind him, convinced by his brother's charisma and promise for a family. Maybe his dad would have understood. Or maybe the tough man would have thought it was a ridiculous pipedream and made fun of him like some of the high school guys did every time he peeled off from their group after practices and headed for the art room.

Instead, Drake remained silent. About everything. No one seemed to notice. In a family as big as his, being the middle child made it easy to float under the radar. All he had to do was what was expected of him: a good job at the garage and stay out of trouble. No one needed to worry about him; he was solid.

In any spare time, he threw his passion into custom paint jobs on the bikes he could convince his club brothers to entrust to his care and artistic eye, and into his sketches, paintings, and projects he kept secret. It helped to be the silent one; no one questioned when he disappeared for hours, or maybe they didn't even realize he was missing. He laughed to himself, a choked sound in his throat, from a man who rarely laughed, while his mind conjured the scenario where he was really missing, and no one noticed. Yeah, that would probably be his fate.

"What are you doing here?" Tiffany appeared from upstairs. She added sarcastically, "Aren't the patch bunnies feeding you at the clubhouse?"

Drake rolled his eyes, not bothering to answer.

"Well, I'm not going to cook for you. I'm out of here," she tossed her hair over her shoulder. The girl couldn't boil water, much less cook anything edible. She threw one more barb at him as she grabbed an apple from the fruit bowl on the counter and headed toward the door, "I don't know why you bothered to move into the clubhouse if you're always back here scrounging food."

Seeming to remember something, Tiffany turned and prowled back toward him, this time with an inviting smile on her face. Drake wondered if she practiced that smile in the mirror. Her brainless boyfriend might fall for it, but he certainly would not. One of the advantages of being the quiet one in the family, he was able to spend a lot of time observing. His sister would be surprised by how much he saw and how much he knew about her.

"Drake, when are you going to customize my car? I was thinking maybe something like 'Princess' would work or some art that would come across like that?" she batted her eyelashes, trying to appear innocent and agreeable.

He blinked. Hard. He couldn't help it. Once he realized she was serious, he snorted and ducked his head into his hands resting on the counter. If he did that for her, their father would have his head.

"You ass! Why do you take care of everyone else but not your own sister?" she whined, smacking him in the back of the head with her open hand. Tiffany turned on her heel and huffed out of the house. Not even a minute later he heard her peel out down the driveway. Good thing for her that their father and grandfather weren't there. That girl was on a one-way trip going nowhere and if she wasn't careful, reality was going to smack her in the face.

The backpack on the stool next to him concealed a sketchbook. He thought about sketching out what he would do to her car and leaving it somewhere his dad would see it. It would be a great joke, but he was sure he would get a lecture about better judgment before he had the chance to reveal the joke. He wasn't the jokester. But it was a good plan in his head that caused him to chuckle silently.

The sound of boots on the hardwood floor alerted him to approaching people. He turned and saw his oldest and youngest sisters come through the living room. Halley quickly schooled the surprise on her face and Scarlett looked overjoyed to see him – weird.

"Are you here to talk to Halley?" Scarlett bounced up to him and threw an arm over his shoulders.

As much as he tried to look annoyed at the teenager, her eyes within inches of his own, he really couldn't hold it. Scarlett's personality was infectious; it even affected him and his practiced grouchiness.

"Scar –" Halley started to reel the girl in, not wanting to scare Drake off on the off-chance he *was* there to see her.

"I am, squirt. What's it to you?" Drake challenged the teenager, only affection in his voice.

"Well, I've got a vested interest in this conversation," Scarlett asserted, causing both Halley's and Drake's eyes to open wide. At their surprise, she blushed, "Well, I hope I do. I might want to work with you two when I'm out of college." Her voice became more and more quiet as she spit out the sentence, realizing they may think she overstepped.

"And what is it you think we're going to do?" Drake couldn't help himself from asking.

Scarlett slid onto a stool next to him, "Custom art on bikes and vehicles. Maybe an art gallery. You're a great artist, Drake. I told Halley that."

"I know I'm your best brother, but how would you know what I can do, Scar?" Drake asked, curiosity piqued. He may be quiet, but the charm and competitive genes ran through his blood.

Scarlett had the grace to dip her head before answering. "Sorry. I used to go through your room and look at your sketches and paintings. Plus, I see the bikes, like everyone else. You really are the best. Ms. Paisley told me you were a once-in-a-lifetime student."

Drake's eyebrows reached high on his forehead. Hearing his high school art teacher's name was not what he expected this morning, especially when he knew he let the young woman down. She was a new teacher when he was in high school, so he suspected she was still in her twenties or early thirties. Uncomfortable, he avoided her when he saw her on the streets downtown or in the tavern with her friends. "Why was Ms. Paisley talking to you about me?"

"Well, I'm in her class this semester and I talked to her about taking more advanced classes next year. I – I want to see if I can be any good," Scarlett admitted.

"You didn't tell me you're interested in pursuing art, Scar," Halley said, grabbing onto the teenager's bicep.

Scarlett ducked her head again, "I might not be any good. I mean, Ms. Paisley says I am, but Drake is the one who's the artist. I'm hoping I might be."

"Scar, you should have told me. About all of it," Drake said. "I can't believe you went through my room without asking. And you should have told me about your art. I want to see it."

"I do too!" Halley jumped in.

"Really? Okay! I'll get my sketchbook. But only if you talk to Hal, Drake, and let her see your art," Scarlett bargained, looking serious as she stared down her brother.

"Really. And yes, that's why I'm here," Drake let a small smile play on his lips, one he saved for his youngest sister when no one else was around.

"Oh, and it's not just your room. I found your studio too. But don't worry. I didn't tell anyone," Scarlett admitted.

It was Halley's turn for her eyebrows to reach toward her hairline as Scarlett ran upstairs to her room. If she had known Scarlett was the way to get to Drake, she would have clued the girl in days ago. "Well, that was easier than I expected."

Drake shook his head. "Sorry. I can be a dick. I'm not used to talking to people. Especially not about my art." He looked worried for a moment. "Dad doesn't know. No one does. Well, except Scarlett, I guess."

"Dad may know more than you think. He knows about the custom bikes you've done. And he wants to see a business plan when I put it together," Halley said.

Drake pulled the sketchbook and a book of photos from his backpack. There was only a slight hesitation on his part. Halley held her breath, waiting for him to decide to continue. He laid both on the granite island and nodded for her to look. Scarlett joined them and set her work aside while they viewed their brother's art. They spent the next half an hour going through what Drake brought to share. Halley asked intelligent questions about his inspiration, motivation, what some of the pieces represented to him, and then got down to what he really wanted in his life. What gave him joy, made him happy, and what he would do if *anything* was an option.

Drake had not allowed himself to dream, ever. Maybe that was his problem, he realized, that he never allowed himself to dream or think big enough. No one ever asked him what he wanted to do. No one ever asked him what made him happy.

"To be fair, rarely does anyone ask those questions," Halley said. "I've come to realize they are the key to happiness and true success. Most people fall into something and then inertia doesn't allow them to leave or think broadly. Change is hard. Just ask me."

She laughed at herself, and her brother and sister laughed along with her.

It was only fair, after Drake laid his soul bare with his art he never shared, that she clue him in on the way she was thinking a business could start. "These are only ideas now. I need to put the plan together and do some competitive and market research. But my gut says this will work, Drake."

"Dad says go with your gut every time," Scarlett added sagely. She had been quiet as her sister and brother talked, completely wrapped up in the discussion and becoming more and more vested in the outcome.

"He does," Drake agreed. "This could really work, couldn't it?"

"It will," Halley asserted.

"My art can be the basis for a business," he shook his head, and his smile grew. Those facial muscles ached, rarely used.

Halley nodded.

"Okay, squirt. You've seen mine, now it's time to show yours," Drake said as he reached for her sketchpad abandoned on the counter.

"I don't know. Yours are so good. You guys are going to think my stuff is stupid," Scarlett slammed her hand down on the sketchpad before Drake could reach it.

"What did I say? Don't do that. Don't run yourself down," Halley whispered. Then she encouraged, "Show us, Scar. Show us what you love."

They viewed Scarlett's sketches in charcoal and colored pencil. She also pulled out her phone and showed some of the pictures of the paintings she did in Ms. Paisley's class.

"These are really good, Scar," Drake said, clearly impressed. He could see where she struggled and was already thinking of how to talk her through the rougher patches.

"They really are," Halley mused. "This business is going to rock!" The other two laughed and got caught up in the enthusiasm.

"I can help you with whatever you need to put the plan together," Scarlett offered.

"How are you with research?" Halley asked. "And do you have time between school and softball?"

"Expert," Scarlett promised. "Please, I'm bored stiff most of the time. I'd love to help. Then maybe you guys will let me be part of this."

"Deal," Halley and Drake replied at the same time. Halley then outlined what she needed for market research and intelligence on any competition for both the custom painting and the marketing sides of the business she hoped to pitch. In the back of her mind, she hoped she didn't end up in federal prison before they could launch the business.

Drake left the house feeling lighter than, well, ever. He was having trouble keeping the excitement from permeating his being, still afraid it could blow up in their faces. This could be what he needed to marry the obligation he lived and the passion he felt. He gave a low, two-finger wave to Maverick as he rode past his club brother on the driveway. Halley disappeared back into her room to begin putting the plan together and Scarlett sat on her oldest sister's bed with her own laptop, beginning the research. Both had kicked off their motorcycle boots, forgetting about the ride they were headed to take when they spotted Drake. Now they were quiet and focused.

Maverick checked on his brother in the stable, half expecting to find Halley out riding, only to be told Tyler hadn't seen her today. He saw Henry, her car, in the driveway, so she was still there. Thank goodness for that. He still wasn't completely sure she would stick by her promise to wait for her security detail anytime she left the house. Not that she would explicitly slip away, but that she was so used to doing everything alone, she might forget.

"What do you need help with?" Maverick asked his little brother. Tyler grinned and handed him a pitchfork.

Chapter 17

THE LIGHTS WERE OFF IN THE LUXURY CONDO WHEN Enzo arrived home. He expected that. It was late. What he didn't expect was the outline of a man sitting in front of the sliding glass door. As he reached for the gun tucked in a holster at the back of his trousers, his cousin's voice rang out in the dark. "You're late. And alone."

"Shit, Anthony. I could have shot you," Enzo huffed. "Where have you been?"

"Around. Where were you tonight? No, let me guess, that speakeasy."

"What if I was?" Enzo shrugged and poured himself a finger of whiskey in a crystal glass made for it. He joined his cousin in front of the large window overlooking the harbor, the lights of Sausalito dancing on the water, and sat in a comfortable armchair. He could see Anthony was in a suit with no tie; his preferred dress when not skulking near the company headquarters.

They sat in silence for a long while. Enzo could sense the waves of coiled tension rolling off his cousin. What he didn't know was why. Possibly the investigation by the feds was finally getting to him. Enzo hoped something would shake the man to his senses. Surely nothing he said so far had sunk in with Anthony.

They were running out of time. His father had left a voicemail earlier in the day. Enzo winced when he thought about it. His father was not a man you let go to voicemail. He would use the excuse of being in the speakeasy and his phone on silent, not that the man would care or believe it. He had a reprieve for the night because his father said he and his mother would be at a charity fundraiser all night, but he expected an update in the morning. That gave him the rest of the night to come up with a plan or come to terms with telling his father the complete truth.

"What are we going to do, Anthony? Why are you obsessed with this girl?" Enzo finally pressed. "Most important, how are you going to return the money and get out of this investigation?" Enzo was under no illusion that the investors and their own family would go quietly and take their losses.

Anthony looked long at his cousin's profile in the dark condo, the only light coming from outside at the marina and the lights reflected on the water. "She's mine, Enzo. Make no mistake. I don't let what's mine go."

"And the investigation? The money – you do have the money stashed somewhere, don't you?" Enzo was desperately searching for some form of good news, or at least not-so-bad news, to share with his father.

"Investments go bad all the time, cousin. If the investors did not have the money to lose, they should not have taken the risk. No?" Anthony spoke as though schooling a child. Enzo had to tamp down his mounting anger.

"Investments didn't go bad this time though, cousin. Did they? This is embezzlement. You've brought too many eyes that could turn to the family," Enzo tried to get through to him.

"Enough, Enzo. You're making me tired going over all this again. I told you; they will blame the dead partner. As far as they know, I could be dead too. I'll come back in a different part of the country with my own name. You'll see. This will not come to me or the family," Anthony said, sureness not masking the tiredness in his voice.

Enzo thought it must be exhausting to have to hide and try to point all those fingers in another direction. He was not as convinced as his cousin but arguing was not going to change the course the other man had set. For this, Enzo lamented all the choices his cousin made over the last year that led to this untenable situation. Anthony was making one bad move after the next. It was never going to end. And, it seemed, that if he got his way, the girl would be back in his grip, which was one more complication they did not need.

"I'm going to bed. See you in the morning," Enzo conceded.

"Good night, cousin."

The next morning, Enzo awoke to a quiet condo. His cousin's bags and clothes were gone, as was Anthony. On the counter, he found a note:

You worry too much, cousin. That will send you to an early grave. Try to loosen up. I'll take care of this on my own; you'll see. You'll all see. I have it handled. See you back home – I'm sure my uncle will call you home now – when I bring this to the inevitable conclusion for which I have been planning.

-A.

"Anthony, you fool!" Enzo yelled into the empty condo and slapped the note back on the kitchen counter. He ran his hands over his face and through his black hair, still wet from the shower. Pulling his phone from his pocket, he called Anthony's burner phone. No answer; no surprise.

Enzo shook his head and went back to his room to change into workout clothes. He would go to the gym and work off the aggression he felt. Punch a bag for an hour or two. Maybe then his mind would clear, and he would see a way out of this mess. Or maybe he would relent and tell his father, the head of the family, the complete story and let fate take over. Fate was better known by the name Leonardo Ricci where he was from – his father.

Luckily, fate did not call that day or the next two. Something else was occupying his father's mind. According to one of his friends who worked the protection detail for his father, shipments were being disrupted in New Jersey, and they had to find out if it was one of the New York families, disgruntled dock workers, or maybe a cartel or gang was pushing their luck in new territory. Enzo did not envy his father the headaches that came with running the business and the family. Sometimes he hoped that spot would not befall him one day, though it seemed inevitable, and he would step up, just as his father before him and his father's father before that.

***

In the small Michigan town, Halley continued to plot out the business plan. It had the added benefit of keeping her mind occupied and her body in the house. Scarlett turned out to be an even better researcher than she claimed, which gave Halley the foundation for the market and competitive intelligence her father would demand. Days Priscilla stayed home, Halley slipped over to her grandparents', mostly with Maverick by her side, though once in a while it was one of his men. They didn't think she saw the others following in the distance, but she did. She had a full security detail. Her grandparents tried and failed to hide their enthusiasm for her new plan.

Gramps practically shoved Maverick out of the way as he moved in to peer over Halley's shoulder. He offered, "You know, Hal, you can run that by me before you go to your dad. You can practice your pitch on me and Gram."

Halley tilted her laptop away from his prying eyes and pretended to glare at him. "Stop trying to read over my shoulder. I'll let you know when I'm ready." Grumbling, the older man moved away and sat at the other end of the kitchen table staring daggers at his granddaughter. Gram put fresh coffee in front of him and patted him on the shoulder in support.

It was all Maverick could do to hold in his laugh. Then his phone buzzed, and he excused himself to take it outside. He listened and curtly said, "Got it" before shoving the phone in the back pocket of his worn jeans and heading inside.

The look on his face told Halley something was up. She was becoming an expert in reading the man's face, even though he rarely showed what he thought. She learned to follow the slow clenching of his teeth, the tightness in his jaw, the tick at the corner of his lips when he held them in a straight line, the slight narrowing of his eyes, the searching gaze. The one she appreciated the most was the small smile he seemed to save for when he thought she wasn't looking. Something clenched low in her belly and she was cognizant enough to realize she may be developing a small crush on her bodyguard. Small? Who was she kidding? This man was everything she ever wanted and never had. No one like him had ever looked twice at her.

"What is it? Just spill it," Halley demanded.

Maverick looked first at her grandparents. Gram had stopped moving in her preparation for dinner and stood motionless, waiting to hear what he had to say. Gramps gave him a brief nod, which Maverick took as permission to talk in front of them.

"Looks like your holiday time is up. Feds are on their way," Maverick explained. He and the MC's executive committee, security team, and their outside attorney had already drilled her on all her movements before she got back to town, with whom she made contact, however brief, what she did, even where she stopped to use a restroom on the journey home. They drilled it so often that she was able to accurately recite the entire time from when the investigators arrived at the startup's office to now. Wire had searched for video footage of places she'd been to back up her story. She was as prepared as she could be for the interrogation that would come.

"No," Gram breathed out quietly.

"It'll be okay, Mrs. McCarthy. Your granddaughter is prepared. We made sure of it," Maverick assured the woman.

"What do we do? Do we go meet them somewhere? I hate that they'll ask around town about me. The rumors will fly then," Halley bemoaned.

"We're going to let them come to us," Maverick stated. "They're going to ask around regardless, Thunder. We've been over this." Her grandparents exchanged a glance at the use of the nickname.

"So, should we let them find me here or at Dad's?" Halley asked, shoulders slumped in resignation. Not even the business plan on the laptop in front of her could keep up her spirits.

Maverick looked to her grandfather, "What do you think? Fewer people here. The more people they meet the more they're going to want to talk to. On the other hand, they'll probably want to talk to everyone anyway."

"Here. I want them here, in my house," Mitchell McCarthy asserted. "Call my boy and tell him the plan." Maverick gave him one quick chin lift and placed the call to his president. The call was brief; Wire already told him the FBI was on the way. James told him their attorney was also on his way and Halley was not to speak to them unless he was present. He would be at the house soon himself.

By the time the FBI agents were buzzed through the gate by the road a couple of hours later and arrived at her grandparents' home, Halley had already pictured herself being hauled away in handcuffs and thrown in federal prison for crimes she did not commit. Gram had cut off her coffee and replaced it with decaffeinated tea. She reluctantly conceded being jittery was not going to make a good impression on the federal agents, who were probably looking for any little tells in her behavior.

After introducing themselves, the lead of the three agents at the door said, "We understand Halley McCarthy is here?"

"She is," Mitchell nodded but didn't move his large body from taking up the entire door frame.

"We need to speak with her, please," the agent said politely.

Reluctantly, Mitchell stood aside and waved his arm in a low swoop, gesturing the agents inside. He took them to the kitchen where Mary, James, Maverick, and their attorney already sat at the large kitchen table with Halley. They all stood when the agents walked in.

Following introductions, the lead agent said, "Ms. McCarthy, we would like to speak with you in private, if you don't mind."

Before Halley could answer, the lawyer cut her off. "As Ms. McCarthy's attorney, I will be present during any interviews with her. Also, everyone at this table is aware of the situation and you can speak freely in front of them."

The agent looked questioningly at Halley, clearly not expecting to face so many people. Halley nodded, "You can ask me anything. They're all family. They've already heard my embarrassing story."

Maverick wasn't sure why, but hearing Halley call him family made his insides warm pleasantly. He knew it shouldn't matter and probably wasn't personal. She grew up in the club and the club was family. It didn't stop his mind or body from taking it very personally.

Clearly not happy, the agents took seats at the table. Before they could say a word, Gram placed mugs in front of each of them, sugar and cream already in ceramic containers on the table, and poured coffee. "Would you rather have iced tea?" she asked sweetly.

"No, ma'am. Coffee is fine," the lead agent replied.

Gram then placed a large plate of cookies on the table and admonished her family to wait until the "guests" had their first choice.

The two agents looked at their lead agent, which Gram read as hesitancy. "Go on now, I'm not trying to poison you. You better try them before this lot demolishes that plate." Reluctantly they smiled and reached for a cookie each. After one bite, they were all reaching for a second. Then Gram, satisfied with her hostess duties, nodded to her family they could eat cookies now too, and sat to her husband's left, waiting for the interview to commence.

The agents began their questioning, around bites of cookies, which made them a little less intimidating in Halley's mind. She absently wondered if Gram did that on purpose. It's not as if this was the first time the feds had been in her house.

Maverick's instincts had been right. She had to explain how she came to leave her job in New York and then walk through the entire timeline of when she discovered the vendors weren't being paid, through the beginning of the company's subsequent investigation, and where she was from the moment she left the office permanently until now. Then she walked through it again, at their request. On the third time, her attorney objected, telling the agents they already got what they asked for and another run-through would be pointless.

"Ms. McCarthy, when was the last time you saw Andres Murano?"

"The day before he disappeared from the office."

"You've had no contact with him since?" the lead agent asked her to confirm.

"No."

"What about Craig Martin?" the agent continued.

"I've spoken with him once on the phone since I left." Halley figured they already knew that if they looked at her phone records.

"Have you seen or spoken with Anthony Martinelli?" one of the agents asked.

"No. Not since the day before he disappeared from the office," Halley replied.

"But he's your fiancé," one of the agents goaded her.

"*Was* my fiancé, past tense. I broke it off with him long before any investigation began," Halley replied evenly.

"Ms. McCarthy, did you start a relationship with Mr. Martinelli, the CFO, so you would have better access to company accounts? Were you the one who drained the accounts?" the female special agent pushed.

Halley frowned and her eyebrows knitted. She ignored her attorney's hurried whispering and answered tersely, "Absolutely not – to both of those questions. Anthony pursued me, *not* the other way around."

"Ms. McCarthy, do you own a gun?"

"I don't see what this has to do with the investigation of embezzlement," her attorney interjected.

"There has also been a murder. As I'm sure you've already heard, Mr. Andres Murano's body was found at the bottom of a cliff on the Pacific Ocean, double tap to his heart and his head." The female agent almost seemed to enjoy recapping the death of the partner.

"My client is not a hired assassin, nor is she a murderer. You have the timeline of her whereabouts. What was determined as the time of Mr. Murano's death?" the attorney asked.

"I'm sure you understand why we have to ask these questions, Ms. McCarthy," the lead agent took control again. He did not answer the attorney's time of death question.

"Not really. I did nothing wrong. In fact, I'm the one who first brought the possibility of wrongdoing to the attention of my CEO. And not that it matters, but no, I do not own a gun," Halley stated.

"I suppose you have no idea where the missing funds were transferred?" the more hostile female agent asked.

"I do not. Haven't your forensic accountants been able to follow the money trail?" Halley asked, pure innocence in her voice. Her father hid his smile. His daughter was holding her own. She would have made a good MC president, in another time, in another world.

"Ms. McCarthy, some of the transfers made their way through your bank account," the female agent stated, insinuating Halley already knew this.

"And, as I'm sure you already know, my *ex*-fiancé drained my bank account, so he found a way to access those accounts and could have used mine as the first stop on the money trail. Have you asked him?" Halley asked, voice hard and even. "Oh, that's right, you said you haven't found him. That might be a better use of your time than going over and over timelines with me."

"As far as we know, you could have killed Anthony Martinelli along with Andres Murano to set them up," the female agent countered. The lead agent sent her a "go carefully" look.

"You don't believe that, or I would have been arrested instead of questioned in my grandparents' kitchen." Halley was getting to the end of her patience, and that woman rubbed her the wrong way.

"That could be arranged," the woman retorted.

The lead agent laid a restraining hand on the agent's forearm and continued in a less threatening tone, "You're sure Mr. Martinelli accessed your accounts?"

Halley nodded vehemently, "Yes. The bank has the security footage for multiple transactions that show him as the one. And before you ask, no, I did not authorize him on any of my accounts. The transactions took place after I broke our engagement."

The agent, who had not spoken yet cleared his throat and asked, "You know his name is not Anthony Martinelli, correct?"

Wire had told her Anthony hadn't existed a few years prior, but no one had told her if that was a mistake or if they discovered he had a different identity. Thinking through it all in the amount of time it took someone else to say "yes" to a cup of coffee, Halley decided her best option was going with what she knew and how she genuinely felt.

Halley looked completely confused, not that it was difficult because that was a very natural reaction to everything happening. "What? What are you saying? Of course, he's Anthony Martinelli. He was at the startup before me. Craig and Andres knew him."

"No, his name is actually Anthony Barone. He's the nephew of the head of one of the Midwest crime families. There was no record of an Anthony Martinelli before five years ago. He assumed the name, probably to funnel investment money into the company from his family's less-than-legal businesses," the agent explained gently. It must have been obvious to him she was either a great actress or was really stunned by the news. It was a fact, and nothing was to be gained at this point without her knowing.

"What?" Halley asked again, her vision narrowing with black dots taking up more of the periphery. Her breathing shallowed, and she couldn't get a deep breath. She squeaked out on lungs deprived of oxygen, "Anthony's with the mob?" This could not be happening. This could not have gotten worse. Every time she thought she had a handle on the situation, a new truth ripped into her and took her equilibrium.

Maverick moved quickly beside her, placing his hand on her back, rubbing small comforting circles, whispering quietly near her ear to breathe in and out slowly with him. The attorney sat on her other side and looked concerned. Her father noticed the change in her face and breathing and leaned toward her from the head of the table at the attorney's left. Gram put a glass of ice water in front of her, but Halley didn't want anyone to see her hand shaking.

"So, this is a surprise to you," the female agent stated, voice full of barely contained snark. Halley could tell she was losing even more respect from the woman, if she had any to begin with. But now, the woman clearly didn't understand how she was duped by a man.

Once Halley regained her breath, she squeezed Maverick's thigh in thanks with her still-tingling hand. She turned to face the female agent, the black spots receding, her vision clearing. "Yes, it's a surprise. Does Craig know?" She wasn't sure she could take one more betrayal. Because Anthony's deception was another clear betrayal. Hearing Craig knew and was a party to it might be her undoing.

The mostly silent agent shook his head, "No. It appears no one knew, not only you. Your fiancé – excuse me, *ex*-fiancé – brought with him a lot of investment dollars, so they didn't dig too deeply into his background."

Maverick thought this agent might feel sorry for Halley, just maybe. He had noticed as the agent's eyes looked her up and down when they arrived in the kitchen – clearly the man at least approved of her looks. That made something in his chest compress, and he shot the man a hard glance, one any other man would read as "back off."

"Well, that's something, I guess," Halley muttered quietly.

After a few more questions, the lead agent must have felt they had gone as far as they could with the interview, rose from his seat, and placed his business card on the table. It read Senior Supervisory Special Agent, clearly the man in charge. "Thank you for speaking with us, Ms. McCarthy. Please let us know if Anthony Marti—Barone contacts you or if you think of anything else. We may have more questions over the next days and weeks."

"Of course. We'd appreciate anything you can share too," Halley responded, back to her polite, even tone. No one would ever know her confidence had wavered with a panic attack minutes before. She moved the agents toward the door with Maverick, her father, and grandfather flanking her.

"Thank you for the cookies and coffee," the lead agent said to Gram sincerely. The older woman then quietly put a bag containing more chocolate chip cookies into his hand. He gave the woman a sheepish smile.

The quieter agent lagged behind and turned to Maverick on his way out. In a low voice, he asked, "You're a former Delta Force Ranger and run the security business, right? Have you got her back?"

"I am, and I do," Maverick answered.

"Good. Good. You've got a keeper with her. Make sure she stays safe," the agent nodded and followed where the other agents were already getting in their dark SUV.

Maverick did not correct him that she wasn't his. He found he agreed with the agent's assessment. He also didn't think the man would have said that if she was truly a suspect, so that loosened part of the tightness in his chest. In his mind, the feds were as big a threat to Halley as was the unknown threat she faced. More and more he thought that unknown threat was her ex-fiancé, though he could not figure out why the man would be gunning for her – unless he was the type who did not like the woman doing the breaking up. He'd met assholes like that before and had no use for them. Or it could simply be revenge for his father's death, an eye for an eye, and make her father suffer through her, though it would make more sense for him to go directly for Irish, if that were the case. Neither scenario sat well with Maverick.

Once the SUV headed back toward the main road and was out of sight, Halley slumped against Maverick. "That was a lot," she whispered. Tears threatened to break loose from her eyes, but she swallowed hard several times to keep them from falling. She hated crying, especially in front of any of the MC members, most especially in front of these men.

"It was, Hal. But you did great," James praised his daughter and pulled her from Maverick's side. His long, muscled arms cradled her against his chest, and she closed her eyes and breathed in the smell of leather, the open road, and her father's Old Spice, all the familiar smells that made her feel safe and loved.

Maverick's phone vibrated in his back pocket. He saw it was Wire and answered it on speaker, "We're all here."

"Check first."

Maverick went back to the kitchen. He searched under the tables and chairs and all possible hiding spots between the front door and the kitchen. "Can't find anything," Maverick reported.

"I'll send one of the guys over to do a sweep to make sure," Wire responded. "All three exited the compound." They had worried one might decide to stay behind in the woods to gather more information, but these feds appeared to be on the up and up.

"Refreshing change," Mitchell growled.

"That one had a thing for our Hal," Gram said with a smirk.

"Gram! That's not true. That was a terrible interview. I almost lost it!" Halley complained.

"You didn't, Hal," the attorney threw in his more hardened and unbiased opinion. "You kept it together, said just enough, not too much, and that near meltdown solidified your innocence with them, at least the two guys. There was no way you faked that surprise. You did great, sweetheart."

Maverick pulled her back to his side, "I agree. You were awesome, Thunder. And now we look for who's leaving the notes."

"Maybe we should have told the feds about that? Will that get me in trouble for leaving it out?" Halley worried.

The attorney replied, "It's fine, Hal. Those two notes don't say enough to indicate a viable threat. They could be from anyone, including any old rivals you may have in town. The FBI wouldn't be able to do anything with it unless it escalates."

One of the security guys arrived to sweep the house as they said goodbye to the attorney. After a thorough electronic sweep, he turned to Maverick, "Good job, boss. Didn't find anything." He left as quickly as he arrived, and Gram clapped her hands from the kitchen and told them to all sit down.

Dinner would be out of the oven shortly. Scottie and Handsy came through the front door just as they gathered at the table. Those two always did have a good sense for when it was time to eat. Gram wordlessly added two more plates to the table, and her smile got bigger. The more around her table, the happier the woman was.

James sighed as he smelled the pork chops and scalloped potatoes. The smell as it cooked while the agents were there almost made his stomach growl loudly. He was surprised they didn't push their stay in order to be extended an invitation to dinner – his mother seemed to have the agents wrapped around her little finger. Even better, he had already told Priscilla not to wait for him and knew he would get a good meal out of it. His wife tried, but her skills in the kitchen were lacking in so many ways, no matter how many times his mother tried to teach her. His more cynical side thought his wife probably did it on purpose so she could get out of cooking more often than not, but that didn't make sense to him since she had to eat it, too. Her cooking wasn't always awful, but it was not good either.

"Excellent, as usual, Gram," Scottie sighed, patting his stomach. "Conor's going to be pissed he wasn't here for this. I get the feeling he's a little tired of fast food and sitting in a pickup. And I think your guy Wolf is messing with him." Scottie grinned at Maverick, showing his complete approval of messing with his little brother.

Maverick's phone rang at that moment, "Speak of the devil… Hey, Conor, you're on speaker."

"And not at the club. We're at Gram's table with Halley, but no outsiders here, so speak," Scottie added.

Conor groaned loudly, "Please tell me you're not eating her scalloped potatoes." The reason for his call was momentarily forgotten.

"I'll make you a special dinner when you get back. And bring that Wolf with you. I think he deserves a few good meals, too," Gram laughed. Maverick appreciated her attempt to help attract his former teammate to town and the club.

"Thanks, ma'am. I may take you up on that," Wolf's voice came through. That was the closest to an affirmative that Maverick had heard yet.

"See you do," Gram challenged.

"As nice as this conversation is, do you have more information for us?" James asked, his father nodding from the other end of the table.

"Something's up with Craig. He's antsier than usual. He wants the driver – one of our guys – at 6:30 a.m. Wolf and I are going to go along as his designated 'company' security. I think he's about ready to crack," Conor reported.

"We don't know if that's in a good way or bad," Wolf added.

"Did the feds find Hal?" Conor asked.

"They did. One of them appears to have a crush on your sister," James replied, chuckling. Maverick found himself pushing a snarl back in his throat. James continued, "The female agent has her own hard-on for her, but the two guys seem to have concluded she has nothing to do with this."

"Huh, wonder if it's the same female agent who's been visiting Craig?" Conor mused. Maverick gave a quick description of the female agent.

"That's her," Wolf replied. "There are a couple others parked on the street."

"Not hidden very well. Not sure if they're trying to intimidate McWussie or keep him from getting offed," Conor added.

"McWussie?" Halley asked.

"Martin – Craig. Your brother amuses himself by giving people nicknames," Wolf responded. Maverick could picture the big man's eyes rolling as he said it; it would be good to have his buddy back with him.

"Good thing you already have one, then," Conor shot back at Wolf.

"Watch it, Conman, you might want to remember what his nickname is," Handsy laughed.

"Yeah, right," Conor grumbled again. "We'll call in after we find out what's going on in the morning."

"You do that. And keep a close eye on Craig tonight. If he's getting squirrely, no idea what he might do," James admonished.

"Copy. Out here," Wolf signed off and pressed *End Call* on Conor's phone.

"What's for dessert?" Halley asked, trying to break the tension she felt fall over the table. Maverick caught Scottie's eye, and both men grinned – their girl was eating without being nagged.

Chapter 18

WOLF WAS READY TO SLAP CONOR IN THE BACK OF THE head if he complained one more time about how early it was. They waited in Craig's SUV for the man to appear. One of the other contractors was in the driver's seat with the chauffeur cap on his shaved head. The sun had not yet touched the eastern horizon of the Oakland Hills, and the air was chilly. What did Conor have to bitch about? It was Wolf who was up all night surreptitiously babysitting the skittish CEO while Conor slept in the motel room not far away.

Last night, Wolf had crept into the house unknown to make sure the man didn't do something stupid and take the whole bottle of pills the doctor had prescribed for him to sleep or the ones for anxiety. He also worried about the handgun he found hidden behind a false panel in the man's walk-in closet that was not there before. Someone at the office had to have slipped the gun to him. He understood the sentiment, given the way Andres had been found, but a gun in the hands of an amateur was never a good idea, especially for an emotionally volatile amateur. That was why he unloaded the gun, hid the ammunition, and then tucked the prescriptions in his pocket before he left the house in the early morning darkness.

Now, they waited. Soon, the door opened. Inside, the house was dark, no lights glowing in the inner recesses, and Craig appeared to look furtively from side to side into the darkness outside before moving quickly to the car. Wolf stood with the SUV backdoor open, dressed as one of the man's security detail. Once Craig slid inside, Wolf hurried to the other side and jumped in before the driver pulled down the drive.

"Good morning, Mr. Martin," Conor greeted from the front seat. Wolf shot him a withering look; jerk couldn't have been cheerier before the CEO got in the car?

"This is early for you. What gives?" Conor continued.

Wolf noticed how Craig's eyes widened as he looked around the interior of the vehicle and his hands trembled. "We swept the car; no one is listening in," Wolf assured the man. He could do nice, when he needed to. It was a simple fact that he was usually used for mean, not nice, but he could play either, when the situation called for it.

Craig seemed to relax a little at Wolf's words. "I think I need to come clean with the FBI."

That was not what they were expecting. They had speculated the man was more likely to ask them to smuggle him out of the country or to find Anthony and have him killed. They were prepared to turn down both scenarios. This one was a surprise.

When neither Conor nor Wolf spoke, Craig's nervousness propelled him forward, "I'm being watched. My home and office are bugged. My office phone, too. I need you to figure out how I can meet with the FBI without anyone knowing."

Conor glanced at Wolf and saw the man give him an almost imperceptible nod. "We can help you with that. What is it you're going to tell them?"

Craig's eyes got big as if he thought, for a split second, they might be there on behalf of Anthony and ready to kill him. Then he relaxed slightly, the drumming of his index finger on his thigh stopped, and his pupils went back to normal. "Anthony got very talkative the last couple of times he came to me. I figure he plans to kill me, too."

"Too? Did he admit to killing Andres Murano?"

Craig's Adam's apple bounced visibly in his throat as he swallowed against the dryness. "He did. He said if I talked to the feds, I would be next. But since he told me, that can only mean he's going to kill me anyway, right?"

Wolf and Conor both nodded at the logic. Craig seemed to be pleased with their agreement. Maybe his thinking was getting a little clearer. It had not been clear since Anthony had first come to the house and threatened him. "He seemed to get off on telling me how easy it was to steal the funds from the company and every step he took. I mean, what was I supposed to do? It was his job as CFO to set up the controls so something like this couldn't happen! He then threatened me with the fact not all my investors were on the up and up. He found that very funny." Craig seemed to relax more as he continued with his story; coming clean seemed to fuel his anger, which was much better than the abject helplessness they had seen so far.

"We'll contact the FBI for you and arrange a meet," Conor promised.

Craig handed him the business card for the senior agent who visited him more than once. He would rather deal with him than the female agent who seemed to despise him. He supposed they all probably despised him, but the senior agent seemed the least hostile, or at least hid it better.

"I want to save my company," Craig said softly.

"I'm not sure anything you can do at this point will bring about that outcome," Conor said honestly.

"Maybe not, but I have to try. My employees deserve better. My investors deserve better. And regardless of what's happening now, the technology is solid, as is what we have under development. That's worth a lot in itself, even if it means I have to sell rather than save the company," Craig sounded stronger, more resolved, as he spoke about the product. That was his love, the research and development. Unfortunately, he had to rely on others for the other functions of the company, such as finance, operations, and sales. He wasn't sure he could ever trust anyone ever again. Maybe Halley McCarthy. He trusted her. However, she would probably never trust him again after he told her to leave in the midst of his meltdown and the company's implosion.

"Regardless of what happens with me, please tell your sister how good I know she is at her job and that I trust her, even though I made an ass of myself the last time I saw her. What I said was unforgivable; I know that," Craig said, on a roll. "Let her know I took care of her in the end."

Wolf scowled. He had not met the woman yet, but he already felt protective toward her after everything he had learned, "What does that mean? How did you 'take care of her?'" he asked, knowing it wasn't his business, but wanting an answer anyway.

"She's still getting her paycheck. I doubt she's even checked. She sounded so devastated when I spoke with her. She's still an employee and a member of the executive committee. That means if I turn the company around and we go public or if I have to sell, either way, she's going to get a big payout – I swear my technology is that good. It will be one or the other. She will be a wealthy woman," Craig explained.

The men in the car let that sink in for a moment. Wolf couldn't help himself when he took one more swipe at the man, "You think that makes up for destroying her reputation?"

"Yeah, man. I don't know where you come from, but in our family, reputation and integrity mean a hell of a lot more than money," Conor added.

"I'm going to tell them everything. Halley will be cleared of any wrongdoing. I'm willing to make a statement for investors stating the same," Craig added.

That was something, but Wolf hoped it was not too little too late.

The SUV pulled up to the building as Craig said, "We're really early. I was thinking we might just go directly to the FBI. Maybe we can go across the street and get a latte?"

"How about I walk you up and stick with you today? Once you're settled inside your office and I've checked the area, I'll go get us a couple coffees – lattes. Conor or the head of our security division will contact the FBI. I think the agents you want may be investigating further out of town, so it may be tonight or tomorrow before we can get you to them," Wolf laid out his plan and rationale.

Conor had to keep his jaw tight, so it didn't drop open. Wolf spoke in full sentences. More than one.

The rising sun still wasn't over the Oakland Hills, but the lights were on at the coffee bistro across the street. Wolf waved to the driver to go underneath and let them out near the private elevator. They had security posted on that level and in the lobby. Those men would know if anyone new or suspicious entered the building this morning. Wolf accompanying Craig was more to keep the man from backtracking than for his security.

"Text when you have the plan," Wolf said to Conor. Conor lifted his chin in response. They waited until Wolf spoke with the floor security, and then the two men disappeared into the private elevator, and the SUV left. Conor asked the man to drive around while he called Maverick and his father.

"Talk. Prez, Red, Wire, Scottie, and Handsy are here, too," Maverick answered the phone.

Conor could tell it was on speaker. He briefly wondered if they had been up all night waiting for this call. He explained what Craig told them that morning and ended with, "Sounds like the guy he wants to talk to is there with you, unless they flew back to San Francisco last night."

"We'll make the approach," James agreed. "Wait for our call. The sooner we get this away from Hal, the better." The other men murmured in agreement.

Maverick hung up and stared at his president. "How you want to handle this, Prez?"

Before he could reply, Wire spoke up and confirmed part of what Craig said. "Damn, she *is* still being paid. She's still an employee."

"Wonder if the rest of what he said is true?" Scottie asked.

Wire jerked his head up and looked at Scottie, "Yeah, brother, I think it is. From what I've gathered, the Department of Defense was salivating over the first product. And the consumer uses are limitless. He's right, the tech is solid. Halley told us the same. What I've heard about the latest developments is that they're of the same caliber. The guy may be a shit businessman and bad at picking friends, but he's a genius at tech development."

James got back to the business at hand. "We need to track down the agents we met last night."

"I've got a tail on them," Maverick told the others. "They stayed at the travel motel just outside of town. About fifteen minutes ago, they went to the diner for breakfast. They're still there."

"Of course, you had it handled," James said, a slight smile playing on his lips. "Okay then. Maverick, you're with me. Let's go visit us some feds. Maybe they'll buy breakfast," James gave a full smile this time. All headed out the door and walked down the street toward the diner. They didn't notice the wary looks from people on the main drag, six large, gruff men in faded jeans, heavy boots, and leather cuts made a frightening grouping in the morning. While the other four got their own table, James and Maverick approached the booth at which the FBI agents sat, voices low, talking among themselves.

"Can we help you?" the woman looked up and asked, the annoyance clear in her voice.

James shook his head at her attitude and turned his attention to the senior agent, "I think I have something you may want."

"Why would you help us?" the woman asked suspiciously. She looked them up and down like they might smell bad.

"Sweetheart, with that attitude, no one is ever going to want to help you," James sighed. He then turned back to the senior man, who scooted over and motioned for James to sit. Maverick grabbed a chair and turned it to the end of the booth, straddling it backward, leaning over the backrest.

"Craig Martin wants a meet," James started. He was immediately interrupted by the woman.

"What did you do? Did you threaten the man? Your goons coerce him?"

The senior agent looked like he wanted to tell her to go stand in the corner but held his tongue.

"Goons? Sweetheart, those *goons*, as you call them, are my son and former Delta Force operators who have been the only men keeping that CEO alive. We've been providing security for him so no one takes him out like happened to his best friend." James was quickly losing patience and any semblance of respect for the woman.

"Yeah, you might –" the woman started, and the other agent cut her off.

"Stop, Caitlin, just stop," the senior agent's patience was as frayed as James'. "Go ahead, Mr. McCarthy."

The younger, male agent, who seemed to like Hal, sat next to the woman. A slight upturn at the corners of his mouth told Maverick the man was not of the same mind as his partner.

"As I was saying, Craig Martin told our men this morning as they drove him to work that he wants to meet with you – he specifically said you, Senior Supervisory Special Agent Bishop," James made sure to use the man's full title. "It will be tricky."

"Why? We can scoop him up right now with one call," the woman inserted again, thumbs over her phone ready to text.

Maverick jumped in, "I wouldn't do that. Someone bugged his house and office. Can't say anything without it being heard. My guess is, if they're not your bugs, and unless the government switched the kind you use in the last six months, they aren't, anything you've said to him so far has been overheard, and they know your play. You pick him up at the office, a sniper can take him out before you get him in a vehicle. Our guys have picked up a tail a few times. My guy said he recognized a couple of them – guns for hire. We have to assume they will be there when we try to hand him off to you." He and James watched as the realization dawned on the agents' faces.

James set his jaw and continued, "So, we need to figure out the plan, and then we can get it to Martin through our guys. He trusts them. But he will only talk to you, Bishop. He particularly doesn't trust Caitlin here; thinks she may be consorting with the enemy or some horseshit like that." Caitlin sputtered but stopped with one look from Bishop.

The younger man, Special Agent Ethan Drury, asked, "Any idea what he has to tell us?"

"We do. And you'll want to hear it. We were actually pretty shocked when he blurted it all out this morning. But our men tell us it's the most clarity he's had since they started protecting him,"

James said. "I'd suggest we get him in protective custody sooner rather than later. He's worried he'll end up like Andres. He also wants to try to get his company back on track, so be prepared for that."

Maverick couldn't resist adding an extra dig to see how they would respond, "If you want us to provide the protective custody, we can take him off grid and keep him safe while he talks with you."

"I'm sure we can handle it just fine," Caitlin piped up once again. "What's the chance this is all you? Maybe you killed Andres. Maybe you're trying to cover up your daughter's crimes. Isn't that what an MC does? Mayhem. Murder. Illegal business."

"You really have bad instincts for a cop, don't you? If you got that chip off your shoulder, maybe you could get some perspective and do your job," Maverick said, shaking his head and not letting her get under his skin. He was sure that's what she was trying to do. "This club hasn't been one-percenters since way before I came on board – decades. Do your research. You don't want our help, just say the word."

James remained silent. Either the feds wanted to talk with Craig Martin, or they didn't. They did. He knew that. So, he waited.

"What's in this for you?" Bishop finally asked evenly.

"Gets my daughter out of the crosshairs faster. Martin's information should make that happen. Also, the sooner that pain-in-the-ass whiner is not our responsibility, the better. I do not understand how Halley worked with him the last three years. If everyone in the company is like him, I don't know how she stayed sane," James snorted, shaking his head.

No one spoke for a moment. Even smart-mouthed Special Agent Caitlin Cunningham had nothing to say. The agents stared at their now cold breakfast, and the MC brothers looked at one another. Neither side trusted the other, but the principle of "the enemy of my enemy is my friend" seemed to be playing out in this instance.

"Before we discuss the handoff, do you know if the Ricci family is involved or if Anthony was acting alone?" James asked. "It's pretty obvious Anthony is behind all of this, even if you don't have all the evidence to prove it yet."

Bishop glanced at the other two special agents. Ethan Drury seemed to encourage him, while Caitlin Cunningham looked as stubborn and defiant as ever. He appeared to come to a decision when he met James' eyes, moved him out of the booth, and jerked his head toward the door.

Maverick started to stand but James placed a hand on his shoulder and shook his head for him to stay. James followed the senior supervisory special agent outside.

"It seems that the Ricci's were funneling both clean and dirty money into the startup as investors, through several shell corporations and individuals. I don't think they sanctioned Anthony to embezzle. That would be plain stupid. I'm not saying all those guys are brilliant, but Leonardo Ricci is nothing if not intelligent and cunning. He's a bit like you, Irish. You both took your organizations in new directions, though your businesses went down the straight and narrow, and he stays in the gray. No, I can't believe he sanctioned that or the murder. Not that we know Anthony was involved in murder," Carl Bishop explained.

"But we're pretty sure he was, right? Murano may have been the only one who knew exactly what was going on, based on recovered emails," James said.

"I won't ask how you know what's in the emails between the two, but since I know Wire's work, I can guess," Bishop said. "I guess you've been a couple steps ahead of us on this."

"We work with fewer rules than you. And maybe only one step," James conceded. "We both want the same thing. Whoever is to blame to pay. That seems to Anthony Barone."

"Your daughter's ex-fiancé."

"I'd rather forget that fact," James winced.

"Yeah, I would too if I were you. But it looks like she was his mark. I don't know why he targeted her originally, probably to make her a fall guy in the scam, but the guy is now obsessed with her, from what people at the company told us. Her breaking the engagement did not go over well with him. She needs to watch her back until we have this under control," Bishop spoke directly, not mincing words, not withholding information. He would have been more circumspect in front of his agents. His instincts told him he and this hardened MC president were on the same side for once and needed one another's help.

"So, about this plan. I was thinking we use more than one SUV that looks the same and leave at the same time. Dress one of my guys who's about his size and coloring in Martin's clothes and keep a security detail with him. Put them in Martin's actual SUV in case the hired guns copped the license plates. They should follow that one, if they are. We'd put Martín in one of my guy's clothes and put him in a separate but look-a-like SUV. Then we have one or two others leave around the same time. We'll take a roundabout way through the city to make sure no tail. Then we head up to Sonoma County and meet at the cabins on that remote road that leads to the cliff where Murano was found. You can either get his story there or transfer to a chopper and take him somewhere else. That's remote enough no one would hear or see it." James laid out the potential plan in a logical fashion.

"Or we could go to the office and pick him up and do our own evasive maneuvers," Bishop countered. "We'd bring him out in cuffs, and they might think we're arresting him."

"You could, but there's more chance of gunfire and your guys getting shot or civilians caught in the crossfire," James argued.

Bishop pretended to think hard about it. He had already decided James' plan was the best but had to counter anyway. "Okay, your plan works."

"I know it will," James said.

The two re-entered the diner and joined their respective people. Maverick rose slowly and joined James at the table with their MC brothers.

"What was that?" Caitlin demanded.

"That, Special Agent Cunningham, was how to form a plan and work with who you need to in order to get the job done. Maverick's right; that chip on your shoulder is getting in the way. You might want to get rid of it." Bishop dug into his cold eggs and bacon. He had wanted to say that to her for a long time, but until recently, it hadn't hindered their investigations. She was young enough that she would either learn or move on.

Caitlin stared at him like he lost his mind while Drury tried to hide his smirk. Bishop gestured toward their plates, "Eat up. We have a plane to catch."

Chapter 19

BISHOP ASSUMED THERE WAS MORE TO THE PLAN, but he did not need to know. He only needed to know where to do the handoff and make the decision on whether they would stay at the remote cabin or get Craig Martin out of the state altogether. Getting him back to DC to either headquarters or one of their safe houses might be the more prudent move.

One of the things James failed to mention was that Wire would take over the startup's video security system and put part of it on a loop while the switch was made. That included the changing of clothes in the private elevator. Martin should love that.

While James, Maverick, and the others finished their breakfast, the diner door opened, and Halley rushed inside. A big smile was on her face when she saw her friend Sarah in a booth at the side. Not twenty seconds later, Tyler rushed through the door, franticly looking for Halley.

Maverick stood quickly. He was at his brother's side in an instant and asked in a hard voice, "What are you doing here?"

"I saw her car take off down the driveway, and I knew none of you were with her, so I dropped everything, jumped on my ride, and took off after her. Mav, she scared me half to death. Why'd she leave without calling you?" Tyler looked like he wanted to be sick.

"Why didn't you call me or one of the security team?" Maverick pushed.

"What didn't you hear about her tearing off down the driveway? I didn't have time, brother. I barely caught up to her. She drives fast!" Tyler was out of breath.

"You did the right thing, Ty. Thanks for gettin' on it," Maverick told his brother and squeezed his shoulder. He then turned on his heel and shoved Halley over as he pushed into her booth. "Thunder, what happened to your promise about sticking with your security detail?"

"I'm sorry. I didn't think. I got off the phone with Sarah, and she was already here, so I ran out of the house. I hate being late. I didn't think about it until I saw Tyler chasing after me. I figured I was okay with him close," Halley tried the innocent look.

"You do not leave here without me. Understand? Things are getting real," Maverick didn't smile, didn't touch her arm reassuringly, just slid out of the booth and gave her his back. Yeah. He was angry.

Sarah's eyes narrowed, and she leaned in and whispered, "What was that about? I swear, Hal, things are weird around here, and you seem to be in the middle of it. Yesterday those FBI agents in that booth over there were asking around. Tell me what's happening and why you're so upset. Why is Mr. Broody all mad?"

It was decision time. She'd already told Sarah and Renee some of what had been happening in her life. She no longer wanted to keep the secrets. She would risk looking like a fool to tell her childhood best friend and hope talking would make her feel better. Keeping it bottled up inside certainly wasn't helping.

With a deep breath and voice barely above a whisper, glad for the crowded diner and the loud volume that came with it, she gave her friend the overview, including the notes left on her car. Sarah's eyes kept getting bigger and bigger. As Halley ran out of steam, her friend narrowed her wide eyes and looked fierce, ready to stand by Halley's side, defend her friend, and battle the criminals. Halley felt like she needed to go back to bed. The glower from Special Agent Cunningham was not helping.

Halley noticed the secretive chin lift between her father and the senior agent as the FBI contingent left the diner and headed out of town. What was that about? Maverick was right; something was happening, and she was in the dark. Tyler kept glancing at her like she ran over his kitten. She felt badly about that. Tyler was a good kid, and he would make a good brother once his time as a prospect was over.

Head dropped into her hands, Halley groaned, "This just needs to be over! I want my life back."

Testily, Sarah asked, "What life is that, Hal? Back on the West Coast? New York? Maybe a new city?"

Halley peeked between her fingers and stared at her friend. "No, Sarah. That's not what I meant. I meant without needing a bodyguard, without wondering if someone is going to shoot me for no damn good reason. I have a new plan, a business plan. But I'd like to make it work without all this hanging over me. And for your information, I plan to do it here."

Sarah looked shocked, but a slow grin spread. "Here? You're planning on staying home?"

"That's the idea. Start a business here. Where I have a family. Support. People who love me. I grew up as a big fish in a small pond. Over the years, I've been a small fish in a big pond. I've been a semi-big fish in a big pond. But you know what I realize? The size of the pond doesn't matter. As long as I'm happy and with people I love, doing something I'm passionate about. I need to be in control of my destiny, in control of my success. I can't get that in a corporation, no matter what they promise. There's always a ceiling, and I hit it every time. On my own, my own business, I create my own path," Halley tried out her explanation, hoping it made sense to more than just her. Judging by Sarah's knowing look, it made sense to one of the people about whom she cared most.

Their food came, and Halley ate, not noticing her brother's and Maverick's watchful stares. Both men relaxed when she ate most of what was on her plate. When she stood up with Sarah, Maverick was immediately at her side. The others in the club were close behind. Tyler's bike was parked next to her car, but she didn't see her father's or any of the other MC rides in the lot. They must have parked by the security office. They accompanied her and Sarah en masse to the lot, and that's when she realized Sarah had no reason to be in the lot either. Her friend could walk to her office.

"I realize I messed up heading to town alone, but isn't this a bit much? I mean, Sarah, what are you going to do if someone attacks me? Poke him in the eye with your high heel? I don't think I need anyone other than Maverick and Tyler to walk me to my car. Do I?" She placed a hand on her jean-clad hip and stared at her father.

Before James could answer, Tyler yelled out an expletive. He turned to the others from beside his bike and pointed downward, "Guys, there's a knife sticking out of the sidewall of my front tire."

"Halley, did you leave something in the driver's seat?" Scottie looked through the side window and tried her locked front driver's side door.

Halley got close enough with the key fob that the door opened. On the seat were a dozen black roses. No note. Halley stared at the roses. There was no doubt about it; that was creepy.

"Get her to the security office," James ordered.

"I'll walk Sarah to her office," Handsy offered. Sarah was rattled enough by what she saw between the black roses and the knife that she went with him without argument.

Maverick noticed Kathy at the back door of the diner, taking out the trash. She had a smirk on her face as she watched the group walk away from the vehicles. When she saw Maverick staring at her, she quickly moved inside.

"How did someone get in my car?" Halley demanded. "The door was locked."

"Did anyone else have the spare key? Do you have the spare key at the house?" Maverick asked. Anthony could have ordered a replica at any time. He had the money, and he had been her fiancé. That was a logical conclusion. Maverick was more worried about the less logical answer, which meant someone much closer, someone in her family, was messing with her or colluding with Anthony. Someone like a jealous sister or a stepmother. Maverick would keep those thoughts to himself until he could investigate.

"No one. The spare is in a jewelry box in my room at Dad's house," Halley said decisively.

While they talked, Wire ran a handheld tester over the car, looking for bugs or trackers. He found a tracker under the trunk and stepped on it with his heavy boot. No bugs in the car. At least that was one less violation of her space Halley had to think about.

James herded the group to the security offices just down the main street. Scottie called the garage to have prospects pick up Tyler's motorcycle and take Halley's car back to the club.

Once sitting in Maverick's office, they called Conor and gave him the plan. Halley sat silent and watchful through the entire discussion. Wire waited to hear from the guys who were tasked with securing the cabin, and once that was confirmed, he texted the exact coordinates to Bishop, Conor, and Wolf. The handoff would not be until the next day. The security team would leave work early, Craig feigning illness – though Wolf thought he wouldn't have to pretend. The man looked like he might hurl or pass out at any moment all the time.

After all the logistics were with everyone who needed them, Halley waited for someone to fill her in on the new part of the story. To say she was shocked Craig was willing to finally step forward and do the right thing was an understatement. She was convinced the man did not have a backbone. He was a brilliant engineer, but he had shown no bent toward courage when everything imploded around him. Maybe he was staying true to form. He probably saw turning himself into the FBI as the more likely probability he would survive. She was back to judging him a coward. Once again, she shocked herself when she realized the bravest and most selfless people she knew were in this town and in this room. They would take a bullet for her; she had no doubt. That thought made her cringe. She did not want to invite that horrific possibility.

Halley realized more and more what she needed in her life and the type of people with whom she wished to surround herself.

Her thoughts were interrupted when Maverick read a text from Wolf. "Craig wants to talk to Halley on the drive home from work today."

"Not unless we're with her," James ordered.

"Agreed," Maverick replied and typed a response.

Seeing no sense in arguing, Halley sat mute. She wondered what the man could possibly say now and if she would be able to be civil. She was over this whole situation, and when Halley was done, that was it; she was done – with the people, with the work, with the details. It angered her that she was unable to completely walk away and that someone was trying to scare her. She settled back on the leather couch in Maverick's office and waited.

Maverick had Tyler call around to all the florists within a fifty-mile radius to see if any had sold a dozen black roses recently. There were a surprising number of mom-and-pop types of florists and greenhouses. After hours of fruitless calls, when Tyler thought the task was a waste of time, he came upon one in a town about 45 minutes south who sold that very thing that morning. The order had come in a couple days before; the buyer wanted to make sure they very specifically had a dozen long-stemmed black roses. They'd had to special order them from their distributor.

The woman had been happy to chat with Tyler, "Around Halloween and Valentine's Day, we always get a handful of orders from people hosting Halloween parties or those goth kids who want to impress their partners. I thought it was odd to get that order at this time of year, but I guess there's no accounting for taste."

"No, ma'am, I guess there isn't. Could you tell me who ordered the flowers? Did they pay by credit card or leave a name?"

"No, it was cash on pick up. No name. I'm sorry."

"Can you describe the man who picked them up?"

"It wasn't the man who called. It was some grungy teenager in a too-big black hoodie and a nose ring, with dirty, ripped black jeans and those skater shoes. He said he was the delivery service."

"Do you have security cameras in and outside your store?"

"I do. Why, is there a problem?"

"No, ma'am. My brother and his girlfriend thought it was strange that someone anonymous had given her such a strange bouquet. They hoped to track down whoever it was," Tyler flinched when Maverick punched him in the shoulder.

"Oh, I'm sorry to hear that. Well, if you want to take a look at the footage, I keep it stored on the internet," the woman sounded sorry she couldn't be more help. She also sounded like she didn't often have people talk to her.

"I'll tell my brother. Thanks for that. You have a good evening, ma'am."

"Stop by anytime. I love your Texas accent. My brother up and moved to Texas. I'd recognize that drawl anywhere."

Tyler flushed, "Yes, ma'am. Thank you." He hung up before she could continue the conversation.

"Got it," Wire waved from his seat behind Maverick's desk. "Our guys installed the security cameras there. Here's the footage. She gave a good description."

"How'd you know which shop I was talking to?" Tyler asked.

Wire rolled his eyes, the long-suffering genius he was having to suffer Troglodytes. "I pulled up your phone and saw the number and cross-referenced it with a street address and business name." He made it sound so simple.

"I've got a few reference points from banks and other commercial security cameras down the street. Oh, and there's even a trial police photo cam at the one stoplight in town." Everyone crowded behind his chair to look at the larger screens. Wire insisted Maverick keep them on his desk. Maverick preferred to use his laptop alone.

"See here? The kid's approaching a dark SUV with tinted windows." They watched as the driver's side window lowered, and a large man with a bald head and a crooked scar running from the top of his skull to the top of his ear, dressed in a black jacket and aviator shades, reached out and set the roses in the passenger seat. He then peeled off a couple of bills and handed them to the teenager, who skated off, probably worried the guy would try to get his money back or, worse, kill him for his trouble.

"That's not Anthony," Red stated the obvious.

"No, but I know that guy. He's a gun for hire. Got blown up and discharged in Iraq. He now goes to the highest bidder. He hasn't been quite right in the head," Maverick announced. Looking at the scar, no one doubted Maverick's assessment.

"He's also one of the guys in the picture from Halley's storage unit. So, this is definitely Anthony behind terrorizing Halley," Scottie stated what everyone was thinking.

"Hey, I'm not terrorized. I'm angry," Halley griped. She memorized the man's face, not that it was hard. But if he wore a hat it might be more difficult, so she pictured him in a hat and stored that in her memory bank.

The men ignored her semantics and continued their assessment. James said, "Still doesn't tell us if Anthony is here or if he's directing the muscle to carry out his orders."

"No, but he's disappeared from San Francisco, so it's a good bet he's come here to carry out whatever his sick plan is, avenging his daddy, or whatever the fuck he thinks he's doing," Red muttered.

Wire discovered Anthony's cousin Lorenzo Ricci, the don's first-born son, was in San Francisco, probably trying to temper his cousin and keep an eye on him for the family. Maverick sent in a two-man team to scour the condo when Enzo was out and see if there was any sign of Anthony. It would have made sense for Anthony to hide in plain sight with his cousin since, until the last few days, no one even knew Anthony was his cousin. The team found their answer easily with the note Anthony left Enzo still on the kitchen counter. The "A" signed on the note had to be Anthony. The problem was he was already gone.

"Wait, what did you say? Who is Anthony's father? What aren't you telling me?" Halley asked.

James closed his eyes, looking for inner strength. Red shot him an apologetic look, but the damage was done. "Not the time, Hal. We'll talk about it later."

"Didn't Anthony ever tell you about his family?" Tyler asked an innocent question that would not have been innocent coming from any of the others. He thought it was strange that two people who were engaged wouldn't know a lot about one another's families and have met them.

"No. We didn't talk about family. We didn't talk about the past. And yes, I realize now that was really weird and should have set off all sorts of warning bells. But there were enough other ones to keep me busy. Plus, we were all about work, trying to grow the startup and get it ready to go public." Halley's excuses sounded hollow even to her own ears, but it was the truth.

Maverick sent two guys to track down the kid. He would be in the skate park or selling pills or powder on a corner of the small town southeast of them. The kid had the look, and his instincts told him the kid wouldn't be too hard to find, especially if they showed his picture around town. They traced the plates on the SUV only to discover they were stolen in Illinois, so that was a dead end.

Suddenly, Halley was exhausted. Breakfast felt like it was hours ago. *Oh yes, because it was hours ago*. She slumped back on the couch and asked, "Can I go to Gram's now?" She did not want to go to her room, not ready to be alone, or face the annoyed glares that came from Priscilla and Tiffany, if they were at the house.

All the men quieted and looked at her.

"I ordered sandwiches from the deli," Scottie said. "As soon as we all eat, someone will escort you." Halley was going to protest, but then her stomach growled.

***

Tiffany attended the away high school baseball game, several hours from her hometown, purportedly to watch her boyfriend and Danny play. Her brother would go to college in the fall on a baseball scholarship and had Major League Baseball scouts showing up regularly, which seemed to add to the large crowd Danny drew these days. Scarlett was on an adjacent field with the varsity softball team. That her sister took sports so seriously made her wonder how they were possibly related.

Tiffany drove herself rather than ride the bus with the other high school spectators. Hands rubbing down her thighs covered in her tightest, cutest, cropped pants, top covered in a light pink spring sweater with a deep V showing cleavage, she looked around the spectators and the parking lot. She secretly hoped her half-sister's ex-fiancé would show up. She told him where she'd be.

There was quite a crowd, so no one would notice her talking to a stranger. The man was dead handsome and had harmlessly flirted with her over the last couple of days. Yes, he said he wanted to keep his presence a secret because he had gotten in a major fight with Halley in San Francisco before she left and was here to make it up to her and win her back. But did he really want Halley? Why? Halley wasn't acting all heartbroken, in her opinion. And Tiffany knew heartbreak; she had broken up with enough boys that she was positive she was an expert on the broken heart – theirs if not her own.

Just like that, thinking about him, Anthony walked toward her. He didn't have on jeans or sweatpants, like everyone else at the game. He wore loafers, dark trousers with a starched pleat, and a dark sweater, cashmere, that stretched across his broad shoulders and lean frame. Tiffany, like her mother, knew fashion. He oozed confidence and charm. Sure, most of the MC guys had confidence, but maybe not the charm, at least not Anthony's charm, and certainly not his sophistication. His smile alone made butterflies attack the inside of her stomach. As he approached, he acted as if she were the only one he saw. His gaze didn't waver, and his smile only got bigger as he approached her.

"Hello, Bella. This is quite the out-of-the-way place for a baseball game, no?" Anthony smiled, using his pet name for her, and kissed her on both cheeks, European style. It made her feel older, more worldly. Why would her sister ever break up with this man? He was perfect.

"It is. But small towns. We have to go a long way to play teams in our league. I suppose you don't know anything about small towns. You've probably lived in cities your whole life," Tiffany said, pulling her glossed lips into her mouth and clamping down with her teeth.

"I have, Bella, other than a couple of years when I was a young child, and my mother and I lived with relatives in southern Italy. That was a small town. But I was a little boy, so it didn't matter so much," Anthony shrugged.

Tiffany loved that he called her Bella – beautiful. That such a sophisticated man even noticed her boosted her confidence. She tossed her long blonde hair over her shoulder and smiled up at him. He was tall. Not as tall as her father or brothers, but close. Tall was nice.

The crowd erupted with cheers and whistles. Tiffany turned to watch her brother round the bases, one arm up waving to the gathered spectators. Another homerun for Danny. At least the moment gave her a reprieve before she had to think of something to say to the handsome man with the expensively cut black hair. They both watched the game.

Anthony's sharp eyes wandered over the crowd. He thought he might see his fiancée here. What better place to get her away from the town and danger than at a teenage baseball game? But he should have realized after he had one of his men lay the flowers in her front seat that those bikers would lock her down. It wouldn't be enough in the end, but he did like to play with his prey. Just like his mother told him his father did.

That familiar anger rose in his chest when he thought about the man he only remembered through broken visions in his memories, pictures, and his mother's stories. To say the woman was bitter was an understatement. She never had believed what her father told her about why her husband had to die. She had practically raised her dead husband to saint status and exaggerated her memories, saying she only knew the sweet man who told her she was beautiful and held her close, playing on the floor with their little boy, promising he was going to earn her father's favor and his rightful place in the family.

Anthony would never forget his mother's tears when his grandfather and uncle came to the door along with their men, breaking down and beating against her father's chest as she slowly slid to the floor. It was less than a week later – his mother little more than a crying, empty shadow of herself – that they were packed with those purple suitcases that his mother had loved and had made his father laugh as he indulged her, and were driven to a private airstrip and hustled onto the private jet.

When he woke up, they were in Italy at the home of his grandfather's cousin. They spent the next two years with their relatives in Italy and did not return to their Chicago home until he was nine. His mother grew stronger in that time and the seeds of vengeance were sowed deep within Anthony. It was always meant to be this way. His mother was the daughter of the head of the family, and she deemed it so. It was his destiny.

The familiar blackness was coming over him. The last time he felt it rise was when he saw those men in Enzo's favorite speakeasy looking his fiancé up and down, appreciating her curves and the body no one should ever see but him. She was his. Even when she foolishly tried to give his ring back and told him never to come to her house again, the blackness had stayed away because he knew it wasn't over; she did not get to break up with him. The blackness was saved for fulfilling the promises he made to his mother as a little boy and, as he discovered with Halley, claiming what was his.

"Sorry, our time was so short, Bella. I must be going. I must meet my associates. You know how it is; business never ends," Anthony directed his gaze to the teenager standing too close to him, trying so hard to look like a woman.

Yes, she was beautiful, but in a one-night kind of way. She would never hold his interest longer than that. Even he would never go there with someone underage, there were too many potential risks. Though, like this one, so many caught his eye and practically threw themselves at him. Two more years, and she would be fair game. He would wait. That would be a good way to punish Halley – with her sister. Maybe his business with this family would not be over so soon. They took so much from him; his entire life was altered. His mother was never the same.

"So soon?" she looked up at him beneath her long blonde eyelashes coated with multiple layers of black mascara, knowing the alluring look worked with her boyfriend – well, ex-boyfriend. She dumped him two nights ago. Maybe that's why he wasn't playing so well today. Served him right for flirting with that freshman. She'd make him squirm a few more days before taking him back. Or maybe she would have an older, more sophisticated man by then.

"Remember to keep this between us, Bella. You wouldn't want to spoil the surprise," he said smoothly as he brushed his lips lightly over her cheek. She quickly lost sight of him as he disappeared into the crowd and made his way toward the back of the parking area.

"Who was that?" her friend demanded in an exaggerated tone and sidled up to her, bouncing her hip against Tiffany's.

"Wish I knew," Tiffany said wistfully as she lied to her friend.

"Me too. But he's kind of old. Wonder if he has a younger brother?" the friend laughed.

Belatedly, Tiffany realized he hadn't returned her sister's spare key fob. That could be a problem. Then again, no one would ever suspect her of taking it. It wasn't as if she paid any attention to the sister who left when Tiffany was one year old and she had only seen a handful of times since.

From inside the dark SUV, Anthony looked at his hired help and said, "Soon. Then we can get out of this god-forsaken place."

The driver, beanie pulled low over his scarred bald head, pulled away, looking in the side view and rearview mirrors to see if anyone paid them too much attention or attempted to follow. Nothing. He relaxed and let the pumped-up peacock next to him talk without hearing what he was saying. So far, the man's money was good. If things got too hot, he was out. He saw those bikers around the town and recognized one or two from his time in the military. His client may think they were small-town losers, but he knew better. He knew their capabilities. The man was a fool. But, as he reminded himself, the money was good. For now, that was enough.

***

Wolf watched through the interior window as Craig paced in his office for more than an hour. The man then stepped purposefully out the door and waved for Wolf to follow him. They ended up in the general counsel's office. The attorney looked harried, clothes expensive and usually immaculate were rumpled. His neat, short hair was sticking up from running his hand through it.

He had been Craig's undergraduate roommate at Stanford, and this job had been fun when they were in the building phase of the startup. Now, the investigation, requests from opposition attorneys, and the feds took up most of his time. Like Craig, he was blindsided and scrambling. Craig raised a finger to his lips, wrote a lengthy note on a legal pad, and showed it to both the attorney and Wolf.

The general counsel raised an eyebrow, but Craig's look was adamant, and the man wrote back in the affirmative. He would have the paperwork ready by noon the next day.

They left the office early. Craig said he had nothing else to do for the day. In the SUV on the way home, Wolf first made Craig call his outside counsel. He was less worried about the outcome for Craig than about the FBI being held to whatever deal was struck and Halley being exonerated.

Craig ensured the attorney would be ready to be picked up by their security team the next day and taken to a secret location to represent Craig in an interview with the FBI. Later tomorrow would be early enough to brief the woman on the details. While they trusted she would keep the information confidential – the woman had been pushing Craig to make a deal from the beginning – money could buy a lot of disloyalty, as could coercion by hired guns, so they needed to keep things to as few people as possible until the last minute.

"Now, may we call Halley, please?" Craig asked politely. Since he made his decision, the man had become more steady, less whiny.

Conor pressed the number for Maverick. No one thought it was secure to use Halley's or Craig's phones any longer. Craig took the phone, pressed it to his ear, and asked for Halley when a man answered. Conor wasn't bothered; he and Wolf both knew the phone would be on speaker on the other end.

"Halley? It's me. Craig. I just wanted to tell you how terribly sorry I am for this whole mess. I didn't have anything to do with it, but I still feel guilty bringing you all the way to San Francisco for, well, for this. I'm also ashamed of the way I acted when everything happened. I know you had nothing to do with it and were the only one trying to raise red flags. I'm going to tell the FBI everything I know and everything Anthony said to me since he disappeared. I'm going to tell them you had absolutely nothing to do with it. I'm so sorry, Halley. You will probably never forgive me, but I wanted you to know I'm trying to make it right."

Craig ran out of breath during the monologue, and Halley could finally get in what she wanted to say. "Thank you for doing the right thing. I know it's not easy. We had a lot of fun and a good run for a while there. Your technology is solid. Please know that." What she didn't say was that his business acumen was another story.

"Halley, please listen to me. I know your father and others are probably listening to this. You are *not* safe. Anthony has gone off the deep end. He was ranting to me the last time I saw him, not only about me not telling the FBI anything important but about you dumping him and how you would be his again. If he couldn't have you, no one would. I … I know he's the one who killed Andres. He said as much, standing in my house when he threatened the same would happen to me. He has some very big, soulless-looking men working for him. They'll do anything for money," Craig's voice pleaded with her to take heed. What he did not tell her was that he urinated himself when the big mercenaries threatened him. That was too embarrassing to divulge, though Anthony had laughed about it over and over.

"Anthony hasn't been in contact in a few days. He's gone dark. But I've seen some of his hired men prowling around. I'm afraid he may be looking for you. Promise me you'll take care. And one more thing – we're almost to my house – no matter what the outcome is, I'm ensuring you'll be all right in all of this. I'm taking care of you. Like I should have done from the beginning. Bye, Halley. You're the best," Craig hung up before she could ask questions or say anything else.

"That was kind of odd," Halley said to the men in Maverick's office. "It's almost like he was saying goodbye. Like he's going to kill himself or doesn't think he'll make it. Did it sound like that to you guys?" She looked at each of the men to see if they seemed as rattled as it made her.

"Yeah, it was strange; I agree," Scottie admitted.

Maverick texted Wolf what they were all feeling. Wolf was already on it and told Maverick he agreed with their assessment. While listening to Craig's side of the conversation, Wolf had decided he would have to sneak into the man's house again tonight and keep a close watch. He had buddies in the service, as well as some when they got out, who suddenly were at peace with everything when their lives had been torment and chaos before – they made a decision and not long after either attempted or succeeded in death by suicide.

It was eerie, and Wolf couldn't get the same feeling out of the hollow of his stomach as he listened to Craig. He believed the man would try to make things right with the FBI and that his attorney would be there to cut him a deal for coming forward, even though Craig had to be convinced to take the attorney with him. But he also believed the man did not intend to make it long after that interview, whether by his own hand or by Anthony's hired guns. What Craig required from the company's general counsel earlier that day made his intuition flare even stronger. Good thing Wolf learned long ago how to survive for days on little to no sleep. He would sleep when this nightmare was over.

At the mansion, Conor and Wolf cleared the house, as good bodyguards would, before they let Craig set foot inside. They agreed to meet at the normal time the next morning, not before the sun rose, which made Conor sigh with relief.

With Conor back at their motel, Wolf would wait until the sun set and the night watch from their team was in place before he made his way through the shadows and slipped into Craig's house. He knew the gun was empty of ammunition, and the pill bottles were still in his pocket, but there were more ways than those to do the job, if someone was so inclined. He was also mindful that the few people they did talk with today, such as outside counsel, could have turned on them. What better time for the hired guns to show up than in the shadow of the night? He would be prepared if they did.

Chapter 20

IT WAS EARLY EVENING BY THE TIME MAVERICK AND James walked into the house with Halley after the call with Craig. She opened the heavy wooden door to her bedroom and used the natural light streaming through the window to look around the room. She wanted to go directly to her grandparents' house, but the men insisted they stop here first.

"It's there, on the dresser," she spotted the small jewelry box that had belonged to her mother. She kept important things that she didn't often use in it, so she rarely opened the box, but it had been one of the first things she packed to put in Henry for the trip across the country.

Her father hesitated as he stared at the intricate design on the solid metal lid. He bought this for Evie on the trip they took to Ireland, one of the few trips they took in their short adult life together.

Halley reached around him and tilted the top open. She moved things, thinking her spare key fob might have gotten lodged under the other things. Her father picked up a picture of her, her mother, and him at the lake. His breath caught in his throat. Halley shifted the matching necklace and earrings that belonged to her mother and that she only wore on special occasions. He saw her lift the small card he wrote to her when he was out of town on club business and missed his family. He didn't remember being that sentimental man. He lost that with Evie.

"It's not here," Halley said, her movements becoming more erratic. James watched as Maverick covered her hand with his, calming her.

"Let me look, Thunder." She moved aside, and Maverick methodically looked through the small box. "Not here. But there's something stuck in the side." They watched as he carefully took each piece out and set it gently on the dresser. Halley smiled to herself. Of course, he would know these things were important to her and treat them with care.

Maverick's fingers worked to carefully pull back the side of the velvet and work out the small piece of hard plastic casing that was wedged in the side of the box between the bottom and the inside wall. He held up the tiny memory stick, "Not the key, but what's this? Important pictures saved on it?"

Halley's eyebrows knit and formed a ridge in the center of her forehead. "I have no idea what that is. It's not mine."

"You sure? Some of this has been in here a long time," James said quietly.

"Dad, I know every piece of jewelry, paper, and treasure in this. This is not mine. I don't know how it got there," Halley insisted.

"And we still don't have the key fob," Maverick brought them back to why they looked in the box in the first place.

"I know I put it in there. When I left San Francisco, I remember putting it in this before I put it in Henry. It was here," she said, her eyes sweeping over the top of the dresser, desk, and nightstands, looking at every flat surface to see if somehow the key fob moved.

James and Maverick exchanged a look. No one had access to the house except family and the club.

"Come on, let's go see your Gram," Maverick jerked his head toward the door.

"I'm coming too. Those sandwiches were a long time ago," James tried to laugh. He would need to keep his father from going old school and calling in markers James never wanted to use. Priss was at her parents' country club for the evening, Scarlett was at her away softball game, Danny had a baseball game in the same town, and Tiffany went to watch. That left him free to eat more of his mother's good cooking and to stick close to his eldest daughter.

When they pushed through his parents' kitchen door, each of their sense of smell was assaulted with the cooking meat, maybe tomato, and baking bread.

"Goulash?" Halley guessed as she breathed in deeply and allowed her memory to conjure the hearty homecooked dish of her childhood.

"Your great-great grandmother's goulash. I make it the old way," Gram replied, tapping the yellowed cover of the old cookbook created somewhere around World War I by the Women's Sunshine Club. Making it the "old way" usually meant it was made with butter – a lot of butter. "Why don't you and Maverick set the table? Make sure to add three extra spots."

"Three, Gram? You mean Dad, Maverick, and me?"

"No. Three more. I'm sure Scottie will show up. Where he is, Handsy will be close. I hear Handsy's sticking with Sarah today after your little incident in town, so I'm sure she'll be along too," Gram said as she tore the lettuce into a bowl for the salad.

"How do you know all that?" Halley demanded. She was sure her grandmother had been in the kitchen all day.

"Know what? I just listen," Gram waved off the questions and cut cucumbers and tomatoes to add to the lettuce.

Halley grabbed the plates and salad bowls from the cupboard and placed them on the table. Maverick pulled the flatware and dinner napkins from drawers under the kitchen counter and followed Halley around the table, setting them in place.

"You're good at that," Halley noticed. "You actually know how to set a table and don't just throw the utensils next to the plate."

"My mother made sure all of us knew the proper knife and fork to use, too," Maverick laughed. Just because he was a biker didn't mean he had no manners. Plus, he paid attention and knew exactly how the elder Mrs. McCarthy expected things to be done. He'd been around her table enough in his time in town.

"Well, excuse my assumptions," Halley tossed saucily at him.

He liked this version of Halley. The one who acted like she didn't have a care in the world. Actually, he liked every version of Halley.

The door opened again, and Scottie walked in with Handsy and Sarah close behind him. Gram called that one. Handsy had his hand on Sarah's lower back as he guided her to the table. She had spent as much time here growing up as he had, but he also spent a lot of his adult life here, too. Halley assumed it was more his protectiveness of Sarah than showing her the ropes. She kept her thoughts to herself so Sarah wouldn't be scared off. Handsy was good for her friend.

The timer on the top oven dinged, and Gram pulled out two loaves of bread she set on the island to settle before she sliced them. A few minutes later, the lower oven dinged, and the older woman pulled out the large casserole dish and set it on the cork hotpad on the table. She slid the salad bowl onto the table next. Before she could call out, James and Mitchell appeared and took opposite ends of the table.

"Excellent, as usual, Gram," Scottie complimented the woman.

"You just like it because you didn't have to cook," Gram batted away the compliment, but her satisfied smile told them all how pleased she was.

Mitchell looked fit to be tied. He knew he couldn't bring up club business with Sarah there and precious little in front of Halley, but it was killing him. The man gave up the presidency years ago, yet still found it hard to keep his hard-forged opinions to himself. James didn't usually mind, but he had no intention of letting his father contact old rivals, at least not yet.

"Thanks for dinner, Mary," Handsy said as dinner finished and he stood. "I should get Sarah home."

"I'll help with dishes first," Sarah offered.

"Nonsense, there's hardly anything to clean up, and Halley and Maverick can handle it," Mary smiled. "Come back anytime. We haven't seen enough of you."

"You'll be seeing a lot more of me again, if our girl here stays in town," Sarah shot a look at Halley.

"Oh yeah? You going to stick, Hal?" Mitchell asked, leaning forward and speaking for the first time since he sat at the table.

Halley blushed. This was not how she envisioned telling her family she'd made her decision. "I'm giving it serious consideration. We'll see what Dad thinks of the business plan." It really didn't depend on that. She knew the business would work, and even if they didn't support her and Drake pulled out, she would start something else. She wasn't ready to reveal any of that definitively.

Mitchell grumbled, "Told you, me, Gram, and Maverick will let you practice on us."

Halley conceded, "I'm going to take you up on that, Gramps." That raised the man's spirits. Maverick was glad to be included in the preview. He thought the elder McCarthy might be conspiring in his favor. Well, if he decided, he would act on what he'd been thinking since Halley came to town. That was a longer conversation with the woman's father, his president, before he would go there.

Maverick and Halley worked in companionable silence to load the dishwasher and handwash what was left. Halley liked how close Maverick stood. His brunette hair was pulled back in a short ponytail, sleeves pulled up to his elbows, and tattoos surrounding his left forearm disappeared under his shirt. She liked how he smelled. It was the leather and fresh air of her father and grandfather, but an additional citrusy scent that must be his shower gel.

"So, we gonna talk about this now?" Gramps growled and sat back down in his place at the head of the kitchen table.

"Pop," James tried to delay the man.

"Maybe I said that wrong. We're gonna talk about this now," the elder McCarthy's voice raised, brooking no room for debate.

"What do you want to know, Pop?"

"This Anthony character. He's really a Ricci?" Mitchell asked.

Halley stiffened at the sink. Maverick put an arm around her shoulders and squeezed. He bent down, mouth close to her ear, "Hey, don't do that. It's going to be okay. I've got you." He should probably have said, "We've got you," but he didn't, and he said what he meant. She needed to know he was there for her.

James blew out slowly. "Yeah, Pop. His grandfather, his mother's father, is the Ricci. He's a Barone. FBI confirmed what Wire found."

"His family behind this?"

"Don't know. Don't think so. They invested in the startup through a bunch of shell corporations, but their being involved in the rest makes no sense. There's no upside for them," James said.

"So maybe they're looking for this Anthony fella, too," Mitch said. "We could join ranks to flush him out."

James stole a look at Halley before responding, "No. We don't know enough yet."

"You'd rather wait until this asshole gets to my granddaughter? Let me make the call," Mitch argued.

"Wait, Gramps. How do you know Anthony's family? I don't even know his family. What am I missing?" Halley demanded.

"Pop," James warned.

"Maybe she should know," Scottie tread carefully.

James glared at his son.

"Not maybe. I need to know what is going on. All of it. No more waiting." Halley moved from her place at the sink and stood next to her grandfather, arms crossed at her chest, glaring at her father. "My life, Dad."

"It's more complicated than that, Hal. You really don't need to know," James tried to assure her.

"Let me rephrase: I want to know. Now." She didn't move, jaw set, so like her father, and she probably didn't realize it. Her blue eyes blazed.

"Sit down, Hal," Mitchell tugged her down into the seat beside him. Maverick stood behind her chair, dish towel over his shoulder.

James looked to the ceiling and closed his eyes. When he opened them again, the pain was recognizable. "Your great-great grandfather ran moonshine and other liquor during Prohibition, across the lake from Canada, rum up from the Caribbean, stills in the woods."

"I already know that, Dad," Halley urged him on.

"What you don't know is that he was in a sort of partnership with a man named Ricci. Ricci was establishing his crime family in the Midwest. It was a violent, bloody time. When your great-grandfather formed the *Phantom Raiders* after World War II, they were still doing some business with the Riccis. Many years later, your grandfather and I wanted out of that business," James explained.

"More your dad and Red than me. It was all I'd known, but your dad was adamant it would all go legitimate for you and your mom and any other kids," Mitchell had the grace to admit sheepishly. "He was right, but I took some convincing."

"Then your mom…" James stopped talking for a moment, and Halley's brain caught up.

"Wait! Did the Riccis murder Mom to send you and Gramps a message?" Her face and hands started to tingle, and her vision began to narrow with those damned black spots. These new panic attacks were beginning to make her really angry; well, they would as soon as she could think clearly again.

Almost immediately, Maverick dropped to squat next to her chair and grabbed her hands to ground her. "Look at me, Thunder. Follow my breathing. Slowly in. Slowly out. Do it again."

The attack passed, and her father continued.

"No, Hal. The Riccis did not go after your mother. She and you were family, innocents. You were untouchable in their world. A man married to the don's daughter came after us on his own. He was trying to make a name for himself in the family. He's the one who attacked and killed my Evie and set the house on fire to try to cover his crime. His name was Dante Barone. His son is Anthony," her father spit out, keeping such tight control of his emotions that he sounded emotionless.

"So…what? You killed him, and this is all some vendetta passed from father to son? Is that why it's a police cold case? This sounds like a movie, Dad. This can't be real," Halley exclaimed.

"We don't discuss club business, you know that, Hal," her grandfather admonished.

"I think it's a little late for that, Gramps," Halley said, sarcasm in full effect.

"I was going to say, before you interrupted me, except this one time," Gramps finished his thought. He felt the pain from his son at the other end of the table and picked up the story, "Dante Barone will never hurt anyone again. The Riccis were after him, too; he broke their rules. I heard after that his wife had a breakdown of sorts, and they sent her and her son Anthony to live in Italy for a couple years while she rested and got through her grief. She never accepted that her husband did what her father and brother told her he did. The man was a complete psycho. Sounds like his son inherited those traits."

"So, what, the mother poisoned Anthony's mind against our family? Did he target me? Reel me in to get back at this family? Did he put Craig up to hire me? None of it was real?" All the possibilities, awful possibilities, swirled in Halley's mind.

"We think she probably did poison his mind. As far as targeting you, we don't know. Craig told Conor he's the one who introduced Anthony to you, not that Anthony asked him to go after you. The job was real, Hal," Scottie assured her.

The tears were in the back of her eyes again, threatening to make an appearance. She could not let that happen. She was not going to cry until this nightmare ended. Then, she would give in to the luxury of tears. That is, if she was alive.

"All this time, I thought the person who killed Mom, brutalized her, was still out there. I had an idea I would investigate on my own. Well, I guess now I'll put all that extra effort into building our new business," Halley swallowed loudly. Letting go of a long-held premise was disconcerting, similar to driving and not knowing where you were headed.

"I still think I should call Lorenzo Ricci. His son Leonardo is head of the family now, and he has a son, Lorenzo, named after the old man. I think he's about the same age as Anthony and may know where his cousin is or what this is all about," Mitchell said, staring at his son.

"Pop, and then what? What if we find out they're behind it all?"

"Well, at least we'd know they're coming," Mitchell maintained. "But I doubt they sanctioned anything to do with Halley. Not their style, against their code. That family still holds true to the old rules."

"Kind of like us?" Scottie broke in, his voice quiet.

"Yeah, Scottie-boy. Like us," his grandfather agreed. "Family is everything."

"Anthony is *their* family," Halley threw in.

"They don't allow family to break the code without consequences," Mitchell insisted.

"Family is everything," Halley repeated her grandfather's phrase.

Maverick squeezed her hands and looked her in the eye before he stood, keeping a reassuring hand on her shoulder, "Yeah, it is, Thunder."

"Okay, Pop. You win. Call your old friend. We'll be ready no matter what happens next," James relented. "But we are not going backward. No deals. No business." James could imagine the Riccis would love to funnel their dirty money through the club's businesses and have it come out clean. That was not happening, not as long as he walked this earth.

"No deals. No business," Mitchell agreed.

Halley's head pounded, but at least she was all caught up now. It was too late to go to the cemetery. Normally, she would sneak in after dark, but now she felt Anthony or his goons might jump out from behind any tree or around any corner. She knew she had to go soon, and it had to be alone. Maverick didn't need to know she might be a little crazy and talked to dead people. She had to talk with her mother and tell her dead grandmother that she had finally found her answers, knew what she wanted.

Gram slammed a pan of apple crisp and a bowl of real whipped cream she had whipped up earlier on the table. Next came the dessert plates and spoons. Silently, she dished it out for each person. Halley tried to decline, but Scottie stuck his spoon in her mouth when she opened it to tell Gram, "No, thank you." Maverick accepted his standing behind her, and every third or fourth bite he would reach down to her plate and hold a spoon of crisp to her mouth.

"You need to savor every moment, Thunder. Lot of people I served with didn't get to come home and enjoy all life has to offer. Now, I take whatever pleasure I can. Sometimes that means apple crisp," Maverick said quietly as she scowled up at him and chewed. He caught Scottie's eye, and her brother gave him a chin lift.

"Damn men don't think I can feed myself," she said to Gram.

Mitchell pushed away from the table and kissed his granddaughter on top of her head. He admonished Maverick, "Keep her safe." Then, he turned to his son and said, "I'll make the call in the morning. You want to be here for it?" James nodded, still not talking. Too much talking tonight. Too much of the past stealing into the light rather than staying in the dark hole he dug for it.

***

In San Francisco, enjoying his flirtation with the waitress at the speakeasy, Enzo felt the buzzing in his pocket. Reluctantly, he looked and saw that it was his father. His stomach lurched, but he knew he could no longer evade this conversation. He motioned that he had to take a call and would be back soon. Then, he stepped outside, where it was quieter, and the air was cool. No one was on the sidewalk to hear him as he answered.

"Hello, Papa."

"Enzo. Tell me," Leonardo Ricci ordered his son.

"Anthony said it's taken care of. That the money trail will lead to the dead partner and then disappear. I don't think that's right. I gave him the space he asked for to work it out, but I think he's made it worse. He hired his own people," Enzo sighed.

"His own people? Hired guns?"

"Yes." Enzo held the phone away from his head, waiting for the yelling and expletives to begin.

Instead, Leonardo was quiet in his response, "Mercenaries. They have no loyalty. They aren't family. They chase the dollars."

"I agree. I told him that. I don't know if one of them did it or if it was Anthony who took out the partner he was paying off and framing at the same time. He promised the other partner, the founder, he would do the same to him if he talks to the feds." His father's silence was more deadly than an outburst. Enzo hesitated for only a moment before he went on, "Papa, there's more. Anthony was engaged. He asked me not to say anything until he could tell all of you himself. But the girl broke it off. They both worked for the company. She's some hotshot marketing executive they originally brought in from New York. He's not taking it so well. He says she's his."

"What's her name, Enzo?"

Enzo didn't know why that was important but answered, "Halley McCarthy. From everything I can tell, she's solid, smart. Some sort of genius who graduated early and climbed the corporate ladder quickly."

"McCarthy?"

"Yes, sir. And I don't know, but my gut tells me Anthony has gone after her. She originally raised red flags about finances to him when their vendors weren't paid. Obviously, Anthony was the one causing the issues, so he ignored her and thought she'd let it lie when he told her he had it handled. She didn't and took it to the CEO. She moved out of her rental and left the area after the company came under investigation and the CEO told her not to bother coming in. The CEO regrets it and now says she had nothing to do with defrauding investors."

"*We* are investors, Enzo."

"I know. I told Anthony he had a good thing going with this company and was doing good by the family. He seems to have lost the plot. As far as I can tell, he wanted access to money himself, and he's obsessed with this girl. He left me a note saying he was leaving and taking care of it. We'd see he could handle it, and nothing would blow back on the family."

"You don't believe him."

"I tried to give him the benefit of the doubt. I tried to stand by him. Now I think he's lost it, Papa. I can't figure him out anymore," Enzo admitted sheepishly. He could feel the heat crawling up his neck and was glad his father could not see the flush that colored his olive skin.

"You've always been soft about him and had a blind spot when it comes to Anthony, Enzo. He's taken advantage of your loyalty. No more. He's gone too far this time. If the FBI traces the investments or the diverted money back to the family, this will be a big problem for us," Leonardo sighed.

"Why don't you sound surprised?" Enzo had to ask.

"My sister has been ranting about how she will finally get justice, and her boy is taking care of it. She poisoned him with lies about his father. He's turning out to be a psychopath, just as his father before him. I'm disappointed but not surprised," Leonardo sighed.

"This model can work, though. I've identified some other companies and potential investments for us," Enzo tried to add some good news to the rot, assuming they were still talking about the business. He didn't know what his crazy aunt had to do with it.

"It's time to come home, Enzo. You can tell me about these potential investments when you get here. Fly back tomorrow. The plane will be at the airstrip at 5 a.m. your time. I'll have the boys pack your condo."

"Tomorrow!" Enzo couldn't keep the shock from his voice. That was so soon, mere hours from now.

"Tomorrow. This thing with Anthony is going to get worse. I can feel it. I want you here with me. We will need to find a way to minimize the damage." Leonardo was leaning on intuition. His crazy sister made a mess of all of this. "Our money guys tell me as far as the FBI goes, as long as he didn't divert any funds to family accounts or companies, we should be clean. They are looking and will scrub if they have to. The possible good news is we will have a hefty tax write-off with how much we lost as investors in the startup." With affection, Leonardo added, "Good night, son. It will be good to have you home."

"Night, Papa. I should have told you my worries sooner, I know. I'm sorry." Enzo knew he had to own up to the delay in talking with his father.

"Like I said, I know you've always had a blind spot where Anthony is concerned. Thank you for recognizing you should have come to me sooner. This can't happen again."

"It won't," Enzo promised. He would never allow himself to be his cousin's babysitter again. Someone else would have to take that job.

Enzo headed back into the speakeasy to settle his tab and let the waitress down gently; she had been sure she was going home with him that night. He hoped to reconnect with her in the future and keep his options open. There was something about her that got under his skin. The familiarity he felt reminded him of Halley McCarthy. That was a first. He and his cousin never had the same taste in women.

At the condo, he shoved Anthony's note into his satchel, then his laptop, tablet, and all his chargers, as well as the book he was reading. Anthony never understood his love of books. Sometimes, everyone needed a place to get away, and for Enzo, that was a book. Besides the escape, he often learned something new.

Next, he carefully packed his clothes and shoes. Not as ostentatious as his cousin, he still had an expensive wardrobe. He carefully wrapped in bubble wrap a painting he acquired for his mother, a bronze sculpture for his father, and a tapestry for his grandparents. He thought about leaving it to his father's men to move, but at the last minute, he took down the framed painting by a local artist that hung over his headboard and wrapped that as well. That was it. The rest the men would handle.

In the early hours, he would shower and pack his toiletries before driving his Alpha Romeo to the airport. He hated leaving the car behind, but his father gave him no choice. His preference would have been to drive it across the country and delay his return by a few more days. The car was pure enjoyment to him – another love he and Halley McCarthy shared.

Anthony found pure enjoyment in nothing. His purchases were all about curating his image and impressing or cowing people with his wealth. Enzo felt sorry for his cousin and wondered where the man had disconnected from the boy he had been. Enzo found joy in many things, but then, his father and mother spoke a lot about happiness, as well as honor and family. He saw in their marriage something he aspired to someday. They were in love. Unlike many of his father's peers, even Enzo's own peers, he knew his father never strayed. His mother was his father's *one*. His father ran the family and the business, while his mother had a strong philanthropic gene and insisted her children not only partake in that work but understand it. It was not an obligation; it was a passion for his mother.

Maybe his father was right. The combination of his father's psychotic gene and his mother's delusions left Anthony with no real chance of being normal. However, that did not sit right with Enzo. His father had taught him that once you hit adulthood, everyone made their own choices, each of which led to its own consequences.

While Anthony's parents were not ideal, he had plenty of role models in their grandparents and Enzo's own parents. Anthony may have tipped the scales into his own delusion; he made his own choices that got him there. Enzo had to stop making excuses for the man. They were thirty-five years old, not twenty with no experience and plenty of runway to learn from mistakes.

Anthony never once owned up to mistakes or took responsibility for his own actions. Everything was always someone else's fault. The family allowed that, giving him leeway because his father was dead, and his mother was frail. Looking at it now, seeing his cousin clearly for the first time ever, Enzo realized how they were all complicit by allowing him to skate by due to the circumstances of his childhood and parental unit.

Enzo slept very little that night, tossing and turning in his Egyptian cotton sheets, fruitlessly running the last few years in his mind, trying to envision different decisions and a different outcome. He knew it would not change anything. He knew it was a waste of time and energy, yet still, he ran the reel in his head over and over. He told himself this was how he would learn from his mistakes and never allow himself to be caught in the same situation again.

When sleep did come, it was plagued with Anthony dancing just out of reach and wreaking mayhem and destruction with everything he touched. The last image that woke him with a start was Halley's face, followed by darkness and a loud scream. When he fought through the sleep to wake, his heart racing, he heard the obnoxious screech of his phone alarm. Anthony again. The man loved messing with his smartphone settings.

Darkness had settled outside, and the sunrise was nowhere in sight. Only the marina lights and a bright moon shone on the water to dispel the shroud of black. When he got on the road to head to the private airstrip in Marin County, across the Golden Gate Bridge, there was very little traffic on the streets and even less when he hit the shores of Marin. At the airstrip, the pilot greeted him, and a worker from the local airport helped load his few belongings onto the private jet.

Soon, he was seated in the butter-soft, charcoal-gray leather seats and accepted the steaming latte in the designer black cup and saucer from the flight attendant. She looked eager to strike up a conversation, her smile bright for the early hour, but Enzo barely noticed her. Staring, unseeing, out the oblong window, he missed the faint glow on the eastern horizon that indicated the sun would rise again this morning.

The coffee cup sat forgotten on the black hardwood table anchored to the carpeted floor. Glancing back in the cabin, he noted how his sister had perfectly designed the interior in a masculine palette that would automatically put his father and his associates at ease. He felt anything but at ease.

The flight attendant quietly reached for his seat belt and secured it low and tight across his hips for take-off. That she brushed lightly against him in a too familiar way, he would not acknowledge, just as he would ignore the bedroom in the back of the aircraft. Stoic and resigned, he readied himself to face fate, better known as Leonardo Ricci.

Chapter 21

WHEN TIFFANY ARRIVED HOME AFTER THE GAME THE NIGHT BEFORE, she was surprised to see two of the club brothers hanging out by the entrance to their drive inside the gates. She was more surprised to find two more standing on the front porch, watching her approach. One of the guys was a prospect she liked to tease and hoped would take her up on her flirtation soon. She made sure to toss her blonde hair over her shoulder and tilt her chin down, so she looked at the men through her eyelashes as she approached the porch, hips swinging seductively, her journey from car to house slower than usual, giving them a good look. Neither so much as cracked a smile. That made her frown.

"What's up, boys? Not enough action at the clubhouse?" she tried a smirk.

"Jailbait," the club brother said under his breath to the prospect, eyes searching the drive and tree line.

"Go inside, Tiff," the prospect said stiffly.

"What? No 'hello?' Not even a smile?" she pouted, standing in front of them, turning from her waist side to side, standing a little too closely to the men. Anthony had made her feel older. More sophisticated. Now, she wanted them to recognize the woman before them.

The front door swung open. Her father stood back in the shadows, “Get inside, Tiffany. Where are Danny and Scarlett?”

“How would I know? They were on the team busses. I drove myself,” she slid inside with a last look and huffed at the prospect. No acknowledgment came in return, and her sexy glide turned into a stomp in the space of one new breath.

James looked at the two on the porch, hardness around his mouth and eyes, “How old is my daughter, Prospect?”

“Sir?” the young man swallowed noisily.

“Tiffany. How old is she?” James reiterated.

“Uh, I don’t know. Eighteen? She said she’s eighteen,” he said more confidently as he remembered when she introduced herself at a club barbecue a few weeks ago.

“Sixteen. Don’t forget it. That is if you still expect to get your patch someday. Maybe you don’t,” James ground out, sounding like he was issuing orders. Maybe he was.

“Sixteen?” the prospect’s voice was small, sweat beading on his forehead and running down the small of his back, even though the night air was chilly. “No, I won’t forget, Prez. I promise.”

James shut the door. The brother looked at the prospect with pity, shaking his head. “Dumbass. Never go after the president’s family. No matter what she offers.”

Tyler listened from his post by the stables, the voices carrying easily in the night air, and grinned to himself. Some people really were too stupid. His fellow prospect may be one of those people. Tyler had already turned Tiffany down multiple times, and Maverick reinforced it the last time by moving silently behind the girl and whispering in her ear, telling Tiffany to stay away from him.

Sometimes, it was good to have a brother of whom everyone was afraid. At least this was one bit of trouble he would not find himself stumbling into. He had made that mistake before with another pretty girl in Texas. The sister of one of the gangbangers had come on to him at school, and he had stupidly followed wherever she led. Where she led was to trouble and his current banishment from the only home he’d ever known. Yeah, he learned from his mistakes.

***

With the first morning light, Halley was in the kitchen waiting for her father. Maverick was already seated at the counter. She wanted to be there when her grandfather spoke to the Ricci patriarch. James came in and saw the two.

Pulling in a deep breath, James said, "You're not coming, Hal."

"Dad –" Halley started.

"No."

"This is my life. I want to hear what Anthony's family has to say," Halley insisted.

"No. You had your chance to meet them when you were together and didn't think it was important then. And thank God you didn't." He muttered this last part under his breath.

"But –"

"No." James spun on his heel, and the next thing they heard was the door closing.

"Let's go," Halley said stubbornly.

"You heard him, Thunder. I'm not disregarding a direct order," Maverick shook his head.

"No reason we can't go and eat breakfast with Gram. And get *good* coffee. I don't have to be in the office with them," she reasoned and headed toward the door, daring him to follow.

Maverick swung off his seat on the stool and followed her, albeit reluctantly. Mary's breakfast did sound good to him. He'd been up for hours and already checked in with all the guys on guard duty and drove the property perimeter himself on an ATV.

James glowered at Halley when she stepped into his mother's kitchen less than a minute after he had. Mary already had bacon frying in one pan and eggs in another. He grabbed three mugs and begrudgingly poured coffee for himself and Maverick and dropped a tea bag into Halley's. "You don't listen well, Hal."

"I listen fine. You won't let me in on the call, but I can still eat with Gram," she glowered back. James nodded in resignation. She was his daughter; after all, what did he expect?

Maverick accepted his mug silently. He knew his prez expected Halley to show up, and it was his job to be with her, protect her … from everyone but her family. That was one area he would avoid. Maverick set his mug on the table, got plates from the cupboard, and started setting the table without being asked. His mother raised him right. Mitch entered the kitchen, hair wet from the shower, and looked from father to daughter before catching Maverick's eye and shaking his head.

"Want to get this over with?" Mitch asked his son.

"Is it too early to call?" James questioned. "Your buddy Lorenzo is retired now."

"Retired, not dead, asshole," Mitch scoffed. "He was always an early riser. His son, the current don, may not be there, though. We may have to have two calls, if Lorenzo wants it that way."

James nodded and followed his father down the hall to his home office. He glanced back at Maverick, "You coming?"

Maverick glanced at Halley before following the men out of the kitchen. He raised his shoulder in a version of an apology. She merely shook her head and waved him away.

"Maybe he'll tell me what's going on if they don't," she griped to her grandmother as she finished what Maverick started with setting the table.

"Pick your battles," Gram said simply and turned the bacon in the pan, cooking everything on low, trying to time it to the end of the call. She was usually pretty good at timing, but this morning's call was a wildcard.

Seated behind his large, custom-made desk with James in front and Maverick leaning against the wall, Mitch pulled a phone from a drawer and set it on speaker before punching in the numbers.

"Who is this?" a gruff voice answered immediately on the other end.

"An old friend, Lorenzo," Mitch replied.

Without waiting for a name, "Well, I didn't expect to hear from you, old friend."

James was amazed they knew one another by voice after all these years. Unless his father was holding out and still spoke with him. No, that would never happen. Not with how everything ended. It would be too painful for everyone.

"Lorenzo, my son is here with me," Mitch said, leaving out Maverick's presence.

"Ahh, not a social call then. You know I'm retired."

"As am I," Mitch replied. Both old men laughed at that. James and Maverick weren't sure what was funny other than both kept their hands in, regardless of turning their operations to the next generation.

"Wait a moment. Let me get my son Leonardo. I saw him sneaking into the kitchen to see his mother." They heard muffled voices as it sounded like Lorenzo opened a door and called down a hallway. There were some rustling sounds through the airwaves, and then the man was back. "We're both here now. To what do we owe the pleasure of hearing from an old friend?"

"We've been made aware of a situation that may involve your grandson. We weren't sure if you were aware," Mitch began.

"Which grandson?" Lorenzo asked.

"Anthony."

"Have you seen my nephew?" Leonardo now spoke up before his father could respond.

"We have not. I was hoping you had," Mitch replied.

Silence met them on the other end of the phone. Mitch raised a finger to his lips, telling them to wait.

"We have not," Leonardo responded. "I guess we have some things to discuss. I was hoping we had bad information."

"You heard he was engaged to my granddaughter, and she called off the engagement? We only found that out recently. It seems they were keeping it from all of us."

"Young people. No respect for tradition," Lorenzo sighed before his son continued the conversation.

"I was only made aware of the situation last night. It seems my nephew has disappeared. My son Enzo was with him in San Francisco, but Anthony has made some bad decisions and gone his own way."

Mitch nodded to James and Maverick. There was the confirmation the family was not involved in any vendetta.

Leonardo continued, "We had what started as business investments. Those have apparently gone wrong. There was no mention of your granddaughter until last night when my son told me about the broken engagement and that she worked at the company.

Apparently, his cousin wanted to tell us himself and swore my son to secrecy. He only realized the other implications yesterday. Anthony left the Bay Area with a note to my son. He does not take rejection well." That might have been the understatement of the decade.

"Was there any indication where he was headed?" Mitch pushed.

"We can only assume it is your direction." There was another hesitation, some quiet conferring in the background, and then Leonardo spoke again, "My sister has been filling her son's head with bad information – apparently for years. We now realize she is delusional and never healed. I can only apologize for my family and our ignorance of the situation. The past should stay in the past. There has been too much hurt on all sides." He sighed heavily.

James spoke up, "If my daughter is in danger, I cannot allow that."

"Nor would I expect you to," Leonardo agreed. "I think it's time for a vacation. I hear there are many nice lakes near you. Maybe some of us will come and partake in nature. We don't have much of that in Chicago."

James hesitated. The last thing they needed were mobsters in their town. But, if it kept his daughter safer, he would agree.

"I understand your son's hesitation, old friend," Lorenzo chuckled lightly. "But please understand, we find ourselves on the same side once again."

"As long as that's the case, there shouldn't be a problem. It's important everyone knows which side they're on," Mitch answered.

"Same side. That will be perfectly clear," Leonardo answered for his father.

"Old friend, maybe we could talk about continuing business with this next generation. Why not combine a little business with my son and his friends' trip?" Lorenzo opened the door Mitch knew was coming.

"We're beyond that, Lorenzo. The younger generations have gone their own ways and taken separate paths. The old agreement remains," Mitch reinforced his son's position without James having to jump in. James nodded once to his father in agreement and wordlessly thanked him for handling the sensitive subject.

"I understand. Can't blame an old man for trying," Lorenzo chuckled again.

Leonardo steered the conversation back to the present predicament, "Can you give us details on what's happened? I learned my nephew hired his own men, which displeases me greatly. Maybe they have already done something of which you are aware? You have the advantage of a few more days sitting with this than I have."

They spent the next several minutes discussing the destroyed storage unit, the anonymous notes and now flowers left for Halley, and some of what they learned from Craig and through Wire's investigation, such as Halley's drained bank account and the direct threat to Craig's life and Andres' murder, without mentioning the FBI or Craig's coming interview with them.

By the time the three men sat at the kitchen table, all were stuck in their own thoughts.

Halley set the full serving dishes on the table and demanded, "Well?"

"Club business, Hal," her grandfather sighed.

For once, James decided to be a little more forthcoming, surprising both Mitch and Maverick. "Your ex-fiancé is acting alone. His family was blindsided, both by what he did with the company and their investments and with his engagement to you. We have to assume he's either already here or on his way."

Scottie had come through the kitchen door and heard his father's admission. He grabbed a plate for himself and sat at the large table, grinning at her, "You sure know how to pick 'em, Hal."

Halley scowled at her brother, "Yeah, I'm aware." Suddenly, her appetite was gone, yet again.

"We may see some new faces in town until this is resolved," James said.

"Friendly faces?" Scottie asked, now serious. James grimaced but nodded in confirmation.

***

Enzo reluctantly stepped into the backseat of the car waiting for him on the private side of the airfield in Chicago. He was even closer to home, and the inevitable lecture that would come from his father. Reluctantly, he admitted to himself it was deserved.

Once through the gates of the estate that looked like Tuscan country homes had come to the shores of Lake Michigan, where his parents, grandparents, and various aunts and uncles had their homes, he stepped from the car just as his mother raced out the front door of his grandparent's house with her arms wide, ready to hug her eldest son. It had been too long since they saw one another in person. His father and grandparents appeared in the doorway and watched as she wrapped him in her welcoming arms. He glanced cautiously over his mother's shoulder and saw that neither man looked angry – that was a good sign. In fact, both smiled indulgently at the display between mother and son.

Once in the house, he was led to the kitchen, and all sat at the large kitchen table where a lunch spread was waiting.

"I missed this," Enzo admitted quietly as he stared at the food and then looked into the eyes of his family.

"Of course you did, Enzo. Who takes care of you like your family?" his grandmother asserted.

Before Enzo could respond, the swinging door that led into the kitchen swung open violently with the sound of a palm smacking the wood. A woman dressed in fitted black dress pants and a tight, black designer blouse, with long dark hair streaming down her shoulders, burst through, dark eyes wild, until they settled on Enzo. She stalked toward him and slapped her hand on the table.

"Why are you here, Enzo? Why aren't you with my boy? Does he have to do everything alone?" the woman demanded.

Enzo's eyes widened. He felt a faint crawl of fear run up his spine as he looked into the woman's eyes.

Before he could answer, his father interrupted, "Stop this, Checa. I called Enzo home."

"He should be helping my son," the woman insisted.

"What have you done, Francesca?" Lorenzo, Enzo's grandfather, interjected. Enzo thought something was going on that he didn't understand but remained quiet.

"What have *I* done?" the woman ranted. "What have *you* done, Papa? Nothing! All these years – nothing. My son has to right the wrongs you and my brother should have taken care of long ago."

Lorenzo did not want to believe his daughter was the root cause of Anthony's madness, but the proof stood before him now, and he could not deny it. "Let's take this to my office, Francesca."

"No. Everyone should hear this. You never gave my husband a chance, and now you disregard my son. He should have just as much chance to take over this family as Enzo. He will prove he's worthy," she ranted.

"Office, Francesca. Now. Enzo, come with us. I'm sorry, lunch will have to wait," Lorenzo stood, brooking no disagreement from his daughter. Leonardo grabbed his sister's arm and led her out of the kitchen.

"Mama, are you going to let them treat me this way?" she looked to her mother seated at the table.

The older woman shook her head in dismay and said nothing; she feared her daughter was beyond saving. She had twenty-eight years to wallow in her grief and descend into the folly of her vengeance. For so long, Francesca appeared to deal with her fate and seemed better, if quiet, but it was all a false flag. All it took was for Anthony to begin his revenge plot on behalf of his mother, for the woman to lose the last threads of her sanity. Or that's the impression she left with her mother.

***

Breakfast had been a quiet affair. Everyone had a lot to think about, and Halley felt the pressure of regret for bringing any of this to her family and her hometown. Now, her father and his club were embroiled in things they left behind long ago.

"Maybe I should leave. Go to New York – or somewhere," Halley said quietly, staring into her mug, unwilling to look into the eyes of those around the table.

"Nonsense," Gram scoffed. The men all looked toward Halley as if she had sprouted horns.

"No, really. If I hadn't come here, you wouldn't be mixed up in whatever this is," Halley rationalized and threw her arms in the air in frustration, finally steeling herself to look up and meet the stares. No anger, pity, or the judgment she expected stared back at her.

"This is coming full circle. Trouble would have come here, with or without you. If anything, I'm sorry you were put in the middle of something that should have been buried," James told his daughter, his own guilt gnawing in his gut.

Halley wasn't sure she agreed but bit her lip to keep from continuing the discussion. She needed to move her life forward. Concentrating on something she could control might help the vulnerability and failure she felt to dissipate. Rational or not, it was what she felt. Pulling out her phone, she texted Drake and Scarlett to see if they wanted to run through the business plan in front of an audience once Scarlett was finished with softball practice later in the afternoon. Both responded, Scarlett enthusiastically and Drake with a simple "K." She then confirmed her grandparents and Maverick would be their willing audience.

***

Wolf was glad the previous night should be the last to babysit Craig Martin. Today was the FBI handoff. No mercenaries had breached the property the night before, and Wolf found no new razor blades, only disposable razors, in the bathroom. He still stayed close, listening for any unusual noises from the man's bedroom and bathroom.

Martin rose early and seemed calm. After waking, he moved to the workout room and spent an hour driving out any last-minute jitters or doubts. Wolf made his presence known and watched the workout, even stopping to correct the tech genius' stance when he used the punching bag. After showering and packing a duffle bag others from the security team would sneak out later, Craig moved to the front door with Wolf and followed the big bodyguard to the dark SUV.

"I just need to sign those documents at the office, and I'll be ready," Craig said calmly. They had already decided to contact his outside counsel by phone to brief her when both were on their way to meet the FBI. It wouldn't allow her much time to prepare, but no one thought she would need to prepare much, considering Craig's stance to tell all. That way, the security team could control any outside contact either he or the attorney might make and purportedly keep him safe.

Once inside, they headed for the general counsel's office, Wolf sticking close behind him while Conor waited by the CEO's office. Craig wanted to see if there were any other documents he needed to take with him. After all, it may be the last time in this office. The last time as the head of his company.

"Are you sure?" the general counsel asked as he passed the documents to his old freshman roommate. It was hard not to remember when they were both fresh and eager to take on the world as the man resolutely nodded and silently took the papers from his hand. After reading through each, he signed. The general counsel had a notary sitting by the coffee table in his office, ready to stamp and witness the signing. Craig was leaving nothing to chance.

Before Craig and Wolf headed back along the quiet executive floor, Craig pulled his old friend into a tight hug and turned abruptly. To his back, the general counsel said quietly, "Thank you. Good luck." The last part was whispered, to Wolf's ears, a prayer.

In his office, Craig shoved into his backpack briefcase the two laptops that had been returned after being confiscated, and no incriminating evidence was found on either. Conor wished Wire could have had a crack at the laptops. He was so confident in his club brother's skills that he believed the man would find something, if there was anything to find, that the authorities hadn't.

They saw Craig palm something small into his hand and slip it into a small side pocket. He lifted two thick file folders and shoved those in as well. Then he looked around, turning a full circle, eyes landing on what was left. He had practically lived here for the last few years since he and Andres left their shared tiny house in Oakland and made it big, ready to make it bigger.

With one last sweep of his eyes, he lifted a framed photo from his credenza. Wolf and Conor could see it was the executive team, obviously before anything went wrong – all were smiling broadly, arms around one another, genuinely chummy. Wolf saw who he assumed was Halley between Craig and who must be

Anthony. The other two were the dead partner, Andres, and the general counsel.

Wolf had heard the executive committee was kept to this tight crew, and everyone else, including others usually part of a C-suite, was relegated to report mostly to Andres and two others to Craig. Craig put the framed photo in his bag and pulled from a corkboard an old snapshot of himself with Andres and the general counsel in front of a small, rundown house. He placed it in the bag's front pocket and zipped it closed.

"It's time," Craig said to his bodyguards. To his assistant – God knows why the woman kept coming in, but she did faithfully – he said with his hand pressed to his temple, "I'm heading home now. I can't get rid of this headache." He gave her a pinched but sincere smile.

He followed Wolf to the executive elevator, with Conor walking closely behind texting Wire to take over the video security feeds. Once inside, another member of their security team waited who looked alarmingly similar to Craig. As they were on the way to the parking garage, Wolf hit the hold button. Craig quickly exchanged clothing with his look-a-like, pulled the baseball hat over his head, and steeled himself for what was to come.

The SUV was pulled close to the elevator bank, and with his head down, the decoy "Craig" hurried into the back, along with two large bodyguards that looked much like Conor and Wolf.

Conor and Wolf pressed Craig between them and launched themselves into the third of the four SUVs they staged in the parking area. Their driver, who went by the name Pace, an experienced member of Wolf's and Maverick's Delta team, had driven in from Nevada for this op, and the bodyguard in the shotgun seat came from Arizona. They wound their way through the city, losing anyone who may have followed.

Given their team picked up tails on the first two vehicles, they weren't surprised no one appeared to follow them. They thought their adversaries would assume one decoy, not three. Still, the fourth vehicle followed closely behind the third as they exited the parking area and turned the opposite way. Craig spent his time filling in his attorney on what he was about to do as she sped toward the remote meeting place with another of their security detail. He wasn't sure, the woman was always so unemotional that she was virtually unreadable, but he thought she was pleased with his decision.

They were careful as they came close to the Golden Gate Bridge. Other than the ferry, it was the only way to Marin County and then on to Sonoma County without driving across another pinch point with the bridge that led to Oakland and possibly taking them hours out of their way. No, this way had to work. Driving around the city enough before heading for the bridge should have exposed any tails. If there were others positioned in Marin County, they would have to deal with them there.

In the third row of the SUV sat two more large men, both heavily armed, with eyes focused outside the vehicle, alert for any potential threat. It was crowded with the six bodyguards. Craig was not a small man, but he was the smallest of the seven. If these men couldn't keep him safe, no one could. Halley told him they would protect him, and they had. Once again, Halley came through.

Miles past the Golden Gate Bridge, a dark SUV pulled out in front of them, their driver waving his acknowledgment. Ten miles down the road, another pulled in behind them. The three made their way quickly on the highway north, rolling evenly spread, precise.

The fourth SUV was at the tech genius' house, purportedly having dropped the CEO home to nurse his headache. Even Conor's nerves were on edge by this point; yet again, he considered enlisting and getting the experience he hoped would put him on par with these men. Soon, this would be over, and he could head home and give serious consideration to his future.

As they got close to their destination, Craig fiddled with the small pocket on the side of his backpack and produced a tiny thumb drive. Wolf was pretty sure that was what he had palmed and hidden when they were at the office. Craig handed the memory stick to Conor. He explained, "In case something goes wrong, anything your tech guy may need to clear Halley or get the truth out is on this. It's got everything I've pieced together, and, well, a statement from me, and something Halley might need later."

Wolf chuckled, "I thought you slipped something into that pocket."

It was Craig's turn to surprise the men, "Well, you saw one, but I pocketed two. They're identical, except for the something extra Halley can choose what to do with. The other I'll give to the FBI guy – Bishop."

Wolf laughed, "We'll take care of it."

"But hope we won't have to," Conor added.

They reached the remote cabins, and Conor could see why his team had chosen this spot – no one came out here. There was no reason to. He didn't see any FBI vehicles either, which made him a little on edge. Sensing his question, Wolf pointed toward a close stand of trees, "See the reflection in the sun? They parked the vehicles out there. Smart. In case someone showed other than us."

Conor texted to let the agents know the three vehicles approaching were them.

Senior Supervisory Special Agent Bishop cautiously opened the cabin door. Quickly, armed agents in protective vests lined the drive, looking for threats. Wolf opened the back door, hands slightly raised, and reached inside to help Craig out. Their own men exited the SUVs and continued the protective detail, their cargo still their responsibility until the official handoff. A woman in dark trousers and a white blouse came to the door, and Craig whispered to Wolf that she was his attorney. He wasn't sure why he whispered, but it felt right.

Conor walked up to Bishop and held out his hand, "Conor McCarthy. I understand you know my dad."

"I do. Good man. Seems you're following in his footsteps. Good to meet you, Conor," Bishop shook his hand. Wolf approached with Craig plastered to his side. Bishop asked, "Any trouble?"

"None. They seem to have taken the bait and followed the other SUV to Mr. Martin's home. They are now parked outside on the street waiting and watching, according to our men," Wolf replied.

Bishop nodded curtly to Special Agent Ethan Drury, "Have them picked up." He explained to Conor and Wolf, "They probably won't say anything, but you never know. If they think they're on the line for Murano's murder, they may talk, give up Barone." Craig felt like an extra appendage at this point. No one had addressed him or given him instructions.

Finally, Bishop looked him in the eye, "Glad you saw fit to do the right thing, Mr. Martin. That is why you're here, correct?"

Craig responded head held high, "I am."

Before he could say more, the attorney spoke up, "He will, once we have an agreement on provisions and immunity."

Craig smiled for the first time all day; his attorney was with him all the way. He turned and shook hands with both Wolf and Conor. "Thanks for keeping me alive. Halley was right about you guys." Then he held his hand, palm outstretched, to Wolf, "Think I can have my prescriptions back now?"

Wolf gave him a half smile and pulled the two bottles from his pocket. He handed them to Bishop, who had immediately held out his hand, rather than to Craig. "I'm sure they will accommodate you if you ask nicely."

Conor spoke so only Craig, Bishop, and Wolf could hear, "Don't forget to take care of Halley. She doesn't deserve any of this."

"That's a promise I'm happy to keep," Craig assured the younger man. Two agents flanked Craig and hustled him into the house, where the door closed behind them.

"Do you want us to stick around? Back up your guys, if necessary," Wolf asked Bishop.

The senior agent shook his head no, "We've got it from here. You can stand down."

"Got it," Conor said. Then he hesitated and asked, "Are you going to keep him here to take his statement or take him to another location?" Conor was worried about what could happen in transit and wanted to leave no room for error, at least until his sister was in the clear.

"I think it's best if I don't answer that, don't you think?" Bishop smiled indulgently. "Tell your dad I owe him one." On that note, Bishop strode toward the cabin and disappeared inside. Agents still covered all sides of the cabin.

Conor, Wolf, and the security team got back into their vehicles and drove away. A few miles down the road, they looked up and saw a helicopter circling and drawing closer and closer to the ground until it disappeared somewhere behind them.

"I guess that answers my question," Conor muttered. Wolf and the others laughed. All were relieved Craig was no longer their responsibility. "Let's find someplace to eat. On me," Conor suggested, knowing the business would reimburse him.

Wolf texted the other two vehicles and then looked up the closest steakhouse with good ratings.

Conor texted Maverick: *Package delivered.* He got back a thumbs-up emoji.

Outside the restaurant, Wolf pulled Conor aside, and their driver, Pace, stayed back with them. "Listen, want to drive to Michigan with me? I just need to pick up my duffle and bike from my apartment, and we can go."

The surprise was evident on Conor's face, "Really? You want to live in small-town Michigan and prospect the *Phantom Raiders*?"

Wolf narrowed his eyes, "Yes. Have a problem with that?"

"Not at all," Conor threw his hands in the air in surrender. "Sure, I'll drive back with you. But we need to get going after we eat. I want to be there to protect Hal. Shit's going down soon."

"I'm coming, too. If that's all right with you," Pace added, addressing Wolf.

Wolf nodded, "Maverick will be glad to have you. Do we need to stop in Nevada?"

Pace flushed slightly. "No, man. Got my bike and stuff already loaded in the back of my pickup. I gave notice to my landlord when I headed out here. Didn't do anything but flop there anyway. Figured I'd stay with you, but I'm cool with going to Michigan." He smiled broadly, and they all slapped one another on the backs as they entered the restaurant.

Chapter 22

THE LAST SLIDE WAS UP ON HALLEY'S LAPTOP IN MITCHELL'S OFFICE. All was quiet in the room. The three siblings held their breath while they waited for their test audience to say something. Drake surprised himself with how nervous he was. It was like coming out to his family; that's how far back in the closet he hid his art. He was amazed at how great it felt, though, to finally talk about it.

Mitchell spoke first, "Scarlett, you did all that research?"

The teenager bit her lip nervously, "Yeah. Did I miss somcthing?"

"Not that I can see. I'm just so damned proud of you!" Mitchell complimented his youngest granddaughter. Then he turned to Drake, not giving anything away, "You really committing yourself to this?"

Drake swallowed hard, "I am."

"It's what you've wanted to do, isn't it?" Gram asked.

"It is," Drake sighed.

"Well, you're damned good at it," Mitchell declared. "And by the look of this, you're going to make money."

Drake let out a deep breath and relaxed. No one made fun of him. Even Maverick looked impressed.

"Anything else we need to add to convince Dad and the executive committee?" Halley asked, not sure she wanted an answer.

Mitchell stared ahead for a minute, giving the question serious consideration. "I can't think of anything else, Hal. The three of you have a solid plan. What do you think, Maverick?"

"I agree. I think Prez and the others are going to see the value and the potential. Hell, I'd like to invest myself, not just with the club," Maverick declared. "Drake, would you show me some more of your pieces?" Drake nodded enthusiastically.

"This is really going to work," Scarlett mused.

Maverick piped up, "I've got the perfect office space for you in our building, when you're ready."

"That may be a little premature," Halley countered.

"I don't think so. But it's there when you need it. I'll show you next time we're in town," Maverick argued. "I figure you'll want a space people can come into, which means not at the clubhouse or on the compound. Downtown would be perfect."

"Okay, let's focus first on the next step. Dad," Halley said and turned off her laptop.

"Dad what?" James asked as he opened the door to his father's home office.

"We want to present our business plan to you," Scarlett declared before Halley or Drake could answer.

"So, you're involved with this too, huh?" James tried not to smile at his youngest daughter.

"Of course. It's a smart move, and I'm a good researcher. And Drake's going to help me be a better artist, so someday maybe I can be on that side of the company too," Scarlett said quickly, her words running together in her excitement.

"Tomorrow," James said.

"Tomorrow?" Halley asked.

"Present tomorrow," James said. "You want to do it at the clubhouse?"

"I thought we could do it in the conference room at the security office. Then they can take a look at some office space, too," Maverick countered.

James glanced around the room, "Okay. One in the afternoon. You only have a half-day of school tomorrow and no practice, right, Scar?" Shocked her father knew the school schedule, she nodded enthusiastically.

That night, Drake escaped to his makeshift studio and looked at the projects he had sitting in the hidden space at the back of the outbuilding. He eyed each piece critically, trying to see how his father might view it upon first look. Not wanting to dwell any longer on something he wouldn't know until it happened, he picked up his sketchpad and started on the surprise he had in mind for Halley, a custom painting for her Harley. When he could no longer keep his eyes open, he laid down on the cot he'd set up in the corner and pulled an old quilt of his Gram's over his tired body.

The presentation to the *Phantom Raiders* executive committee lasted longer than Halley expected. They had a lot of questions for each of the siblings. They even got into the nitty gritty of the average time it took Drake to complete a custom piece and how long it took to come up with a concept. Then, there were practical questions about whether they needed to look for another mechanic and train someone to do the regular paint jobs if Drake wouldn't be regularly available anymore. They also wanted to know if they should look to hire other artists right away or if they could let the word get out and have the artists come to them – Halley preferred the second method for talent, at least to start.

Halley kicked herself for not asking who the current executive committee members were before entering the room. The committee she remembered was not the same as now. One of the older members, their secretary, had retired and moved to Florida – it was that or get a divorce; he moved and relinquished his committee position. Her brother Scottie took his position until, presumably, he became president.

The former treasurer, a good friend of her father's and Red's, died of cancer two years before, and Handsy took his place. That worked because when Scottie eventually took the reins as president, everyone expected Handsy to have that position.

Her dad had created a new position on the committee specifically for Wire, called technical director. James' rationale was that it was a new era, and Wire would need to be privy to the inner workings anyway; having him as an official part of the executive committee saved time.

Red remained as vice president. The road captain was the same good-natured, mild-mannered man who had gone to high school with her parents.

The bigger surprise was that Maverick was the sergeant at arms. She should have spent more time examining the patches on his leather cut. For someone relatively new to the club, he had to be held in high esteem to be given the position and also run one of their most complex businesses. She just wished she had known before she did the run-through with him in the room the previous day.

By the time the meeting was over, Halley was exhausted. She waited for Maverick in his office, since leaving without her bodyguard was no longer an option, even though two others were in the reception area waiting for her.

"I'm hungry!" Scarlett exclaimed as she flopped on Maverick's leather couch.

Drake dropped next to her and put her in a chokehold. "I suppose I could take you out, squirt. What do you want? Burger? Pizza?"

"Pizza! You're coming too, right, Hal?" Scarlett laughed with her brother's arm still around her neck.

"Yeah, that sounds good to me," Halley agreed, smiling at the easy camaraderie between the two. She was amazed at how different Drake was than the young man he was even a week ago. With his secret out in the open, his churlishness mostly evaporated. She suspected he would keep the artist's temperament, but she could work with that.

They heard their father's voice call from down the hall, "Halley!"

When all three stuck their heads around the office door and looked toward the conference room, they saw the executive committee headed their way.

"Yes. The answer's yes. You're the newest club business. Of course we'll take it to the club for a full vote, but they'll agree." That had to be the fastest vote on a new business in the history of the club.

The presentation clearly laid out that Halley, Drake, and eventually Scarlett, if she was still inclined, would own the business, and the club would be a partner, which made sense since Drake was a club brother. They had Sarah work on all the financial models with them so they would be correct, clearly represented, and easily understood by the committee. The plan showed the first five years and how they intended to grow in increments within that span. With Drake's talent, Halley truly believed it was a matter of getting the word out about him and carefully managing the business.

"Drake, would you mind showing me more of your artwork?" James asked quietly.

Drake's jaw dropped before he broke out in a huge grin. "Absolutely. Uhm, I kinda cleared out studio space in one of the buildings behind the clubhouse and have been hiding in there."

James smiled, "Well, maybe we better see if that space is adequate or what else you might need." He threw his arm over his son's shoulder and gave him a half hug.

"I'd like that."

"Hey, we're going for pizza; anyone else coming with us? Now it's a celebration!" Scarlett asked, her stomach growling loudly.

They made their way down the block to their favorite pizzeria, bodyguards in front of and behind the group. Halley noted what she considered overkill but, for once, kept her thoughts to herself. If Anthony really had killed Andres, the security detail was probably warranted.

Halley had a hard time reconciling the man she had been engaged to with a cold-blooded psycho. Sure, he had been overbearing, controlling, and sometimes unreasonable, but never would she have thought he was a murderer. His charm and sophistication were all surface level. She knew that now. For all the right reasons, she had finally listened to her instincts and broken it off with him. Wishing she had never gotten involved with him in the first place was a waste of time.

Why did she have to think of him now? Tonight was a celebration. Tonight was the start of her new life. Could she really move on until this was all behind her? She was certainly trying.

"I know that look, Thunder. You're thinking too hard," Maverick whispered next to her.

"Am not."

"Darlin', I see your lips moving," Maverick challenged her, playing up his Texas accent. He noticed that when she was caught in her head, her lips were often moving as if she were having a conversation with someone only she could hear. Sometimes she said those things out loud. While he found the habit somewhat charming and often amusing, he knew what caused it tonight was disturbing. He wanted to give her one night where she wouldn't have to worry.

Maverick moved them toward the back of the restaurant, away from the front picture windows, where he had a clear sight of the front and side doors. It was hard not to smile and laugh with the ridiculous banter thrown around between club brothers and Prez's kids. Scarlett was going to be a handful when she was fully grown. Maybe if Tyler didn't have an ol' lady by the time she was out of college – many years down the road – she would give his baby brother a chance. The kid already had her father and brothers wrapped around her finger.

"Scarlett, how come I don't see you at the stables?" Maverick asked. He knew the girl was an athlete, and she seemed to like all the same things Halley did; horses should be a natural for her.

Scarlett grimaced and glanced at her father and saw he was in a conversation with Red and a couple of the other guys before she looked at her plate and answered in a low tone, "My mom says I have to ride English-style and wants me to compete. I prefer Western, so I'd rather ride my dirt bike."

"Gotcha," Maverick said, completely understanding the girl was avoiding an argument with Priscilla.

"Maybe you can go riding with me," Halley offered. She felt her temper flare. Priscilla tried to do the same thing to her when she was a child, but Halley simply ignored her and did her own thing. Scarlett would have a harder time. But she could ride with her big sister, right? Halley was sticking with that line of thinking and going to stay positive.

Scarlett perked up and agreed, "Yeah, I'd like that a lot."

"Maybe I'll come too," Drake added. He rode alone when no one was around. He needed the silence at times. Going with his sisters sounded like it could be fun, and he assumed Maverick would be there too. The tough guy was growing on him.

An hour later, Handsy suggested, "Maybe we should move this party to the clubhouse." He felt exposed in the downtown after dark.

"Me too?" Scarlett asked, hope in her voice.

"You can see Drake's studio with me, and then you're going home," James compromised.

Outside, Maverick felt the hairs on the back of his neck rise. Someone was watching them. No one would be stupid enough to make a move with a group this large. He herded Halley and Scarlett to the middle of the men as they walked toward the parking for the security office. They had retrofitted underground parking as well as an outside lot that was gated. He didn't want to worry Halley but nudged Scottie and got James' attention. He saw Prez's chin lift toward him, confirming that the man felt something, too.

Maverick would feel a whole lot better when they were inside the compound. He looked forward to Conor being back and for his two former teammates to join them. This whole situation would be better with Wolf and Pace here.

Half the guys had their rides, and the others climbed into the club SUVs. The sound of the pipes as they made their way through town should be enough of a deterrence for tonight.

Anthony watched from one of the empty storefronts across from the security building. He had a realtor show him the property and had jammed the lock on the way out so he and his men could use it as a downtown observation post. It was all he could do not to run out shooting at those barbaric men standing too close to his woman. The way she laughed and smiled, joking with them, grated on his nerves. She was not supposed to be happy. He worked so hard for her to be dependent on him; all his work was being undone. He could see that plainly. "That will not do, my darling. You are mine," he said out loud as he watched.

The two mercenaries with him tonight rolled their eyes behind his back. They already figured out the man had a screw loose.

But his money was good. Soon, though, that would not be enough. They were coming to that tipping point. He didn't realize how close they were to leaving. They would give it a couple more days. If his behavior became even more erratic, they were out.

***

The next morning, Halley told Maverick she had a stop to make and needed to make it alone.

"Not happening, Thunder."

"Fine, you can check the area, but I need you to give me space after that," she argued.

Before she said where she wanted to go, he already knew. The cemetery. He texted part of his team to clear the area and make sure no one was there who shouldn't be.

Halley jumped into the driver's seat of her car before he could direct her to one of the SUVs. One of these days, he intended to have her on the back of his Harley. Or maybe they both would take their rides. That was something to which he looked forward.

Maverick's team checked the perimeter and drove the interior drive around the cemetery, looking in the groves of mature trees for anyone hiding before he and Halley arrived. They texted him the *all clear* before Halley parked. When he got out, she glared at him.

"I need some space, Maverick," she insisted.

"I'm just going to hang out by the tree over there, okay?" Maverick pointed to the trees a few yards from her mother's grave, one particularly large where he hid behind the trunk the last time, not that she knew that.

Begrudgingly, Halley agreed. She intended to first stop with her mother and then spend a longer time with her grandparents. Maverick didn't need to know the details. He'd follow anyway.

When she got to her mother's grave, Maverick heard a gasp and a small cry escape her lips before she dropped to her knees in front of the headstone. Moving quickly to her side, he looked her body over to see if she was hurt and didn't see any blood. Her eyes were focused straight ahead, unblinking.

"What's wrong?" He felt his heart speeding up, trying not to panic. He didn't panic. Never. Halley lifted her arm and pointed forward toward the headstone. Maverick followed the line of sight. He and his men had been on the lookout for men; this was considerably smaller. A child's doll, one with the old-time porcelain face and velvet dress, sat with its back leaned against the headstone. The eyes had "X"s drawn over them with black permanent marker. There was a note pinned to the hem of the dress. *Your turn…*

"What does that mean? Is he planning to kill me now? Either he wants me back, or he wants to kill me. He can't have it both ways," Halley sputtered, her anger rising past the initial shock. That vile man had desecrated her sacred space. Her mother had suffered enough at the hands of Anthony's father; at least her body deserved to rest in peace.

"He's not getting you, Thunder," Maverick put his arms around her and held her until her shaking stopped. He wouldn't tell her that in Anthony's mind, having her or having her dead could be the same – he would have her in death, was one interpretation. No, Maverick would not let his mind go in that direction. As she stood up again, he took a picture of the scene and then pulled a bag from his pocket to drop the doll in.

"I hate creepy dolls," Halley shuddered. "I told him that once. I never was a girlie girl who played with dolls. They all kind of gave me the creeps, especially that type with the porcelain faces like my great-grandmother had. I bet that's why he used a doll." She didn't know if he even remembered she told him about her loathing of dolls. She doubted he did, but it still got a rise from her.

Maverick looked around. His team cleared the place. They wouldn't have been looking at graves, only for intruders. "Do you still need some time?" He hoped she wanted to go. He felt too exposed here. It was starting to rain, spitting for now, but the sky could open any minute. He noticed that about Michigan weather, you could get all four seasons in one day, and major temperature changes within a matter of hours or even minutes were not uncommon.

"No. I'll come back when this is over," Halley stated firmly. "We should check my grandparents' plots, though. Make sure there aren't more messages."

They walked the couple of rows over and stopped at the foot of her grandparents' graves. There were no messages. The raven was on the branch again, this time silent, no coughing or calling to her, merely turning his sleek black head to watch as they walked.

"It's him. That's why he picked my mother's grave. It means something to me and to him. He wouldn't know to come to my grandparents because we never talked about our families or the past," Halley said resolutely.

She took Maverick's offered arm and slipped her hand through it. As they walked away, she called back in a whisper, "I'll be back soon to tell you all about what's been happening. I have some good news. I made some discoveries. But you probably already know that."

Facing forward again, she then glanced up at Maverick to see if he was laughing at her or thought she was crazy, "I know you probably don't understand –"

"You talk to people you love. I have no doubt they hear you, Thunder. I could tell you stories of stranger things I've seen and heard. This is mild," Maverick assured her. He wouldn't tell her the stories of men from his team who didn't come home or those they couldn't save but visited him in the dark of night in his dreams, and even some nights when he was awake.

Halley gave him a closed-lipped smile, an unspoken thank you for understanding. She didn't know many people who would understand. The rainfall was picking up.

As they got closer to the car, Halley's phone vibrated in her jeans pocket. She pulled it out and saw the name of a headhunter she had dealt with in the past. Curious, she answered and handed the keys to Maverick to drive.

"Halley McCarthy," she answered in her business voice. She never thought she had a business voice until Anthony had pointed it out and Craig and Andres laughed at her outrage and agreed with him. Listening to herself, she thought they were probably right.

"Halley, it's Laura Jones. I'm so glad to catch you. I've got an opportunity you won't want to miss," the woman's excited voice came through the phone.

"You do?" Halley asked incredulously.

"I do. I would have called sooner, but that blip in San Francisco made my client hesitate. But the CEO said he recommended you highly and that you had nothing to do with the problems at the startup, so my client asked me to reach out," the executive recruiter explained.

"Sorry, it's taking me a moment to catch up. You heard from Craig Martin?"

"My client did. He called him directly while talking about potentially selling the company or at least the technology. He said they would make a huge mistake if they didn't scoop you up while they could," the woman enthused.

"Wow. This is unexpected. What's the position? Is it in San Francisco?"

"It's for the Chief Marketing Officer, reporting to the CEO. And no, it's not San Francisco. This would be in London. Would that be a dealbreaker?" the woman hesitated at the possible hiccup.

"London?" Halley repeated.

"London. I know you wanted to get European experience and live there. Here's your chance to be an expat," the headhunter sounded sure she had Halley hooked. "Listen, I know this is hitting you out of the blue. Let me send you the job description and the company prospectus. Take a look, and if you like what you read, I'll set up a call between you and the CEO right away. This job is yours, as long as you and he get along when you talk."

"Thanks, Laura. I'll take a look and get back to you," Halley said, regaining her composure. She hung up and stared out the passenger window as Maverick moved out of the cemetery grounds.

"London, huh?" Maverick said. "So, your career is back on track?" He tried to keep his tone even and impartial.

"Seems so," Halley answered, still staring out the window. "Craig must have called them after he talked to the FBI."

"He's going to be talking to the FBI for weeks, is my guess. But he could have called while he's with them," Maverick guessed. "When do you have to decide?"

"Right away." Halley's voice sounded as far away as her thoughts.

Maverick told himself he didn't have any reason to feel the protest rising in his gut. She never actually promised she'd stay. However, after the business plan was approved, he thought that would be the result. Maybe that was her contingency if something else didn't come through.

They were almost to the turnoff for her father's house when Halley loudly yelled, "UGH!!! Why now? Why am I being tried this way? I've wanted to work in London my whole career. I already decided a different path, and *now* it comes up. Why?! ARGH!" She brought her fist down on the passenger door in her frustration and immediately winced in pain.

Maverick stayed silent, assuming her rant was rhetorical.

"Go to Gram's. I don't want to see Priss," Halley directed, still staring out the window.

Maverick made the turn, and by the time he parked, the rain was coming down hard. He turned the car off, and they both sat, her staring to the side and him staring through the windshield. The front porch light blinked on and off several times.

"I think your gram is signaling," Maverick said, leaning forward in his seat and squinting, trying to stare through large raindrops pelting the car in a constant beat and the sheet of water pouring down the windshield.

"Of course she is," Halley scowled. "Let's go before she walks an umbrella out herself – or sends Gramps with one."

Maverick held back a laugh. Seeing the big, grizzled biker carrying an umbrella to the car would be funny. The two leaped from the car and ran toward the side door to the kitchen. Mary McCarthy was waiting with two towels. They accepted gratefully and wiped the dripping rain from their faces and hair. She handed each a pair of sweatpants and a sweatshirt.

"They're your grandfather's, but you should be able to cinch them in while I dry your clothes," Mary said.

"You don't need to do that. I'll dry eventually," Maverick protested.

"Nonsense. Go change," Mary insisted, accepting the kiss on her cheek from her granddaughter. Then, almost as an afterthought, Maverick leaned down and shyly kissed her other cheek before heading to the half bath in the hallway. When he came out, he had the bag with the doll and set it on the counter, waiting for his brothers to arrive. He had it protected under his shirt when they ran into the house. As much as he wanted Halley to be able to forget, even for the time it took to drink the tea her grandmother left steeping in the mug, he couldn't do that.

The rain was back to a drizzle when Wire, James, and Red arrived; Scottie and Handsy arrived less than a minute later. All stared at the creepy doll with X'd eyes staring blankly through the plastic of the bag.

"Nice clothes, guys. Did you raid Gramps' closet?" Scottie asked; anything to distract from that doll.

"Haha," Halley scowled. She stared in her mug, hands wrapped around the outside, absorbing the heat. The sweatshirt slipped off her right shoulder and it hung almost to her knees when she stood. The sweatpants pooled at her ankles. When she came out of the guest bedroom and watched as Maverick walked to the kitchen, she was fascinated that the sweats Maverick wore hung a little loosely, but the sweatshirt pulled across his chest. Her grandfather was always larger than life in her mind. To see that Maverick was close to his size was shocking.

Scottie turned to his father, "There are vehicles with Illinois plates at the motel outside of town and others at the hotel at the other end. Could be tourists, but I doubt it."

"I ran the plates," Wire added. "They belong to the Ricci family companies." He looked to Scottie and shrugged, "I didn't have time to tell you when we got called over here."

"Should we meet?" Handsy asked.

James pondered that and then shook his head, "Not yet. They'll look for him and let us know if they find him. We'll do the same. If Anthony's watching, I don't want him to know we've joined forces."

"Lot of firepower in our little town," Red stated uncomfortably.

"Lucky for us they want to stay under the radar as much as we want 'em to," Mitchell said as he joined them in the kitchen.

Maybe there was some sort of tax break he could claim since this seemed to be the new club meeting place. "Hal, you okay?"

"Fine, Gramps." At the similar look on all their faces, she shrugged, "Okay, I'm a little freaked out. But I've got all of you at my back, so we're good, right? I really don't want anyone else to get hurt because of me."

"Don't even think about leaving town again, Hal. We will handle this," James admonished as if he could read his daughter's thoughts.

Indeed, she was thinking London might be far enough away to escape and lead her deranged ex-fiancé away from those she loved. But did she want to go back to the corporate life? She acknowledged in her brain she would still hit that damn ceiling sooner rather than later, regardless of how exciting living in London sounded. She would not be the one in ultimate control – again. She really did like control. Why did this have to come now? Was it to lead Anthony away?

"Stop!" James said loudly.

Halley's eyes went wide. Did she do it again? Think she was talking in her mind and said it out loud?

"Yeah, Thunder. You said it out loud," Maverick said quietly, moving to her side and sitting next to her at the kitchen table.

"What the … Hal! London? Why would you go to London?" Scottie asked, the hurt apparent in his voice.

Halley sighed. "I didn't mean for you to hear that."

"Yeah? Well, we did," Red sputtered.

"This morning, as we left the cemetery, I was offered a possible job in London."

"So, you weren't serious about the business here and marketing Drake's art?" Handsy's voice held the accusatory tone she knew everyone else felt.

"Princess, London has enough of its own royals, they don't need ours too," Red spit out.

"No, stop. I was – *I am* serious about working with Drake. This was out of left field. Something I've always wanted was dropped in my lap this morning at a time I see all of you – the people I love – in danger because I'm here. I haven't had time to process any of it. But don't tell me I'm not interested in what I want to build because I am deadly serious. More serious than I've ever been," she huffed angrily, gathering steam the more she talked. The more she talked, the more it felt right in her skin. She needed control. She liked to build things. She liked working with creative people. The life she carved out that could be built here fit what was most important to her. It helped that she truly believed in her brother's talent and could already see ways of expanding what they would build.

"So, no London?" Scottie asked.

She glared at him, wanting to say she was still thinking about it, just to be disagreeable. But she wouldn't. Things were tense enough as it was. Adding to it was not productive. "No London, Scottie." Saying it out loud, the tension in her chest and the pain that was growing behind her right temple faded.

The room let out a collective groan of relief. Each man hugged her over her chair from behind and from the side, placing kisses on top of her head. Maverick watched with interest. The way she held her own with the bikers, handled her independence, and discovered who she was as she rose from the ashes all made her even more alluring.

"Proud of you, Hal," her father muttered in her ear.

Maverick thought, *hell yes, that's what I feel, proud of her*. He hoped none of his brothers noticed the goofy smile before he schooled his face.

Mitchell nodded to James, and the MC president got everyone's attention. "It's time we go on offense, brothers. We've been playing defense, and I'm done. No more messages. No more creepy gifts. We find this chickenshit bastard. This stops." Expressions of agreement echoed in the kitchen.

Any feelings Halley had for Anthony were long gone, if they'd ever existed. Now, she wasn't sure if she hoped his family or hers would find him first. Either way, it needed to be soon, before anyone else got hurt. One murder was more than enough. It made her sick to her stomach.

Chapter 23

GENTLE BUT CONSTANT RAIN FELL ON THE INLAND LAKE. Each raindrop caused its own outward movement, eventually coming together with all the others and joining with the wind, creating small whitecaps. The rain brought out the smell of the water, the pine trees, and the black earth. It was making him queasy. Too much nature. Anthony knew one of his hired mercenaries was around the corner of the cabin. He had appropriated the dwelling north of the small town to which his fiancée had fled. He could see the man's breath in the chilled early morning air. Fool.

The realtor had proven to be a good source of information. He mentioned maybe buying a cottage or cabin in the area in the near future, and she had been more than happy to drive him by several that were either seasonal homes for their owners or that she knew were unoccupied and for sale, as well as providing the listings for others. It really was too easy. All he had to do was force the lock, and he no longer needed to stay at a motel or hotel where he and his hired guns could be more easily detected. Electricity from a generator and heat for the furnace were fueled by the large propane tank near the driveway. There were no neighbors within sight or shouting distance. As much as he detested the country and country ways, he had to admit the current setup was perfect for his plans.

"This is taking too long," the man with the bald head and scar said tersely from the doorway.

"It will take as long as I say," Anthony bit back.

"There's no longer surprise on our side," the mercenary argued.

"No. There's fear," Anthony declared, satisfaction clear in his words.

The man shook his head and moved back inside the cabin. Arguments were futile with this kind of client. He thought he knew it all, that he was smarter than everyone around him. What the mercenary knew was that delusional men like his client had the hardest falls. Anthony thought he was playing with his prey, but he was giving her family and those bikers time to find them. It was only a matter of time. Now, he needed to make sure he was long gone before the fallout. He recognized Maverick and had no desire or reason to go up against the other veteran. The mercenary had a solid ego, but he knew who they were dealing with, even if Anthony was too blind to see it.

"What are you doing?" Anthony asked, leaning against the door frame. The mercenary was in front of him, stuffing clothes in a duffle bag.

"I'm out."

"I'm paying you."

"Paid me for what I've already done. You have the others. I'm out." The big man didn't stop his movement, throwing the bag over his shoulder after adding his extra firearms and ammunition to a separate duffel. There were four other hired guns here in town, and more were still in the Bay Area working at Anthony's whim.

"I'll pay you more," Anthony upped the ante.

"Not interested."

"I'll double what I've already paid."

"Can't spend dead."

"I'll triple it," Anthony countered. "Why would you be dead? I was told you're the best. I'm paying you to be the best."

The mercenary stood straight and sighed, "You learn in this business, there's always someone better. You may not know who you're up against, but I do."

Anthony scoffed. He knew who he was up against; his mother had drilled it into his head since he was seven years old. He was better. He expected who he hired to be better. "I didn't take you for someone who runs from a fight. There may not even be a fight if I get my fiancée, and we leave the country first."

"There are special forces operatives in that biker gang," the man tried to explain.

"This is a problem?" Anthony rolled his eyes.

"Could be," the man admitted.

"Triple," Anthony reiterated.

The others were part of a company of mercenaries set up to take on allcomers anywhere in the world. He was a free agent and was paid separately. He liked it that way. He could come and go as he pleased and give the client the finger if he got fed up.

"Fine. Three days."

"Fine. I need to move up my timeline anyway," Anthony revealed.

"I want the money now." He wasn't sure Anthony would be around to pay at the end of whatever this was. "Maybe if you told me the entire plan, I could figure out how best to help you."

Anthony didn't trust anyone. Money only bought temporary loyalty. That's why he was the puppet master, and his puppets only moved when he pulled the strings, not before, not with prior knowledge. He needed the big man, though, so he'd give him a little, "I'm going to use the sister to get to her." He went to the bedroom and came out with stacks of cash that he handed to the hired gun.

"The blonde?"

"Tiffany. She's enthralled with me. I'm going to use that," Anthony confirmed.

"She's a kid," the mercenary brought up. He had very few lines he wouldn't cross, but he did not mess with children.

"I'm not going to sleep with her. Just use her to get Halley to come to me. Since when did you get morals?" Anthony sneered.

"I don't mess with kids, man."

"Well, glad to know you have your limits," Anthony laughed. He unlocked his phone and sent a text to the burner he gave the girl when they first met. She had been more than happy to think she was pulling something over on her big sister.

A: Lunch plans?

Tiffany: Not anymore

A: Meet me?

Tiffany: Love to. Diner?

A: Bella, somewhere more private. And I need to return the car key

A: I'll send you the location after I set up our lunch

Tiffany: I'm waiting… (smiley face)

Tiffany could barely keep the smile from her face. Anthony may be her sister's ex-fiancé, but she was the sister he wanted to see. That meant something. He was sophisticated and beautiful. Finally, someone who appreciated the same things she did. Quickly, she texted her friends that she couldn't meet them at the diner. But it didn't hurt her parents thought that was where she was going. Everything was coming together nicely.

***

Duffels packed with clothes and others with weapons sat inside the door to the previously unoccupied apartment. Two apartments were above the security offices owned by the club. Maverick kept one. He eventually hoped to buy or build a house in the area but hadn't been motivated yet. The other now housed his two friends, brothers forged in battle, and, with any luck, soon brothers in the *Phantom Raiders*. Conor, Wolf, and Pace had arrived minutes before. Per Maverick's instructions, Conor dropped them at the apartment.

Maverick recently thought he might be getting through to Wolf, but when Conor texted that both men were coming with him and were considering prospecting as well as full-time security employees, Maverick was overjoyed. With these two by his side, he felt even more ready to face whatever was to come with Anthony and his mercenaries. He would take them to the clubhouse and introduce them later.

"What do you think? There are two bedrooms. This work for you for now?" Maverick asked, looking around the furnished apartment, pleased to have a place for his friends to land. "You can have rooms at the clubhouse if you prospect, but thought you might want a little more privacy."

"Perfect, Mav," Pace nodded. "Only need a place to put my head. Been drifting the last year since I got out. Feels good to maybe belong again."

Wolf felt the same, "Yeah, this is great, man. When do we meet your prez? He going to be cool with this – with us?"

"Oh yeah. He knows I've been trying to get you here, Wolf. When I told him Conor said Pace was coming as a bonus, he was stoked," Maverick assured the men. "You want to get some shuteye before meeting the guys?"

Wolf stood by the front window, looking down at the main street. He stiffened, "Mav, that looks like Anthony's cousin headed into the diner." Once they realized Anthony's real identity, Wire had sent pictures of possible associates, including Enzo, to the team in San Francisco. Wolf was one of the guys who broke into Enzo's apartment.

Maverick and Pace joined him at the window and watched as two more men followed Enzo into the diner. "The Riccis aren't involved. Anthony went rogue. They're here looking for him for the same reason we are."

Pace whistled lightly, "Remind me never to get involved with a family like that."

"I think we'll pass on the sleep for now. Just need a five-minute shower. Seems like there may be some work to do first," Wolf answered Maverick's previous question.

Maverick couldn't help but grin. The enthusiasm, the dedication, was something he appreciated in the men, his men. "Appreciate that. Why don't you catch a few hours while you can? Pretty sure things are going to pop off soon. Want you at your best."

With a quick nod, Wolf picked up two of his bags and headed for the bedrooms. He said as he walked, "Come get us when you're ready." Pace smiled at Maverick and went to his own bedroom.

***

Tiffany passed by the diner on her way through town. She had to make it look like she was going where she said. Her father's men were always watching these days. Through the window, she saw her friends already at a booth in the front, laughing and making sure they looked cute in case any of their major crushes walked by. She thought she saw Anthony walking into the diner with two men in front and two men behind him. On a second glance, she realized it wasn't him; it was just someone who was his size and had the same dark, wavy hair. The clothes were all wrong, and the way he walked was wrong – she should have noticed that straight away. Her mother would have.

She kept driving out of town toward a small park on a lake that no one ever went to before summer. She'd been to several high school parties there, but always in the summer and fall. He must have a picnic planned for her. Sometime she would tell him she preferred restaurants to blankets and bugs, but today, it sounded romantic, and she wouldn't ruin the mood.

The park area was several hundred feet off the road. It's why it made a good high school partying spot – it wasn't visible from the road. A large SUV was parked near a tree, and she could see two large men sitting in the front seats when she drove further along. A tingling sense of caution ran up her spine, but then she saw Anthony's back, where he was sitting on a picnic table staring at the lake. She parked in the designated parking area, afraid to drive any closer because the mud was usually deep and treacherous this time of year. The last thing she needed was to have to call her father or brothers for a tow.

"You came, Bella," Anthony stated without turning around when he heard her approaching steps.

"I did. Are we going somewhere else for lunch?" she asked as she looked around and didn't see any food, cooler, or picnic basket. Now standing in front of him, he still stared at the lake.

"Are you that hungry, Bella?" Anthony asked, finally meeting her eyes.

"Well, no, but I thought…" her voice trailed off. She didn't know what she was supposed to say.

Anthony raised his hand in the air, and one of the men brought a perspiring bottle of champagne and two glasses from the SUV. The man stood between Tiffany and the picnic table. She heard him release the cork and pour the two glasses. The man left it on the table and returned to the truck without a word. Anthony picked them up and handed her one.

"Don't tell me you've never had a drink before," Anthony looked at her mockingly. "I forget you're still a child."

"Of course not. I'm not a child," Tiffany huffed and took the flute from his hand. She waited for him to raise his glass to his lips and followed suit. Her nerves made her gulp half the flute.

"Before I forget, here is the car key fob. I wouldn't want you to get into trouble," Anthony held it out to her. She reached for it and put it in the pocket of her cropped pink jean jacket. She would have to sneak it back into Halley's jewelry box while her older sister was out of the house. Anthony captured her fingers and pulled her closer to him.

"A toast, Bella. To becoming good friends." Anthony raised his glass to hers and took a sip while Tiffany drank the rest of her glass. He filled it again and pulled her to a seat on the bench.

"I have food for you, Bella, but this will work better on an empty stomach," Anthony said, staring back at the lake.

"What do you mean?" Tiffany asked. As she said it, the world tilted a little. Then she thought she saw two of Anthony. That made her remember the man in town who looked so much like him. She opened her mouth to tell him about the strange likeness, but her tongue would not work. She took another drink, trying to lubricate her mouth and vocal cords. It didn't help. She tried again. Now, the glass was tilting in her hands.

"Whoa there, Bella. Let's not spill your drink," Anthony said, taking it from her hand and tilting it to her lips.

"Wha –" Tiffany fought to get the words out.

"Sshhh. Relax. As long as your sister does as she's told, you'll be fine," Anthony consoled her, slipping his arm around her before she slid off the picnic bench. With his other arm, he motioned to the men in the SUV. They came quickly, secured her hands behind her with zip ties, another at her ankles, and fixed a gag around her mouth. Anthony didn't want to listen to her whining voice when the drug wore off, and she could speak again. He looked her up and down as the two men carried her to the back of the SUV and threw her inside.

What a pity she was only sixteen; he really needed to work out some stress, and what better way than with a beautiful woman? He had to remind himself not to cross that line. He had sent the large mercenary with the bald head and scar to town to watch things from there, not wanting him here when he took the girl. The man showed too much distaste for the use of children, and Anthony couldn't afford to trust him with this part of the mission.

Anthony left the bottle of champagne and the two glasses sitting on the picnic table. The earlier rain had stopped, but everything was still damp. He thought the setting looked like a romantic scene and perfect if his adversaries tracked her there. He fleetingly thought they should drive the car into the lake, but why? It wasn't as if they could track her with it. She would be long gone. And no random tourists were going to happen upon the scene – no one had been in this area since before winter.

Chapter 24

THE MERCENARY WITH THE BALD HEAD AND SCAR WALKED INTO THE DINER, purportedly to pick up food for himself and the other hired guns watching the main street from the empty storefront. It was amazing to him that no one thought to check the empty buildings more often. He placed the order at the counter, then looked around the room. He noticed Enzo and what must be more of the Ricci family and their associates.

He then saw Maverick at a table with the girl with whom his current client was obsessed, Halley, and three other men wearing the *Phantom Raiders* cuts. Maverick watched him closely, and the scarred man took a deep breath as he made his decision. He indicated to Maverick with his head and walked down the hall toward the bathrooms.

"Long time no see, Bull. Surprised to find you in this neck of the woods," Maverick greeted him.

"Maverick," Bull said in greeting back. "First, want you to know I had no idea that was your girl." Maverick didn't correct him and waited to hear what else the big man had to say. "Also want you to know I'm leaving town. I want no part of where this is going."

"Where's it going, Bull?" Maverick pried, teeth clenched.

"Nowhere good, man. I don't know what's happening, but I think that crazy psycho Anthony is going to kidnap that little tramp Tiffany in exchange for your girl. I don't mess with kids. I'm out of this," Bull said, disgust showing on his face.

"What's his plan?"

"Wouldn't tell me. Just got a feelin'," Bull explained. He ran his hand along the back of his neck nervously and then dropped it to his side. "Listen, Tiffany's been meeting up with him. I think she's got a crush on the guy. Seems to want to prove she's better than her sister or some shit."

"Where's he staying?"

"Remote cabin." Bull gave him the lake and which cabin. "Doubt he'll take her back there, though, but who knows? He's losing it."

"What are you going to do?" Maverick asked. The guy wasn't right in the head a lot of the time, but he did do the right thing this time and didn't seem to want to cross Maverick.

"I'm picking up lunch for the two morons who work for that security force team in Georgia, and then I'm getting in my truck and driving out of here. I'm not looking back until I get to Tennessee. Think I'll spend some time at my granddaddy's cabin until this is sorted. Don't want trouble with you or any of your guys," Bull explained.

"How many other guys does he have with him?" Maverick was determined to get as much intel as possible before the man bolted.

"Other than the morons down the street, two more with him now. I heard the other guys talking, and four others from their team will be in from San Francisco within the next hour or so," Bull replied.

"Gotta ask, Bull. Did you off the partner in San Francisco?"

Bull turned slightly red and seemed to fight his temper, "Hell no, Maverick. That was Anthony. I wasn't there, but one of the guys told me he waved his gun around, screaming all sorts of nonsense, and then double-tapped him. That wasn't the plan. He almost had the guys draw down on him. They thought he went crazy." Looking a little amused, he continued, "But I am the one who made that other

CEO guy, Craig Martin, piss his pants when Anthony told me to scare him. I didn't even do anything, just moved toward him, and he lost control of himself. I don't like that guy. He's a wuss."

Maverick knew Conor would agree with Bull on that point.

"I gotta get back with the food. We've been set up in that empty storefront across from your offices so we can watch the town," Bull started moving toward the front before Maverick stopped him with a hand lightly on his shoulder.

"Thanks for the heads up. I won't forget it," Maverick said and reached to shake the mercenary's hand.

Bull gripped the offered hand, "Don't want to be on opposite sides with you and your guys, Maverick. You saved me over there. I may have forgotten most everything else in my life, but I never forgot that."

Maverick took a split-second to assess the giant of a man and said, "Listen, if you ever decide you want a permanent place to land, give me a call."

Bull smirked, "Be part of a motorcycle club? I don't know. I'm not always in the best control. Probably a good idea if I stay by myself."

Maverick could tell he was tempted. He smirked back, "Sounds like half our guys on a Friday night. But seriously, we have each other's backs, and we'd have yours. You wouldn't have to work for scum anymore, either. We keep our standards pretty high."

"I'll think on it. But thanks for the offer even if I don't take you up on it. I'm kinda used to being alone now."

Maverick gave him a chin lift as they both walked to the front. Bull paid for his food, waiting in a sack at the counter, and walked out the door without a backward glance. That was some confidence he had, banking that neither of the two tables of angry men would put a bullet in his back.

Bull delivered the food and told the two hired guns he was making a scouting run before getting in his SUV and driving away.

Maverick grabbed a chair and sat at the end of the table the Riccis occupied. Wire and James joined them. After quick introductions, Maverick gave them the rundown of what Bull told him.

James pulled out his phone and called Priscilla. She informed him Tiffany was at the diner meeting her girlfriends. James looked up and saw the booth with Tiffany's friends by the window. Tiffany wasn't with them. He marched over to the table.

"Do you know where Tiff is?" James asked the girls.

"She was supposed to meet us," one of her friends said.

"Yeah, but she texted about an hour ago and said she got a better offer. I don't know what that means unless she got back together with Greg," one of the girls huffed out snottily, mentioning Tiffany's secret boyfriend and Danny's fellow baseball teammate.

"Could she have gone to the game?" He knew the boys had a Saturday away baseball tournament. Scarlett had a softball tournament in the same town. Neither teen should be home until late that night.

"Maybe, but I doubt it. She's still pretty mad at Greg," yet another girl informed him.

"Let me know if she contacts you. It's important," James stressed, knowing the girls would think Tiffany was in trouble and probably not tell him.

"Okay, Mr. McCarthy," her best friend agreed.

James shook his head when he got back to the Ricci table.

"Let us know if you hear anything," Leonardo requested. "Our men are trying to locate him, but so far, no luck."

Wire was busy looking down at his phone. He glanced up briefly, "I've got a location on her car."

James moved toward the door with the brothers behind him. He told Halley to stay put and motioned Tyler, who had just entered the diner, to stay with her. He told them Red and Handsy were on their way and would be there shortly. Halley didn't even have time to protest or ask questions.

"Do you know what's going on?" she asked Tyler.

"Nope." The look on his face was as confused as hers, so she knew he was telling the truth.

The table her father and Maverick had joined shifted as two of the men moved to stand at the end of theirs. Halley looked up at two men who were very similar in facial structure, hair, and eye color to her ex-fiancé. Tyler shifted in his seat, uncomfortable with the strangers paying attention to Halley.

"Halley McCarthy, I presume? I'm sorry we didn't meet under better circumstances. I am Leonardo Ricci, Anthony's uncle, and this is my son Enzo," the older of the men introduced.

"Oh, hello," she replied shyly, not sure what to say to the people who could have been her in-laws. She stared at Enzo for a moment, and recognition crept across her face, "Hey, I've seen you before. In San Francisco, in that speakeasy. But we never met."

"No, and I'm sorry for that, Ms. McCarthy. I also apologize for my cousin's appalling behavior. You deserve much better," Enzo said. He looked very sorry for his cousin's actions and also maybe that he hadn't met her properly when he saw her in San Francisco. Halley remembered him because she thought he was so attractive and looked a lot like Anthony but less fussy.

"We'll go back to our seats now. But if you don't mind, we're going to help your friend here look out for you until the others return," Leonardo explained. He did indeed move back to his seat with Enzo close behind.

"What was that about?" Tyler whispered, not liking the look of any of them or that he had the responsibility to take care of Halley when he had no idea what was going on. At least they sounded like they were on the same side, but you could never know for sure.

"I'm not sure," Halley replied as honestly as she could. She sighed with relief when Sarah ran into the diner with Handsy two steps behind her. They both slid into the booth. Red arrived only a minute later and positioned a chair at the end of their booth.

"Will someone please tell us what's going on?" Halley demanded.

"Not sure, princess. Just got the text to get my ass over here and watch yours until your dad is back," Red said smoothly.

They found Tiffany's car at the park. Embedded in the mud, they saw one other set of tracks that had peeled out of the area; the tires looked to be for an SUV. Tiff's car was open. Inside, they found her purse, but then Wire noticed another phone, a burner, in the cup holder.

Maverick viewed the champagne bottle and two glasses left on the picnic table. The bottom of one looked like something was mostly dissolved. He was pretty sure a lab would prove the drink had been drugged. A logical conclusion was that it was Tiffany's. He could see more than one set of fingerprints on each glass. Maverick bagged the bottle and glasses after taking a picture of the setup. He doubted they'd need evidence, but if they did, they'd have it.

"Let's get back to the office. Maybe I can get something from one of these phones," Wire said. At the same time, Maverick slipped behind the wheel of Tiffany's car to follow Wire and James back downtown. James drove their SUV, his jaw clamped so tight Wire thought he might break his teeth.

Maverick stopped back at the diner and had a quick word with the Riccis before joining Halley and the others. Two of the men sitting with the Riccis disappeared down the hall toward the bathrooms and the rear entrance and didn't return.

"Somebody better tell me what's going on, and it better be now," Halley whispered tersely.

"Not yet," Maverick whispered back. His brothers sitting around the table kept quiet, though they were as anxious as Halley. Maverick threw several bills on the table and gestured to the others to get up. As agreed with James before they left the park, he said, "Let's head over to *Raiders Roost*."

Getting Halley and club members out of the diner in the middle of the downtown, where tourists and townsfolk alike were likely to wander, was a priority. They could go to the security office, but, as Bull told him, the mercenaries were watching the street and would see them. They could go to the clubhouse, but the town was a more central location for the time being. *Raiders Roost Tavern* wouldn't have many outsiders at this time of day, and they could easily hustle anyone out, if need be.

They reached the tavern. James and Wire walked in after them. Wire, hanging onto a laptop with a mobile phone connected to it by a cord, immediately sat at a table off to the side. Other than club members, Halley, Sarah, and Jana, only two regulars were seated in a booth to the far side, away from everyone.

James stood at the booth where Halley was seated. "You may hear from Anthony soon."

Wire strode to stand next to James with his laptop resting on his arm. He grimaced and steeled himself when he said, "Prez, she's been in contact with him for a while. Here's the text stream. It ends today when she agrees to meet him at the park."

James read from the laptop, and Maverick stood next to him doing the same. Scottie stood behind his father, reading. The longer they read, the angrier each of the men looked.

"Will someone please share or explain," Halley said exasperatedly, looking from one man to the next.

"Anthony has been in contact with Tiffany. It looks like he's been using her to get to you," James said.

Halley's breath left her chest. She felt the pain of betrayal hit her in the sternum.

"We think he may have kidnapped her today to get to you," James laid it out, no sugar coating.

Conor heard the explanation from where he stood behind Scottie. As soon as he got to the clubhouse earlier, he heard Red had been called to town and turned around to join his brothers.

"Conman, can you get Wolf and Pace from the apartment? Stay out of view of the main drag," Maverick said. Without a word, Conor headed for the door.

"I'll try to get a location on this number that texted Tiff," Wire said and moved to his table, shutting everyone out as he worked feverishly. It was a long shot. The phone could be untraceable, or the man could have turned it off.

"What about this cabin he's been staying at, the scary dude told you about? Shouldn't we head out there?" Scottie asked, having been brought up to speed.

"We've already sent some of our guys out that way. They'll stay out of sight and call if there are any vehicles or anyone there. Two of Ricci's guys went with them," James said.

Halley sat in the booth unmoving, taking in everything said around her. This could not be happening. She caused this. She came home. Now, everything was out of her hands. There was nothing she could do.

"Stop, Thunder. This is on Anthony, not you," Maverick said tersely. He could see the changing emotions as they flew across her face when her father gave them the situation, and Wire provided the proof.

"This would have come with or without you, Hal," James reinforced Maverick's statement. "We know from his family this has been twenty-eight years in the making. It's all on his psycho father, delusional mother, and him. Not you."

Halley's phone dinged with a text message. It came from an unknown number. Well, that made sense; she had blocked Anthony's number long ago when he wouldn't accept their breakup. James reached for her phone, but she swung it away from him and faced the back of the booth while she opened the image. Her gasp had all the men and Sarah leaning in.

There was a picture of Tiffany, bound and gagged, mascara streaks down her face, eyes unfocused. It looked like she was staged against a tree.

"Handsy, would you take Sarah and Jana to their homes? They don't need to be part of this," Scottie said, his words terse as he tried to control his emotions.

"Like hell I'm going anywhere. I'm here for Hal," Sarah declared, refusing to move from the booth when Handsy tried to pull her out. She reached out and gripped Halley's forearm in a show of support.

"What she said," Jana declared equally forcefully from behind Scottie. At some point she had abandoned her post at the bar and was part of the group gathered around the booth. She gestured between Sarah and herself and said, "You said we're family. So, we're either family or we're not. If we're family, we're staying."

Scottie sighed heavily and reluctantly nodded his head. At the very least, if they were with them, they knew the two women would not be new targets in Anthony's sick game. Who knew how much he knew about who was close to Halley or any of the McCarthy family.

A second text came.

Unknown: Tiffany is safe…for now. The rest is up to you

"I have to answer him," Halley said, beginning to type.

“Do not press send until we know what you’re saying,” James ordered.

Halley: What do you want, Anthony?

James nodded his assent.

Immediately, she saw the three dots that indicated he was responding.

Unknown: What I’ve always wanted – you

Halley: We aren’t a couple

Unknown: That’s where you are wrong. This was destined 28 years ago

Halley: Let her go

Unknown: Only when I have you. But I am willing to talk first

Halley: Where should I meet you?

Halley pressed send on the last text before her father or the others could object.

Unknown: I’ll come to you, my darling

Unknown: Bring my thumb drive. I know you have it. We’ll need it

Unknown: Do tell your father and those heathens he associates with not to shoot me, or you’ll never find your precious sister

“How does he know where I am? What thumb drive?” Halley asked, her hand shaking while she clutched her phone. Maverick slid into the booth and put his arm around her. No one answered her questions.

Wire moved in and handed the thumb drive they found in Halley’s jewelry box to Maverick, “I copied it. But don’t give it to him until the exchange. I suspect this is what he really wants.”

Maverick raised his eyebrows but didn’t have a chance to ask more.

James had his phone to his ear, “Yeah, he made contact. He’s coming to her but won’t have Tiffany with him, so we can’t stop him. *Nobody* can interfere until both my daughters are safe.” He listened for a moment and responded, “Understood.”

When he hung up, he looked at his guys and said, "Two down." Leonardo had his men dispatch the two in the empty storefront.

Conor came through the door with Wolf and Pace on his heels. Introductions were quickly made.

"Good to have you both here," James welcomed them. That's all they needed to hear from the president.

Wolf leaned down to Maverick and said into his ear, "There was a van in the alley next to the door of the empty store across from the office."

"Cleaners. Ricci's," Maverick responded. He was impressed. Leonardo Ricci must not leave anything to chance. He had his cleanup team already in town. He must have planned all along that it would not end well for his nephew and his mercenaries.

James spat orders. Men moved quickly out of the tavern. Some changed seats to the bar and strategic locations throughout the room. Red was on the phone issuing other orders for the bikers to set their trap; he made sure the McCarthy family was covered, moving Priscilla to her parents' home two towns away and ensuring Scarlett's and Danny's shadows were ready at the tournaments several hours away – they were probably safe, but they had to be sure. James gambled on where Anthony would want to be two steps down the game board. He had no doubt the man saw this as a game. Maverick called in their security force members who were not part of the club and added their numbers to the club brothers, where they assumed it would all culminate.

"You sure about this, Irish?" Red asked his president and best friend.

"I am. He's so stuck in the past, it can't end anywhere else," James replied. If he was wrong? Well, they would deal with that when the time came.

"I'm going to allow Leonardo and his people to be there. Any objections?" James asked the men closest to him. They all thought for a moment and then shook their heads – no objections.

"They aren't going to get sentimental, will they?" Scottie asked the only question any of them had.

"From what I've seen and heard? No. There will be no hesitation," James stated and sent a text to Leonardo.

A minute later, Halley's phone signaled more texts.

Unknown: I'm coming in

Unknown: I want to sit with you and that man who never leaves your side; everyone else move away

Halley braced herself to keep her emotions at bay and showed the text to her father. He moved to the booth behind hers. Maverick stayed where he was. Conor was at the door when it opened. Anthony took one step inside.

"That's far enough," Conor said and frisked the man, removing his two weapons. "You might get these back when you leave."

"I would have done the same," Anthony said simply, as if this was an everyday occurrence. The bikers had to hand it to the man; he was supremely confident coming to them on their own turf. But then, he did have the president's daughter held hostage.

Anthony slowly slid into the booth, his eyes never leaving Halley. If Maverick had to describe it, he would call the look reverent.

"Finally, we're together again," Anthony smiled his most charming smile at her. He reached across and put his hands over hers, which were clasped on top of the table. Halley pulled hers back slowly, not wanting to show any fear, hoping her manner was devoid of emotion. If anything came through, she wanted to project disdain.

"We are not together, Anthony. We never will be. We never really were, were we? This was all some sick game to you, and I was your pawn for a while," Halley said evenly.

"My darling, I was attracted to you before I realized who you were. Then, well, yes, then our involvement became even more vital," Anthony said, his voice smooth.

"Release my sister," Halley insisted, not wanting to revisit their torrid relationship.

"Now, now, Halley darling. That's not how this will work. I will give you a location, and we will exchange you for her. Then you and I will travel by private jet to our new home," Anthony explained as if she were a child. "If any of your father's men waylay me, my men will kill her. If I'm not back by the designated time, they will kill her. If you refuse to meet me, they will kill her."

"I'm to meet you, not go with you now?" Halley asked, knowing Maverick was not going to be happy with her suggesting it, as if there were a choice, but she had to know. Anthony was precise with his words, and this did not make sense to her.

"My darling, I want you to come to me of your free will. I would be no better than these bikers you've surrounded yourself with if I merely took you from here against your will," Anthony said, apparently believing his own deluded logic.

Anthony continued, "I can see you're confused. Let me back up and explain. My uncle and grandfather insisted I either start a company or join one that would make money for our family. I met Andres in New York at a fundraiser my aunt had sponsored. He introduced me to Craig. They obviously did not have the financial acumen, so I offered my assistance and brought in large investors – not only my family's business. As you know, the technology is solid. I was getting bored, though. When you joined, I knew it was our destiny. Both of our lives changed when your family killed my father."

"You mean when your father raped and killed my mother," Halley interrupted, her temper briefly flaring.

"That was not the case, my darling, no matter what lies your family told you," Anthony dismissed her. "To continue … You seemed estranged from your family. I wanted to make you part of mine. Then, you had to display your conscience and go to Craig with your concerns over payments, which caused greater scrutiny of my operations. I was almost done. I was setting aside a nice nest egg that would last for the rest of our lives and the lives of our children.

"Your irrational action to try to give my ring back was childish. I knew you would eventually come to your senses. But with investors and federal agents descending on the company and Andres' disappearance, I had to disappear as well. I was angry and made a trail that would lead to you, but it was one I knew would not hold up. I only wanted to punish you for not standing by me. Then I had to take care of Andres and get Craig in line. That's why it took me so long to come to you," Anthony smiled apologetically at her.

Halley couldn't tell if he believed his own story or if he was trying to con her.

"I am nothing that you want, Anthony. You made that clear when we were together."

"You misunderstood. I had to make sure you depended on me and only me. You are willful. Anything I suggested would only make you even better," Anthony explained.

"I want my sister back. Now. Have your men bring her here," Halley commanded.

"That's not the plan, Halley. You should know by now that you follow me, not the other way around."

Maverick could feel her tense next to him and was afraid she might slug the arrogant bastard in the jaw. No one kept his woman down. His woman? When did he start thinking Halley was his? He told himself that now was not the time for those thoughts. He, however, did want to clock the guy and knock him out himself.

"Well, let's get to it then, Anthony. You've had your say. Let's exchange me for my sister," Halley said stubbornly. "I can't believe you would come on to a child. That's low. I never thought that was your style. It's disgusting." Halley thought that was exactly his style but wanted to provoke him to action. She was done with this whole game.

Anthony looked directly at Maverick for the first time, "Darling, your new plaything thinks you'll provoke me. But we both know that you are simply a passionate woman. I am not easily incited."

Halley felt satisfied that she did indeed rattle the man. He would not have acknowledged Maverick otherwise. It also made her realize she was closer to the truth than she suspected with her taunt. That made her want to squirm with unease, but she forced herself to remain still. She prayed the man across from her had not violated her sister. How like his father was he really?

"The exchange, Anthony," Halley prodded, her jaw clenched.

"My thumb drive, darling."

"Did you leave it in my old jewelry box? If so, I can bring it to the exchange."

"You did find it then?" Anthony asked.

"If it was in there, then yes. I found it a couple of days ago when I looked for my extra key fob," Halley admitted.

"Did you see what's on it?"

"No. I forgot about it until now. Someone left me disconcerting gifts and my mind was elsewhere. What's on it?" Halley replied coldly.

Anthony laughed. A chilling sound that would have been better suited to a horror movie. "It's our future, Halley."

"The exchange, Anthony. I'm growing bored with this," Halley sighed dramatically.

"Ah, yes. That. Well, I will see you soon, my darling," Anthony smiled indulgently at her. Then he raised his voice, "James McCarthy, if I see anyone following me or if my men spot a tail or anything we could construe as a tail, I will kill your other daughter. Expect my text with the location for the exchange."

He reached for Halley's hand before she could pull back and raised it to his lips in a soft kiss, "Soon, my darling. None of these men are worthy of you. It's me or no one. Understand?"

"I understand you think that's the case, Anthony. I'll be waiting for your text," Halley pulled her hand from his grasp and sat straight and still until he reached the door, got his weapons – emptied of their ammunition – from Conor, and slipped outside.

Halley slumped, putting her head in her hands when she heard the door slam closed.

"You did great, Thunder," Maverick's voice was soothing but far away over the sudden sound of rushing water in her ears – the start of another panic attack she fought away. She slowly looked up. Her father, Red, and Scottie had slid into the booth and were staring at her expectantly. Jana and Sarah raced back from where they sat at the far end of the bar.

"I'm not going to collapse," Halley said, rolling her eyes at them all. Her forced bravado made them smile but didn't fool anyone.

Drake ran inside the tavern and pushed Maverick over. "I was under a car, and the music was loud. I hadn't seen my texts until now. Are you okay? I saw that asshole pull out. Please tell me we aren't trading Halley. You have a plan, right, Dad?" They all stared at him open-mouthed. It was the most anyone had heard Drake speak at one time in years, other than when they presented the business plan.

"Yeah, son. We have a plan. Both your sisters will be fine," James assured him. Drake's forehead was lined with worry, and it lessened somewhat with his father's words. If anyone could figure this out, it was James McCarthy. James understood why no one at the shop told Drake what had happened – they wanted all McCarthys out of the line of fire. He could see the mechanics at the bar, heads low, embarrassed they left Drake behind, even for his own good.

Chapter 25

ANTHONY HAD HIS DRIVER DRIVE AROUND TOWN FOR several turns before heading back the way they came and making their way to where they held Tiffany in a swampy area he found by chance. There was only one way in, and the two-track was practically invisible from the road, it was nearly impossible anyone could slip in behind them at this location. He needed to keep his hostage secure until the exchange. Truthfully, he didn't care if the girl lived or died. But alive would make the last move in his game easier.

Tiffany was awake now. She had given herself a black eye and split lip with her thrashing around and the subsequent crash into the large, exposed root of a larger tree. With her mascara dried in rivulets down her cheeks and the bright red lipstick with which she hoped to seduce him long since smudged around her mouth, she looked quite the fright. It was amazing how she appeared to be a child trying to play grown-up.

Her captors took the gag from her mouth when she threw up and then experienced continued dry heaves from being drugged. Anthony admitted to himself that she may also have a concussion.

"Why are you doing this?" Tiffany asked. "You don't need Halley; you could have had me," she said, the vitriol evident when she spoke her sister's name. She knew she was more attractive than her half-sister – her mother had told her that for years.

"You? You're a child," Anthony laughed at her protestations. "You, Bella, pale in comparison to Halley. No, I need the challenge of breaking a *woman*. You are no challenge at all. You would be putty in any man's hands. That is not interesting to me."

Tiffany sat quietly. She had nothing else to say. Nothing else to give. Whether he killed her or not, she irrationally knew her sister had caused this pain, even if she was the one who had been gullible. If Halley hadn't broken the engagement with Anthony, none of this would have happened.

Anthony was no longer paying attention to the girl. He was busy talking with his men and texting the ones waiting on the other end of town. The two with him glanced at one another, their questions about the veracity of the plan unspoken. Their boss told them to give the man anything he wanted – he was paying well beyond the normal rate for the privilege of unquestioned authority.

The men loaded Tiffany into the backseat of the SUV. They were gentler this time, hoping it may gain them some leniency in the hellfire that was sure to come. She tried batting her eyes at them, hoping to convey her desire to be freed. It didn't work. They still put her in the backseat, barely glancing at her. Anthony climbed in the other side next to her. He sent one more text.

"Let's go. I want to be there before them," Anthony ordered.

They spent several minutes getting back to the side road from the swamp. Then headed toward the McCarthy residence.

Halley received the final text from Anthony, and her eyes grew big. She looked to her dad and noted he registered no surprise. He and Maverick exchanged a look.

"You knew?" she asked.

"I guessed. In his mind, this would bring it full circle. He doesn't have to know it's not the original house, just that it's our home. Where it all started, for him," James sighed, resigned to what would come next. He called the men guarding the gate at the drive leading through the trees to the house and instructed them to open it and allow the vehicles to pass unhindered.

Maverick grabbed James and pulled him aside as they all moved toward the door. "Prez, bad timing, but I want you to know, I'm gonna ask your daughter out once we're through this. I want to make sure you don't have a problem with it – with me."

"Thanks for the respect. But I already figured that out and am more than fine with it. I think you better ask my daughter though. She's independent that way, if you didn't notice," James said, giving Maverick a half smile and clap on the shoulder.

Halley backed up when she heard the words that weren't meant for her ears, glad to concentrate on something else for the few seconds reprieve they would give. She took the opportunity to give Maverick a hard time, "You didn't just ask for my dad's permission, did you? This is all me, buddy. My life. My decisions. Get used to it." She turned and moved toward the door.

Maverick grabbed her bicep and held her back, "Well?"

Saucily, she tossed her shoulder-length hair and pulled toward the door again, "Ask me when this is done. You know, after I save your life."

Maverick shook his head and followed her out. Yep, she was his Thunder.

Outside the tavern, the small crowd of bikers not already positioned elsewhere mounted their motorcycles and followed behind the SUV driven by Pace, which carried Maverick, Halley, James, and Scottie. Maverick had sent Wolf ahead with Conor. Before he slid into his seat, James acknowledged Leonardo and the two SUVs waiting to follow them with a quick nod.

"Why is the new guy driving?" Halley whispered to Maverick.

"If you knew what he did in the military, you wouldn't ask that question," Maverick responded with a smirk.

Anthony and his men drove through the gate without a problem. The two bikers standing to the side didn't look happy, but they didn't try to stop them. As they wound down the drive and got closer to the house, Anthony thought he saw a white-haired, little old lady who had to be pushing eighty come out the front door and disappear into the woods down a side road past the barn. He remembered the elder McCarthys had a house down the road within the same compound. That must have been the grandmother. He was glad she was gone. One less complication.

"Stop here," Anthony ordered. It was at a spot in the drive between the house and the stable. He had the men take out red cans of gasoline from the second SUV carrying the men who had just come from California. They set half next to the house and half near the stables. He wasn't sure why his men from town hadn't shown up yet. Maybe they were following behind the McCarthys to make sure they didn't bring the FBI.

"Wha – what are you doing?" Tiffany stuttered.

"Making things right," Anthony muttered. He roughly pulled her out of the vehicle before remembering her ankles were bound by the zip tie and her hands bound behind her back. She fell to the pavement and cut her knees and shin. Angrily, Anthony called for one of the men to cut the ankle tie so she could walk.

"Stop that annoying crying," he gritted out and pulled her to stand, sheltered behind the broadside of the SUV. They could look over the hood and see any vehicles coming down the drive. Anthony assumed they would be no more than fifteen minutes behind. He was correct. They made it in eight minutes. The sky grew dark with rain clouds that threatened to open the heavens upon them.

The lead SUV drove too fast into the driveway, turned quickly, and stopped, leaving the vehicle sideways, much like the one Anthony stood behind. The motorcycles stopped behind the safety of the SUV. And the two Ricci vehicles pulled in straight next to the sideways one driven by Pace.

While James exited the vehicle, Maverick counted six mercenaries. Two stood beside their SUV, guns visible and flat across their chests, not aimed at them or at Tiffany, while two sat in that vehicle in driver and shotgun positions. The two closest to Anthony and Tiffany looked ready to bolt, based on their eye movements. The driver got back in the vehicle, and the other had the passenger door open before he slipped inside. Anthony was focused on James.

"Tiff, it'll be okay. Stay calm," James implored her. Her only response was a loud sob.

"Where's my fiancée?" Anthony demanded, jerking Tiffany closer to him, a handgun held loosely in his other hand.

"If you're talking about me, I'm right here," Halley called. Maverick had pulled her out of the "safe" side of the SUV, but Anthony didn't see her until she stood by the vehicle's hood. Pace fingered his weapon, ready to do what needed to be done.

"Tiffany and Halley will start walking at the same time. Tiff toward me and Halley toward you," James said.

"You're not calling the shots, McCarthy. Do you think I'm stupid? As soon as I don't have your daughter, your men will shoot me. I think not. When Halley comes to me, I'll let this one go," Anthony demanded.

At that point, the two Ricci vehicles both opened their doors, and all but the drivers stepped out. Anthony stiffened, thinking an attack was imminent, but he immediately relaxed when he saw Leonardo and Enzo. His uncle ran his hands over his shirt to smooth non-existent wrinkles. Enzo looked pained, though was dressed more like the bikers than a Ricci. His cousin never did have his good sartorial sense.

"Uncle, I see you've come to join me. We will finally have vindication. And I want you to meet my fiancée," Anthony smiled toward the man.

Maverick's head pivoted toward the mobsters, clearly worried they may have switched sides. He breathed again when none of them made a move. Leonardo looked pained by his nephew's words. He wondered how long it took to master the long-suffering expression he sported. That would be a good one to learn and use with future children. Wait, why was he suddenly thinking about children? He had only just adjusted to the fact he had met the woman with whom he wanted to spend his life.

Giving himself a mental headshake, he gripped his handgun. He looked toward the top of the stable where a box that resembled a bell tower with a small widow's walk around it sat with a weathervane on top, but couldn't see Wolf. He was sure that's where the man set up his sniper's perch; it's where Maverick would do it. He knew his club brothers and security team were spread out, covering the entire area, but none of them were visible either. He loved his brothers and his team.

"Anthony, let the girl go and stop this foolishness. Come back to Chicago with us and put this behind us," Leonardo said calmly.

"Is that what you want too, cousin?" Anthony asked angrily, looking at Enzo.

"Yes, Anthony," Enzo simply responded.

"Not without my fiancée."

Halley moved forward before Maverick or James could hold her back. She heard their hissing voices behind her. She was ready for this to be over. Her sister was hurt, and she was done waiting. "As soon as I reach you, Anthony, you let Tiffany go. She's got nothing you want."

"No, my darling, she does not. She is a pale substitute for you. I can hardly believe you're sisters. You have much more loyalty to her than she does to you. Your protectiveness is misguided, my love," Anthony responded.

Tiffany blanched at his words. She looked up at him as if he slapped her, and more tears ran from her eyes. "You liked me. I helped you," she whispered.

"You did. I used you, Bella. There is a difference," Anthony replied while watching Halley's march forward with rapt attention.

When she was within two yards of him, Halley stopped. "You can let her go now. Tiff, move away and go to Dad."

Anthony roughly pushed the teenager away. She faltered on her cut legs and scraped knees and ankles but limped toward her father, turning halfway to look at the man she thought she knew. Anthony already grabbed Halley's arm and pulled her to his side. Halley gritted her teeth and fisted her hands to keep from slugging the man.

"Get in the vehicle, Anthony. Let's go home," Leonardo tried again. "You have Halley now."

Anthony laughed, "We'll meet you there, uncle. I'm not so foolish to ride with you today. My fiancée and I have a lot of catching up to do." He turned to Halley and whispered, "Do you have the thumb drive, my love?"

Halley had forgotten Maverick had given it to her in the car, and she had shoved it in the front pocket of her jeans. She reached in and held it loosely with two fingers, "Is this it – this tiny memory stick?" Anthony's face broadened into a wide, maniacal smile at the sight of the small plastic casing. Halley extended her arm toward him but bobbled the bit of plastic. It dropped to the ground, bouncing under the vehicle.

"Oops!" Halley exclaimed and dropped to reclaim it. At the same time, Anthony lifted his gun, presumably to point it at her, but never got that far. Two shots rang out, one right after the other. The first hit him center forehead and the other at an angle through his heart. He fell to the ground backward from the impact of the shots, with a quiet exhalation of breath, eyes wide open.

One of his men moved to shoot one of the gasoline cans closest to the stable but was taken out by the same person who made the heart shot. All the others dropped their guns. The ones in their vehicles leaned outside and dropped their assault-style weapons through the windows, keeping their hands clearly visible on the dash. The client was dead; they didn't intend to join him. Besides, their boss had already been paid.

After the initial inertia from shock, everyone seemed to move at once. Enzo and two of their men moved to Anthony's body. Enzo stood between Halley and his cousin's lifeless form, blocking her view, and reached down to help her from the ground, where she squatted motionless. She peered around Enzo in shock at the man with whom she had once been intimately involved. He was going to kill her. She was sure of it. Either there or when he got her to the private plane he had waiting. He wanted to punish her and punish her father. Or maybe he really did want to drag out the revenge and make her miserable for the rest of her life, nothing but a trophy to him.

No one worried the gunshots would attract undue attention. In the country, random shots cracked regularly. Many residents target practiced on their property, and others had full shooting ranges, not to mention the hunters and poachers that prowled the woods and meadows.

Scottie cradled Tiffany in his arms, whispering softly to her as her sobs became more pronounced. Conor ran toward them from the stables. Drake ran toward Halley. Handsy, Wire, Hairy John, and Munch, as well as a few of the others, moved to secure the mercenaries who were still alive. Wolf strode out of the stables toward Maverick with his hands raised shoulder height, palms up, asking without words where the other shot came from; his was the heart shot.

Maverick, Wolf, James, and Leonardo looked toward where the initial headshot was initiated. It was clearly friend, not foe, but they didn't know who it was.

After a few moments, they saw movement in the old treehouse that had been last used when Scarlett was twelve. Short legs covered in black jeans, with small black motorcycle boots, climbed carefully down the ladder behind the tree, the upper body covered in a black sweatshirt with a rifle slung over the person's back. When the figure moved around the thick trunk of the tree, the white hair stood out in stark contrast to the darkness of the bark and the green of the grass and tall weeds. Mary McCarthy smiled and lifted her chin in acknowledgment. Mavericks' smile was huge as she walked surely and confidently toward them.

Leonardo stood next to James. He asked, "Is that your mother?"

"It sure is," James said in quiet amazement.

Leonardo grinned and said, "I think she should meet my mother."

They heard a loud shout from further down the road, "Woman! What the hell do you think you're doing? You were supposed to stay in the house with me!" Mitchell's long strides had almost caught up to his wife.

She turned to him and looked up defiantly, "Old man, do not use that tone with me. I was taking care of my granddaughters."

Rather than get angrier, Mitchell broke out in a wide smile, "Well, did you save them?"

"You bet I did."

Mitchell reached down and picked up his wife, crushing her body to his and kissing her long and hard, embarrassing every grandchild and son in the vicinity. "That's my Mary. Best shot in the entire state."

"I've still got perfect vision and perfect aim. Good thing we sighted in my rifle this week," Mary responded proudly. A dark look passed over her face as she said, "No one messes with the people I love." Maverick needed no convincing of that. When Mitch set his wife on her feet again, Maverick picked her up and swung her around, kissing her on the cheek.

"That's enough, Maverick. You may be a grandson-in-law someday soon, but my wife is off limits," Mitchell scowled at him, his following small smile letting Maverick know he was teasing.

Wolf held out his hand to Mary, "Ma'am, I'm Wolf. I work with Maverick and will be prospecting with the club. I want to say that was a fantastic shot. As good as any I've seen in my tours of duty. It's an honor working with you." Maverick was shocked by the sincerity in Wolf's tone and the deference he showed the older woman.

Mary gave him a bright smile and reached up to pat Wolf's cheek, "You can call me Gram. It was good working with you, too. Maverick did good bringing you here. I'm glad you made the right decision. You'll fit in fine."

James checked on Tiffany. The club doctor, who had been a patched *Phantom Raider* since before getting his MD, approached and quietly told Scottie to take her to her room, where he would check her over and see if she needed to go to the hospital. They would make sure she had her story straight later. For now, the doctor thought he was going to have to give her something to calm her down since the sobbing hadn't stopped, and she didn't respond to anyone who tried to talk with her.

Enzo walked Halley away from the body and toward their fathers, Maverick, and her grandparents.

"Hal, you okay?" James asked, wrapping his arms around her in a tight hug.

"I'm fine, Dad," Halley assured him. "I dropped that stupid memory stick on purpose and was going to pull the knife Maverick gave me out of my boot while he was distracted. Someone got to him first." She really didn't want to kill anyone, but she had wanted to take control and give him a piece of her mind. Now, she'd never get that chance.

"That would be your gram," Mitchell stated with a hint of pride in his voice.

Halley's eyes rounded as she noticed the rifle strapped to her grandmother's back. "Gram?"

Mary hugged her and whispered, "It's all right, Hal. It's over now."

Halley hugged her back, astonished. "Wow! Gram's a real-life badass." When she looked around, she saw Wire move in close to her father, and that reminded her, "What's on that stupid thumb drive?"

Wire smiled, "Only all the transactions, banks, account numbers, routing numbers, and every move he made setting up his new life."

"Can we access the accounts?" Leonardo asked. "I can get my tech guy on it."

"Well, we can, but I wouldn't be too surprised if the feds follow the trails. I suggest the money he embezzled miraculously turn up in the corporate accounts again." Wire waited for the wisdom of that suggestion to take root with James and Leonardo. Halley caught on the most quickly, and she smiled brightly.

"Then the investors can get their scheduled payout, late, but still get it, and the vendors will be able to be paid. The feds would probably never legally be able to access and recover all the offshore accounts themselves; at a minimum, it would take years. It should make the investigation easier or maybe go away altogether," she rushed out.

"Yes. Anything outstanding will more than likely be pinned on Anthony or Andres, and because they're both dead –" Wire was interrupted by Halley before he could finish.

"– it will be easier. The feds will find better things to focus on," Halley concluded.

"That's the idea," Wire agreed.

"You can make this happen? Without it coming back to us or you?" Leonardo asked.

"Yes. Just get me Anthony's laptop, and I'll take care of it now," Wire promised. Enzo went to look in Anthony's SUV. All his cousin's things had been absent from the remote cabin when their men got there.

Leonardo and James walked away to talk about what to do with the mercenaries. Leonardo leaned toward getting rid of them. James thought they could be persuaded not to talk, given they were already paid, and if the club or James wanted, they could have them charged with the federal offense of kidnapping and intention to blow up his house and stable. The forensic evidence would be irrefutable. "There's no upside for them ever talking about this situation. It would be very bad for their business. As we know, men like them are only motivated by money."

"So, ready to start a life with me, soldier?" Halley boldly asked Maverick. James spun around and stared at his daughter. Maverick's eyes almost popped out of his head; he recovered more quickly than anyone else.

"And here I thought I was going to have to wine and dine you," Maverick smirked, stalking toward her until he was towering over her.

"Why wait when you know what you want? I'm done holding back. We're not getting any younger," Halley teased. It was amazing what watching your life flash before your eyes could incite.

"Are you asking me to marry you, Halley McCarthy?"

"I am. Are you saying yes?"

Maverick bent and kissed her, softly at first and then with heated passion. Halley realized she just proposed to a man with whom she hadn't even shared a kiss. If this kiss and the fireworks it started in her body were anything to go by, she wasn't worried.

Leonardo smiled widely. He pulled his son forward and faced Halley. "Everything always comes around to where it's meant to be. The universe rights itself. It may take a while, but it happens. Like the Indian concept of karma. The real magic is to be in control of your own destiny and to be happy, to seize those things and not let go.

"You are the new generation. Listen to me when I say that generations-old vendettas are a waste of time. Sure, watch out for those who are out to destroy you, but it makes more sense to build something of your own and move forward than to look backward. And always take care of family."

Halley smiled shyly. She reached out and clasped Leonardo's hand between both of hers, "I couldn't agree more."

Leonardo tilted his head and looked from Halley to Enzo, "Could I talk you into being interested in my son?"

Halley laughed, and Maverick sputtered, pulling her more closely to him. Enzo whispered in embarrassment, "Papa!"

"I thought not, but I had to ask. You are a special woman, Halley McCarthy. My nephew was a fool," Leonardo declared. He leaned down and kissed her on both cheeks and returned to his conversation with James and ordering their men.

The non-descript van with no windows suddenly showed up. People in hazmat suits stepped out while Leonardo lifted his eyebrows to James, looking for permission. James nodded his okay. The cleanup began. That included melting down Gram's rifle in Drake's expanded studio, which James had cleaned out and properly set up for the artist.

Chapter 26

THE CLEANUP TEAM WAS AIDED BY THE HARD RAIN THAT STARTED; at least Maverick thought it would be a help. Maybe not. The blood was washed from the driveway in a matter of minutes. Most of the club members went back to the clubhouse to blow off steam, and Ricci's people went back to their respective hotel and motel. Leonardo decided they would not leave that night; there could be more to discuss with James the next day.

Maverick had the security team take the mercenaries to the basement of the clubhouse, where they would hear their options. Leonardo and James argued over which one would call the head of the security firm for which the mercenaries worked. Maverick was pretty sure it was going to come down to a coin toss, or they would call together and pose a double threat.

Sarah and Jana showed up at the house with Tyler and another prospect who had been left at *Raiders Roost Tavern* to protect them. They couldn't have kept the women from coming to the house if they tried; they didn't. Both women ran inside to where Halley sat at the gigantic kitchen table with Gram, while Mitchell, Maverick, and Wolf hovered over them, fetching tea, homemade chocolate chip cookies, brandy, and anything else the women wanted.

"I have a whole big dinner prepared at home. I turned off the stove when I left. I'll warm it up," Mary said, pushing up from the table with the full intent to bring the food to her son's house.

"Leave it for tomorrow, Mary," Mitchell ordered.

"We have an army of people to feed," Mary argued.

"They can order pizza," he grumbled.

"I like pizza," Maverick agreed with the former president.

"Me too," Wolf echoed.

Mary looked at Wolf, "Well, if you're sure. I hate this is the way you're welcomed to the club. You deserve a hot dinner."

Wolf smiled, something he rarely did, and it even reached his eyes, "Tomorrow would be better."

Mary nodded, reassured she wasn't falling down on the job, and sat in the chair.

Doc came down the stairs with Scottie at the same time James and Leonardo entered the house.

"She's sedated. I think we can say confidently that she was drugged. She says she wasn't raped, and it appears that's true, thank God," Doc assured them.

Halley broke in, "Good thing, or I would kill him all over again myself!" Her face was a snarled mask of anger, and her fists clenched on top of the table.

"My girl," Gram said quietly, no more than two words on an expelled breath, and patted her eldest granddaughter's hand in comfort.

Doc continued, "I stitched up her leg and cleaned the other abrasions. We left her with an ice pack for her eye and lip. She's going to be sore but should heal fine. It looked a lot worse than it was. It sounds like she did most of the damage to herself, thrashing around. I don't think she has a concussion. If she does, it's very mild." Doc got quiet for a minute, staring from James to the floor, and then added slowly, "We may want to bring my colleague out to talk with her. I can get her to make a house call."

"The therapist?" Scottie asked, and Doc nodded.

Maverick had no doubt Doc could get her to make a house call. They were all wondering when he was going to claim her as his ol' lady. He didn't seem to realize his brothers knew he was in love with the woman.

"Yeah, do that. Thanks," James agreed.

Conor had a mischievous look in his eye when he turned to Sarah and Jana, "Hey, did you two hear? Halley proposed to Maverick. He said yes."

"You did what?" Sarah practically screamed at her best friend.

Halley shrugged and tried not to look embarrassed. "So? Life's too short to waste when you know it's right."

"Well, that settles it. I know you're not leaving town now!" Sarah beamed and hugged her friend. Halley rolled her eyes.

Handsy appeared from the living room and took Sarah's hand, "Does this mean I can tell them you finally agreed to go out with me?"

Sarah rolled her eyes even more dramatically than Halley had. "We've been going out for days, big boy. Catch up." At that, Handsy leaned down and kissed her, relieved it was official. He'd been waiting for this since he was in middle school and first noticed girls weren't another version of boys.

Scottie looked to where Jana hugged his sister and added her congratulations, glad Jana was fitting in not only with the club but with his family, not that there was much distinction.

"You know, I always wanted to be president of the *Phantom Raiders* when I was a kid, until Dad squashed my dream," Halley said mischievously. "I was thinking, maybe we should start a *women's* motorcycle club. You all would learn to ride, right?" She looked to her friends, who nodded enthusiastically.

"Not happening!" Handsy, Scottie, Conor, and Gramps all shouted at the same time.

"I actually have my eye on a sweet ride already," Jana said loudly to the women at the table, ignoring the guys, though Scottie glared daggers at her. She wanted to stir the pot even more than Halley.

"Ooohhh. I'll go with you to check it out," Halley offered.

"Never say no to a McCarthy woman, boys. Haven't you learned that yet?" Gram winked.

That night, after numerous pizzas had been delivered and eaten, Gram and Gramps wandered back to their house, and Leonardo and Enzo left for their hotel. Danny and Scarlett arrived home late, buzzing from coming out on top of both their tournaments, ate what was left of the pizza, and went to bed. James was grateful they didn't ask many questions. Announcing Halley's proposal to Maverick seemed to keep them pleasantly sidetracked. He'd deal with the explanation about Tiffany tomorrow.

Everyone else – Scottie, Conor, Handsy, Maverick, Tyler, Drake, Sarah, Jana, Wolf, Pace, and Doc all stayed at the house, falling asleep across the living room couches, chairs, and Halley's room. He was surprised his sons didn't take their old rooms and that the others didn't use any of the guest beds. They all seemed to want to stay near one another for the night. James was the last one awake and surveyed the house before turning off the last of the lights and setting the alarm. He felt at peace for the first time in a long time.

Priscilla would return, and he would deal with that. She would either want to remain a biker's wife or not. She hadn't faced any real trials in the almost twenty-eight years they'd been married. This would be the true test, especially once she saw Tiffany. He would make sure his wife clearly understood Tiffany had made the choices that led to her kidnapping and that her own treatment of their daughter had created the entitlement the girl wore with pride. He would also tell his wife and daughter the teenager lost her car for the foreseeable future.

***

The next morning, Maverick waited, already showered and dressed, when Halley got out of the shower. No one but James was awake, and he had the real coffee made with two travel mugs ready for them – Halley might need something stronger than her usual tea.

"Where are we going?" Halley whispered. Her father winked at her and watched as Maverick pulled her out of the house. As they walked across the drive hand-in-hand toward the stable, Halley glanced around. The pavement was still wet from the night rain, and the blades of grass glistened with the leftover raindrops. The pictures of the horror from the day before ran through her mind like an old-fashioned movie reel. It was hard to see the calm that existed now and believe what happened yesterday. Even the red gas cans meant to destroy the house and stable were gone. Instead, Halley smelled the scent of fresh straw and horses. Tyler held the reins of the saddled Lightning and Lady. They set off at a leisurely pace, letting the horses choose the speed.

"I have something I want to show you," Maverick said, keeping his secret until they had ridden over a few rises toward the large lake near the northwest end of the property, bordered on three sides by stands of pine, birch, and maple trees. On one side of the lake, where a gentle hill rose up from the shore, trees lining a natural meadow on the hillside, Maverick dismounted and stared out at the lake.

"What do you think?" he asked.

Halley said quietly, "You've brought me to my favorite place on the property. When I was a kid, this is where I told Dad I wanted to build a house someday."

Maverick chuckled, "No wonder your dad laughed when I brought him out here and asked if I could buy this piece of land to put a house on."

"You did?" Halley said, wide-eyed and jaw dropped. "We want the same piece of property?"

"Appears so, Thunder. Maybe Ricci was onto something when he said everything works out and comes around," Maverick mused.

"So, we're going to do it? This is where we'll build our house?" Halley asked.

"It is. Your dad said the club retains ownership of the land, but we'd own our house. It's the same deal with his and your grandparents' place. We just need to decide on the blueprints and hire the contractor."

Halley whooped and jumped up to grab Maverick by the shoulders and kiss him – she had to jump to reach. A new business to build doing something she loved, a house to build in the spot she dreamed, and the right guy with whom to build a life. She couldn't remember a time when she was this happy.

When they got back to the house, Wire was there, and her dad took her in his arms and hugged her tight. "I almost spilled the surprise. I knew you were going to love it." Halley noted how much easier it was getting to hug her father; it felt normal.

"The money made its way back to the company, too, Hal. So that's more good news," Wire told her. Wire now treated her like family, not the outsider he saw when they first met.

Halley's mind was firing in all directions. She would have to try to reach Craig today, even if it meant going through Senior Supervisory Special Agent Bishop. She would also call the company's general counsel, since he was the last senior person still in the office. It shouldn't be so difficult now that she knew she was still an employee. Given the time difference, she would wait until late afternoon to make her calls, though she didn't know in what locale they were hiding Craig.

That afternoon, James' phone rang. It was Senior Supervisory Special Agent Bishop. James stepped into his home office to take the call and pulled Maverick and Wire in with him. All were stunned by the man's news.

Craig Martin had gone through his complete statement three times over the last few days, with his attorney present, clearly placing the blame for the embezzlement and murder on Anthony. Apparently, Craig had reverted to his teenage hacker years and was able to trace most of what happened in the days leading up to talking with the FBI.

He gave Bishop a thumb drive for safekeeping with all his evidence on it, should anything happen to him. Wire mouthed to James and Maverick that it was the same drive Craig had given to Conor that last day just in case something happened.

They had Craig in a safe house, where they intended to keep him pending any trial. They had issued an arrest warrant for Anthony and were still looking for him. They didn't interrupt the man; no one mentioned Anthony's whereabouts.

That morning the agents found Craig dead in his bed during a shift change, a gun with a silencer by his side. It wasn't making much sense why he would take his own life. It also didn't make sense for him to use a silencer. Yet there did not seem to be any way an assassin could have gotten past his protective detail and into his bedroom, though there was a window and a balcony in his room.

The external security cameras had glitched for more than thirty minutes when they went back and looked at the footage. Craig had gone to bed early the night before, and no one had seen or heard from him the entire night.

Everything about this investigation was going sideways, including the general counsel insisting this morning that the money was back in the accounts. Bishop was headed back to San Francisco.

Maverick told Wolf once the call was over, and both shook their heads. None of that sounded above board to them. Craig's behavior pointed to knowing he was going to die. They may never know if it was suicide or murder.

"Uh, Maverick!" Halley yelled from across the house. They ran to her. After everything, everyone was still on edge. She held out her phone. He took the phone and saw what looked like a legal document.

"What is this?" Maverick asked.

"It came from the general counsel," Halley said, stunned.

Wolf nodded knowingly, "Bet I know what it is. Craig had the head lawyer draw up papers for him to sign right before we left for the FBI handoff. He was adamant that's the way he wanted things."

"He signed all his shares and any shares that revert to him on the death of the other two partners to me and the general counsel. He gave us complete control of the company," Halley confirmed. She dropped to a seat at the kitchen table.

James put his arm around his daughter's shoulders and squatted down on the floor next to her chair. "Hal, Bishop just called. They found Craig dead in his bed today. Gunshot. No idea if it was suicide or suspicious circumstances."

"Why? Why would he do that? Anthony's gone. The money's been returned. He should have waited!"

"We don't know that he did anything, Hal. This could have been something Anthony set in motion days or weeks ago, and we may never know," James comforted his daughter.

"So now I own the startup? Partially, anyway," Halley asked, staring at the email attachment. The last couple of days – really the last few months – were overwhelming. She should just go back to bed and pretend none of it ever happened.

"How about we get the club attorney to take a look at the documents, explain the details and what options you have, okay? You don't have to make any decisions today," James reminded her.

Halley nodded numbly. She would wait to call the general counsel until after she talked with the club attorney. He would have just found out one of his best friends was dead, his Stanford roommate. The man would be devastated. He'd lost his two closest friends in less than a month. *Oh crap, please don't let him be suicidal.*

The day's drama wasn't over. The prospects monitoring the gate at the end of the driveway called to say Leonardo and Enzo were on their way to the house with two of their men. James met them at the door, and the father and son entered the house. Their men stood in their neat, dark clothes, hands clasped in front of them, on either side of the front door, not seeming to notice the side-eyes the bikers in their worn leather cuts and faded jeans gave them.

"We had some disturbing news and have to get back to Chicago. However, this news should give you even more peace of mind," Leonardo started after accepting the cut crystal glass of top-shelf whiskey Scottie offered the man and his son from his father's private bar. Leonardo took a sip of the whiskey, his eyes closing for a moment as he savored the rich flavor and deep burn. When he opened his eyes, he sighed and started again, "My sister Francesca, Anthony's mother, tried to reach her son many times yesterday and last night. Please understand that this week, my father has been arranging for her to be committed to a private, secure facility. We realized how delusional she had become and how she influenced her son to go down this unfortunate path."

Halley thought there were better ways to describe it than "unfortunate," but she liked Leonardo, and he seemed truly distraught, so she kept her thoughts to herself and waited for him to continue. She braced herself to hear Francesca had disappeared and was heading this way to kill her. Maverick squeezed her shoulder, his arm stretched protectively across her back.

"My mother told her Anthony was gone late last night after she became obsessed with reaching him and demanded a car to drive her here. Francesca broke dishes and smashed vases until my father had her taken to her room. She cried and promised she just wanted to sleep. She shot herself in the heart and left a note saying she had nothing else to live for," Leonardo forced out. When he looked up, he wasn't sure what he had expected, but it wasn't the horrified looks on the faces of the bikers and their family. The shock turned to something he did not often see in his life: compassion.

"Oh, Mr. Ricci, I'm so sorry. She may have been sick, but she was your sister," Halley said sincerely. She wasn't sure what she felt toward the woman who at one time could have been her mother-in-law, maybe relief, but she did feel compassion toward the woman's brother and nephew. They were stuck in the middle of something they didn't start or want.

"Thank you, Halley. Are you sure you wouldn't like to date Enzo?" Leonardo said, weakly trying to lighten the situation. Halley shook her head no. Enzo shook his head in disbelief at his father's preposterousness.

Leonardo met James' eyes and said in a strong voice, "It truly is over now, my friend. Your family can breathe easily. There is no one left to carry on this ridiculous agenda. That branch of the family is no more." Leonardo stood and motioned for Enzo to follow him. "We must leave now. You understand, my parents, while relieved her torment is over, still mourn their lost daughter. My plane is waiting at your private airstrip. I was pleasantly surprised your town had one of those."

Halley hugged the frightening mobster before he stepped out of the house, as she would a beloved uncle. He found her mixture of relief and compassion endearing. Once they were gone, James scrubbed his hands over his face.

"It's over, Dad," Scottie declared in a soft voice. James nodded his head, words escaping him.

***

A few days later, Senior Supervisory Special Agent Bishop called again. This time to tell James Anthony Barone's body had been dredged up by a boat in the Chicago River. The body was bloated and badly damaged by boats and fish, but death had been by gunshot, though neither wound contained the bullet. They surmised it was a mob hit, the family taking care of its own. Bishop wanted Halley to know she was no longer in danger from her ex-fiancé. Bishop was sure Craig's death had been a hit, too, but couldn't prove it. His superiors had already assigned his team to a new case with live suspects. No one wanted to spend the time or resources on this one.

***

Halley spoke with the general counsel and assured him she did not want to run the company and would not move back to San Francisco.

"I want out too, Halley," the general counsel said sincerely. "This all made me realize what's important, and it's not how much money I can make or how impressed investors are. I miss my friends. My wife and I want to move to Montana near her family, and our kids can grow up with their cousins."

"I'm surprised, but not really. I feel the same way," Halley told him. "What will you do there?"

"Maybe open a small law practice. Maybe ranch with my brother-in-law. Maybe nothing. I don't know. I just know I can't do this anymore," he said, sorrow tinging his words.

"Well, I know Craig had someone in London interested in buying the technology. Maybe now he'd buy the company? It'll no longer be at bargain-basement prices, but he was really keen on getting his hands on the technology and Craig's research team. I also have Craig's notes for his new product development that he left on the thumb drive he gave to my brother," Halley admitted. That was something he left off the one he gave to the FBI. "I'm pretty sure the Brit would love to get his hands on that too."

The general counsel gained enthusiasm, "Let's make this one last great deal, Halley. I'll get our outside mergers & acquisitions team to sketch out the paperwork for a deal. It would be a start. Do you want to contact the guy in London to kick things off or have the M&A team make the approach?"

Halley thought for a moment. "He wanted to talk with me about being his Chief Marketing Officer, so I guess I'll make the first call. Wish me luck."

"No luck, Halley," the man said. "We may not want to do this anymore, but the technology is sound and worth a fortune. You can do this."

Halley sat in her new office in the security company building and read the company profile the headhunter had sent before on the London enterprise and then searched everything she could find about the CEO. She took a few deep breaths and picked up her phone, pulling his direct phone number from the email the headhunter had sent her when she thought she would be interviewing. It was past end of the day in London, but she suspected the CEO would still be in the office.

"Mathis," a pleasant, masculine voice answered.

"Mr. Mathis, this is Halley McCarthy. I'm not sure you remember me –"

"Ms. McCarthy, of course, I remember you. Did you reconsider? Interested in my company and living in London now?" She could tell by his voice he was smiling.

"Not that, but I think I may have something you'll be interested in," Halley began. She spent the next hour talking with the man. He was aware the startup's circumstances were no longer so dire, but he was still interested in the technology and could be open to acquiring the company and technology. There would be some regulatory hurdles to cross due to the defense applications, but nothing insurmountable since they already worked with some of the same clients. Halley was able to forge the beginning of trust with the CEO and start the process for the acquisition. He asked her to keep in touch with the new small business she was creating – he rode a Harley and was interested in the custom art her brother could do. He was also intrigued by Halley's ideas for new, more creative campaigns.

Once, everything was wrong. Now, everything seemed to be turning around. *Everything comes around,* echoed soothingly in Halley's head.

After the call, Halley called the general counsel, her current partner in the startup, and passed on the good news. He would push the M&A team to hurry with the opening deal documents and then shepherd the process through to the conclusion. He was motivated – Montana was waiting.

With legs kicked up on her desk, she leaned back in her chair and stared sideways out the window to the main street. Maverick stood in her open doorway and took her in with his eyes before making his presence known. "Slacking off already, Ms. McCarthy?"

"Hardly. I may have begun the process of selling the startup," she said smugly. "I deserve a break."

"How about I take my fiancée for an early dinner?" Maverick suggested.

Halley was still getting used to using and hearing that word. For so long, *ex-fiancé* was used as a curse in her vocabulary. Yet there was nothing alike between the two men and nothing similar in her feelings for them. Even when everything had been somewhat good with Anthony, she felt nothing as deep or passionate as she did for the rancher turned former special forces operator turned biker. She realized she had been lonely, feeling left behind by her friends who coupled up in New York, and Anthony's interest in her was convenient. Eventually, she would get over it, and the term *fiancée* would no longer bother her.

"I need to make an overdue stop first," Halley said.

"I'll come with you," he offered.

"You don't have to," she responded shyly.

"I know I don't have to. I want to," Maverick assured her. When she shoved her laptop in her bag and stood to leave, he said, "Cemetery."

"You knew," she tipped her head and gazed at him in wonder.

First, they stopped at the greenhouse, then took Maverick's Harley to the cemetery. As much as she loved her own ride and the freedom she felt as the wind rushed over her, she found she equally loved being on the back of his, arms gripping his middle and thighs snug against his thighs. It was its own sense of intimacy and never disappointed in giving her a thrill.

If she asked, Maverick would tell her pride surged in his chest when she rode her own bike alongside his on the country roads. But when she hugged him, molded to his back on his bike, he felt immense love and joy.

Halley strode purposefully, first toward her mother's grave. An involuntary shiver crawled over her body as her eyes darted to the headstone. She sighed in relief when no ghoulish gifts greeted them. Maverick touched her back, and she knew he understood and probably felt the same way.

The only thing there was a single yellow freesia lying across the top of the headstone and a bunch of white daisies in the buried vase – both her mother's favorite flowers. Evie claimed she was a combination of simple and elegant, and James loved both. Her father left the flowers; she knew in her bones it was true.

"You want me to wait over there?" Maverick asked, pointing to the large tree he once hid behind.

"No, stay," Halley gave him a small smile. She set her own bouquet of spring wildflowers at the bottom of the headstone. "Hi, Mom. I guess you already know; Dad probably told you, but it's all over. No one is coming to get us anymore. Anthony is dead. His mother killed herself. I want you to meet Maverick. He's to me what Dad was to you," she said in a quiet voice. "I'll always love you, Mom."

They moved the two rows over to her grandparents and set a bouquet of red regular size roses with yellow and white baby roses at the base of her grandmother's headstone.

"Well, I'm back. I'm safe. This is Maverick. We're getting married, and before you say anything, yes, I asked him. I didn't hesitate. I went with what felt right. Just like you used to say," she grinned at that and felt the pink flush crawling up her neck and face. Maverick moved behind her and pulled her back to his front, quiet, supportive.

"You were right. I was stupid when I first came home. No one saw me as a failure but me. I guess success isn't what the younger me thought it was. Sure, money is nice, but it's no longer in my top five measures of success. Instead, I guess it's all about loving the people I'm with, being passionate about what I do, making a difference in someone's life or a lot of lives, having enough of a challenge to keep my interest, and doing it in a place I enjoy and feel at peace. That's it. No great revelations you didn't already know."

She turned to lie down directly over her grandmother's grave site, back against the short, cropped grass and damp black earth and looked up to the sky while she continued talking. Maverick moved to sit under the tree only a few feet away, where the raven stood watch on his branch above him. "Success can come in all different forms, I guess. Who knew – well, besides you? I found out I'm strong, Grandma. I can survive anything and go on to build something special. Especially with my family around me."

Rising from the plot, she nodded and reached for Maverick's rough hand to pull him up and walk back to his Harley. She glanced over her shoulder at her forebears resting place and added in a voice no more than a whisper, "I'm happy, Grandma. So…this is what it feels like, huh?"

The wind picked up, swirling a mini tornado of dried grass and leaves, whipping her shoulder-length, wavy, light brown hair with sun-kissed highlights into her face. It was probably the wind, but she heard clearly "*yes, this…*"

Startled, Maverick's head shot down to her face, eyebrows knitted closely together, "Did you hear something?"

Halley laughed and pulled him toward his ride, while he continued to surveil the area with his eyes.

The raven precipitously coughed loudly, echoing against the trees and headstones, and flew away, the low sun catching the color of his feathers as he dipped his magnificent blue-black wings to them.

Acknowledgments

It took a village to come to this place. From the moment I made a hard left turn and gave up my corporate suits and paychecks for the life of a novelist, there were those who stood up and loudly encouraged and supported me. No one was more in my corner supporting the change than my mother, Loree Ann Richardson Noel, who always has my back and was first eyes on my book; my sister, Melanie Nolan, my lead cheerleader; and my brother, Chris Morris. My surprise was beyond pleasant when my brother said the magic words, "Just come home." Where I come from, family takes care of family.

Torin Lee, part of my chosen family, has been my creative partner since we met a quarter of a century ago and kept one another sane during the corporate years. The Aquarian that she is calmly talked me down in my times of doubt, while suffering through my questions, such as "What is the word that feels like…?" This novel was written primarily at her Connecticut kitchen table. Her Zen Creative stepped up when I finally decided on the indie route and promised to be by my side – my ride or die.

Thank you to Callaghan Publications, who provided the team for tangibly bringing my first novel to fruition with project management, editorial, design, and marketing teams. This has been a learning experience.

Penny Parkin has been a patron when that term and practice seemingly went out of style centuries ago. More than that, she is chosen family we all love. Her encouragement and prayers come from a good place, and our discussions are as intellectually charged as they are sometimes goofy and inappropriate. It's always fun to have someone who "gets" the international part of my background.

Steven Garcia, business owner and book club leader, has kept up the drumbeat, asking in his happy and nudging way how much further I am in my writing, always supportive and eager as a beta reader. I knew I was onto something when he texted me after so many pages of *Comes Around* and said he didn't want to put it down.

AnneMarie Laorenza has been with me since I made the hard pivot to this new endeavor, focusing on the business side and ensuring this creative pursuit would march toward success. It was through her I met PR guru Bob Cavosi, who, in the early days, called upon his contacts, and we learned about the publishing industry and got feedback on style, story, and ability to triumph.

I would be remiss if I didn't thank Mid-Michigan Writers for introducing me to my local tribe, after I'd been gone from my hometown for decades.

I will forever be grateful to Dario Ciriello, bestselling Author of *Aegaeon Dream*, editor, and former publisher, for getting me in the right mindset to take this leap into the indie world, which was greatly facilitated by his encouragement and, most particularly, taking the time to go through the pros and cons of indie versus traditional publishing – his Indie 101 tutelage was invaluable.

Lenore Troia has been my touchstone for commercial viability and approaches to marketing. As a successful indie musician, many of the tricks and lessons of her trade are easily convertible to the world of books. I also appreciate her night owl biorhythm that matches my own and talking with me into the wee hours about the business side of being an artist, as well as being a good friend and like-minded soul.

Finding such a gem in a small northern Michigan town made me believe my luck continued when I got to know the bestselling Author of *Hannah's Dream,* Diane Hammond. She remains my close friend, confidante, gripe partner, world watcher, deliverer of copious notes, and a constant source of belief and support. Our hours-long chat sessions at the local Starbucks are renowned.

Michael Salsbury, another new friend and author, actor, educator, has an infectious enthusiasm. He read manuscripts, gave notes, and championed *Comes Around* as a book with broad appeal. He was the first to insist it could be a series, if only to rid that world of the characters he believes need their comeuppance. Down the road, some of the characters from *Comes Around* may appear again…but I'm getting ahead of myself.

Another compatriot, Laura Bender, opened her house to all of us to discuss not only our latest work but also the art and business of writing and simply bask in the presence of other creative spirits. She has listened to and participated in our energetic discussions and debates around plots and characters, and her own insight and ability to cut to the chase is much appreciated.

Nancy Renko is a beta reader whose notes and comments I anticipate. Her thoughtful comments and suggestions are spot-on and always constructive. That this discerning woman is interested in reading my drafts and suggesting ways to make them better is a gift I do not take lightly. Her commendation that "this is a book I would buy" is one I await with bated breath.

Scott Willems has been a constant champion for my move to writing books fulltime. He encouraged, pushed, and prodded me to follow my passion and believe the rest would follow. He continues to reach out at precisely the opportune times to remind me to live in the moment, enjoy the journey, and most of all, keep writing.

Michael Lage met me in the business world, and in friendship, he followed me to this next act. He has been an avid beta reader and supporter. I have an entire drawer full of Sharpies from Michael in his great anticipation that I will need them when signing books.

Joan Beck, a voracious reader and book club member who possesses a no-nonsense sensibility, agreed to be a beta reader and has offered her opinions and support throughout this process. She and her friends represent a market of readers who understand the need to immerse themselves in a fictional world and be left feeling better because of it.

Through my husband's last years and death – and any time since – Kerrie O'Connor and her wisdom have been on my side. She is more than her gifts. More than fifteen years ago, she knew that this was what I should be doing with my life if I was brave enough to take that step and write the first book. She has been in my corner, cheering and prodding all the way, especially when I told her I made the leap. Carrie Konyha reinforced that same direction and gave voice to how to rid my mind of the "shadow thinking" that holds back so many people. The abundance they both see for my future is enabling, and I am grateful.

Since 1991, Tony Coady, an exceptional Irish artist and goldsmith was calling for me to "chuck it" all, move to Ireland, devote myself to the pursuit of the written word, and quit "wasting" my talent. He will be delighted I finally gave in to the longing and leapt.

When I took up this endeavor, my potential readers were at the heart of what I would produce. While my writing offers twists and turns, emotional roller coasters, suspense, and the joy and angst of connection, I always try to provide an uplift, wanting to leave everyone with hope and perhaps the impetus and courage to be as strong and resilient as some of the characters in my pages. It is with all of you in mind that I will continue to write books for years to come.

My children are always on my mind and deserve their own line. Ciara Cowan, who probably wished she didn't live so close when I made her listen to different passages while I wrote and who always gave me her unvarnished opinion; Benjamin Cowan, who insisted I have an audio version of my book if I wanted him to "read" it; and Jamie Cowan, whose enthusiasm for reading what I've written and belief in me is humbling. Love you all infinitely.

Lastly, my late husband, Irish musician Gerard Cowan. I am finally fulfilling the deathbed promise to write the books and do what I've always wanted instead of what I had to do.

See? It takes a village…

For more information on the Author and her books, or if you'd like to invite her to speak with your book club, women's group, etc., visit www.MichelleSMorris.com

About the Author

Michelle S. Morris is a storyteller driven by characters, providing a glimpse into motivation, inspiration, and the power of resilience and connection. She writes novels that are general fiction, women's fiction, and suspense/mystery. Her books abound with strong women, a diversity of characters, a little suspense, multi-generational family – both blood and chosen – timely issues, and timeless topics.

She's had many careers, initially in politics – first job at the White House – and as a journalist, then as a corporate communications executive with global companies, before deciding to write novels full-time. Born in rural northeastern Michigan, she has lived most of her adult life up and down the East Coast from DC to Connecticut, with a few years in the San Francisco Bay Area, and a magical year in England.

Michelle's late husband was an Irish musician from Dublin, Ireland, and they have triplets whom she adores but who frustrate her as a competitive sport. She enjoys travel, reading, sailing, good conversation, cooking, exceptional breakfast tea, story-telling lyrics, Impressionist paintings, and finding inspiration in the landscape, people, and world around her. Having traversed the globe, she's learned to embrace her inner nomad and considers Northern Michigan and Southeastern Connecticut home.

Made in the USA
Columbia, SC
15 June 2025

24a0a1d4-c17f-4065-8818-610820736990R01